Sinew and Bone

Gitte Tamar

BTW LLC

To those who base their worth on vanity, remember that beauty is subjective. It comes and goes; it is not guaranteed, and in the eye of a different beholder, it can decide to flee.

If left in the dark, unable to see, intellect is much more stimulating, and with it, you can add meaning to the world, breaking the chains of hypocrisy.

Only once narcissism is dead, as a nation, can we finally be free.

Hello to all,

Thank you to every last of you, whether your part was big or small.

Thank you to each of my family and friends; you already know who you are, so I will refrain from listing each of your specific names. Just know I will forever be thankful for each of you who gave me never-ending love and emotional support.

Thank you to all my readers for continuing this journey with me. I am forever indebted to you.

Yours truly,

WARNING: This story includes situations of violence, gore, death, and swear or curse words.

Contents

Epilogue   1

1. Porcelain   9

2. Fresh Meat   21

3. White Gloves   31

4. Get on with it   41

5. Chilled to the Bone   55

6. Cold Introductions   71

7. Be Proper   79

8. Initiation   93

9. Blessings   107

10. Peculiar Ingredients   117

11. The Golden King   133

12. Death to the Wicked   149

13. I do not Recall   173

14. Fresh Start   187

15. The Drawing Room   199

16. Surprises   209

17. One of us   233

18. Who is There?   251

19. Where are you From?   273

20. Deceased   291

21. Familia Secrets   309

22. Lurking Shadows   333

23. A Nice Bath   347

24. Innocent   363

25. Pick a Straw   369

26. Run   387

27. Soft Whispers   411

28. Mummified Lies   423

29. Deadly Eyes   441

30. Shattered Portraits   459

31. Ichor Smiles   471

32. Dinner Plates   489

33. Blink Twice   499

34. Do not Move   519

Afterword   534

About Author   541

Epilogue

Cannibalism is alive and well, my dear friends; do not let anyone fool you into thinking differently.

I have witnessed the acts, and I fear a part of me has changed. I cannot un-see what I have seen. The gruesome sight of someone you are acquainted with being devoured seems to drain your very essence.

Lately, I find that when gazing upon the dead, I feel nothing. The sight of a lifeless body no longer riddles me with sickness. My complexion does not grow pallid, nor does my skin turn green. Every ounce of sadness and remorse has vanished.

For the first time in my life, nothing provokes an emotional reaction from me; I am entirely apathetic.

Interestingly, though, when I poke and prod a dead body, I am met with an indescribable sensory experience—a strangely pleasant sensation. The dullness of their pupils is captivating, and within them, I discover tranquility.

There are so many intricacies of a corpse that vex me.

Did you know fingers sometimes flinch when a body is postmortem? I have discovered that through my observations.

Following death, the soul tends to linger, causing subtle twinges and twitches. Occasionally, as one exhales their final breath, a gently whispered word escapes their lips. Most often, it is *help,* but other times, it is gibberish that I cannot understand.

I believe that every soft murmur and gentle wiggle reflects the poignant last-ditch effort of a dying individual to rouse themselves one final time before coming to peace with their circumstances and releasing their grasp on life.

If I were in their position, I am certain I would do the same. I can only imagine the confusion that comes with detaching from your body, especially if the death is traumatic and unexpected.

Directly upon encountering a dead person, I am compelled to touch their hands, regardless of the corpse's condition. I like to close my eyes and attempt to guess how they spent their last breaths. Sometimes, I even imagine them uttering the tale of their final moments.

It is fascinating to fill in the blanks of how one dies. The notion that anyone can go in the blink of an eye adds an element of surprise. I liken it to an after-dinner game, which brings me to my next point: the cause for this brief lament.

By the time you read this, my time likely has come. I am almost certainly deceased, and after they handle my body like the others, I will not be found. They will devour me, crushing my bones and spreading my remains like jam across a piece of morning bread.

Therefore, I must confess all that I know so that even without a proper burial, I can rest in peace, and my soul can fly free to the heavens, where I long to find tranquility.

My life experiences have made me tired. Rather than filling my head with happy thoughts of lace and ivory, everything after my marriage to Hugh McKinley has been wrought with trauma. The toxic remnants of each experience have ensnared havoc within the confines of my mind.

Some of my accounts are dreadful and so dark the edges of my heart have turned to jade. Perhaps that is why I am so at ease with death.

The deceit of others has ignited a swirling madness in me, leaving me adrift in a sea of uncertainty. Trust has become an elusive concept, and it seems there is no escape from the relentless and sinister forces that bind me to this harrowing destiny. Despite my desperate attempts, these suffocating ties show no sign of relinquishing their grip.

The moment I entered this place, I realized how my naivety had closed my eyes to the malevolent darkness that resides in the world. Even in my worst nightmares, I could not fathom that the abhorrent act of cannibalism would be so prevalent among the affluent members of our society. The desire to indulge in the remains of others is cleverly concealed behind a facade of opulent attire and impeccable public display.

It terrifies me I have lost all understanding of this awful place and the people I am with. Everything around me feels like nothing but a deceptive illusion. I feel completely hopeless, living life in a darkness that I know will soon swallow me whole.

Every time I seek comfort in positive thoughts by shutting my eyes, my mind is flooded with distressing images that plague me both day and night. I cannot escape from the torment that engulfs me.

Imagine extending your arms into the pitch-black and feeling nothing — not even a wall meeting your fingertips. As panic sets in, you only have your smell to rely on, and the aroma that laces the air is reminiscent of a catacomb.

That is my daily existence. I am certain it is foreshadowing someone's death, perhaps mine. I am nothing more than a caged animal awaiting to be euthanized.

On each page of my accounts you are about to consume, evil looms, so if you choose to read further, you must be careful not to let it attach.

Carefully survey your surroundings. Scan from the far left to the far right, and do not forget to check behind, in front, above, and below. Take a moment to confirm that no one, living or dead, is observing you.

Once you feel confident that you are alone, check again. Take a deep breath and attune your ears to the quiet. Listen for any subtle noises.

If you detect any, it may be wise to make a swift exit. If nothing catches your attention, consider yourself fortunate, as it means that, at least for the present, you are shielded from the entities eagerly awaiting your arrival in the other realm.

Now, quickly find a match and bridal-white candle made of beeswax. Light the wick within three strikes of the match-stick, and as you watch the flame dance, ensure all other lighting in the room is extinguished.

Be vigilant and focused so you can discern any barely perceptible whispers that might tickle your ears or the subtle shivers that raise goosebumps on your arms. If you do not encounter any of these sensations, congratulations! You are quite lucky indeed.

I am about to share a secret that will satisfy your craving for intrigue.

There is something sinister lurking among us. A wicked existence of vanity, I fear, will eventually swallow humankind whole. Untamed, it will engulf the forthcoming generations, devouring every ounce of our morality. In return, it will make our judgment lawless.

According to philosophers, human remains contain a remedy for various ailments and are even capable of reversing the aging process. As we age, our yearning to regain our youth grows stronger; for some, it becomes an obsession. This drives many to embrace any potential solution eagerly, regardless of how unusual or unsettling it might be.

As privileged women, we were taught from birth that beauty is highly esteemed and that being attractive is more valued than intelligence.

The longing to preserve our youthful glow intensifies with each passing day, leading many to eagerly take a daily prescription of the remedy for old age—a gritty, ash-like paste.

Upon reflection, I now recognize that we have all been grossly misled.

Regrettably, it is now too late, as our deepest, darkest selves have been set free, driven by an unquenchable thirst for more, and now, even I am not immune.

The relentless misery that I carry feels inescapable, like an unwelcome shadow that haunts my every moment. It lingers in the stillness when my eyes open and shut, leaving me with scarce moments of respite. It taints every connection that I once cherished, rendering them mere hollow echoes of their former selves.

In the past, I found great joy in introducing myself as Genevieve Ellsworth. My name was a source of immense pride, signifying a strong sense of identity and heritage.

However, as the years have passed, that pride has dwindled, and my once-cherished name now feels distant and disconnected from who I am today.

Assuming the persona of Genevieve McKinley plunged my life into a sinister and terrifying journey.

The following accounts will detail my horrifying experiences.

This is my story.

One

Porcelain

1646, Endmill, London

The winter sky stirs, frosting all the leaves on the trees with ice.

Sitting in bed, I feel the frigid chill, and wrapping the blankets tighter around my body, I follow the sunlight entering the room.

The glass windowpanes have a light dusting of slush on their exterior surfaces. It adds a beautiful glossy overlay to the view of the foliage on the other side, creating a picturesque scene.

As I gaze at the snow-covered landscape, I joyfully sing, "Oh, what a wonderful day it shall be."

Every word transforms into an echo, dancing through the sunbeams illuminating the room. I smile and close my eyes to listen.

The euphoric ambiance is cut short by a muffled squawk.

Startled, I glance back to the window, and my heart races.

Outside, a raven flaps its wings, attempting to find a perch on the icy ridge of the window ledge.

I smirk as I stare into its tiny black marble eyes through the frost. "Hello, there, little fellow." Interrupted by its beak tapping against the glass, a wave of guilt washes over me. "You must be chilled to the bone."

The piercing, high-pitched caw of the bird grows louder and more intense, creating a frantic and distressing rhythm that fills the air.

In a swooping motion, I fling the covers from my body, and shivering, I sense the frigid air hitting my teeth. "Hush, little bird, with your caw, caw, caw. Do not fret; everything will be just fine. I will help you."

As I feel the cold floor beneath my bare toes, I scrunch my nose while continuing to observe the raven's struggle. Quietly, I tiptoe closer, careful not to startle it, hoping to get a better look. The raven tilts its head, watching my nightgown sway with each step.

When I reach the window, a wide smile spreads across my face. "Here we are," I say, unlatching the hinge; I push the pane open.

As the icy seal breaks, winter's frozen remnants tumble to the ground, and a chilly wind enters the room.

The raven stands motionless, its feathers rustling in the breeze.

My teeth chatter from the cold, and my throat burns with each wintry breath. "Come closer. Don't be shy," I say. Barely able to squeeze out my words, I curl the long sleeve of my nightgown over my fingers and pat the window.

With an even-louder caw, the bird flutters its wings and hops sideways.

I slowly extend my hand. "Trust me, it is much more pleasant here."

Clicking its tongue, it glances at my fingers.

"There is no reason to be afraid. Jump on like a twig," I say, wiggling my digits and urging it to hurry.

It peers at me with a curious gaze and inches closer.

"That's it," I say.

There is a delicate knock on the bedroom door.

Startled, I quickly glance over my shoulder. "Who is it?" My voice quivers as I attempt to mask my pain, feeling a sudden sharp twinge in my pointer finger.

"Pardon me for the interruption, miss. Is everything satisfactory in there?" It is the chambermaid, and her voice sounds concerned.

I nervously chuckle. "Yes, of course, Fran. Just give me a moment." Feeling tingling in my fingertips, I quickly glance toward my hand, still hanging outside the window.

The raven is gone.

I recoil in response to the biting cold, feeling the frost redden my skin. As I retract my hand, I become fixated on the sight of a tiny drop of crimson on my finger. "It bit me," I whisper, sticking my finger in my mouth to clean the wound. While pulling the window shut, I glimpse movement in the frosted tree.

The bird's dark eyes still linger, but unlike before, a splash of red taints the tip of its beak.

A click resonates from the latch of the bedroom door.

My eyes widen at the unexpected sound, and I nervously scan the room from one corner to the next.

As the doorknob turns, I become acutely aware of the soft fabric of the nightgown caressing my skin. Feeling a sudden surge of self-consciousness, I hurry back to the snug embrace of my bed. I fumble for the hand mirror on the bedside table and anxiously inspect my reflection. With utmost care, I adjust the curls that frame my face, ensuring every wisp of hair is in place.

The door swings open, bumping the wall and causing the large chestnut wardrobe to rattle.

Squeezing my eyes tightly closed, I instinctively flinch at the sudden, urgent sound of Fran's rushing footsteps as they draw nearer, echoing through the room. I feign a yawn, pretending to have just awoken.

She rushes toward the bed, her kitten-heeled boots echoing against the hardwood floor. Noticing my flushed cheeks, she grows concerned. "Are you unwell, miss?"

The reassuring sight of her black dress with a white ruffle adorned with eyelet lace brings a smile to my face. I move my thick braid from my left shoulder to the right and untie the forest-green ribbon from its base. "There is no cause for concern. It is just a bit chilly in here," I say.

"We cannot have you falling ill," she says. The skin of her scalp is pink at her hairline from the strain of her taut bun.

"I am certain that you told me that on the day I become a lady, you would be a bit freer in your appearance," I say, snickering, noticing the slicked-back sheen of her hair and how tightly it is pulled back. "You know it will only make you wrinkle faster."

She matches my smirk. "Only one of us needs to meet the suitors' appearance expectations," she says, laughing, "and we both know it is not me."

I can't help but roll my eyes as she pulls out the chair at the vanity and pats the cushion. "All right, up you go. You have a long day ahead of you," she says.

Flinging the covers back off my body, I feel the cold air against my skin once more. "These winters are going to be the death of me," I mutter as I step onto the freezing floor and curl my toes in discomfort.

Fran dismisses my complaint with a pointed remark. "If you dedicated as much time to your appearance as you do to complaining, perhaps you would have better luck attracting a suitor who owns a grand estate with even more fireplaces," she quips, lightly patting the vanity chair's cushion.

Hurrying, I sit and direct my attention to the mirror. I pinch my cheeks to draw color. "I daresay I do not look a day over sixteen." With a laugh, I look at Fran. She smirks, making brief eye contact with me. "Would you not agree?" I ask.

She swiftly unravels my braid. "Indeed, and no one will be the wiser," she says while combing my locks with her fingers.

As I analyze my face for fine lines, I inch closer to the edge of the seat. "You know, that's what my mother says. I am certain you have heard her gossiping about it. I daresay that even if I were old and wrinkled, if she had her way, she would not allow me to celebrate a birthday past sixteen."

With graceful swiftness, I raise my finger to gently smooth out a crease. Fixed on the mirror, I point with authority, and my voice echoes my mother's pitch. "A young lady must never tell a man her true age. There is simply no good reason they need to know. If you can bear children, that is all that is important. So, from this moment on, when we introduce you into society, you will tell everyone you are turning seventeen on this birthday. That is the perfect age for finding an eligible match."

While running a boar bristle brush through my tangling waves, she shrugs and says, "She might be onto something." Struggling to keep a straight face, she adds, "Men tend to prefer younger women. And besides ... the age difference from twenty to seventeen is not significant."

Pausing, I lean closer, scrutinizing every minute sign of aging etched on my skin. "My mother always said it provided me with extra time to accomplish more."

She listens, continuing to brush.

I steal a glance at her with a mischievous twinkle in my eye, and chuckling, I add, "You will not believe what else she told me. She admitted she pulled off the same thing to secure her position in this household."

As Fran continues to ready me for the day, she remarks, "It seems like it has worked out well for her. She appears to have settled into a comfortable life."

"I suppose you are right, but what if people find out?" I ask. "What then?"

"You scarcely have left this house. No one will know the difference," she says.

Staring at my reflection, I watch her meticulously pinning up my hair. "I don't know what I would do without you. You always know the right things to say," I mutter through gritted teeth, my words laced with a tinge of pain as she pulls my hair tighter.

After Fran finishes placing the last curl, she rushes to the wardrobe.

I watch her select a cream and earth-tone satin dress adorned with royal blue roses paired with a matching blue bustier. "This will complement your porcelain skin perfectly," she says, and with a smile, grabs a matching crème hat.

Nervously, I scan the delicate netting that adorns the hat's brim. "Yes, that will be perfect," I say with a hint of relief in my voice.

She signals me with a side nod. "Come on, let's get you dressed. Your mother is waiting."

Her eyes lock on me with a look of insistence. "Make haste!" she shouts, motioning for me to move.

Feeling the chill, I quickly stand up, eager to put on something warmer. As I rush to the wardrobe, I briefly peek at the window.

Perched on the second branch, the raven maintains its steady stare.

I pause, redirecting my attention to it.

"Something the matter, miss?" Fran asks.

As I hear her footsteps gradually drawing nearer from behind, I find myself shaking my head almost involuntarily and clearing my throat to speak. "No, everything is fine. It is just that the way the bird is gaping at us is so peculiar and unsettling." I glance toward her.

Fran peers over my shoulder to get a look. "What bird?"

"The one over there," I say, turning to look; I pause, staring at the empty, frost-bitten branches.

The bird is gone.

"Oh, silly me." I chuckle as I clench my fists in a pulsating grip. "I ... I must be imagining things," I nervously add. "How foolish of me."

She rushes past me to continue her work, carefully arranging the clothes on the bed. "I believe that all you need is a good meal to refresh your thoughts," she says.

"I am sure you are right," I say. "I am probably just a little peckish." As I walk toward her, I look at the finger that was pricked and sense the dampness on my sleeve.

I can't avoid sensing an unnerving presence, as if unseen eyes are fixed on my every move, sending a shiver down my spine.

Fran motions for me to lift my arms, and I swiftly comply. As she helps me dress, I catch a fleeting glimpse of the raven's wings flapping as it departs from the tree.

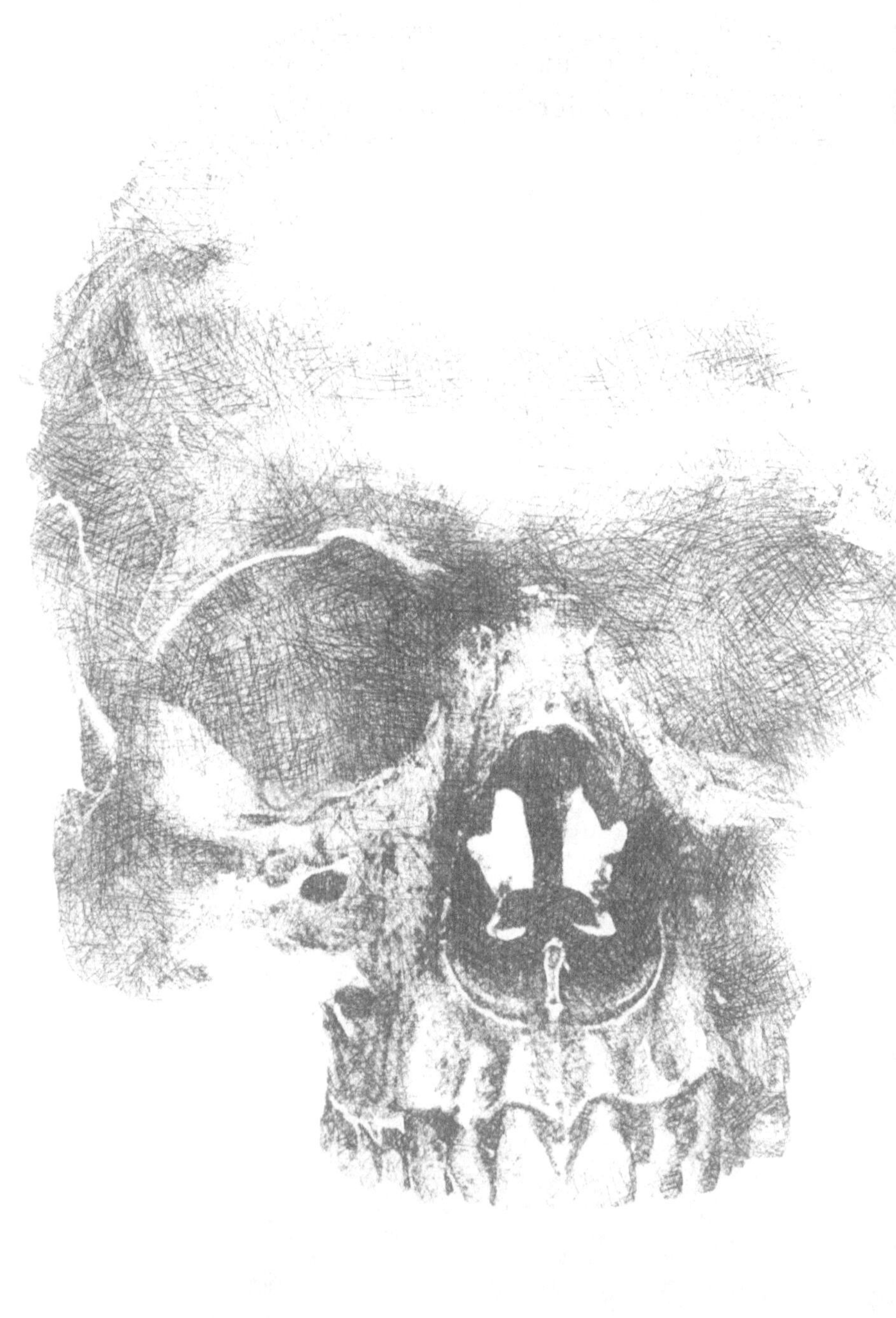

Fresh Meat

We are running behind schedule, and Fran urges me to hurry as we sprint down the stairs.

My dress's voluminous skirt trails behind, swaying from side to side, pressing against my hips with its weight. We enter the opulent dining room without a moment to gather my thoughts. I glance at the intricately designed oblong dining table as I approach, noticing the room's draftiness.

Then, my eyes are drawn to the sight of my mother and father. They are seated at opposite ends of a meticulously crafted, long wooden table. Their polished, heeled, pointy-toed shoes, adorned with elegant buckles, create a subtle but rhythmic tapping against the floor as they wait impatiently. A hushed atmosphere envelops the room as we pause beneath the ornate door-frame. At the cue of our arrival, their heads pivot in unison, and the butlers, clad in tailored black suits, swiftly respond to their unspoken command.

I take a quick breath, forcing a smile as I speak. "I understand the importance of being prompt ... but on one's birthday, I have heard that rules regarding tardiness do not apply." Adding a slight, graceful curtsy, I let my eyes momentarily flick toward the floor.

A hushed silence falls over the room, saturating the air with tension. Confused by the lack of laughter at my remarks, I lift my gaze to look at my parents.

My mother's long ebony hair is artfully arranged in an elaborate updo, embellished with dainty blue rosebuds woven throughout. She looks radiant, wearing a refined royal blue satin gown accentuated by elegant white ruffles adorning the collar.

My father is wearing royal blue knickers, a matching vest, and a white ruffled shirt that complements my mother's attire. His long white socks perfectly match the color of the curls in his hair.

As I examine the scene, I notice a pattern and begin scanning the room for more details.

A blue satin runner adorns the center of the dark wooden table, accompanied by sterling silver cutlery and elaborate floral dishes aligned in front of each chair.

"We seem to embrace a similar theme," I remark, stealing a quick look at my gown.

As Fran fights back her snickers, the staff's eyes bulge with disbelief.

My mother scrutinizes me from head to toe before glaring past me. She is looking at Fran.

"Where are her gloves?" she asks, snapping her fingers. "Did I not instruct for her to wear them?"

Fran's posture stiffens, and her heels click together as she stands at attention.

Preparing to strike, my mother lifts her eyebrow. "A proper woman cannot be seen without all her accessories," she hisses. "It is as though you want her to be received improperly in society!"

With a sudden burst of urgency, Fran rushes up from behind me and anxiously scans my hands. Realizing her shameful mistake, she tilts her head toward the floor as her complexion turns pallid. "No, I would never ... My apologies, Ms. Ellsworth. I will fetch them immediately. I promise it will not happen again." She quickly pivots to prepare for her departure.

My mother clears her throat, stopping Fran in her tracks. "Before you leave, there is one more thing I would like to bring to your attention," she says, her chair scratching against the floor as she pushes away from the table.

Fran slowly turns around. "Yes, ma'am?" Her words barely escape her lips as she trembles with uncertainty.

Mrs. Ellsworth rises to her feet, savoring each second of her ascension. The chambermaid finds herself intimidated and unable to avert her eyes from the imposing presence of her slender and tall stature.

Towering over the table, my mother tilts her nose to the ceiling and looks down at her. "Allow me to offer a piece of advice: although I may tolerate your carelessness, others will be far less forgiving. The man who ultimately becomes Genevieve's husband will not display the same level of leniency. Committing such a mistake could cause grave consequences for you, such as being forced to leave your home or something even more dire."

I look at my mother's disapproving expression with disgust.

As Fran fights her shaking knees, she curtsies. "Yes, I understand; thank you, ma'am." With haste, she darts out of the room.

My mother smirks while gracefully taking her seat.

Her heartless behavior sends a surge of heat through my veins, making my blood boil. "I implore you, Mother, stop your cruelty and show kindness! That unfortunate young girl is scarcely older than I."

My challenging words make her snap, and with a boisterous laugh, she whips out a navy-colored ostrich feather fan. As she takes her frustration out by waving air to cool herself, she cackles, "Quite the contrary. That girl is at the age when one should be the most severe. The younger they are, the more impressionable. You must strike while the iron is hot and mold them into submission."

In disbelief, I glance at my father and bulge my eyes, hoping he will speak.

He refuses to look up from the table. Pretending to be preoccupied, he fixates on his empty plate, pushes up his reading glasses, and remains silent.

My mother raises her voice to ensure she is heard. "Trust me—if you disregard my advice, your marriage will suffer. The biggest threat to a man's fidelity comes from unruly women who do not know their place. If she lacks understanding of her role, she will ultimately betray you."

I gasp. *"Mother."*

With a flick of her wrist, she closes her fan. Her silence fills me with relief, but I am still in shock. I shift my eyes to the table, trying to collect my thoughts.

"And another thing...!" she exclaims, raising her closed fan in the air.

I flinch, recoiling at the motion.

"I forbid you from ever suggesting that you are remotely close to that girl's age again. You are and will remain only seventeen years old, still far from your twenties," she continues, her tone brimming with repugnance.

I roll my eyes. "But..."

She sneers and snaps her fingers to silence me. "Now ... take a seat, child. You are making a spectacle not only of yourself but of us by association."

A server springs from the wall, pulling out the empty chair from the table with a bow.

Quietly, I approach the man, concealing my contempt with a fake smile; I nod in gratitude. I feel my mother's disapproving glare as I settle into my seat.

Before a word is uttered, three kitchen staff members hurry to serve our first course. In perfect synchronization, a pastel-orange liquid fills our bowls. "To begin this joyous occasion, we offer you a delightful butternut squash bisque," declares a man with a well-groomed mustache.

I watch the steam rise, and feeling it caress my cheek, I gently pick up my spoon.

"I requested the addition of turmeric to your dish, as it is believed to help maintain your youthful appearance," my mother says through slurping lips.

Her sudden voice startles me, and I cringe in embarrassment as my hand slips, resulting in my spoon clattering noisily into the bowl.

Smacking her mouth, she ignores me, continuing to eat.

As I extend my hand toward the delicate silver spoon, the scent of the fragrant seasoning fills my nostrils, enveloping my senses. A sudden surge of nausea overcomes me, leading me to place the spoon back on the table silently, attempting to regain my composure.

My mother clears her throat mid-bite and turns her attention to my father. "Have you received any news from the McKinley boy?"

Unsure of what she is talking about, I look at my father, who is already halfway through his potage.

"Yes, after I called upon him, he promptly sent a reply," he says, slurping another spoonful.

Her eyes widen. "Speak, my dear! Tell me what he had to say. You must finish your thought before gorging yourself."

Irritated, he grabs his napkin from his lap and hastily wipes his mouth. "He shall visit today," he says, over-enunciating every word.

She squeals with excitement, "Oh, marvelous! How splendid."

"If your conversation pertains to me, please enlighten me on the matter," I say.

A grin forms on my mother's lips. "Well, I suppose since it is your birthday, I can disclose the details," she says, her words flowing out with excitement. "We have been orchestrating this for some time now ... an arrangement of sorts. This is our grandest birthday present for you. If all goes well, you shall be engaged to Hugh McKinley this evening."

As each word pours from her mouth, a wave of nausea washes over me. "What?" I inquire. "Are you referring to the same McKinley family that is connected to my brother? Other than the brief mention you made about Phillip's acquaintance, I know nothing about him."

"Is it not enough that you know you are to marry him? What other information could you possibly need?"

"Well, to begin with, do you know his age?" I inquire.

Slurping her soup, she dismisses the question. "Foolish child! The age of the man is of no consequence. All that matters is that he makes at least five thousand a year. Nothing else should concern you."

In desperation, I look at my father. "He cannot be a day over forty," he says, stopping briefly to cough up phlegm while eating. "Your mother is right. That is the least of anyone's concerns at this table. Age is but a number ... and besides, the man was one of your brother's closest acquaintances ... and his brother-in-law, for goodness' sake."

Struggling to control my anger, I shift my focus downward onto my plate. "When do we meet?"

The room's chill has caused the food's steam to dissipate.

"That's the right attitude," my father says. "I daresay it won't be long now. They departed a few days ago and should arrive anytime."

"Very well, then," I reply. "If that is what must be done, so be it."

As the staff clears the first course dishes, I glance around the room, longing to leave. "May I be excused from the table? It appears Fran has yet to return, and I need my gloves so that I am put together for the occasion."

"You will miss the charcuterie, but if you must go prepare, then that is what you must do," my mother replies.

Despite my eagerness to escape their company, I maintain my composure.

"Your perfect presentation is of the utmost importance," my mother adds.

As I stand, my corset constricts my breath, making it challenging to speak. "Thank you," I mutter. "You are too kind."

I rush out the door, avoiding eye contact.

Three

White Gloves

The thought of my future already being decided leaves me at a loss for words. Despite my profound awareness of the societal expectation of marriage, I envisioned myself having a wide range of possibilities when choosing a life partner. I had also hoped that my personal interest and influence in shaping my future happiness would be considered, or at least respected.

In a haze and trying to ignore my spiraling mind, I rush up the stairs, my corset tightening with every step. Overcome by dizziness, I desperately grip the railing, wheezing and struggling to regain control of my breath.

The sensation of dizziness intensifies as I struggle to find my balance, the room blurring and tilting wildly. It feels as if the entire world is crumbling around me.

"Fran," I call. Overwhelmed with panic, I gasp for breath. "Fran!"

A series of soft footsteps echo through the quiet.

As I turn my head to look, the staggered paintings lining the stairway catch my attention. In the center of the lineup is a young man's portrait; its size is more prominent than the rest. Not having seen my brother in some time, I hardly recognize him.

The stunning likeness captures him in his finery on the day of his elopement. He stands tall in a distinguished coat and cape, exuding quiet confidence. His endearing dimpled chin, carefully styled curled chestnut-brown hair, and impeccably groomed sideburns emanate an undeniable air of refinement and sophistication.

"You do not know the suffering a woman endures." I stare at his effortless appeal and analyze the details of his eyes.

The chandelier's glow bounces off the glossy finish of his pupils' brown-and-green paint, making each appear moist, almost lifelike.

Feeling overwhelmed by unexpressed emotions, I find my words spilling out in a rush, eager to be heard. "Maybe if you were not so impulsive, you would still be here, and I would not be in a position where I must secure my future by marrying a man whom I know little about. I could choose whom I want, when I want, without having to lie about my age."

The painting gazes out at me with a calm and unwavering expression.

I observe the stillness of his body, and a surge of grief washes over me as I sniffle. Inhaling deeply, I divert my attention to the top step, willing myself not to cry. "Where is that girl?" I ask, gritting my teeth.

A slight crackling noise comes from my right rib. I wince and clutch my side as the pain aches through my bones.

"Genevieve," a voice whispers.

I freeze, listening to the word linger. My skin turns ghostly white.

There is a familiarity to its masculine tone.

The feeling of terror grips me while I cautiously watch the portrait from my side glance. My breath escapes in quick, shaky exhalations, creating a misty cloud before me. "Phil ... Phillip, is it really you, my brother? Have you returned?" I stammer, my words spilling out in a rush. "But that's not possible. It simply cannot be."

A haunting stillness plagues the air. As I strain my ears, a faint rustling reaches me from the distance. With a blend of hope and uncertainty, I call out, "Fran?"

A subtle tap sounds against the wall, causing each paint stroke to shift, warping the portrait's integrity. Little by little, the corner of Phillip's lips curls into a smirk.

Frightened, I bolt up the last few steps, my eyes locked on the welcoming entrance of my bedroom. As I try to keep my composure, I walk faster; the looming sensation of being followed is overwhelming.

Reaching my destination, I dart inside and take cover behind the doorframe. I poke my head out of the doorway and scan from left to right. Seeing no one, I direct my eyes to the portraits.

The sun's rays streaming through the window at the far end of the hall capture my attention. As they bounce off the snow outside and pass through the glass, they create a serene atmosphere that fills the space, easing my fears.

As my rapid breaths slow, the ache in my ribs lessens. I softly close the door and find Fran standing motionless across the room. Her arms are strangely bent in front of her as she stares out the window, her glare locked on the trees.

"You will never believe what just occurred." I giggle. The room's silence makes me uneasy.

Her gaze does not waver. As I look closer, I can make out a faint glimpse of white gloves clutched in her hand.

"I see you have found the gloves my mother insisted upon," I say, taking a small step forward.

The floorboard beneath my foot creaks, and, giving no verbal response, she stiffens her posture.

Desperate to lighten the mood, I attempt to apologize for the way she was treated. "I know my mother can be overbearing … but she means well, or that is what I like to tell myself."

Her shoulder twitches as she hears my awkwardness turn to laughter.

"I have some interesting news to share." I move closer. "It appears that we will not have to tolerate her presence much longer. After you left, I was informed that a husband has been chosen for me. Soon, I will marry, and as my lady's maid, you will accompany me on my journey to a new home, leaving this place behind."

She raises her shoulders in response.

A smile spreads across my face as a wave of relief washes over me. "We can never stay angry at each other for long," I say while quickening my steps. I reach out to retrieve my gloves and touch her hand.

Her body spins around, and she meets me halfway.

Instead of the smoothness of imported silk, my fingers are met with feathers. The body of a mangled raven rests in her arms. Its beak hangs open as it stares back at me, its tongue sprawled to the side.

Horrified, I hastily withdraw my hand and scream, "Get—get that thing away from me!"

Fear fills her eyes. She looks as though she has seen a ghost. Shifting her hand from underneath it, she tries to cover my mouth. "Sh…. shhh. I did not know what else to do," she says, clutching the bird tighter.

I bat her hand away. "Don't touch me," I scream as my gaze remains fixed on the tiny creature's shattered body, brutally maimed and covered in blood. It appears a wild animal has attacked it.

Overwhelmed, I hyperventilate. "Fr—Fra—" Unable to get out a single word, I take a breath to calm myself.

"Please, let me explain, miss. It's not what you think," she says. "I didn't do this. I could never do something like this."

Unsure of what to believe, I take a step back.

"When I came to fetch your gloves, I noticed an icy chill in the room. The window was wide open. As I rushed to close it, I heard a terrible noise from your bed," she says, fighting back tears. She runs and pulls back the comforter. "That's where I found the poor creature nestled into your sheets."

I gasp; the white cotton bedding is smeared with blood.

"I am telling the truth, miss, I swear," she says. "I believe it may have entered to find protection from the cold or to avoid being hunted by a predator." My eyes shift from the gore to the window and then to her.

There is a loud, forceful knock on the door.

We both look over in panic.

I promptly clear my throat and ask, "Who is it?"

A woman answers, "Mr. McKinley is in the parlor to see you, miss."

I glare at Fran. "You must get rid of it. That thing cannot stay here. It must go Now!"

She clutches it tighter. "But, miss, the poor thing is on its deathbed."

Directing my attention back to the door, I shout, "Let them know I will be right down!"

"Very well," the woman replies; her voice trails off as she turns and heads down the hall.

As I look back at the bird, the horrid encounter from the morning haunts me. "That is the creature I offered my hand to earlier, and it bit me, drawing blood. Throw it out this minute!"

"But ... it will freeze to death," she says, holding the bird toward me. "Look at it."

I swat her hands away, remembering my mother's words. "Don't make me ask twice!"

"Please, miss," she says.

Once again, the woman returns and knocks.

Overwhelmed by stress, my voice breaks as I shout, "Yes, coming!"

Then I turn to Fran and seize the raven by its neck. A look of terror plagues her face.

Swiftly opening the window, I toss it outside and observe as it slowly sinks into the soft, powdery snow. The act overwhelms me with a mix of emotions. "Now, wipe those tears from your face and fetch me a fresh pair of gloves," I say, snapping my fingers.

Tears continue to pool in her eyes as she responds with a sniffle. "Yes, miss."

As I embrace the cold winter air on my skin, I hear her footsteps dashing to the wardrobe. I lightly pinch my cheeks, adding a rosy hue to my face. There is a newfound exhilaration coursing through me, unlike anything I have ever felt before. Not only did I stand up to the creature that attacked me, but for once, I was in control.

Fran hurries toward me, head down. "Here are your gloves, miss," she says.

Taking a brisk inhalation, I shut the window and, turning around, force a smile. "Thank you," I say, grabbing them; I rush to the vanity mirror to check my appearance. Fran, unsure of what to do, follows close behind.

Walking toward the door, I carefully slide the silky gloves over my hands and up my arms. The way they fit snugly against my skin gives me a sense of completeness.

"I will not require your assistance downstairs this evening. It would be best if you stayed here and tidied up." Her footsteps stop, and I grin.

Without looking back, I reach for the door handle and remark, "Those sheets will need a thorough scrubbing."

Four

Get on with it

Shutting the door, I race down the hall-way to the stairs, pausing briefly to take a quick glimpse at the paintings.

Each portrait remains motionless, devoid of life.

The meticulous arrangement of brush-strokes appears to mock me, as though the painting itself is sneering at my very sanity. Clutching the railing, I straighten my posture and fluff the hoop underneath my skirt.

Miss Milton, the head of our house staff, waits at the bottom step.

My attention is drawn to her uniform, which is identical to Fran's, and my thoughts drift to our icy encounter. "I say, the sooner I can leave this place, the better."

Miss Milton signals for me to hurry. Her face flushed with stress.

With my head held high, I declare, "I refuse to let anyone rush me." Gliding down the staircase, I quietly add, "Onward and upward, Genevieve."

Upon reaching the last step, I catch sight of her vigorously waving. "To make a favorable impression, you must hurry," she says. "Make haste, dear. Make *haste*."

I gracefully make my way through the grand foyer. "You know what they say, Miss Milton: good things come to those who wait." She places her hand on my back and scoffs, ushering me forward.

Her sense of urgency irritates me, but I bite my tongue.

She swiftly breaks away, dashing ahead, and quickly opens the door to the sitting room before entering. "May I present Miss Genevieve Ellsworth," she says, curtsying and averting her gaze to the floor. Holding her position, she waits for me to enter the room.

As I step inside, the sight of my parents triggers my nerves.

Both sit on a luxuriously cushioned loveseat, each holding a dainty teacup adorned with hand-painted tulips and roses. I am familiar with the set, which is exclusively reserved for special occasions.

Sitting across from them is a man whom I can only assume is my suitor. He sets his teacup on the side table and rises to his feet.

While attempting to remain subtle, I observe my mother's eyes widening. Already aware of what she is thinking, I am pleasantly surprised. He is much more attractive than I expected.

His dark brown hair possesses a captivating richness. The sides are trimmed short, while the longer strands on top are styled with a tousled curl. His sideburns are neatly maintained, precisely shaved with a razor-sharp edge.

My father stands to introduce the guest. "Hugh, allow me to present my daughter, Genevieve, to you."

As I glance at the subtle swoop of his hair gracing his forehead, the enchanting gaze of his hazel eyes captivates me. "It is a pleasure to meet you," I say, curtsying and extending my hand in greeting.

He accepts my offer with a grin, and his lips gently caress the back of my hand. "I am pleased to make your acquaintance as well. I have heard so much about you, but the descriptions fail to capture your true beauty," he remarks, a hint of smolder lingering in his expression.

Fighting back a smirk, I gracefully take my seat. "Oh? Is that so?" I ask, watching everyone sit as well. Trying to be coy, I shift my attention from him to my mother.

She purses her lips. "Before you joined us, dear daughter, we were deeply engrossed in a conversation of the utmost importance. Hugh has just informed us that his father has fallen ill," she says, pausing to take a sip of tea. "He wishes for Hugh to be wed quickly, before his demise."

My heart sinks. I knew that marrying was on the horizon, but I never imagined it would happen so soon. The thought of having my freedom snatched away causes a sickening feeling in the pit of my stomach.

To mask my panic, I shift my focus toward him. "Please accept my sincerest well-wishes for your family through this difficult time."

He clenches his jaw. "I appreciate the sentiments, but I am afraid his health has been declining for some time now, so it is not completely unexpected."

As I listen to him, trying to lighten the mood, I nervously glance at the floor and notice his attire; he is dressed in tones of royal blue, matching the decorations. I change the subject. "Did they tell you it is my birthday?" I ask.

He adjusts his frilled shirt and straightens the sleeves of his coat. "I must confess," he states with a mischievous grin, "a little birdy may have let slip the secret."

I glimpse at my mother.

"You just turned seventeen?" he asks.

I return my attention to his chiseled jawline, and I nervously gulp. "Indeed, you are correct," I say in a reassuring tone. The lie quickens my heartbeat, and I chuckle. "It is quite peculiar, though. Today feels like a moment of déjà vu."

Intrigued, he slowly leans forward. "Is that so?" he asks.

I playfully cup my hand around my mouth as if I am about to tell a secret.

My mother nudges my leg with her knee, then promptly rises to her feet. "If you would excuse us, your father and I have a few matters to attend to," she says, casting a quick glance at him to get his attention.

As she speaks, I anxiously listen, struggling to maintain my composure. With a mischievous glint in her eye, she turns to give a sly smirk and says, "We need to review some instructions with Miss Milton for dinner ... don't."

My father quickly stands. "Ah, yes," he says. "That is correct."

"I do not mind a bit. We shall manage just fine," Hugh says. "I am certain of it."

My mother lifts her eyebrow. "Very well. Come along, now," she says, motioning for my father to follow; they exit the room.

With just the two of us left, the room falls into an awkward silence.

Clearing my throat, I inquire, "I assume your journey here went smoothly?"

He grins. "It was precisely as expected," he says. "I have no complaints."

I grab an empty cup and saucer, add a sugar cube, and pour the tea over it. The sensation of steam wafting against my cheeks is comforting. "That is splendid," I remark, taking a sip.

His gaze shifts toward my lips. "Although we are not very familiar with one another, I believe it is imperative for us to discuss our arrangements," he suggests.

I flirtatiously take another drink. "Do tell," I say.

"Given that I have already sought permission for your hand in marriage, and considering the circumstances, I would prefer for us to depart as soon as possible. I am unsure of the state of my father's health, and we have a bit of a journey. He longs for nothing more than to witness our wedding," he says.

He springs to his feet, causing me to startle and nearly choke on my tea. "When you say 'soon,' do you mean now?" I ask, voice stifled.

"There is not a moment to waste," he says.

I gently set my teacup on its saucer to hide my trembling hand and glance across the room. "Oh, dear ... Um, I am just taken by surprise. I ... I have not had time to pack my things," I say.

"Oh, yes, well..." He looks at my outfit. "Although that is pretty, I have already spoken with our seamstress about designing your new wardrobe. The society you will be woven into has certain tastes, and I want to ensure you are warmly welcomed."

"I see," I say, rising to my feet. "Should I notify Fran of our departure?"

Hurriedly, he walks toward the door and, with a tone of confusion, asks, "Who?"

"My chambermaid," I reply. "I expect she will accompany me to assist with my daily duties."

He pauses and looks at me. "Ah, of course," he says.

In an instant, his mood shifts, and his smile vanishes. "I already have plenty of staff, so it won't be necessary."

A feeling of panic consumes me, and my eyes dart from him to the door. "But ... we have a lifetime of shared memories. I cannot envision leaving her behind."

He cringes, showing his irritation by clenching his jaw. "Genevieve, this is not the way to start our journey. I understand you may lack experience in these matters, so I will overlook your naivety this time and make an exception. However, understand that in the future, I will not tolerate any challenges. You will be a wife, not a business partner. From this moment forward, I control all decision-making."

"I understand and appreciate your generosity," I reply, averting my gaze to the floor. "I promise not to overstep again."

He swiftly opens the door. "I will summon my driver to move the carriage to the front. We can continue our conversation during our travels, as there is much to discuss." The heavy front door closes with a thud, echoing through the foyer.

The sound evokes a sense of finality as tightness grips my chest. "You'll be okay, Genevieve; it's just a matter of adjusting to this new chapter in your life," I whisper, though the words ring hollow in my ears.

My heart races while I fight to catch my breath. A sudden, faint creaking sound from behind startles me, prompting me to turn around.

Fran is ascending the staircase while carrying an armful of clean sheets.

My eyes widen. "Fran," I say as I dash to her.

She pauses and turns to face me.

I reach out and clutch her arm, my breath coming in ragged gasps. "Come quickly; we must go. *now*!" I see the confusion in her expression and hasten my words. "I don't have time to explain."

She looks at the sheets in her hands.

"Leave them on the stairs," I say. "We must depart without delay." Worried about taking too long, I anxiously glance at the front door.

After a brief hesitation, she carefully lays the linens on the steps and rushes toward me.

My heels echo against the wood floor as I dash toward the door. Fran follows closely behind. "Where are we going?" she asks.

Trying to catch my breath, I squeeze out my response. "I am to be married, and we are leaving now."

Startled by the news, she warily looks back at the staircase. "Should we not start packing? Do we need to collect our belongings?" she asks, frantic.

I pull on the heavy door's handle. "We have time for none of that. We will get new things when we arrive at our new home," I say.

As I step outside, the cold engulfs my body. Horses in shades of brown and white stamp their hooves on the cobblestones while I stare at the dark wooden carriage they are hitched to.

The enclosed box is grand. Swirled gold leaf designs with intricate carved detailing are etched into the glossy wooden panels.

With caution, I step toward it, almost slipping on the icy ground. I look to see if anyone noticed, then set my sights on the coach and, braving the elements, walk. Halfway there, I hear a clicking sound from the passenger door. I pause, startled by its opening.

Hugh leans out from the entry, his eyes lighting up. "There is my beautiful bride-to-be," he remarks with an infatuated smile. But then his eyes wander past me. "You didn't mention she was so pretty," he remarks, a mischievous sparkle in his eyes.

I shift my gaze in the direction he is looking, and as I turn back to face him, I plaster on a forced smile. "What are you implying?" I inquire while making my way toward him. Fran keeps a distance behind me, oblivious to the tension between us.

His beaming smile widens as he continues to watch her, and seemingly unconcerned with my existence, he barely moves to let me inside. I squeeze past him to enter the carriage and settle onto the burgundy velvet seat.

Ignoring me, he maintains his gaze on her youthful appearance. "Your chambermaid is quite attractive. She seems to be around your age," he remarks.

I am shocked, as I have never considered her to be pretty. "I beg your pardon; she is considerably older than I ... by at least five years," I reply indignantly.

He stretches his hand outside the carriage and into the frigid air as if preparing to usher her inside. "I typically require staff to sit with the driver, but seeing how cold it is..." he says.

I draw back the curtain from the window and witness my parents standing on the porch, bidding their final goodbyes.

Fran dabs her handkerchief against her cheek to wipe away a tear while remaining ignorant of the unfolding scene.

Upon shifting my focus to Hugh, I notice an intense interest in his eyes toward her. It sends me into a frenzy, causing me to reflect on what my mother told me about unruly women and the wandering eyes of men. "No. No, she is quite all right," I say, grabbing at his coat. "She should receive the same treatment as any other staff member."

He retracts his hand and turns to face me; I quickly continue. "Besides, a little cold never hurt anyone. In fact, I have been told it is quite good for the staff. When mixed with fresh air, it can strengthen their immunity and boost productivity."

The ends of his lips lift to a soft smirk. "Well, that settles it," he says. Patting the side wall, he calls for the driver. "Benny!"

I peer out the window, attempting to see what is happening.

A big, burly man, clothed in a black woolen coat and wide-brimmed hat, hastily reaches out and grasps Fran's trembling arm.

Hugh calls out from the carriage toward him, his voice brimming with exuberance as he says, "Please escort her to the front."

Then, with a hearty laugh, he turns and playfully slams the door shut behind him.

I give him a coy smile.

He trembles, feigning an attempt to shake off the chill, and sighs. "Now, where were we?"

As he takes his place opposite me, the carriage starts its journey. I glance out the window, and the sudden momentum pulls me back into my seat. Flakes of fresh falling snow skew the image of my parents waving goodbye. They appear pleased, and, nodding to acknowledge them, I push the curtain over the glass.

Trying to erase the thoughts of my chambermaid, I engage in conversation. "Let me see ... I believe you were just about to tell me about you," I say, redirecting my attention to his eyes.

Fascinated, he gazes at me intently. "Where should I start?"

I grin. "From the beginning."

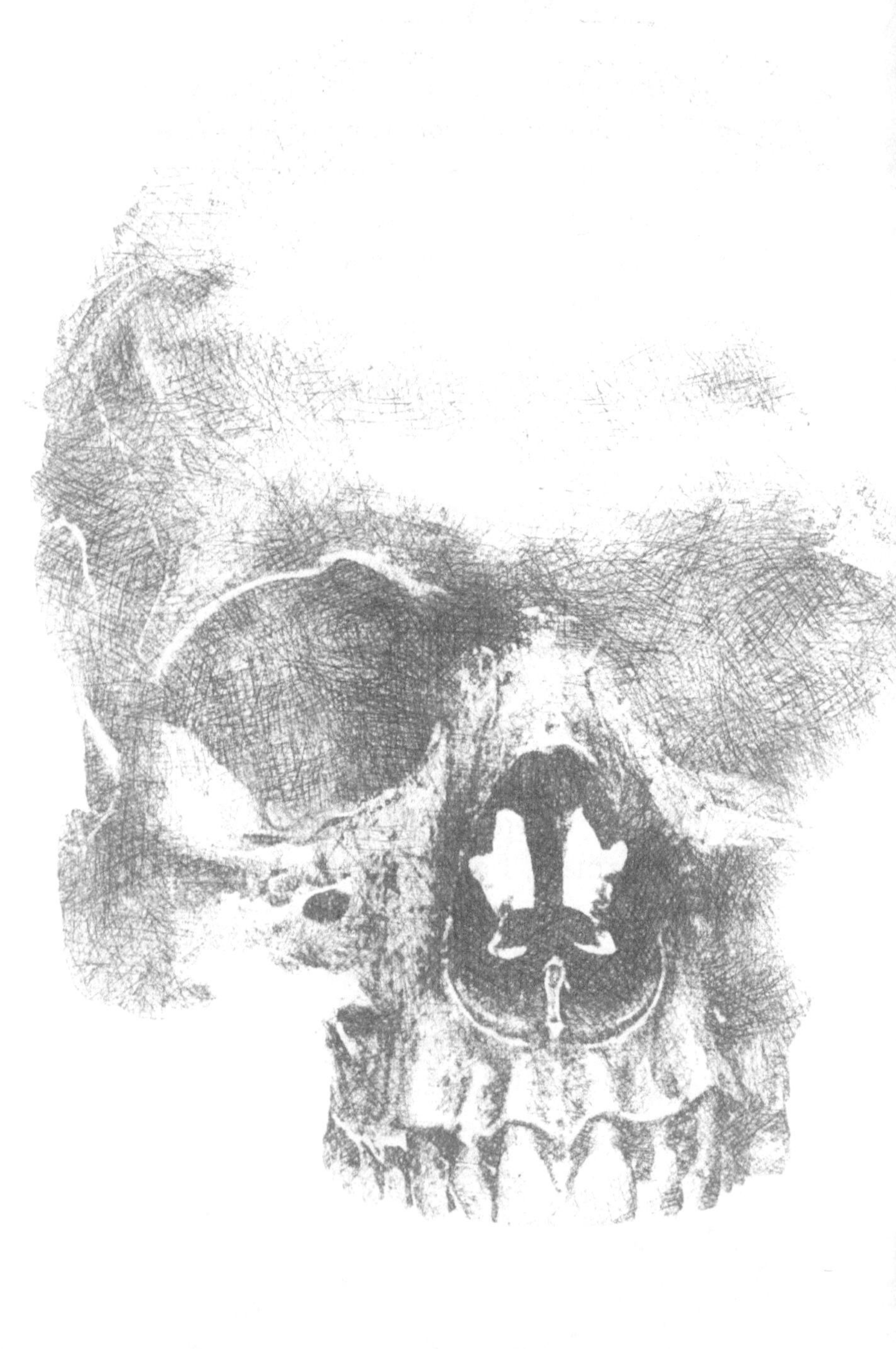

Five

Chilled to the Bone

The path to his estate is quite lengthy; at certain points, there are serene pauses for reflection, while lively conversation fills the air at other times.

Even though our exchange of words is sporadic, he possesses a captivating hold over me I have never experienced before. He crafts each syllable with such eloquence that it mesmerizes me. There is a quality about him that makes me crave his approval, leading me to do or say things to command his attention.

As I stare into his eyes, I cannot help imagining my new life. I want to know more.

Hungry to paint a picture, I run through the questions in my head. *"There is so little I know about you. Could you share more about your family? How many siblings do you have in total?"* Without realizing it, I blurt out my thoughts, only to cringe at the volume of my excitement.

A soft chuckle escapes his lips as his eyes methodically scan every corner of the carriage. He pauses, allowing a moment of silence to fill the air as he mulls over his thoughts. "I am one of four—the only boy among sisters, most of whom are already out and married."

Nodding, I smile.

He sinks into his seat with a heavy sigh and continues, "Being the only son is difficult. The pressure to carry on the family name is excruciating for me. There are moments when I feel like the weight of the world has been placed upon my shoulders; most days, my father makes me feel like a failure. He has made it his mission to drill into my head that it is my sole duty to carry on the McKinley lineage."

Caught in a daydream, I grin. "You know, I'm envious of you. I have always dreamed of having a sister, let alone three. Growing up, I would have cherished the company and conversation, as being trapped indoors with only the servants as my companions was nothing short of dreary."

Fidgeting, he adjusts his seat. "Certainly, there are some dull aspects to not having siblings, but let's not jump to assumptions too quickly."

Intrigued, I lean in. "What do you mean?"

His gaze intensifies as he grows more serious. "Well, it is simple: I fear you may retract that statement after you meet mine."

I giggle. "We often tend to be more critical of our own family, so I'm certain your perspective might be slightly exaggerated. I believe they cannot possibly be as bad as you describe them."

Hugh briefly averts his gaze. "I prefer you form your opinion when you meet them, so I will refrain from sharing much more. However, I believe their upbringing could have attributed to their behavior."

Clenching his jaw, he continues, "I have found that when money abounds, it can turn one's mind mad, and with all the time on their hands, they fixate on perfectionism." My thoughts spiral, thinking of my father's reminder of my brother's connection to him, and countless questions boil beneath my skin. "Do you think that could be what happened to my brother?" I interject. *Did he go mad? Perhaps he is in an asylum as we speak. We have not heard a peep from him since his elopement.* My mind races with thoughts of his whereabouts.

Like he's seen a ghost, he shoots straight up on his bench, and his eyes widen.

Immediately, I cover my mouth in embarrassment and stammer, "I am—I am so sorry; I do not know what possessed me to ask such a thing."

Hugh clenches his jaw tighter and, in a burst of energy, pulls back the curtain on the window.

Cowering deeper in my seat, I carefully observe his demeanor. "You know, he wasn't just my brother-in-law. He was one of my greatest friends," he says, his cold expression making it difficult to gauge his emotions. "He taught me the importance of cherishing every moment, as we have no control over when we will be plucked from this earth or whom God takes." The floor of the carriage shakes as he anxiously taps his toe.

Able to sympathize with his uneasiness, I soften my tone. "You know that my mother and father never told me what happened to him." Pausing, I notice his glossy eyes harboring his sadness. "One morning, as I sat at the dining table, waiting for my breakfast to be served, they told me he was gone. You can only imagine my bewilderment; I was speechless and did not know what to think.

There was no funeral or period of mourning. Oddly, we seemed to continue our lives as if he were still living, and after that day, his departure was never spoken of again. Not because of a lack of grief, but I believe it is out of maintaining sanity. It was easier for everyone to pretend he was just on an extended holiday."

"If it gives you peace of mind, none of us know," Hugh says.

I pause, feeling perplexed by his response. "I'm sorry. Could you please explain what you mean?"

His attention darts to the corners of the carriage as he nervously brushes away the moisture from his brow. "From my understanding, he was dealing with something far greater than we will ever know—these … these things, these monsters that lived inside his head," he says. "One day, it became too much to bear, and he disappeared, leaving no trace."

"Mo—monsters," I say in disbelief.

He flinches at the sound of the word. "Yes, it sounds absurd, but it is true. He said they made him feel dreary and confused," he says, gripping the cushion beneath him and shaking his head. "Despite their being invisible to the naked eye, we attempted to eliminate them. However, time only seemed to exacerbate the situation, and eventually, they took Phillip away from us."

I gulp. "They 'took' him? What do you mean?"

"I believe that's sufficient for this conversation," he says, straightening in his seat with a sense of manic energy as he swiftly pulls the curtain shut. "Let us transition to a topic of a more uplifting nature."

Abruptly, the carriage hits a bump on the uneven country road, causing the wheels to bounce and slide on ice. Feeling queasy, I rest my head against the wall behind me and force a painful smile. "Of course, yes, of course. Let us not discuss it anymore."

Regaining his composure, Hugh stares intently at me and resumes a comfortable reclined position. "Are you all right? You look unwell," he says.

Quickly, I use the back of my hand to pat my cheeks, trying to draw color. A spell of dizziness causes my vision to blur. "You must excuse me. I am feeling rather poorly."

"It's probably a bout of road sickness," he says. "Some rest will do you good."

Knowing the truth of where my illness is genuinely coming from, I hold back my rebuttal.

He fumbles through his pocket. "Hold out your hand," he says, placing a black pill on my palm.

"What is it?" I ask.

"Those, my dear, are referred to as stones of immortality," he says with a gentle smile as he takes another from his hand and carefully squeezes it between his fingers, examining the intricate patterns on the casing. "Sister's husband is a philosopher deeply knowledgeable about the healing arts. He recommends that our resident doctor keep them readily available because of their incredible effectiveness and medicinal properties."

I gently roll the object in my palm, carefully surveying its surface as he speaks.

"Despite their small size, these miraculous gems can swiftly ease every discomfort and ailment upon ingestion, providing quick aid."

Longing for relief, I place the pill in my mouth and swallow. "I've never come across anything like this before," I murmur, punctuating my statement with a resounding yawn.

His excitement grows. "I have even found they help with sleep." He shrugs and, without hesitation, consumes it. "We shall wake up nice and rejuvenated."

As his voice fades, I desperately try to keep my eyes from closing. Warmth prickles over my body; his smile turns fuzzy. "You ... uh ... um ... don't ... um ..." I struggle to speak, my words slurring as I helplessly shut my eyes.

He snickers, resting his head against the seat.

I feel myself transported into a state of lunacy. The more lost I become in the abyss, the greater the silence surrounding me.

Then, suddenly, the tranquility is shattered by an unidentifiable presence, releasing a sharp exhale.

Before I can react, a sensation of something crawling on my skin overwhelms me. Despite my body's instinct to fidget, I find myself completely immobilized. All that remains is my sense of hearing, the sole sensory connection to the outside world.

With every laborious breath, the intruder grows more prominent. Its chest heaves, pushing saliva through the unnatural fissures in its throat and producing a faint crackling sound with each exhale. As the carriage wheels turn, their motion creates a gentle sway, stirring up a cloud of musty dust that permeates the air.

As I take a gasping inhalation, a dense fog fills my nostrils. The atmosphere is thick with the aroma of burning cedar and roasted flesh.

I fight to let out a scream, but with every futile attempt, the carriage seat engulfs me like quicksand, causing my slouched form to sink deeper into the upholstery.

A hiss penetrates my confusion. "Genevieve," a man's voice whispers.

My heart races as the weight of my body pushes me further down in my seat. With no escape from my paralysis, a flood of chaos enters my mind. I want to speak, but I cannot make a sound.

The carriage's gentle rocking gradually comes to a stop, leaving behind a serene stillness that envelops the surroundings.

At that moment, as I heave a sigh of relief, a sudden harsh, grating noise shatters the tranquility, jolting me back into a state of apprehension.

"Listen closely, little Vee," a voice says.

Hearing my childhood nickname evokes a wave of sickness through my gut, and its familiar tone instantly conjures up memories of my brother. *It cannot be.* Yet, it sounds so much like Phillip.

I flinch as I feel something grabbing onto my dress. My eyes burn as the weight of the entity slowly shifts to my thighs.

"Ice sickles cascade from the sky, striking the gaze of the wicked eye. They slice through the corneas of those who are weak and pierce the hearts of the inquisitive who seek the answer to secrets others wish to keep. And when the monsters depart, leaving you lifeless in the frigid cold, all will know they arrived to claim yet another soul," the voice moans. Its deep laugh rumbles through the cabin.

I wriggle uncomfortably, shutting my eyes even tighter.

"Open your eyes," it hisses.

I feel an immense pressure bearing down on my chest while a sharp, stabbing pain radiates through my ribs. Overwhelmed by panic, I fight against my paralyzed limbs, willing my eyelids to open. Suddenly, they break free with a gasp, and I am startled when I am met by Hugh's gaping stare.

He is kneeling in front of me, his hand on my knee. "Wake up, Genevieve," he says, smirking.

My eyes open wide, and my breath quickens as I sense the menacing presence departing past me, its warm breath brushing my ear.

Hugh, filled with enthusiasm, grasps the corner of the curtain and gives it a tug, causing it to open rapidly and reveal the outside world. I shield my eyes from the sun's intense glare reflecting off the snow. "Welcome to your new home," he says.

"Have we arrived already?" I ask, yawning.

"After you took the remedy, you slept peacefully, like an angel," he says.

The driver opens the carriage door, letting in a gust of wind. "It appears my body was desperately craving rest," I murmur as the icy air envelopes me in its chilling embrace, instantly sharpening my senses.

With a twinkle in his eyes, Hugh extends his arm, pointing to the door. "After you, wife-to-be," he says.

In an instant, I become bashful and find myself at a loss for words. "Um…" I say, smiling. I avoid eye contact and divert my attention to the purple carpet covering the carriage's floor. My cheeks flush with embarrassment as I adjust my skirt and approach the exit. With a slight stammer, I utter, "Thank you, kind sir."

The driver helps me down, then gently touches my waist to guide me. I clench my jaw; the position of his fingers triggers a jolt of pain in my corseted ribs.

I give a nod of thanks, acknowledging him, then take a few steps forward.

Hugh swiftly dismounts behind me, and he and the driver engage in conversation.

I brush myself off while admiring the estate's grandeur. It surpasses all my expectations, and I am overwhelmed. The home is surrounded by impeccably maintained grounds and boasts a spacious layout with multiple wings. Its exterior, with its intricate gray stone wall, is unlike anything I have seen before. Even though I grew up in a respectable household, from the outside, this manor appears to triple its size. Most women could only dream of being the mistress of an estate as magnificent as this.

Halfway through counting the number of white shuttered windows, I gasp. *There must be at least thirty rooms.*

Seeing my stunned look, Hugh dashes toward me and grabs my shoulders. "Roar," he shouts.

I jump in surprise and laugh. "Didn't your mother teach you not to sneak up on others?"

He smirks. "That depends on the context of the surprise," he says.

I smile back and reply, "I suppose."

Swiftly, he presents his arm for me to take. "Shall we?"

I gently touch his elbow, and as I do, I hear the carriage wheels shift against the cobblestones behind me. "Wait," I say, turning to look. I notice the driver seated alone in the front, commanding the horses and urging them to move forward. Snow dusts his heavy woolen overcoat.

"What is the matter, my dear?" Hugh asks.

My attention turns to the stone steps leading to the estate's entrance. Outside, the staff forms a line dressed in gray dresses and woolen coats to welcome us. I quickly scan their faces.

"Where ... where is Fran?" I ask.

As Hugh glances over his shoulder, his posture stiffens. "Who?"

Joining in with his joke, I laugh. "My chambermaid."

With a huge grin, he rubs my arm. "Oh, yes, of course, the girl you brought with you," he says. "Yes, yes, indeed. The staff have already taken her to their designated quarters to warm up by the fire."

"You are so kind. How thoughtful of you," I reply.

As the snowfall intensifies, I find myself gripping his arm even tighter. Amid the swirling snowflakes, he looks deeply into my eyes. "Anything for you, Mrs. McKinley," he says.

"I like the way it sounds," I respond, mirroring his smile. "It seems to roll off your tongue so effortlessly."

"Mrs. McKinley," he says again.

There's something about the tone of his voice and his handsome features that instantly puts me at ease. I cannot resist but be captivated. "Yes?" I ask, unable to hide my intrigue.

He pulls me closer. "Shall we?"

His words sound like music to my ears, and I gleefully reply. "We shall."

As we set foot on the path, the piercing squawk of a bird resonates through the air, abruptly shifting the staff's demeanor. Their faces brighten with a cheerful expression, and they wave eagerly.

From the edge of my eyesight, I discern the origin of the call: a mysterious black-feathered raven perched on the rooftop's edge, its glossy plumage glistening in the sunlight as it emits its haunting cry.

I smirk, keeping my gaze straight ahead. "You cannot torment me here," I utter under my breath, "for I am home."

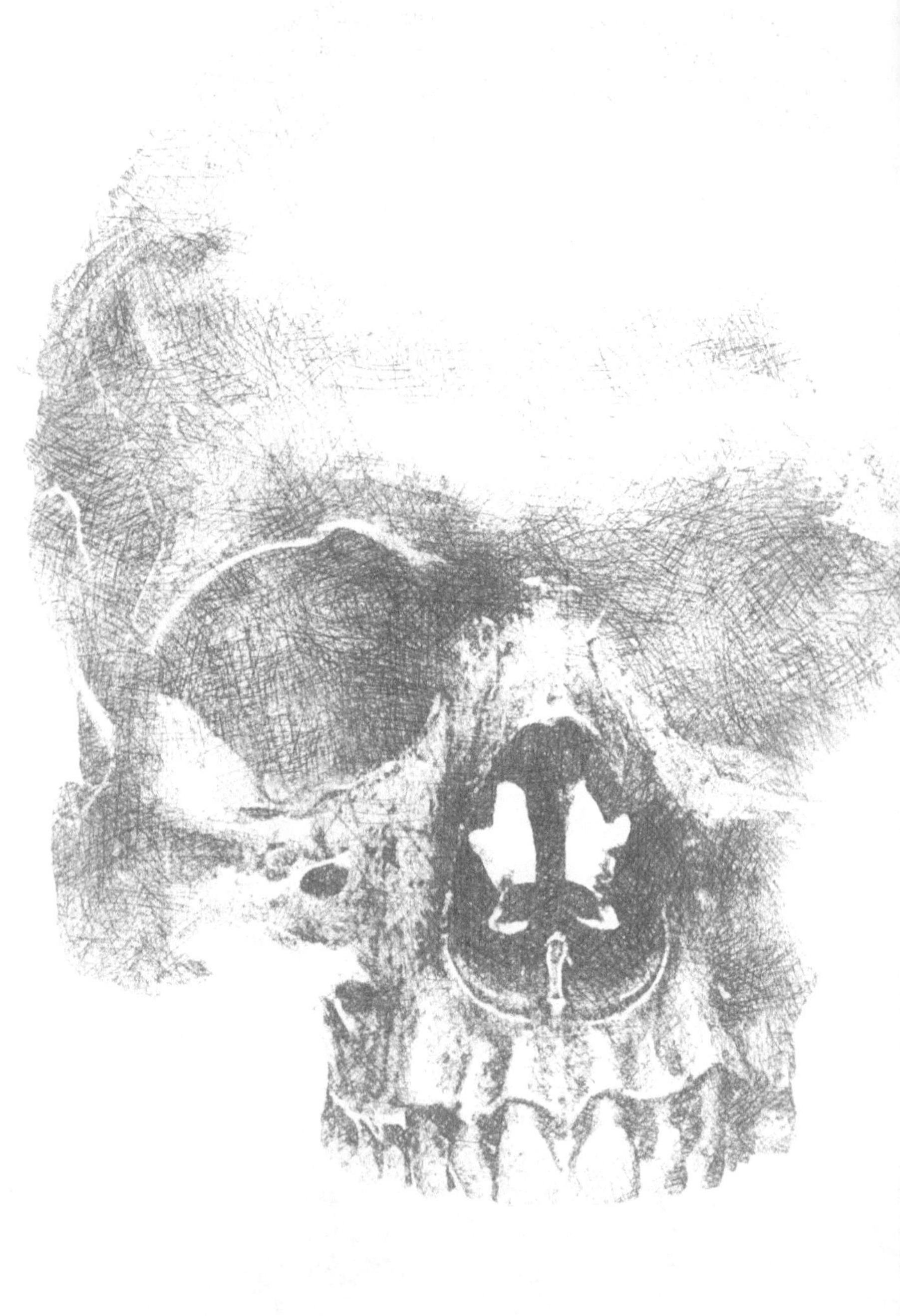

Cold Introductions

In a rush to escape the piercing cold, we hasten our steps as we ascend the flight of stairs. The staff's silence barely registers as I glimpse their pleasant expressions, prompting me to offer a nod of acknowledgment.

As we step through the magnificent entrance and enter the foyer, I am filled with awe. The sheer enormity of the space overwhelms me, as it is nearly three times the size of our dining room back home.

The massive doors close behind us, echoing a loud thud between the marble floors and lofty vaulted ceilings.

Startled, I swiftly spin around and stare in bewilderment at the vacant space before me. There is not a servant in sight. "Where did they go? They were just..." I ask, my voice tapering off in uncertainty. "Are they not planning to come inside?"

I glance over at Hugh and catch sight of a man in a sleek, formal gray coat silently extending his hands toward us. While Hugh hands him his coat, he chuckles and remarks, "They were the greeting staff."

"Greeting staff?" I ask.

He looks at me and, noticing my obvious confusion, continues, "It is precisely as it sounds. The staff stationed outside has one simple task: to give you a warm welcome. They create a friendly atmosphere for us and our guests as we come and go. After they are done with their greetings and goodbyes, they head back to a separate entrance on the west wing and retire to their quarters."

"I am quite curious. Do they ever come into the main house?" I ask.

"Why would they? They have no task that requires their presence in here," he replies.

"Oh, I see," I say, my voice tinged with uncertainty as I attempt to comprehend this unfamiliar concept.

I shift my focus to the man hanging up Hugh's coat, intending to introduce myself as I would in my childhood home.

Hugh catches sight of me as I prepare to speak. Before I can say a word, he interjects, "What are you doing?" he asks, his expression conveying disbelief.

I immediately stop. The floor squeaks under my shoes as I pivot to face him. "Oh dear, did I do something to offend you?"

He clenches his jaw as he strides forward with brisk steps. "Everyone on the premises has already been alerted of your identity. There is no need for introductions or small talk," he says. Motioning for me to follow, he continues, "All staff members have been clearly instructed not to speak."

"Oh, I was not aware," I say as I rush to keep up. "I'm sorry..."

He speaks louder. "Am I understood?"

"Yes, of course," I say, keeping my eyes on the floor. "I promise you; it will not happen again."

His attitude abruptly shifts, and he laughs. "In due time, you will understand why it is better that way ... It allows us to keep our privacy."

Hearing a rustling commotion, I glance over my shoulder to see what is there, fully expecting to be greeted with a spectacle of the older gentleman battling the coat.

Oddly, the entryway is bare. Not only is he gone, but so is the jacket; all that is left is the ornate brass coat rack. I turn toward the door while maintaining a slow, backward pace.

My heart races as I try to recall the echo of his footsteps. *Perhaps he left when I was listening to the rules of the home?* My thoughts spiral as I scan the perimeter of the grand foyer, and suddenly, I collide with something.

Hugh sternly grabs my shoulder. I recoil at his powerful grip as he forcefully turns me to face him. "Bloody hell, Genevieve," he says, lifting his foot. "You must pay attention." An angry red hue spreads across his face.

Feeling my intestines twist into knots, I stammer, "S-sorry." Quickly, I lower myself to clean the scuff on his shoe.

He gasps in horror. "Abysmal girl, act with class!" He says as he drives the sole of his shoe into the side of my ribcage.

I skid across the floor, the pain of the impact bringing tears to my eyes. Seething, he approaches, speaking through clenched teeth. "I am not marrying the goddamn help. Do not embarrass my family name. Pick yourself up."

Terrified of his abrupt personality shift, I avoid making eye contact.

"I said get up!" he shouts, glancing around to ensure no one is watching.

With a sniffle, I get onto my hands and knees. Then, fighting the pain on my side, I stand. Until now, I have only witnessed his occasional outbursts, but nothing quite like this.

"Now, brush yourself off," he instructs, and filled with frustration, he gestures with his hand through the air. "You look like you have been tousled about like a two-pence whore."

Not wanting to trigger any more anger, I quickly nod. I slide my hands down my skirt to straighten it and lift my trembling fingers to fix the curls framing my face.

His eyes remain locked on me. "That will do," he says.

Everything in me wants to get back on the floor, coil into a ball, or run far away.

His lips slowly shift into a grin. Still shaken by his ability to turn his emotions hot and cold, I force a smile to match. There is an element about him that makes me yearn for his approval more than ever.

The sound of bare palms suctioning the marble floor breaks the silence. I look down at the noise and cringe.

On all fours, a young woman wearing a long gray dress clutches a white hanky, frantically shining the scuff off his shoe.

My attention fixates on the familiar tight bun beneath her bonnet and slim fig-ure. *Fran?* Her failure to acknowledge me causes my heart to skip a beat. I would do anything to have her comfort me right now.

Abruptly, the happiness exits Hugh's face. "What is taking you so long? Have you never polished a shoe before?" he says, rolling his eyes.

Finishing the task, she keeps her head lowered, avoiding eye contact.

Unaccustomed to witnessing her in a submissive state, I study her. As she rises to her feet, my attention is drawn to her hand, clutching the handkerchief. The flesh is covered in purple-and-black pigments; the unforgiving frost has burned her delicate skin.

Although I cannot see her eyes, I can tell something is terribly wrong. A wave of guilt washes over me, and though I want to apologize, I am paralyzed, unable to say a word.

Keeping her gaze averted, she squares off her body toward us. As she curtsies, I get a better look at her features and notice her shaking knees. My complexion turns green, and acid from my stomach travels up my throat.

Visible beneath her bonnet, severe swelling consumes the lower half of her face. Not only is it damaged by frost, but it also bears the marks of severe bruising in black, purple, and blue hues.

I clench my jaw and swallow, determined to battle the overwhelming urge to vomit. More than anything, I want to hold and comfort her. If I had known this would be her treatment, I would have left her behind. I struggle to hide my intense emotions as I recognize my role in hurting her.

Then I glimpse Hugh.

He is observing me, awaiting my next move.

I maintain an icy demeanor as I move around her, trying to hide my emotions, but the overwhelming feeling of my heart being torn from my chest is impossible to ignore.

Hugh extends his arm with a grin. "My father is waiting and eager to meet you," he says.

Despite my reluctance to get near him, I accept his offer and lightly touch his elbow, keeping my gaze forward. "Please, show me the way," I say.

As we step away, I hear nothing but the unsettling silence that lingers as Fran remains behind.

Seven

Be Proper

There is nothing cozy or warm about the manor's enormous size. At every turn, there is another stone inlay wall or extravagant tapestry; when those are not present, the space is filled with paintings and decorative battle armor.

The intricate web of corridors weaves a bewildering maze around me. As we venture deeper into the heart of the home, each pathway's striking resemblance to the next makes it increasingly challenging to memorize our route. I find it hard to fathom navigating through this labyrinthine of corridors alone.

The ill-tempered climate of the large, drafty halls makes my body compulsively shiver. As I watch Hugh, I notice him picking up his speed, and despite my sore feet, I focus on what lies ahead.

He widens his stride, ushering me to walk faster. With each passing step, the pain intensifies, growing more unbearable. Just a short distance ahead, our progress abruptly halts as we arrive in front of a magnificent staircase. A woman wearing a gray servant dress stands at its base. Her hair is tightly pinned up.

Hugh drops my hand and excitedly nudges my arm. "Allow me to present your chambermaid." He gently pushes me forward and mumbles, "She will tend to your needs."

Confusion sets in as I timidly walk toward her; I had assumed Fran would be assigned the position.

"After she has readied you, we will meet at this spot. Then, we will go together to see Father."

I hear Hugh's words echoing from behind, and, ready to escape him, I quicken my pace toward her.

The wilted skin around her warm brown eyes scrunches as she grins to greet me. Even though she does not say a word, there is a comforting element of her gaze. It is as if she can read my disdain.

As Hugh's footsteps fade, she graciously lifts my skirt to aid me, and we proceed up the stairs.

I concentrate on the burgundy carpet beneath my feet, trying not to trip. "So rich," I say under my breath.

Then, as I direct my eyes upward, I am taken aback. I can honestly say that I have never witnessed anything quite like this before. The magnificent staircase splits into two separate paths, and the ceiling above displays intricate dark woodwork that beautifully frames a mural of a vibrant blue sky.

As we reach the landing, the breathtaking beauty of the surroundings leaves me in awe.

A set of exquisitely upholstered settees adorned in luxurious pink satin and vibrant pinwheel cushions sits gracefully in front of a grand, arched window. Although winter snow blankets the land, the view overlooking the garden is pristine, and I am hypnotized by its beauty.

As I drift off in my thoughts, the chambermaid tugs my skirt, steering me toward the left staircase, breaking my fixation.

Upon ascending the last flight of stairs and stepping into the hall, my gaze is drawn to the paintings that decorate the walls.

Every gold-leafed frame is exquisitely carved and houses portraits of women dressed in cascading ball gowns. Each delicate brush-stroke makes them appear lifelike. Their ensembles are embellished with extravagant jewelry, and from time to time, they carry ornate lace parasols to complement the overall scene.

Positioned beneath the works of art are glass display cases that house family heirlooms interspersed with elegant cream-colored fainting couches.

As my focus remains on the painted women, their poise leaves me speechless. There is an element to how they carry themselves that makes me envious. Even though I know nothing about them, I want to be them.

Halfway down the wall, the chambermaid stops in front of a large cherry wood door. I look at the wall beside it; there is a blank space. My imagination takes hold, and I cannot help but visualize my portrait being grander than the rest, filling the void. There is a part of me that craves the satisfaction of seeing the other women envious of my status.

While savoring the glorious moment, my daydream is suddenly shattered by the sound of jingling keys. As the door is un-locked, the chambermaid hastily enters, and I follow her inside. The ornate fire-places' crackling embers draw me closer, and as I feel the warmth, my eyes widen in delight.

Everything is glorious. The walls are decorated with salmon-pink flocked wall coverings featuring a stenciled design of tulips and spring lilies. Paintings with flo-ral themes framed in white-painted wood enhance the elegant motif. The chamber has an abundance of windows adorned with cream-colored curtains, allowing am-ple natural light to permeate every corner.

As I scan the room, the bed immediate-ly captures my attention. Its tall wooden posts proudly display carved flowers, and its canopy is made from imported fabric with a golden fringe that drapes all sides.

Seeing a gown lying across the pink quilted duvet, I break away from the warmth of the fire toward the French silk brocade garment made in ivory hues. The low neckline, intricate quarter sleeves, and velvet bows mirror the fashion style of the paintings.

I grasp the bottom of the skirt and feel the rich fabric between my fingers. "Isn't it the most breathtaking sight you have ever—"

Before I finish my sentence, a sudden and forceful tug at my waist takes my breath away, stopping me in my tracks. To my surprise, the chambermaid is un-cinching the laces of my corset.

Dropping the material from my hands, I screech, "*Ouch!*" After collecting my composure, I turn to face her. "My apologies for making such a racket." I chuckle. "I believe you caught me a bit off-guard."

She continues silently, pulling and prodding with an expressionless face.

I look down at my dress and hoopskirt, now lying at my feet. Left with nothing but my undergarments, I hastily clutch my body, trembling with cold and desperately trying to maintain a semblance of modesty.

The chambermaid swiftly drops to her hands and knees, and she crawls toward my feet with determination.

Her assertive actions as she removes my shoes and stockings startle me, causing me to lose my balance and stiffen uncomfortably. To calm myself, I concentrate on the soothing sound of the crackling fire and visualize standing beside it, feeling its warmth.

Swiftly, the woman jumps up and seizes me by the arm, tugging me behind her. We make our way to a white-painted door on the opposite side of the bedchamber. As she pulls me inside, I shudder as the icy marble floor contacts my bare feet.

She dashes across the room toward a sizable copper tub filled with soapy water and immerses her hand to assess the temperature. Small splashes echo through the frigid air.

"Oh, you ... you must be mistaken," I say, my words coming out in a nervous stammer. Realizing she is not listening, I anxiously watch her continue to mix the tub's contents. In a state of panic, I nervously giggle. "Thank you, but I am not in need of a bath. I just washed the night before my birthday."

She pulls her hand from the bubbles and pats her wet palm against the outside of the tub.

I cringe at the sensation of warm water droplets hitting my face. *Why is she ignoring me?* Forcing a grin, I politely walk toward her.

In a swooping movement, she grabs my chemise undergarment at the bottom of its skirt and yanks it over my head.

I gasp. In shock, I look down at my naked body. Quickly trying to cover my breasts, my fingers brush my ribcage, and pain shoots through my bones. I glance at the injury from my corset, and it is even worse than I remembered. Immediately, I try to hide it with my elbow; the entire piece of flesh covering my side is black and blue.

Hearing a splash, I look at the water. As a layer of steam rolls off the surface, evaporating into the air, the chambermaid pats the top of the bubbles again, signaling for me to get in.

Shivering from the cold, I step inside one leg at a time. Rather than immediate relief, the drastic temperature change feels prickly against my ice-cold skin. Slowly submerging each limb, I sit, slumping further into the tub until the waterline touches my neck.

The chambermaid dips a washcloth into the water and begins polishing my back. With my eyes fixed ahead, I hear the water splashing against the tile as it spills from the tub.

There is a brief period of silence.

"You know that we are alone. It is only you and I in here," I say, hugging my arms around my calves. "There is no one else around."

Listening, she shifts her eyes to me, then back to the water.

"To put it simply," I say, turning to face her as I inch my body closer to the side of the tub, "we can break free from those boring, old rules." Lowering my voice to a whisper, I continue, "It shall be our little secret." As she slows down her scrubbing, I cannot help but smirk, sensing the bond forming between us. "No one will ever know."

Avoiding eye contact, she lifts the rag from the water and begins wringing it out. I watch as her jaw clenches and the lump in her throat moves slightly as if contemplating speech.

"I promise," I say, my voice filled with anticipation, "whatever you tell me will stay between us."

As the tension releases from her jaw, I quickly shift my gaze, respecting her need for privacy. Abruptly, the sound of the damp rag whacking against the side of the tub breaks the silence. Startled, I jump, flinging suds into my eyes.

The chambermaid's cheeks bulge with air as she attempts to suppress a cough. I cannot help but cringe when I hear her hacking. The bizarre incident unsettles me, making me feel like there is no one I can confide in.

She rushes to a shelf to grab a bath sheet and, standing over me, extends it to its length. Skeptical of her, I stand up as thoughts race through my mind. *Is she no better than him? Why would she ignore me?* As I force a smile, I lift my arms and let her wrap the cloth around me.

Assisting me out of the bathtub, she dries my limbs and then places a dressing robe over my shoulders to keep me warm.

While I wrap the robe tighter around myself, I watch her fold the damp towel and place it on the tub's edge. Though I had not thought it possible, her movements have become even more rigid than before, making me question if I unintentionally upset her. "I did not intend to offend you. You see, I am used to things being different. My former chambermaid was my best friend and confidant," I say.

Squinching her face, she looks to the floor, trying to conceal her emotional turmoil.

"I never thought it possible, but maybe I'm feeling a tinge of homesickness." I chuckle nervously, taking a small step toward her.

However, before I can say another word, she swiftly spins around. Clutching a handful of my robe, she leads me back into the bedroom. She guides me to a large vanity adorned with beautiful roses and positioned near the window. As I sit, I notice my weary eyes staring back at me in the mirror.

She pulls out my hairpins and skillfully shapes my curls into an elaborate style, leaving a small section to frame my face and cascade down my back.

My attention shifts to the three brass dishes on the table; each has a lid with a tiny knob. She reaches over my shoulder to pull one covering off and, snatching out a powder puff, douses it in an ash-colored crème.

"What is that ... " Before I can finish speaking, she dabs the mixture onto my lips.

As she works across my face, she skillfully blends the product into my complexion. Moving on to the second jar, she dips her fingers into the rouge and gently rubs it onto my cheeks.

I observe myself in the mirror. Whatever she is doing appears to conceal the tired expression I had been fixating on.

She picks up a small stamp tool and removes the lid from the last jar. She dips it into the contents and applies a small dot of black ink above my right lip, creating a beauty mark.

I look at my reflection in the mirror as she puts everything back in order. I find every element of my image unrecognizable; rather than myself, I look like the women from the portraits in the hall. Being cautious not to disturb the powder on my face, I brush my finger against my lips and release a giggle, remarking, "It is amazing. That was all it took."

Then, while watching me, she wipes her rouge-covered fingers on her skirt and dashes to the bed.

A clap rings through the air, and swiveling my body to look, I see the chambermaid waving for me. She has meticulously arranged the rest of my garments, including a pair of coordinating ivory satin shoes.

With a burst of enthusiasm, I leap to my feet and rush over, lifting my hands above my head to prepare for being dressed.

Without hesitation, she throws the layers on me one by one, starting with my undergarments. Then, fastening the fresh corset around my ribs, she tugs with all her might to cinch my waist.

As tears fill my eyes from the pain, I instinctively widen my nostrils to prevent any drops from escaping and ruining my makeup. My ribs and hips lose all sensation with each tightening yank of the corset ribbons. "Oh, the suffering we must endure," I mutter.

Getting down on her hands and knees, the maid shimmies the shoes onto my feet. I shift my weight from heel to toe, feeling the wood floor beneath them as I work to break in the tight fit.

She then secures a hoop skirt to my hips and carefully drapes the final layers over the top, completing the ensemble. I should feel like I am glowing in the magnificent gown, but the heavy weight of the material, the stiff corset, and the ill-fitting shoes bring me nothing but misery.

She snatches an item from the bed that I overlooked before—a lace bridal veil. In a sudden rush of naive panic, I realize that the dress's color carries a more profound meaning beyond a simple preference. Stammering nervously, I utter, "Oh, no … I… I did not realize. Are you certain this is what Mr. McKinley desires? I was under the impression that we would have at least a week to become familiar with one another prior to our wedding."

The chambermaid pushes down on my shoulders, guiding me to lower myself while skillfully securing the veil's comb into my half-up hairdo on top of my head. With a nervous smile, I straighten my posture. "Well, if that's how it must be, then I guess I have no choice but to comply."

She gestures for me to adjust the veil over my face, and when I do not respond quickly enough, she reaches over my head and does it herself.

As the white shroud covers my eyes, my heart races. There is a suffocating feeling surrounding it. I exhale deeply, observing as a gentle whoosh of air sweeps the fabric from my lips. "Ah, that is much better," I say.

Then, sensing a gentle tug on my skirt, I obediently follow the chambermaid out of the door.

Initiation

I notice Hugh standing at the bottom as we descend the spiral staircase. His presence commands attention, as he is adorned in a pristine white coat and elegant cape, paired with knickers and ivory satin shoes that perfectly mirror my attire.

Tapping his foot, he checks his pocket watch and, lifting his gaze, his attention locks on my descent. "There she is … my beautiful bride," he says, his lips tilting into a devious grin. He watches the chambermaid finish escorting me down the last step. "White suits you well. It complements your complexion beautifully."

Letting my skirt hit the floor, the chambermaid circles me to fluff it. I nervously smile at him. "Thank you," I say.

He snaps his fingers. "You are free to go. I will take it from here," he says. Seeing her continue to fluff my skirt, he clears his throat. "Are you deaf, woman? I said you are no longer needed. You can return to your quarters!"

I watch her from a side glance; I do not wish for her to get into trouble, but I also hate for her to leave.

His irritation builds, and his cheeks redden. Leaning forward, he waves his hand. "Off you go, now," he says, shooing her away. "Go on."

She springs to her feet and gives me one last glance. Her eyes reveal a deep sadness, as though she is concealing something from me. Despite my curiosity and desire to uncover the truth, Hugh's intense glare fills me with panic and draws my attention.

"Let us make haste," he says, grabbing my arm.

Reluctantly, I turn to face him. "Of course," I respond, nodding. As I advance a few steps, I cannot escape the image of the chamber-maid's unsettling look in her eye.

The quick pace of our walk echoes through the corridor. There is an eerie stagnancy that lingers between our footsteps, sending shivers down my spine. A strange realization dawns on me as I listen more closely—I have not heard the chambermaid's departure. Hugh gives my arm a forceful tug, distracting me from my thoughts.

Amid the brief silence, an eerie and unsettling sensation envelops me as if an unseen watchful presence looms in the shadows, observing my every move.

A subtle hiss cuts through the air. "Genevieve," a woman's voice whispers. "Genevieve."

Wincing, I hold my breath and quickly glance over my shoulder.

Both the hallway and staircase are empty.

My racing thoughts mirror the pounding pace of my heart as I come to a sudden stop, catching the weight of Hugh's penetrating gaze. Shifting my focus back to him, our eyes connect; in that moment, a tangible sense of discomfort fills the space between us.

With a grin, I anxiously clear my throat. "It's all so lovely," I say, and, holding myself back from saying more, I watch his look of skepticism dissipate, returning to its normal rigid tone.

Navigating through the expansive estate feels like maneuvering through a spider's web. With each turn, our pace quickens, and the more we delve into the east wing, the more challenging it becomes to recall our path.

We walk down a long corridor, then abruptly stop, turning yet another corner.

Trying to lessen the pain of my fresh blisters, I shift my weight between my feet and distract myself by scanning the artwork on the walls.

The decor differs from the other halls. It is much more elaborate. Rather than splashes of royal purples and blues, dark green and golden accents coat the moldings. Each portrait depicts the same man at various points in his life, from young to old, and he bears a remarkable resemblance to my future spouse.

Hugh releases his grip, and my arm drops to my side. Directing his gaze toward a painting of a youthful version of the man, he beelines toward it. "He is only slightly older than me in this portrait," he remarks, snickering sarcastically. "That was during his prime, in the glorious days of his youth."

As he ponders it, I keep my words under my breath. "Striking resemblance," I say.

His fingers reach out, making gentle contact with the weathered wooden frame. They lightly trace the intricate patterns etched into the surface as if reading a story written by time itself.

After a moment, he withdraws his hand and observes the delicate accumulation of dust, each particle appearing suspended in time, like tiny artifacts of bygone moments. "Well, I suppose the time has come to ensure you are acceptable," he muses.

Turning around, he flicks his fingers, sending the dust swirling into the air like a miniature sandstorm before it settles back down, forever changed. I nervously inspect my dress. Even though I cannot find any flaws, his words trigger my insecurities, and I check again.

Hugh watches the last remaining particles drift through the air. He clears his throat, and with a skipping step, the heels of his shoes kick the floor. "My father can be quite the critic," he says, stopping beside me. "That is why you need to look your very best." He directs his attention to a door at the end of the hall, and all the glee leaves his face. His expression resembles that of a frightened child preparing for a lashing. Something about his raw vulnerability makes my heart ache for him. It causes me to rethink the monstrous side I saw earlier. Maybe there was a reason for his cruelty.

As he slips deeper into his thoughts, his breathing becomes heavy. I carefully place my hand on his back. His posture stiffens under my fingertips without shifting his attention from the door. I embrace the moment, and keeping quiet, I lean in a little closer.

He instantly lifts his shoulders to his ears. Noticing his discomfort, I retract my hand and survey his eyes, which are still fixed on the same spot. With a sigh, he fluffs the collar of his shirt and glances in my direction. "Shall we?"

"Yes, of course." I nod and scan the young portrait of his father once more. There's an undeniable allure in his eyes, captivating my attention.

"All right, then," he says, startling me. "Let us not keep him waiting."

As I briskly walk, following closely behind, I sense the eyes of the paintings watching me as I pass. The further we progress down the drafty hall, the more pronounced the cobwebs become, clinging to the corners of the ceiling.

Dust coats the picture frames and his father's chamber door. The unkempt nature is unsettling. It makes me conflicted; I am unsure what to think. "Do you visit him often?" I ask.

We stop in front of the dark wooden entrance.

As I listen to the silence, I cannot help but wonder if my words were lost in our footsteps. I clear my throat to speak louder. "Your father? Do you visit your father often?"

He responds with a nonchalant shrug, then reaches into his pocket. "I ... well… uh, I must confess…." As he mumbles, he pulls out a skeleton key and sticks it in the lock. Sweat drips from his hairline. "Not nearly as much as I should."

With a twist of the key, the lock clicks. Taking a deep breath, he grasps the doorknob and tries to open it, but the door remains stubbornly shut.

He exerts more effort with a grunt. "You see, every time *we* would speak, *we* would butt heads with one another." Pausing, he puts his body into the metal knob and, with one last heave, says, "It just grew to be too taxing on my *nerves*."

The door gives way, and the unoiled hinges screech. "There we are," he laughs, placing the key back in his pocket.

I seize the moment to ease his nerves. "Hopefully, things will improve once you are married."

He chuckles. "Yes. One can only hope."

His complexion turns pale as he pushes the door open to a crack. Reluctantly peering inside, he shouts, "Father, it is I, your son!" He gets louder. "It is Hugh."

I hesitantly smile, hoping to make a good impression, but instead of hearing the cheerful voice of an older man, there is only silence. Hugh perks up and loudly laughs. "Father, you are quite funny!"

I chuckle, joining in.

He opens the door a bit further. "I must confess, old man, you nearly fooled me! For a moment, I believed the reaper had arrived to relieve us of your presence."

I stand in silence, straining my ears to listen, but I cannot hear a thing.

Hugh speaks louder. "Yes ... indeed. True to my promise, I have arrived with the woman I intend to marry. Allow me to introduce Genevieve. The clergyman is expected to join us shortly, and with you and God as our witness, he will unite us in matrimony."

Still only able to hear Hugh's voice, I shift myself closer.

He opens the door a bit more. "Now that it is settled, may we come in?"

As I peer into the darkness, the pungent odor of mildew and decay overwhelms my senses.

Hugh yanks the door open the rest of the way. "Very good, then. Here we come!" Entering, he motions for me to follow.

A wave of rotten stench hits me, causing me to gasp and stand frozen in place, holding my breath.

Hugh turns around and sticks his head back out the door. His glare sends a wave of panic through me. "Exercise your man-ners, *woman* ... say something."

As I listen to the hiss leave his clenched smile, I release the oxygen in my lungs. "My apologies," I reply.

He enters back into the darkness and waves for me to follow. Struggling not to cough amid the noxious fumes, I inch my way through the door. Despite feeling ill, I force a smile, concealing my sickness. "Hello … sir. My name is Genevieve. I am honored to make your acquaintance. I must say, the grounds of your estate are quite stunning."

Hugh seizes my arm and pulls me inside. He closes the door, surrounding us in darkness. I glance through the shadows and, finding the shape of the windows, notice the heavy velvet curtains have been drawn to block out the daylight.

Hugh stomps his foot, and directing his attention to his father, releases his grip. "I see you have been ignoring the doctor's orders again."

I pulsate my fist to ease the ache in my arm.

He rushes across the room toward the curtains. "Do you not remember what the doctor told you? You are supposed to be leaving these open, not sitting in the dark like a nocturnal beast." With a heave, he pulls at the heavy material. "Just like plants need natural light to survive, our souls also crave its nourishment in order to thrive."

The winter sun trickles into the room. I watch perspiration forming on Hugh's brow as he finishes tying back the heavy velvet drapes.

"I know how you dislike repeating yourself," he says, dramatically pausing. "Well … for that matter, everybody does. However, it is quite obvious that she did not hear you, so if you don't mind saying it once again for her benefit, it would be greatly appreciated." Stopping, he clears his throat to ensure he has my attention.

"Oh!" I gasp, immediately prepared to offer my apologies.

Hugh talks louder. "Father, it is important that you speak louder."

"Oh, I am terribly sorry, sir. I did not mean to…" Straightening my posture, I swiftly turn toward bed. Black satin sheets are tightly tucked around the man's body. Afraid of seeing the disapproval on his face, I quickly divert my attention to the floor as I speak. "I … I… I apologize if I offended you in any manner."

Stammering, I stop and, knowing I must show respect, look at the only visible portion of his body—his head. As our eyes meet, my body goes into a state of shock.

Propped up by a mound of pillows, his wrinkly face appears frozen, petrified in place, resembling a parched piece of driftwood. His moisture-deprived pupils are sunken deep into his skull.

As I struggle to move forward, fighting to keep my knees from buckling in fear, I am startled by heavy footsteps rapidly approaching from behind.

Hugh scrambles past me toward the bed. "Yes, yes, I know. You made it clear that you desired an accomplished woman to be my bride ... and she truly is one. I swear on it," he shouts.

As I try to comprehend the situation, my gaze fixates on the sheets, desperately seeking any sign of breathing. Yet, as I find no evidence of the man's chest rising and falling, my attention turns to the unfolding charade.

Hugh lowers his voice, leaning closer to his father. "Between you and me, I believe she is still exhausted from the lengthy journey."

Is this a morbid joke? I take a slow breath to calm myself. Not only is this my first time seeing a corpse, but my husband-to-be is conversing with him like the living.

As he breaks his attention away from the man, Hugh's face turns red with frustration. "*Well*, Genevieve?!"

The sound of my name nearly startles me out of my skin.

Suddenly, without warning, he rushes toward me and seizes my arm. "You must say something to father. He is threatening to send you back!" he says, talking faster while pulling me behind.

I wince as my eyes remain fixed on the corpse. Inch by inch, we move closer; the reek is unbearable. Hugh pulls harder to combat my dragging feet. "Yes, Father, I told her." He grunts.

We stop at the foot of the bed. His hand forcefully presses against my back, and I cannot help but release a startled gasp.

"I concur; her beauty is more striking when viewed up close rather than from a distance." He chuckles, giving me a playful push to walk closer.

What am I supposed to say? How do I spark a conversation with someone who is lifeless and cannot speak? I try to think of what to do, but my thoughts spiral out of control.

Hugh impatiently taps his foot; he wants me to speak.

I nervously clear my throat. "I daresay it is chilly in here." Pausing, I gaze at the bedposts. "Perhaps it would be best if you were not left resting in the cold ... Shall I bring you an extra blanket?"

Hugh breaks the silence with a loud laugh. "I told you she was a rare find."

Hearing the happiness in his voice, I pretend to listen for his father's reply and lean closer to the bed. "Oh? Is that so?"

As I touch the sheet covering his shoulder, the bedroom door abruptly opens, and I hear an unfamiliar man's voice rumble against the walls.

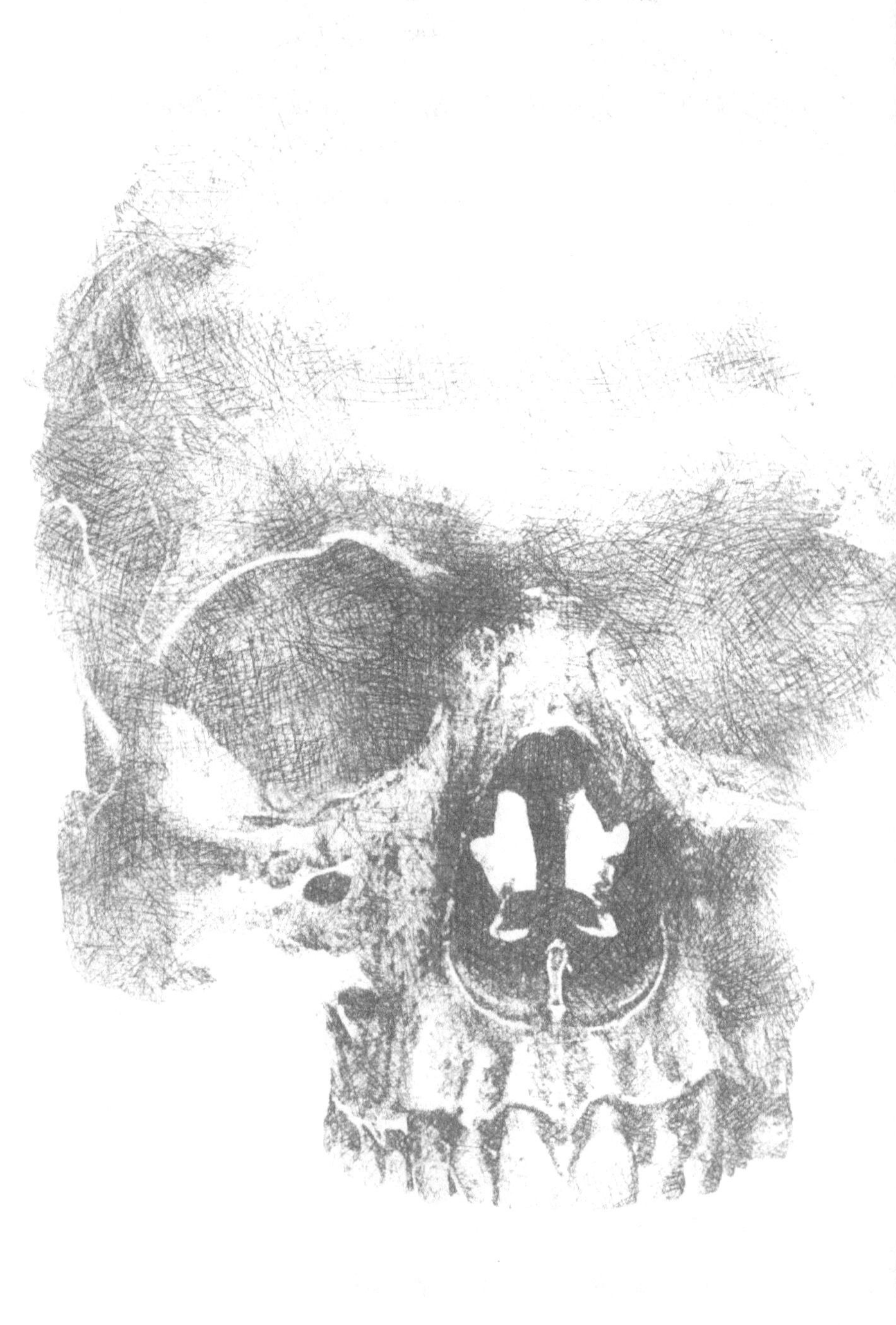

Nine

Blessings

The arrival of the clergyman brings with it a sense of solemnity as he enters the room adorned in his clerical attire—a gown, cassock, and cap. "Please accept my sincerest apologies for my tardiness," he says, catching his breath as he closes the door behind him. "One of my regular parishioners, an unrelenting octogenarian, would not cease to engage me following the conclusion of the service."

As I shift my gaze toward him, our eyes meet. He is an older gentleman with hair that is almost white and skin that sags around his cheekbones.

"There we are! Now, where were we?" he asks with a smile. His attention slowly drifts to the bed beside me, and his eyes bulge in surprise.

I pull my hand away from the corpse.

Hugh smiles from ear to ear. "We are so pleased to have you here to officiate our wedding!" he says, rushing to greet the clergyman. His words tumble out quickly as he motions to the bed. "You are already well-acquainted with my father, so I see no need for an introduction." He chuckles. "As you can see, he is here to witness our matrimony."

The Clergyman's face pales.

Hugh talks faster. "Yes, and beside him is my beautiful wife-to-be, Genevieve."

I nervously stumble forward, my eyes fixed on the floor while trying to curtsy. "How do you do?" I say.

Hugh races toward me. "I am just as surprised as you to see how well they get along, considering they have just met. It seems that my father has taken quite a liking to her."

Still focused on the bed, the clergyman stammers, trying to speak. "He ... um... he is... well..."

"Oh, yes! I believe the last time you saw him, we thought he would not make it another minute, but here we are. I say he has made quite the turnaround in recent months," Hugh says, his excitement building. "He seems to be the most lively he has been in quite some time. Wouldn't you agree?"

As the enthusiasm of his voice fills the room, I watch the clergyman's expression. The Bible shakes in his hand; he is rattled by the sight. "Phil ... Phillip?" he says with a stammer while watching for a response.

I am frozen, listening to the name. *What a strange coincidence.*

"Come now, father! Is that any way to greet an old friend?" Hugh takes a step closer to the bed and touches his shoulder. "We all know you are tired, but that does not mean you can't be pleasant." He directs his attention to the clergyman. "I am not sure how much more my father can handle today. So, shall we speed things up?"

The clergyman anxiously forces a smile. "Umm ... well... if he requires rest, should we postpone this to another time? Perhaps when he is feeling better?"

"What?" Hugh asks, and as he catches the clergyman glancing at the door, he quickly grabs my arm. "Why in the world would we even consider doing that?"

Sweat drips down the clergyman's forehead. "Uh ... yes, um, let me see. Yes, well, to begin with, for your marriage to be recognized in the eyes of the church, you will need another witness."

Hugh tightens his grip. "Father's frailness does not make him any less of a man!"

"But ... he is.... um ... he is de..." As the clergyman searches for his words, he stumbles.

"*Deserving* of respect!" Each of Hugh's heated words spews spit. "Which you are not giving him!"

"Young man, you cannot have a dead witness!" the clergyman exclaims. With an exhale, he closes his eyes and, catching his breath, continues, "Your demands are unholy, blasphemous, and I will *not* condone such behavior." His body stiffens as he lets out a frustrated exhale.

"What are you saying?" Hugh shouts.

My arm aches from his coiling grip.

"Are you implying that I am a liar?!"

With a shrug, the clergyman nervously looks from side to side. "No! Of course not! I meant to say we all process grief differently, and some ... like in your case, some ways are more extravagant than others."

Hugh's jaw tightens as he takes a step closer. "You, sir, are a disgrace to the church and a coward in the eyes of God," he says, sneering, his voice filled with contempt. The clergyman retreats, and Hugh continues, "I will reveal your sins to the congregation." A thud sounds from the clergyman's back, hitting the door.

"The choice is yours," Hugh says.

As the clergyman winces, sweat drips into his eyes. "Threats are the Devil's words," he says.

Hugh laughs. "That's where you're mistaken. Threats are what propel us in society. They serve as catalysts for change … they are the driving force behind success."

He squeezes my arm tighter and drags me toward the clergyman.

"Now, take out your quill and ink," Hugh says with a smile. He points to our clothing. "As you can see, we are ready to marry. We do not wish to be late for our celebratory dinner."

The clergyman realizes he is backed into a corner. "Of course," he says, frantically searching his pocket. He talks faster. "I wouldn't want to cause any disruptions during this joyous occasion."

Hugh slaps his shoulder, and the feeling of his skittish body jumping makes him chuckle. "Ah, you see? I knew you would come around."

I watch the piece of papyrus in the clergyman's trembling fingers. "By the power of God, I pronounce you man and wife," he says. Signing the sheet against the wall, he apprehensively passes it to me.

The moment I finish signing, Hugh rips the quill from my hand. As he starts to sign, he glances at the cleric. "It looks like you've seen a ghost," he says.

The clergyman observes him carefully, his gaze shifting toward the witness line, where Hugh's father's signature now occupies the space.

"Here you are, then," Hugh says. With a smile, he hands the clergyman the finished contract. "Now, you can be off on your merry way."

The Clergyman folds the contract for safekeeping and tucks it in his Bible. His eyes scan the bed, and he suddenly freezes.

The corpse's right hand now rests on top of the sheets. He nervously gulps and fumbles for the doorknob, all without mentioning it. "May you both have a prosperous life and happy marriage," he says, letting himself out and hurrying down the hall.

With a smirk, Hugh sighs. "He shall be the one who needs daily devotional, not us." Clearing his throat, he takes a few steps toward the open door. "Come on, dear wife; we mustn't keep our guests waiting."

As I am about to take a step, I hear something tap the floor behind me. Swiftly, I turn around to see what it is. To my surprise, I find a quill lying on the ground beside the bed.

I instantly recognize it from earlier and chuckle. "I am surprised no one has looked for you." As I walk to retrieve it, a feeble voice stops me.

"To the joyous union." It says.

My eyes drift over the corpse, and suddenly, I spot the source of the clergyman's fear - its mummified hand now lying on top of the sheets.

"Tell my father we must depart!" Hugh shouts from the hallway. "There is no time to waste!"

I instantly shift my attention to the door. "Yes, my love!" I shout, and without looking back, I dart to the exit, abandoning the quill.

As I escape to the hall, the sound of something shifting in the bed resonates from behind me, triggering me to move faster.

Glancing back at the room from the corridor, I take a deep breath to regain my composure.

Hugh slams the door shut. "You will quickly learn that my father has the gift of gab," he says. "He will keep you for hours if given the chance. That is why I do not bother with goodbyes … They are pointless."

As he continues speaking, he takes the key from his pocket, inserts it into the lock, and slowly turns it. "At times, he can be quite unpredictable. So, this is for his good."

My heart races as I strain to listen for the reassuring click.

With a grunt, he pulls on the door, ensuring it is securely latched. Then, he tucks the key away in his pocket and gives it a playful pat.

I notice the light seeping from beneath the door abruptly disappear. Whatever is inside has closed the curtains.

Hugh ramps up with excitement. "One down and six to go!"

"Wouldn't it just be four?" I ask, lifting my gaze from the door with an anxious chuckle.

Thinking, he tallies on one hand. "Well … there are my two sisters and their husbands. Then, our house doctor … Oh, and Mother, of course."

His mention of his mother catches me off-guard and leaves me looking bewildered.

"Ah! You thought Mother was dead, didn't you?" he laughs.

I quickly glance around the hallway, trying to hide any signs of my confusion. "No, not at all. That was the last thing on my mind…. I, um, I was thinking about how grand everyone shall be."

"Hmm, I could have sworn otherwise…" A bemused expression crosses his face before he continues. "Everyone always looks their best in this household, so they will be quite grand indeed." After a brief pause, he extends his arm and says, "Now, come along, wife; let us join the others."

I smile, taking his arm. "Yes, yes, of course … Let us go."

With a grin, he leads the way down the hall.

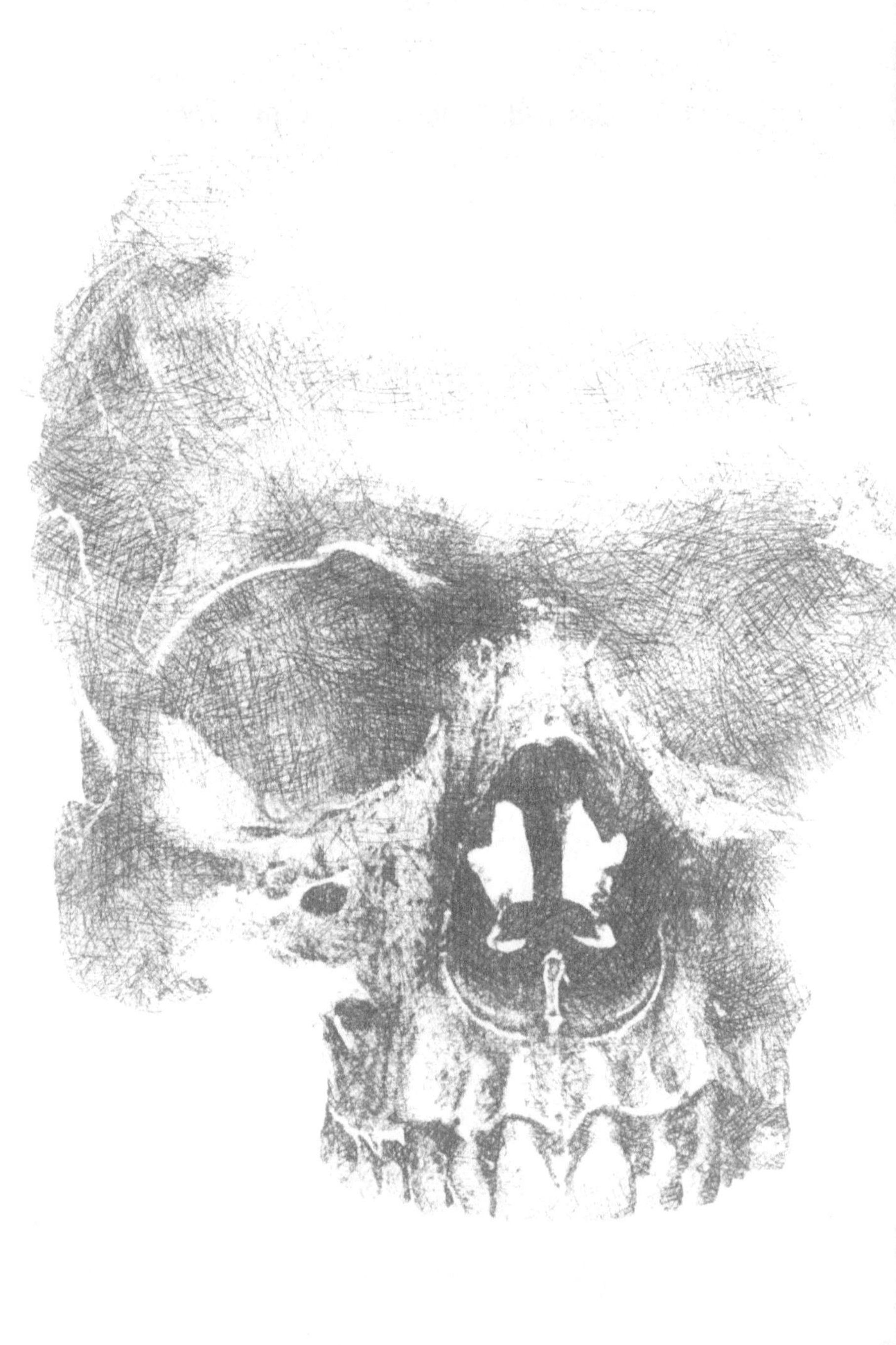

Ten

Peculiar Ingredients

S hrill cackles from gossiping women echo from the dining room.

The sound makes me wonder what they are chattering about. *Is it me?* My thoughts heighten my insecurities.

Hugh stops us in front of an impressive entrance adorned with magnificent golden accents and beveled edges. "Are you ready?" he asks, his voice filled with anticipation.

As I mirror his widening smile and nod, I cannot help but be mesmerized by the intricate floral patterns carved into the door's surface.

"Very well, then. Look alive," he says, reaching for the handle. As he pushes the heavy entrance open, the voices from inside abruptly cease.

Like the rest of the manor, the space is much larger than I could ever have imagined, more closely resembling a ballroom rather than a place to share a meal.

Gold-gilded cherry wood beams vault the ceiling above the table, interwoven with a mural depicting an array of beautiful women with different shades of long, flowing, wavy locks. As they lie down, eating grapes and fruits, long strokes of blue simulate a breeze that meticulously blows their curls over their exposed breasts.

Stunning white rococo grand floral arrangements, with a mix of willows and roses, scatter the space, making it smell of spring. The room is adorned with intricate gold and white lace, creating an atmosphere of elegance and nuptial celebrations.

I glance at the small crowd of women and men perfectly spaced around a long, oblong banquet table in the middle of the sprawling room. The table and chairs are crafted from cherry wood and intricately carved to replicate the pattern found at the entrance.

Each place setting is layered with various sizes of white porcelain plates hand-painted with a floral garden motif. On top are the utensils wrapped in white silk napkins and tied with delicate bows made of tulle. Rather than silver, the forks and knives poking out from the top of the bundle are gold.

As we make our way into the room, the anticipation is palpable. Suddenly, Hugh snaps his fingers and booms, "I propose a toast!"

His loud shout echoes in my ear as he vigorously nudges my arm, and I notice everyone's stare.

A group of waitstaff rushes through a small door from the kitchen carrying crystal glasses filled with champagne. I divert my attention to them and nervously smile, taking a drink from one's hand.

Hugh proudly lifts his glass toward the sparkling chandelier, almost spilling his cup. "Today is the most joyous occasion," he says. "With immense pleasure, I introduce you to the new mistress of the esteemed McKinley Estate," he proclaims, with a grin extending from ear to ear. "To my beautiful bride … Let us drink and be merry!"

Whispers break out across the room.

I anxiously glance in their direction and find everyone at the table grinning while looking me up and down. As I take my initial sip, the crowd applauds, and I look over at Hugh, who is raising an empty glass in triumph.

We approach the table, and I quickly scan for an unoccupied chair, eager to relieve my aching feet. Only two seats remain, each positioned at opposite ends of the table. Wondering why we are sitting at such a distance, I turn to Hugh, but a sudden, powerful tug on my arm by a servant silences me before I can ask the question.

Hugh motions for more champagne and gives a sarcastic wave. "Till we meet again, my beautiful bride." He laughs.

To avoid causing a commotion, I reluctantly comply and put on a fake smile while noticing everyone return to their gossiping gazes. Something about the looks in their eyes frightens me. Their hissing voices cut through the air, leaving me feeling like an innocent mouse that has mistakenly ventured into a pit of snakes. I avoid making eye contact with them while taking my seat. Then, with feigned confidence, I lift my head and survey the guests sitting on either side of me.

Both women wear frilled lace dresses like mine, with velvet bows securing their sleeves. The woman sitting on my right catches my attention with her lavender attire. She has styled her chestnut locks into an elegant updo made of curls and adorned with delicate willow buds. Her face exudes youthfulness with its rosy cheeks and supple, smooth skin.

The woman to my left is dressed in coral tones. Her beautiful hair is a delightful mix of blond and brown, elegantly pulled back into ringlet curls that cascade down her neck.

I give a slight nod. "How do you do?" I say, awaiting a response, only to be met with their silent stares. I continue by adding, "I assume you must be Hugh's sisters. I have heard a great deal about you."

They look at one another and burst into a fit of laughter. I listen to their high-pitch cackles reverberate through the cavernous room.

"How fresh that is!" the woman on the right says. Clutching her heart, she screams, "She thinks we are sisters!"

The other chimes in. "That is gold!" she says. "She must be further from the countryside than we have thought!"

Confusion washes over me as I look at them, my mind racing with panic over saying something wrong.

Hugh appears amused from the other end of the table. "What is so funny? I must know!" He shouts.

Both women turn in unison toward him. "She thought Mother was your sister!" the one dressed in lavender says.

"I ... um... I..." I struggle to utter a single word; the mistake is unfathomable.

"Well, I suppose whatever Doc is doing must be working!" He laughs.

As more members of the table chime in, my attention shifts to Hugh's mother. I study her eyes and forehead, searching for any hint of age. Assuming she should appear around the same age as my mother, I stare in astonishment. There is not a single wrinkle on her face, and her skin is completely free of any signs of sagging.

My embarrassment causes me to sink lower into my seat.

She clinks her glass with her large emerald ring, and everyone falls silent. "Let us not make the poor girl feel melancholy on her wedding day," she says. "How would she have known, with her only example of aging being her mother?"

I slouch so low that the nape of my neck hits the top of the chair. "It is true ... I did not mean to cause offense. My sincerest apologies."

"You'll learn. Now, sit up straight! Slouching hinders blood flow and causes you to wrinkle faster," she says, snapping her fingers.

"My apologies," I say, looking at the table; I quickly fix my posture.

"Allow me to introduce myself properly. I am Adeline, your husband's mother."

I glance at her. "Yes, of course. It is an honor to meet you."

She continues. "The young woman sitting next to you is Henrietta, my eldest daughter. We affectionately call her Ettie, and her husband, Clinton, is seated beside her."

"I'm pleased to make your acquaintance," I say, looking at them both.

Her husband is not at all what I had expected. His skin tone is deep, and he has dark, curly hair tied back with a bow. His attire comprises black knickers and a lilac tailcoat that perfectly complements his wife's gown.

"He is a philosopher of sorts ... arguably, the best this generation has seen. I am living proof—look at me. His studies have proven quite beneficial to my appearance. Wouldn't you agree?" Adeline says, pointing to her cheek with a laugh.

Unable to hold his tongue, Hugh chimes in. "Indeed, he was the person I mentioned to you in the carriage."

Adeline continues, "Beside him is our house doctor, whom we refer to as Doc." My eyes are drawn to the quill tucked in the pocket of his pristine white coat and the glasses resting on the bridge of his broad nose. His hair is gray at the temples, parted to one side. He smiles at me.

"Beside Hugh sits Lucius, the husband of my other daughter, Hattie, and, of course, her

beside him. Lucius came to us from the prominent Burgess family, who run most of the trade
industry here," she says. Like the other husband, he also wears black dress knickers and a
baroque patterned coat that matches his wife's
dress.

I steal a quick look at Hattie. Her outfit is a
sky-blue variation of her sister's gown, and their
hair is styled almost identically. "I have never
witnessed such an uncanny resemblance between sisters," I say. "It is nearly impossible to
tell you apart."

Adeline snickers. "Well, I suppose God
would not have done his job if you could decipher them from each other, for they were born
together from the same womb. They are twins."

The two sisters simultaneously burst into
laughter, their voices blending seamlessly.

"From birth, they were assigned wardrobes
tailored to match the colors they are wearing
now, ensuring that everyone could easily distinguish them from one another. It was quite a
challenge for a new mother—quite unnerving
indeed," she says.

"And what of your other daughter? To my
understanding, you have one more daughter?"
I ask.

My question causes Hugh's body to tense
and the room to fall silent.

Adeline glares at the silk napkin in front of her. "Yes, Theodosia. Of course. She doesn't really look like the others because she is from my first marriage. Unfortunately, we have not seen her much since your brother's ill-fated circumstance. She has isolated herself in her chamber and has made it clear that she wants nothing to do with us at the moment. We hope it is just a phase, and she will come around soon."

"Enough of the gloom. Let us eat!" she says, forcing a smile. "I am ravenous, and I am sure everyone else must be as well."

With a loud clap of his hands, Hugh springs from his chair. The staff enters the room one after another through the swinging door, each carrying gold trays above their heads. The head butler leads the way, holding a large soup tureen.

They circle the table, displaying the first course. The spectacle of the glistening gilded platters transitions me away from my melancholy thoughts of Phillip.

A servant stops behind each of our seats, awaiting their next command. Hugh raises his hand. The waitstaff expertly places a dish in front of each of us with great precision. "Our evening will begin with a delightful bisque," he says. "Enjoy."

I look at the shallow bowl sitting before me.

As they pour a single scoop of liquid into each dish, they are expertly timed to one another.

Adeline swiftly removes her napkin from beneath the cutlery, and the rest of the group follows suit, carefully draping the smooth white cloth onto their laps. I am mesmerized by the steam swirling from the vibrant red soup. I have never witnessed such bright-colored food before, and I cannot help but wonder about the flavor.

The sound of slurps surrounds me.

I place my napkin on my lap and picking up my spoon; I take my first bite. As it flows across my tongue, I am unsure what to think of the taste, but noticing everyone watching me, I make noises of enjoyment. "Mmm."

The soup is relatively flavorless, and the texture is perplexing. As I gently swirl my spoon in the bowl, the others continue devouring the rest of their serving.

Before finishing the course, the next set of staff rushes through the kitchen doors, holding a second round of trays.

Hugh stands and announces. "For our next course, we will enjoy seasoned greens cooked in tallow and tossed in a vinaigrette dressing." After the introduction, he takes his seat.

As they clear away our bowls, they effortlessly swap them for the next dish, already beautifully plated.

The colorful display astonishes me. Not only does it appear much more appealing than the last, but I find comfort in recognizing each vegetable on the plate. Everything about it is delightful.

Forks clack against the porcelain as everyone consumes their meals.

I startle at the sound of the kitchen door swinging open behind me. As I take my last bite, I hear Hugh's chair legs scraping the floor.

He pushes himself from the table and springs to his feet, barely controlling his excitement. Fighting back his snicker, he puffs air into his cheeks, trying to contain himself.

"Now, the moment has arrived for our main course! The one we have all been waiting for … I proudly present to you…" The staff take their cue and pull the lids from their trays; steam rolls from the hot dishes and wafts above their heads. It smells of pot roast and buttered starches.

Hugh lifts his hands. "Behold, the blessed roast!"

As the staff sets the pre-plated entrées down, everyone applauds; drool hangs off their lips.

On each plate sits several slices of roasted meat dressed in au jus beside a whipped heap of potatoes.

Listening to their chuckling whispers, I am uncertain about what everyone finds so amusing. Suddenly, I hear everyone eating voraciously as I take my first bite. Instantly, my mouth is filled with a burst of rich flavors, unlike anything I have ever eaten before. The food is incredibly tender and fresh, and I can't resist devouring it.

"Isn't it delightful?" Adeline asks as she finishes her last mouthful.

I swiftly finish my final bite. "Marvelous," I say. "Just like the previous course, it is simply marvelous."

"Just wait. You think you feel amazing now. Later this evening, you will feel even better. Not only will you get the best sleep of your life, but it will be filled with the happiest of dreams." She laughs.

I smile and, glancing in her direction, notice Hugh at the other end of the table. "That sounds wonderful," I say; I wince at the sound of him starting to clap.

He stands up, trying to get everyone's attention. "What do you think? Shall we proceed to the drawing room for dessert and port?"

Everyone pretends not to hear him and avoids eye contact.

"We have yet to serve dessert," he states as he walks toward the door. Not hearing any footsteps following, he stops halfway across the room. His words become more theatrical as he talks faster. "Come on! What is everyone waiting for? Get up!"

As Ettie stares at the table, she dramatically sighs. "If I am to eat anymore, I fear that someone will have to loosen a string of my corset."

"Only one, sister?" Hattie laughs. "I fear it will have to be two or three."

Hugh races back to the table, irritated, and tries to pull them from their seats. "Come on, you two! A surprise awaits us for the special occasion. It is more than dessert. So! Do not be sour, ninnies, and get up off your rumps."

They fight him, swatting his hands. "'Sour ninnies?' What are we, children?" They laugh louder.

I watch their husbands' reactions as they remain unfazed, sitting comfortably in their seats, simply enjoying the show. Clinton leans forward. "I would listen to your brother. I caught a peek of the surprise earlier when I was taking my morning stroll through the halls, and it was quite spectacular. I must confess I am very excited. We both went to great lengths to make this happen. You will be sour in the morning if you miss it."

"Is that so?" Ettie asks, glancing at Hattie. With a smirk, she continues, "He rarely gets aroused by such things, so it must be quite impressive indeed."

As their cackles echo through the room, he playfully grabs her waist. "You! You, my dear, enjoy trying me, don't you?"

"Isn't that why I married you?" she asks, giggling. She turns around, and they stare into each other's eyes.

Hugh clears his throat. "I believe today is meant for my romantic endeavors, not yours."

Clinton releases Ettie from his arms.

Hugh smiles. "Now, let us proceed so my new bride may delight in her gift."

The waitstaff swiftly enters through the kitchen door, prompting everyone to stand and observe as they carry small ornamental trays with champagne flutes filled to the brim. The head butler leads the processional, holding a clay canister.

As they approach, I reach to grab a drink, and the sound of clinking spoons echoes in the room. Beside each glass is a small golden dish holding a tiny spoon. I glance at the rest of the group, observing how the butler moves from person to person, each scooping a spoonful of the mixture from the container and stirring it into their drinks.

"One a day to keep the wrinkles away," Adeline says. Putting another heaping serving of powder into her champagne, she stirs the sludge, trying to get it to dissolve. "Two a day, you will stay ailment-free, from a sore toe to a bad knee."

The waitstaff lingers nearby while the butler brings the container closer. He extends it to me, and I carefully remove the lid, my eyes fixed on the powder, which is a mixture of black and gray. "What is it?" I ask, sifting my small spoon through the contents of the hand-painted pottery.

Adeline rushes over. "Here, this is how it's done." Then, cupping my hand that holds the spoon, she scoops a heap from the canister and dumps it into my drink.

I notice some of the ashy substance tumbles onto the tray, and what makes it into the glass turns into a sludge that slowly sinks to the bottom.

She forces my hand to rattle the spoon from side to side in the mixture. "Now, give it a good stir," she says.

I nervously glance at the murky champagne flute before me, continuing to swirl as she releases her grip. "Thank you," I say. "That is very kind of you."

She takes a sip of her champagne. "Don't worry; you will catch on quickly." The liquid leaves a dark shadow hanging from the top of her lip.

Hugh grabs my arm as I set the spoon back onto the tray. "Are you ready for your surprise?" he says.

I gasp, almost spilling my drink. Then, noticing him pull a handkerchief from his pocket, I nod.

He takes a sip from his glass and motions for a servant to approach. He hands the handkerchief to them. "You mustn't peek. For I want you to be amazed." The staff places the silk square over my eyes, and my vision darkens. They securely tie it tight.

Hugh clutches my arm tighter. "Now, let us go," he says. "Carefully, follow me."

Eleven

The Golden King

Laughter echoes all around me as we exit the room. The boisterous tone reveals that the others view the matter as a game.

As I gather my bearings, I try not to spill my champagne, but each cackle skews my sense of direction, and every step makes me more nervous than the last. I attempt to count the number of steps and turns, yet I cannot compile a mental map. Their laughter makes it impossible for anything to stick in my mind.

We enter another room, and I feel the floor's surface shift beneath my feet. I sense the darkness through my blindfold; I hear the echo of crackling flames.

The door slams shut behind us; everyone gasps.

My heart races as Hugh unties the handkerchief from my eyes, and my attention darts to the grand fireplace and then scans the dimly lit surroundings.

Tiny flames flicker from a handful of cream-colored candles scattered across the floor. Although they are randomly placed, their flames dance in unison, and each flicker of light illuminates more of the room's bareness. It appears all the furniture has been pushed against the chamber's outer edges, creating a large open space.

In the center, an enormous table sits alone, displaying a sizable, elaborately decorated wooden object. It is unlike anything I have ever seen before. I am captivated by how the candle's light dances on its gilded shell, prompting me to move closer.

Hugh watches closely from behind and fights back his snicker. "Isn't it glorious?" he asks. Barely able to contain himself, he talks faster. "Is it not the most exotic thing you have ever seen?!"

I take a step nearer, mesmerized by the candles' flickering light as they reflect off the object's unfamiliarity. I am especially intrigued by peculiar drawings painted on the sides. Although they look otherworldly, something about them appears oddly familiar.

As everyone talks quietly, their hushed whispers slowly escalate, creating a cacophony that fills the room.

I turn to Hugh. "What ... what is it?" I ask. "What is that thing?"

His face lights up with excitement as he rushes forward. "That, my dear wife ... *that* thing you see lying on the table before us contains royalty."

I turn back to the table and feel my breath sucked from my chest. "Royalty?" I ask.

He chuckles. "Yes ... royalty. I told them I would accept nothing less for my bride. So, that is what they assured me I would get. Do you like it?"

As I stare in silence, my anxiety grows, and I tremble. The champagne in my glass sloshes from side to side. It is the most elaborate thing I have ever seen, with its sculpted form resembling a body at rest.

Hugh passes by me to admire the object. "It took a considerable amount of time to get my hands on this. Well ... that and money." He laughs.

My heart sinks to the pit of my stomach, and as I step forward, I struggle to breathe.

He playfully pats the wooden feet. "Behold, my dear. This is a sarcophagus plucked from a

golden tomb and transported from the mysterious land of Egypt."

Everyone's whispers persist, their murmurs
filled with excitement.

I examine the shell's exterior, which is decorated with gold, brown, black, and blue accents. Depicted on the side closest to me is a
row of stoic men painted in black, marching to
the left. Their serious demeanor and coordinat-
ed attire give off an almost militaristic vibe, as
if they are protecting something.

Hugh takes a sip of champagne. "You know,
in the past, they used those crude illustrations
to tell stories—quite uncivilized, if you ask me.
Instead of having a proper conversation, they
would resort to caveman drawings to document
history. Believe it or not, those rudimentary depictions were equivalent to the penmanship we
use today."

I watch as Hugh slowly runs his fingers
across the top of the sarcophagus, tracing the
full-size depiction of a man.

"And this is a pharaoh, wearing his head-
dress of gold. It's hard to believe that at one
time, he ruled all of Egypt." He chuckles. "I
hope he is watching from afar. That way, he can
be humbled by the realization that he has lost
all importance and is rather small in this new
world."

As I listen to him, my eyes wander to one of the marching men, and I notice a peculiar patch of paint around his waistline. It stands out against the antique yellow background and glistens oddly under the candlelight.

Clinton also notices it and quickly comes up behind me, using his fingertip to touch the spot. "What is this, brother? What is on the hieroglyph?" He pulls his thumb away and stops, holding it close to a candle's flicker. "Is this wet paint?" A layer of light-yellow stamps his skin.

Hugh edges closer to see what he is referring to. "Oh, that? Well … um…" He swiftly scans the room before whispering, "I had to make a few modifications."

I look at the streak left behind on the wood; underneath where the paint had been, there is a thick black line that extends straight from its pelvis.

Clinton looks at the smeared paint with fear. "Why would you do such a thing?"

Hugh restlessly paces around the table. "Well, if you really must know, those little men you see parading about were incredibly inappropriate. It felt like witnessing a Shakespearean farce played out … in Cheapside." His sisters snicker as they overhear his dramatics. With each gasping breath, his face grows redder.

"They had no shame in exposing their cocks like animals."

"Look, sister! It's so tiny." The girls point at the smeared wet paint in unison and laugh.

Hugh slams his fist against the table. "Stop it! Stop looking at it!" Racing toward me, he covers my eyes. "I cannot have my wife greeted with such filth on our wedding day. It is most inappropriate!"

I wince at the sensation of his words projecting spit onto my cheek.

With a shrug, Ettie giggles. "Well, I suppose you should have become a better artist. Ever since we were children, painting has never been your strong suit. Isn't that right, Mother?"

Clinton seizes a candle and brings it closer to examine the other men, only to find that they, too, have been painted in the same fashion.

The paint does not achieve the desired result; it only draws more attention to the small phalluses. The extra-thick coating elevates the objects, further setting them apart from the rest of the artwork.

"The writing is rather unusual," Clinton remarks, his voice trailing off as he continues reading the hieroglyphs. "I have studied this subject extensively, and yet I have never encountered anything like this before." I try to see what is happening by peeking through the gaps between Hugh's fingers.

Clinton's eyes remain fixed on the sarcophagus, his lips moving silently as he reads in a foreign tongue. Suddenly, he stops; his eyes bulge, and his face turns red with stress. "Oh, dear God, Hugh, what have you done?" With frantic eyes, he scours the artifact as though he were a man searching for a key to flee a jail cell before his execution. "I told you not to touch it without me present! That was our agreement. That was the one thing you promised."

"Relax, brother." Hugh removes his hand from my eyes and points to the men. "I would expect thanks if anything, for I have made the thing much more bearable."

"'Bearable?!'" Clinton turns to confront him. "'Bearable?!' You defaced writings you know nothing about!"

Hugh glances at the others and laughs. "That is a very generous description. I would hardly call those things writing. I, myself, would refer to them much differently than that. To me, they are nothing more than piss-poor drawings or scribbles. Look at it … it is all gibberish!"

"Awe, Hattie, look!" Ettie measures a tiny wet paint splotch with her fingers. "I fear these little men made our poor brother feel insecure. That is why he covered them." Hattie chuckles.

Hugh becomes furious. "No, it did not! Those little figures have nothing on my manhood. So, you take that back, you witch!"

Suddenly, Adeline's voice breaks through the bickering. "Silence, children! I have had enough of your antics for the evening!"

Everyone falls quiet. "You are at the ripe age of adulthood, and you must act as such!" she says. "I have taught you to behave more appropriately."

They glare at one another, and after a moment of pause, the squabbling resumes.

Amid their ongoing banter, I notice an unusual scratching noise joining with the chaos, and my attention becomes locked on the artifact. It sounds as if it is coming from within.

I swiftly move closer to the table. Stealing a quick look at the others, I see that they are preoccupied. I place a hand on its surface and press my ear against the wood.

They continue to argue, seemingly oblivious to the disturbance.

The coffin shifts beneath my palms. Terrified, I push myself away, my heart pounding. As I stare at the almond-shaped eyes on its painted lid, the sound inside suddenly stops.

I gasp for air, desperately attempting to form words. "Is ... is something alive in there?" I ask.

The room falls silent.

With all eyes on me, Lucius breaks out into a loud fit of laughter and says, "Absolutely not! The contents inside are ancient! It has been deceased for so long that it is hard to conceive it was once human. The body is completely dried and withered, like rotted fruit!"

Everyone joins in the hilarity, sending my nerves into a spiral.

"When it is opened, you will see," Lucius says.

Wanting to escape ridicule, I avert my gaze from the group and fixate on the intricately outlined eyes. The flickering candlelight reflects off the paint, causing a gentle sparkle that captivates me.

Adeline raises her champagne glass and taps her foot, trying to hurry this thing along. "For God's sake, Hugh, open it up already and let the girl see what's inside!" She laughs. "Even though I do not look my age, I still need my beauty rest, and we are passing the witching hour."

The room's excitement grows, and voices escalate into a chant. "What's inside, what's inside, what's inside?"

Another scrape sounds from the shell.

I gasp. "Are you ... certain it is... dead?"

Everyone falls silent and glares at me. Lucius rolls his eyes. "Yes! For the last time, yes!"

His shouting sends my heart into a frenzy and leaves me feeling paralyzed.

"Now, open the thing, Hugh! I am usually patient, but this is taking it too far! I am the one who put their family's name on the line to get this thing through the harbor, not you! Therefore, I should have the most say when it should be opened!"

Ettie rushes to rub his shoulders, reassuringly saying, "He will, dear. He is opening it now." She glances at her brother in an irritated panic, asking, "Isn't that right, Hugh?"

I shudder as the room turns more hostile, and three sharp knocks rattle the wood.

My stomach churns with unease as I scan the room, my mind racing with thoughts of whether anyone else has caught wind of the noise. I see Clinton peering out from a dark corner, staring at me. It seems like he is hiding from something, making me wonder if he also heard.

"All right, everyone, settle down! We shall open our dear friend on this table straight after a toast." Hugh raises his glass.

I glance at the others and, following along, nervously lift mine.

He continues his speech. "May the contents we discover inside captivate us with sheer delight and retain our youthful vigor. May it quell our inner demons and awaken our hidden desires. And, finally, may it devour our ailments and nibble away at our wrinkled skin."

The others smile and shout a resounding "Cheers!"

As Hugh chugs his drink, finishing every drop, I look at the sludge-laden champagne in my cup and cringe.

The beating on the coffin grows louder.

My eyes scan the room, and I notice something. Next to the table's leg, a champagne flute sits filled to the brim. "Clinton," I mutter under my breath.

Hugh throws his glass against the floor. "Cheers!"

Startled by the sound of shattering crystal, my cup slips from my hand and smashes into fragments near my feet.

"Did everyone finish their drinks?" Hugh asks, and hearing my breaking glass, he chuckles. "Well, I know my wife has! As for the rest of you … you know the rules. Drink up!"

I swiftly look at Clinton, his eyes bulging as he lifts his fingers to his lips.

The pounding from the sarcophagus grows louder.

"Do you not hear that? Can you not hear that dreadful noise?" I become frantic, speaking so quickly that my words blend together.

Hugh laughs, and then his face turns stern.

"It sounds like something is trying to get out!" I scream.

Hugh grabs my hand and pulls me closer. "Come now, dear, calm yourself. That drink will soon make everything feel better."

I grit my teeth and hold my breath while enduring the sounds coming from the coffin.

"Breathe, my darling, breathe." Hugh plugs my nose. "It is important to inhale while you still can."

I fixate on the gray sludge trickling down his chin, and, in desperate need of oxygen, I gasp. "What ... what does that mean?"

He licks the goop from his lips with a smirk and sighs. "Let us gather around, everyone. It is time."

As everyone quietly chants, they create a circle around the table. "What's inside, what's inside, what's inside?"

I notice their odd stares. All are looking at me, their lips twisting into grins.

Adeline grabs my hand; her irises are enlarged. "How are you feeling?" she asks. Her demeanor appears manically happy. "Are you sleepy, my dear?"

I start to speak but stop when I feel her grip tightening.

Everyone stomps their right foot, creating a synchronized beat as she interjects. "It is all right, my child ... There is no need to respond. Just understand that this is for everyone's greatest good."

The others chant.

I scan the room in panic. Adeline laughs, joining in. "What's inside will cure our hideous imperfections and wash away our flaws. With this newly found flesh, we ask to stop aging and for the beauty that we lost to be restored. Bring back our youthful years and rewind the clock."

As Hugh pries open the lid, a sudden break in the seal releases a monstrous crack that echoes through the air. He sings, "We thank you, Lord, for this flesh and blood."

The rattle of the coffin stops as he opens the lid the remaining way. A cloud of dust fills the air, billowing over the sides of the coffin, creating a thick black fog that makes it difficult to see and breathe.

Amid fits of coughing, Hattie glances beside her and is met only with the sight of Ettie and Adeline. "Clinton? Where is Clinton?" She squints, scanning for faces in the fog.

I look back at the corner of the room where I saw him last. Darkness blankets the furniture he had been hiding behind.

Ettie screams. Reaching for the lid and inhaling a clump of soot, she hacks between her words. "You must close it; my husband is missing! You must shut it tight! Put it back the way it was!"

Hugh slaps her hand. "Damnit, Ettie, control yourself! You are making a mockery of us all!"

Her voice falls to a whisper. "Shut it, brother. *Please.*"

A dark, smoky substance continues to boil out of the sarcophagus, flooding the air; its weight dampens the candle flames around us, snuffing some and causing others to flicker.

Hugh's presence fills the room as he stands taller, pushing the lid to the floor with a resounding thud. "I said no! And that is that!"

Ettie grabs her mother's dress and collapses to her knees. "Please, Mother … Tell him to close it. He must put it back as it was."

Adeline stares with disgust at her groveling. "I pray for you to stand, child."

Ettie sniffles, burying her head deeper into her mother's shoes.

Adeline nudges her with her foot to get away. "Do not act foolish. Desperation does not suit you."

As her icy demeanor lingers, a high-pitched hissing noise pierces the air, stealing everyone's attention. It is coming from the open casket.

Hattie covers her ears and shouts. "What in God's name is that dreadful sound?" Trying to calm her aching head, she kicks the legs of the table. "Make it stop, brother! Silence that thing!"

Hugh looks at the others, then at the sarcophagus, and mutters, "Dear God. Clinton … what have I done?"

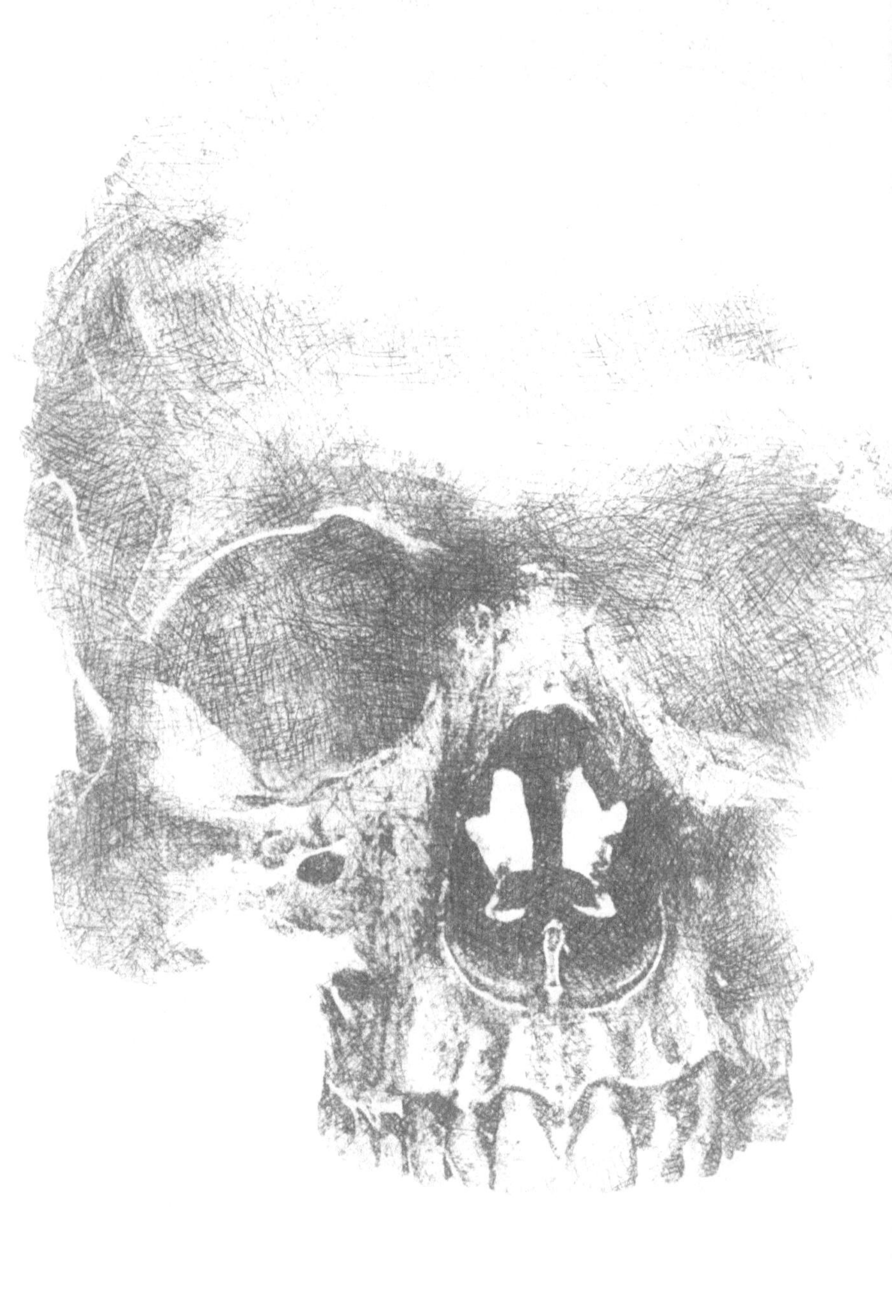

Twelve

Death to the Wicked

Whispering words, speaking in tongues, resonate from every direction. Each break in the speech pattern accompanies another fizzling wick; it is like something's inhalations are consuming the flames.

As I gaze upon the fire, a strange sensation courses through me as something creeps along my skin.

Tiny hisses grow in abundance around us. The sounds of little scurrying legs escalate from the coffin as insects crawl from its opening, tumble to the table, and descend like a tidal wave onto the floor, dispersing in every direction.

"Get them off!" Lucius squeals, swatting at his legs.

"They are everywhere!" Ettie and Hattie scream. They flick at their arms, and lifting their dresses, stomp the floor.

I pluck a tiny body from my arm. Pinching it between my fingers, I hold it closer to the fire's glow. "What is it?" I ask.

Its little legs squirm as the warm light reflects off the blue-black sheen of its back.

Hugh looks at me and squeals, "They are scarabs! Do not touch it! What are you doing? They carry diseases!"

I drop the bug onto the floor and frantically begin brushing them from my skirt.

"Clinton! Where in the bloody hell is Clinton?!" Hugh rushes around the murky room, shouting. "Ettie, you need to find that husband of yours! Now!"

As Adeline swishes her skirt, she climbs on the furniture at the side of the room, trying to escape the attack.

"She has the right idea." Lucius rushes to join her, and everyone follows suit.

A heavy thud sounds from the table. The noise makes me stop and slowly turn around.

"Genevieve…." a cryptic voice moans.

It beckons me, enticing me to come closer and captivating me in a trance-like state. I am compelled to search for it, venturing deeper into the dark abyss.

"Darling, what are you doing?" Hugh shouts. "Get away from there!"

As I turn my attention to him, a bone-chilling moan echoes from behind. Everyone looks at the open coffin, their eyes wide with fear and mouths agape. A cold gust hits the back of my neck, sending goosebumps down my arms.

Hugh lifts his finger to point. "Run!" His word lingers.

Adeline's shock transforms into fury as she climbs over the furniture toward her son, her eyes piercing him like daggers. "I thought you had this managed! If she drank her poison, why is she so alert?! You have ruined everything with your incompetency!" She strikes his face with a backhand.

He folds upon impact, clutching his cheek.

"I thought she did, Mother. She broke her glass! You heard it!" Hugh looks back at me, standing in the middle of the room.

"After her brother, I told you not to choose her. That bloodline has too many ideas of its own. We would have avoided this situation if you had chosen my option."

This cannot be happening. This must be a horrible nightmare. My heart pounds loudly in my chest as I try to comprehend what they are saying. *Were they planning to kill me?* As the noise of my palpitations rattles my head, I nervously smile to cover my fear.

"We all heard it! We all heard her throw her empty glass to the floor." Almost out of breath, Hugh frantically looks at his siblings for confirmation.

Ettie glares at him while Hattie angrily folds her arms, and he wildly flails his hands.

His voice whistles like a boiling teakettle, becoming louder and shriller as his stress grows. "Bloody hell! Nod or something; I am not talking to myself!"

I stare at the ceiling, wishing for a way out.

Suddenly, their eyes lock on me, as if they can hear my thoughts. The whites of their irises eerily glow in the darkness.

This is happening. I take a deep breath. *Oh, God, this is happening.* I try to maintain my composure as I listen to their bickering escalate.

Adeline points at me. "Well, clearly not; just look at her! She is wide awake! That girl looks like a raccoon who found snuff in the trash!"

Both daughters nod and look at me in agreement. "I daresay Mother is right," Ettie says.

Hattie squints her eyes. "Yes, indeed, that girl appears refreshed."

As they continue to stare, Adeline chimes in. "Dear Lord, help us all … This family cannot afford another scandal."

Hugh's face loses all color.

His mother looks at him and clenches her jaw; a crazed gleam consumes her eyes.

Despite her efforts to be discreet, I can hear every whispered word, and they make my stomach drop.

"Fix it." Clearing her throat to get Hugh's attention, Adeline motions her head toward me, getting louder. *"Now!"*

He grimaces in response, infuriated by her demands. "Don't harp, Mother. I already said I would take care of it." With a dramatic exhale, he wipes the sweat from his forehead and squints at me.

I glance from my peripherals to see if there is anywhere to run. The sound of a chair's legs sliding against the floor grabs my attention, and I return my gaze to Hugh; I catch the end of his dismount from the stack of furniture.

His eyes narrow in on me, and he brushes off his pants.

I carefully feel the floor with the toe of my shoe to ensure nothing is behind me.

He takes a giant step forward and grins.

I mimic backing up, only to be startled by a strange moaning sound behind me.

My face falls pale as I delve into my thoughts; the cryptic voice triggers its accompanying whispers to grow louder.

Hugh inches toward me and extends his hand. "Come here, wife; let us put this all behind us and get you somewhere safe." His smile grows wide, thinking my look of despair is for him.

My heart quickens as I hear the table's legs shift against the floor's wooden planks, followed by a loud thud. Another moan rumbles from behind my back, and I wince at the sound of a footstep creaking a floorboard. I freeze; each unnerving noise exacerbates my trembling.

The last candles fizzle around me as I stare into Hugh's eyes. His pupils appear much darker than I had remembered, and his granite-toned irises are filled with a wicked craze.

He waves his arm, motioning for me to come a little closer. "Come along, my dear, take my arm." His measured approach reminds me of a predator luring its prey.

I step back into the roiling fog, hoping to hide and bide time.

"Genevieve, you dreadful girl, get over here *this instant*!" His harsh tone reminds me of the encounter in the foyer. With each passing moment, his fury grows.

"Stay—stay away from me!" I scream.

"Feisty or not, I will catch you. Your fate has already been sealed." He lunges forward, trying to grab me.

I jump back, dodging him.

"You have the choice to make it difficult and experience suffering or make it easier and endure a bit less … suffering," he says, grunting.

The closer he gets to catching me, the louder his family's mocking voices grow, emanating from the barricade of chairs.

"What's taking so long?" Ettie and Hattie bellow. "Hurry! Come on and get on with it!"

Their anticipation is palpable, mirroring the enthusiasm of a crowd at an execution.

With my eyes locked on Hugh's approach, I am startled by a second creaking sound behind me.

Hugh tiptoes closer, taunting me with every step. Sweat rolls down his forehead and into his mouth as he smirks.

I take another step back, and my voice grows louder, commanding, "Stop it this instant! I dislike what you are trying to do, and I will not stand for it. Do you hear me?!"

As he continues his stalking dance toward me, my back presses against something solid. A ghostly groan infiltrates my ears, accompanied by a breath that reeks of death. Its coldness sends a shiver through my body. Quickly feeling with my hands, my skin brushes across something with an unusual texture, and I stop.

Hugh lunges toward me. The air remains murky, making it difficult to see. I swiftly evade him by dropping to the floor and crawling away as fast as I can, but he oddly does not follow.

He stands frozen, his eyes fixated on the dark void where I once stood.

Lucius throws up his hands in frustration. "She is getting away, you imbecile!"

Having nowhere to go, I look toward the corner of the room where Clinton vanished, and I crawl faster, hoping to vanish as well.

The others join in chanting at Hugh to move. "Get her ... get her...get her!"

As I get closer, I focus on the shadows cast by the furniture, looking for a safe hiding spot.

Clinton pops his head out from behind a chair. His abrupt movement startles me, stopping me dead in my tracks. We exchange anxious expressions, unsure of our next steps.

Hugh's eyes remain locked on whatever is lurking in the darkness. A flood of liquid is pooling at his feet.

His sisters laugh and point at the spectacle. "He's bloody pissing himself!" Lucius adds, his laughter echoing through the room.

Clinton silently signals for me to hurry, and with no other choice, I scurry deeper into the darkness.

"Move, brother! You must move!" Hattie cackles.

Ettie gestures toward the corner. "She disappeared somewhere that way! You must find her!"

I crawl behind the safety of the furniture while trying to catch my breath; Clinton's eyes tell me that something is gravely wrong. He glances around the chair toward the center of the room, his hands shaking as he observes what is happening.

The puddle of liquid grows larger near Hugh's feet, and his knees quiver. Petrified, he stutters, "It—it's—" His vocal cords constrict.

I jump at the sound of his bloodcurdling scream, then reluctantly pivot my body to look. As the smoke dissipates, a wave of terror courses through me as I catch sight of the sinister figure that was lurking within the coffin and is now standing, tightly gripping Hugh.

Orange flickers of the fire's light illuminate a tall, thin creature resembling a human form, completely wrapped in dingy brown strips of cloth from head to toe. The structure of the head is elongated, with a slight point to its skull.

My thoughts race, replaying the footsteps and moans I heard behind me. I clutch onto the chair, peering around it, trying to see anything I can see of the creature. As I observe how its hands ruthlessly latch onto Hugh's arms, I shudder at the thought that a single misstep could have placed me in his position.

Then, with no warning, the thing lifts Hugh off the ground, causing his feet to dangle in the air. It leans close, voraciously tears off a portion of his cheek, and chews, blood running down its bandages.

My breath catches in my throat as the room fills with his bloodcurdling screams. Clinton hears my gasp and lunges toward me, forcing his hand over his mouth.

The creature snaps its head toward us, its eyes locking on us.

Neither of us moves a muscle.

I cannot tear my eyes away from its gaping mouth. Its teeth, discolored from rot and covered in bits of juicy flesh, bear deep crimson stains. With its hideous snarl, it slowly shifts its attention back to Hugh.

Clinton lowers his hand. Then, leaning toward me, he lifts his finger to his lips. "Shhhh, it will hear you … It is the mummified body from the sarcophagus," he whispers, monitoring the creature's every movement.

I watch Hugh's feet struggle, kicking the air, trying to free himself. "Please," he begs.

The creature's sinewy fingers reach into his mouth, gripping his tongue and slowly stretching it from his jaw.

Hattie's and Ettie's piercing screams merge with Hugh's agonized wails, creating a cacophony of torment.

The mummy looks at the women and howls, its breath creating a vortex that clears the air like the wind.

Hugh's body hits the floor with a resounding thud as the mummy discards him. He frantically crawls to get away while the flames of the fireplace illuminate the gruesome details of his face: a chunk of flesh is missing from his cheek.

Ettie heaves and then vomits. She staggers and catches herself by grabbing onto her sister. Hattie gasps, her eyes widening as she peers past her sister's shoulder. "Sister, sister...." she says.

Hearing her voice rise with terror, Ettie turns to face where she is staring.

The top of the mummy's skull is stretching, bursting out of the discolored wraps, and two pieces shaped like ostrich feathers sprout. Adding to the display is a tall spherical dome in the center that tapers to a point. Together, they create the unmistakable shape of an Atef crown, a symbol of ancient royalty.

The twins clutch onto one another, staring at the mummy in horror.

Clinton trembles. "It … it can't… it can't be," he mutters. His eyes grow wild with fear.

With a deafening roar, the mummy's form elongates, and the bone of its chin breaks through the bandages, transforming into the likeness of a pharaoh's beard.

Wondering what everyone is gasping about, Hugh flips his body over. Seeing the mummy's distorted features, he pushes through the pain and crawls as fast as he can to distance himself from the thing. As he approaches his family, themes shine on his red gouged cheek fireplace's flame.

His deformities make them cringe in disgust. "Get away!" they hiss through clenched teeth.

"Do you not see that I'm bloody injured?" he asks, grabbing a chair to support himself.

Adeline lifts her dress and frantically kicks her foot at him. "You … you are a horror… now shoo!" She steps on his fingers. "Stay down there, where you belong."

The mummy tilts its head toward the ceiling and inhales a gust of air. As it releases a howl, the bone of its palm pushes through the bandages, crafting a large crook.

I scoot closer to Clinton, trying to remain quiet. He nervously glances at the fight occurring among the family. "This cannot get any worse. That thing is Osiris," he whispers.

Adeline's daughter joins in, kicking at Hugh as he attempts to climb closer.

The mummy swings its crook from side to side, the sharpness of the blade.

Clinton shakes his head and mutters while rocking back and forth to comfort himself. "Oh, dear God, he has come to claim us all and drag us to the underworld. This is the end. We are done for. The time has come to pay the price for our tomb raiding and desecration of the dead."

I scamper back closer to the wall, watching him.

Lucius steps away from Hattie, preparing to run.

The mummy approaches the fireplace and lunges its hand into the flames, lighting a small strip of bandage on fire. As the cloth disintegrates, unveiling the desiccated skin and bone underneath, a wind spirit manifests around him, swirling cinders and ash.

Hattie nervously stares at it and notices her husband slowly retreating from the corner of her eye.

The mummy opens its mouth, inhaling the aroma of fresh blood wafting through the air, while scarab beetles crawl from the decayed crevices in its leathery skin.

"Where do you think you are going, Lucious?" Hattie angrily whispers. "Hmm? What was the plan? To leave your poor wife here to fend for herself?"

Lucius panics and steps back, accidentally bumping into a chair, which falls from the stack and crashes to the floor.

The mummy instantly turns its head, swinging its weapon toward the source of the noise. Then, leaning forward, it dips its henna-dyed fingernail into the ash. Using a streak of black, it skillfully draws pupils on the bandages over its empty eye sockets while its jaw forms a mischievous grin.

Hattie and Lucius freeze, their bodies unmoving, hoping the creature cannot sense their presence. They watch anxiously as it gets closer, only to come to a halt right in front of them.

Hattie quivers, trying to remain calm as it leans toward her, sniffing the air.

She holds her breath.

As the creature gets a whiff of her essence, a growl resonates from the pit of its stomach. Its grin grows wider, and its breath is so near that it blasts its rot-filled breath against her face. As it speaks, its deep voice roars, causing the walls of the room to rattle. "I am Osiris, ruler of the dead," it declares.

Hattie remains frozen in fear, her body trembling uncontrollably, while a tear trickles down her cheek.

Ettie gasps and shuffles closer to her mother.

The corpse follows the sound and abruptly pivots, facing her direction.

Like the Great Sphinx of Giza, she stands motionless, her eyes darting back and forth, tracing the sharp edges of its crook as it swings it like a pendulum.

"Punishment awaits those who desecrate the dead," it says with a snarl.

"Disturbing the sacred remnants of one's existence hinders one's journey through Duat, altering one's afterlife path."

The mummy points its crook toward the fire, and it flares and sparks.

Each dancing flame casts hieroglyphics on the walls, depicting a moving scene. It enacts the journey into the underworld, beginning with a mummified body laid in a sarcophagus and placed within a tomb. As its soul separates, it is greeted by a man with a canine head.

I cannot take my eyes off the beauty of the shifting depictions; something is mesmerizing about the storytelling style. It is visually captivating.

Clinton notices me leaning closer to get a better look. "That is Anubis," he whispers. "He is the God of the mummification process and the afterlife. He serves as the guide to the underworld, leading the newly deceased into the hall of judgment. Inside the room, Osiris awaits to oversee the ceremony, standing beside a large golden balance scale. They will weigh the heart of the deceased against a feather of Ma'at to determine its weight. If the heart is lighter, they are deemed pure. However, if it is heavier, Ammit will devour their soul." He points to a lurking creature depicted in the hieroglyphs. "That is her … the sinister goddess of the Underworld."

My eyes sweep over Ammit's body, taking in every detail. She has the hindquarters of a hippopotamus, a crocodile's head, and a lion's forequarters.

The heart on the scale sinks lower than the feather.

I wince as Ammit lunges forward and devours him. I cannot help but imagine the horrifying sensation of being consumed alive, causing me to shudder and shield my eyes.

The mummy sweeps its crook, motioning to the ends of the room, and the flames of the fire die down. "Their soul becomes trapped in the treacherous underworld, never to be born again."

The hieroglyphs dissipate from the walls.

"After their torturous death, their judgment day is erased."

Ettie quickly removes a single earring and chucks it on the floor near Hugh.

As the pearl skips across the ground, the mummy swipes the blade, turning toward the noise. "Death is the only equivalent worthy of the crime by one who is unnamed."

Hugh hears its footsteps approaching and paws at the chair faster. Adeline kicks his fingers. Frantically clutching his injured knuckles, he whispers under his breath. "Bloody hell, Mother … What is wrong with you?"

"His name is Hugh! It is him!" She points to him and yells louder. "That man is the untalented artist you seek! He was the one who painted over those well-thought-out drawings … I told him not to, but did he listen?" She looks at the others, nodding at them to agree.

The mummy grips the crook more tightly.

"Isn't that right, girls?"

They nod, pointing at him. "It was all him."

The mummy looks in their direction.

Adeline shouts, "He is near my feet!"

The mummy follows her voice, looking toward the floor.

Frightened, Hugh scrambles backward, his words stuttering out in a flurry of apologies. "My—my—apologies. I assure you, I did not intend to ruin someone's deathly slumber."

The mummy continues its approach.

Hugh frantically scans the room, and his attention lands on the fireplace. "Uh … but… um, the imagery on your container was unsuitable for the occasion! You must understand that you cannot just have phalluses on display at one's wedding celebration … It… um…"

"Silence!" the mummy commands, raising his weapon, ready to strike, beetles spitting from his lungs.

Adeline grabs for the wall.

Hugh makes a sprint for the fireplace.

With a growl, the mummy faces in his direction and points its crook. "The one marked with the kiss of death has sealed a fate far worse than the rest."

Struggling for breath, Hugh loses his footing and slides on the puddle of urine from earlier, steadying himself by grabbing onto the bronze fireplace screen. "Mother, tell him he must understand!" He turns to look at her and meets with Osiris's swinging hook.

Ducking to the floor, he quickly crawls through the mummy's legs and, turning around, pushes him into the flames.

As his wrappings catch fire, the flames swallow his ominous words. "May those who partook in altering another's state be plagued with a curse sealing their fate."

Hugh runs toward the door, and the others follow, kicking over candles and knocking over furniture.

Clinton grabs my arm, pulling me with him. "We must go."

I plant my feet, unsure of what to do. "But they tried to kill me," I say.

"What other choice do you have?" He pulls harder. "Come on!"

My eyes widen with fear as I catch sight of the mummy emerging from the flames. We sprint across the room and out the door.

Letting out a bone-chilling howl, the mummy charges toward the exit in pursuit.

Clinton slams the door, locks it, and, with a trembling hand, tucks the key in his pocket. He jumps at the sound of the mummy slamming its body against the other side.

I slowly back away, trying to catch my breath. As my back hits the wall, I fearfully scan my surroundings.

"I wouldn't worry about seeing anyone. They are probably long gone, hiding in their quarters by now," Clinton says.

I exhale a sigh of relief.

"You will learn. That is a normal occurrence." My eyes widen as they dart to the door, certain he is referring to the mummy. He chuckles. "Oh, God, no, not that. I am referring to their behavior ... You cannot rely on a single one of them or... trust them with your life. In this place, people only care about themselves ... and their inheritance, of course."

The rattling door ceases. Clinton glimpses it before redirecting his attention to me, appearing deep in thought.

"Regarding the mummy, I had heard rumors about such occurrences but had to see it to believe it. From what I was told, all the best mummies have been taken, leaving only the defective ones behind. As an added precaution, I warned Hugh not to do anything reckless with the sarcophagus. However, I'm sure you've already realized, in the short time you've known him, that he has a stubborn mindset," Clinton remarks.

"How did you become so knowledgeable about the culture?" I ask.

"As you can see from my distinctive complexion, I did not originate from this part of the world. The reason I am so well-versed in ancient Egyptian culture is quite simple," he says, chuckling to lighten the mood.

"Similar to the horrifying creature you witnessed, my bloodline originates from Egypt. It is what drives my fascination. That is where my ancestry lies."

He locks eyes with me briefly before his gaze wanders to the end of the corridor. "It has been quite an eventful night. The others may be onto something," he says, taking a step. "It is probably best if we retire for the evening."

As my words boil beneath my skin, I blurt, "Why did you choose not to drink your champagne?"

He stops and turns toward me. "Do you know what that ashy powder is made of?" he inquires, his curiosity evident.

I stare at him with a blank expression.

"I see," he says; reading my confusion, he shakes his head and smirks. "Well … I shall enlighten you, then… That gritty substance is called Mummia."

"Mum—Mummia?" I ask.

"To be fair, I must tell you that what was in your glass wasn't limited to just that … A few other things were also added."

My eyes widen.

"Next time, you must look at how the top fizzles. If it simmers, you are a winner; if it boils, you must recoil." He continues, "Mummia is a substance derived from the powdered remains of mummies. Some believe it to possess therapeutic properties." He clutches the back of his neck and shrugs. "Many people ingest it for its health benefits, and others, like Adeline, believe it is the fountain of youth. As for me... I believe it is quite apparent why I prefer not to partake."

My eyes widen, and I frantically wipe my lips, trying to remove any remnants of the horrific revelation.

"After the unwrapping this evening, which went terribly wrong, that corpse was to be used to replenish their stock, but given the circumstances..." He stops and chuckles. "I suppose they will need to be creative and devise an alternative solution to appease their hunger."

His unsettling words make my heart race.

"Anyway, it's best we get to bed. Everyone likes to have a prompt breakfast in the morning."

I quickly glance at him, feeling anxious about being left alone.

"Come along, now. Let us go." He waves his hand for me to follow. "I will show you to the staircase that leads to your sleeping quarters."

An uneasiness runs through my gut. I remain frozen, replaying everything that occurred.

He chuckles. "Rest assured, with the amount of alcohol and other substances in their systems, none of them will even remember this evening's events."

I force a smile and place my hand on his extended arm.

"Trust me," he says with a confident smile. "Tomorrow morning, it will be as if none of this ever happened." With a skip in his step, we begin our walk.

Hoping for the best, I follow him as he leads me down the long corridor.

What other choice do I have?

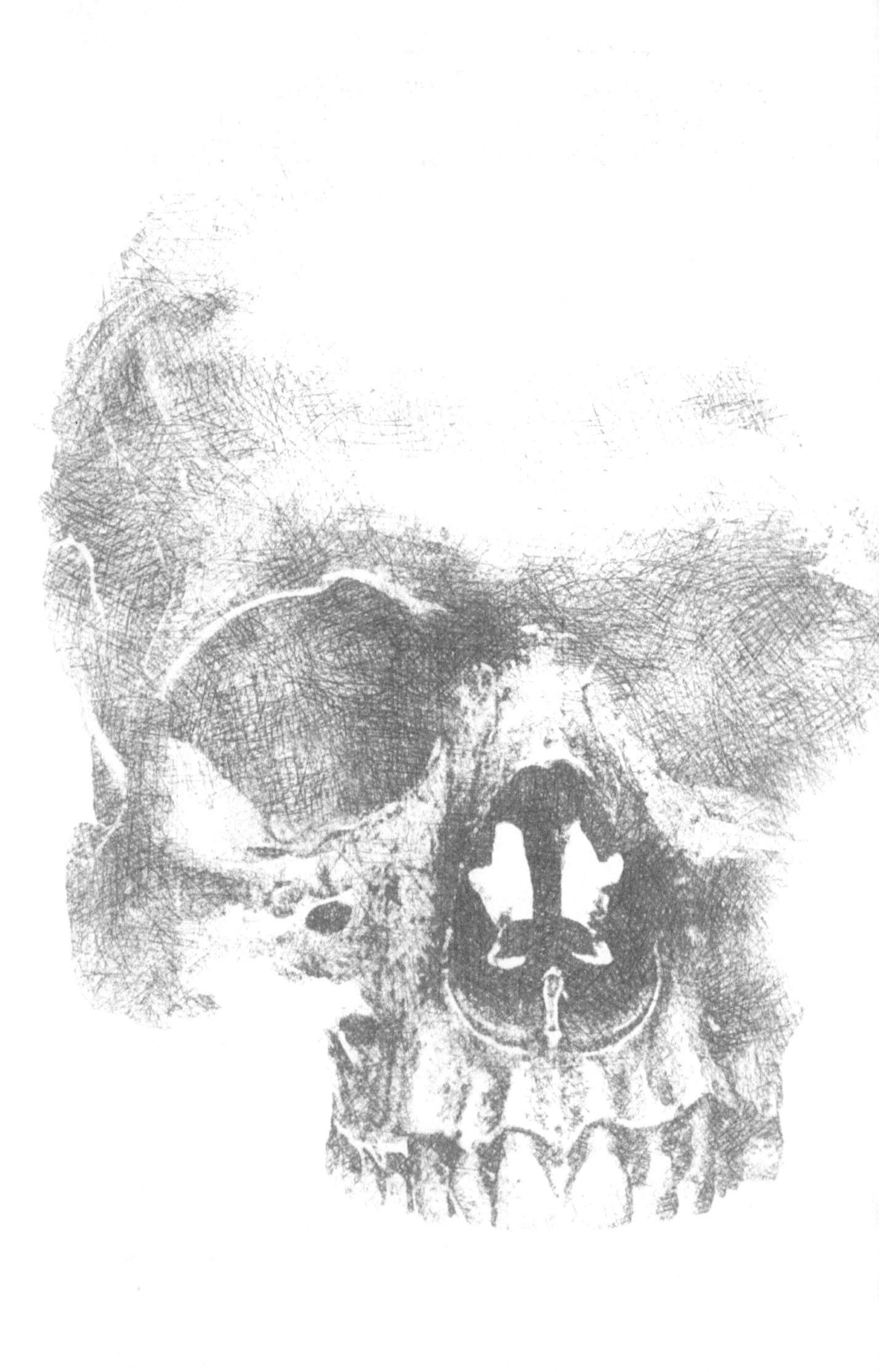

Thirteen

I do not Recall

W alking in silence, my attention is drawn to the floor, where I find solace in counting my steps.

Clinton clears his throat, shattering the quiet and making me jump. I anxiously raise my eyes to the staircase ahead.

"Ah, there we are," he says. "It looks like she is right on time."

I glance toward the familiar face of my chambermaid. She stands at the bottom step, avoiding eye contact.

We hasten our pace and stop beside her. He passes my arm to her. I notice an anxious look in his eyes as they dart around, scanning the vicinity.

"I believe she will take it from here," he remarks, and with a nod, he departs, his footsteps fading into the distance.

The chambermaid gives my arm a heavy tug. I nearly trip on the first step and grab the railing to regain my balance as she pulls harder.

I fumble, following behind her until we reach my room. Everything feels like a blur; the night has left me exhausted and filled with a sense of disillusionment.

Every stage of my bedtime routine is muddled as she prepares me for bed, and the moment my head hits my pillow, my vision goes black.

Yet my moment of rest is brief.

I am jolted awake from a stone-cold sleep, gasping for air, my heart pounding. I close my eyes, hoping to be greeted by the cheerful melodies of singing birds, but instead, an eerie silence engulfs the room.

My stomach churns as I open my eyes and stare at the ceiling.

The room is bathed in darkness except for the intermittent moonlight filtering through the windows and the soft glow of the fireplace.

I hear the flames crackle as the heat projects warmth onto my skin as it circulates through the air. I try to turn my head to look at the windows, but nothing responds. Remaining entirely still, I lie stuck, frozen in place.

In the distance, a floorboard squeaks.

Hello? I try to say, but my words are trapped behind my limply touching lips. It is as though the hinge of my jaw has been locked tight.

I listen intently as the silence is broken again by the sound of another floorboard creaking, now even closer than before.

The sizzling blaze adds to the air of suspense.

A fit of hyperventilation consumes me as I lie in anticipation of another footstep.

Then I see it: the dark silhouette of a man lurking near the corner of the room.

I observe any movement from the edge of my eye while listening to a series of quick-paced steps come to a stop. A sense of being trapped engulfs me as I helplessly stare through the abyss. Despite my desire to flee from my bed, my body stops me. My muscles and joints remain motionless and numb.

From the shadows, it watches me, relishing every moment of my struggle.

I frantically rummage inward for any strength I have left and try again to move, only to see the shadow slink further toward the fireplace. As it approaches the center of the room, my panic intensifies. Each footstep is reminiscent of a ticking clock, counting down the dwindling moments of my existence.

Suddenly, the shadow lunges forward with a swift step, outpacing the others. The motion throws off the lumbering rhythm.

The unpredictability shakes me, leaving me feeling powerless and in control of nothing.

A prickling heat caused by the emotional tension building up inside me consumes the underside of my skin, creating an unbearable discomfort. I feel as if I am burning from the inside out, sweltering in misery. *Just let it be over, please. I beg of you.*

A hacking noise pierces the air, coming from the shadow figure.

I silence my thoughts, listening to each of its raspy breaths between the snapping of flames of the fireplace. In a frenzy, I work harder to wiggle my fingers; all I want is to garner a movement, even if it's negligible. I just need enough range to defend myself.

The footsteps grow increasingly heavy, creating an ominous stomp as they approach. Unexpectedly, they stop at the edge of the bed, and I instantly feel a heavy sensation pressing against my chest, making it difficult for me to breathe. The entity lets out a tormented moan, shaking the bed violently and drowning out my grunting struggles.

The shadow's aggression grows with every passing moment as he menacingly proclaims,

"In your stomach I sit." His words hang in the air, and with each passing moment, he becomes more aggressive, exerting greater pressure on my chest. I gasp, trying to fill my lungs.

"In your stomach, I sit! In your stomach, I sit!"

The pressure on my chest forces all the air from my lungs. I monitor the shadow's movements from the corner of my eye.

"In your stomach, I sit! In your stomach, I sit! In your stomach, I sit!" His voice grows more possessed, shifting another minor octave and inundating the room from all directions.

He stops his movements and looks directly into my eyes.

Still paralyzed, I shift my eyes from his and toward the ceiling, and the voice stops. *There is no need to worry; it is all good now. There is absolutely nothing to be concerned about. It was just a silly dream, nothing more.*

As I work to calm myself, I focus on the rhythmic thumping of my heartbeat resonating in my ears.

I try to move my hand again, desperate for the encounter to end, as another piercing scream abruptly echoes in my ear. "In your stomach, I sit!"

As I strain to break free, my eyes become fixated and unable to blink. The shadow lingers in my peripherals, beside my head, his icy breath brushing my cheek.

"In your stomach, I sit!" He hisses, the putrid stench of rotten meat emanating from his discolored teeth.

Near the point of defeat, I summon every ounce of strength to make one last attempt at regaining control over my body.

At last, my eyes shut.

All falls quiet except for the sound of my hyperventilating breaths.

Gradually, a tingling feeling takes over my fingers, then spreads to my chest and eventually reaches every limb, restoring my ability to move.

I slowly sit up, keeping my lids closed for a moment more, not ready to see what may be there. The only solace I find is in the comforting crackles of the fire.

Finally, I force myself to peek, hoping to be free of the horrid nightmare. I stare at the door, and though there is silence, an unsettling feeling remains in the pit of my stomach.

Someone is watching me.

Without turning, I quiet my breath to listen.

Abruptly, the raspy exhalations of the man return, accenting the popping wood in the fireplace.

I take a quick glance, afraid to move, fearful of drawing attention. And then I see him with greater clarity—a man standing near the fireplace, his tall stature draped in a long black robe. With his back turned, he lingers, swaying from side to side as if preparing to turn around.

I hold my breath.

"In your stomach, I sit," he whispers.

I gasp, and the hairs on the back of my neck stand on end. The familiar voice strikes a nerve, confirming my suspicions. *The clergyman... what would he want from me?*

His movement abruptly stops, and I watch in horror as he slowly pivots to face me.

His head tilts as if surveying me.

I stumble for words. "What ... what do you want?" I ask.

He remains still.

"If ... if you desire money... you have come to the wrong person, as I do not have any."

His grating exhales grow louder.

I quickly continue. "You ... you would need to speak to my husband about that."

He takes a deep breath, causing the flames of the fire to rise and hiss.

As the heat wafts against my skin, I panic, blurting, "I will scream if I must. I will wake this entire manor. If you plan to do something foolish, I warn you that—that—"

His voice reverberates through the air with a screeching tone. "In your stomach, I sit!"

What does that even mean? Unable to make sense of what he is saying, my thoughts run rampant with speculation.

He steps toward me, and the floorboards howl with each stomp. "In your stomach, I sit."

The flames in the hearth roil.

I scream, clutching my hair as my heart races in my chest. "Stop it! Please, I am begging you to stop!"

The clergyman cackles. "In your stomach, I sit!"

A multitude of voices speaking in tongues converge on the room.

Something scurries near the bed.

My head snaps to look, and I'm startled to see the clergyman crouching just a few feet from where I sit.

Horror courses through my veins.

He swiftly stands and races around the bedpost. He grips my shoulders while staring into my eyes with unwavering intensity.

I recoil, looking in terror at his backlit body.

The flames from the fire illuminate the sides of his face, where bits are missing, and what is left of his features sag like melted wax. His jaw hangs lopsided below the drooping skin of his once robust jowls. Disconnected from the bone, it dangles at the level of the Adam's apple. "You did this," he whispers. "All of you."

Frantically, I wiggle my shoulders, desperately trying to escape as blood seeps from beneath his palms, staining my nightgown.

"Get off me!" I scream.

He tightens his grip, his voice a venomous hiss. "Acknowledge your sin and the suffering you have caused. You must repent for what you have done," he insists.

"I have done nothing to you," I reply, struggling to squirm free.

He grabs ahold of my cheeks, his nails digging into my soft flesh. "You partook in the sin, just like them."

As my lips are forced into a pucker, the scent of iron wafts into my nose, and I fight his grip.

"Look into my eyes, child, and you will see the fiery depths of hell that await you." His irises are embedded with intricate cuts, forming the sign of a cross. Hymns in tongues accent his thunderous tone.

I unleash a piercing scream, tightly shutting my eyes in refusal.

He suddenly releases his grip, and I tumble backward, landing on the plush cushion of the mattress. "I did not do anything. I am innocent," I say under my breath. Once more, an eerie silence fills the room. Overwhelmed by the need to escape, I struggle to untangle myself from the twisted sheets that are wrapped around me and entwined between my legs.

Then, small taps emerge.

The noise appears to be originating from the window. I instantly sit up to see the cause and am blinded by daylight.

Another round of tapping sounds echoes from the glass.

I shield my eyes and squint, finally spotting the culprit: a large raven perched on a window ledge.

Disoriented by the sudden change from darkness to daylight, I quickly gaze toward the crackling fireplace, seeking confirmation that I am not losing my sanity. But the site offers no reassurance.

The flames have burned out, leaving only charred pieces of wood.

But it was just burning.

The thought of the attack by the clergyman consumes me, and I wildly scan the room, but he is nowhere to be found; checking the shoulders of my nightgown, I see they are perfectly white.

Nothing makes sense, and I question whether it was simply a nightmare or if it indeed took place.

The bird's tapping resumes, and I turn my attention toward the window once more.

We silently lock eyes with one another.

"What did you see?" I ask, my words filled with desperation for answers. I slide off the edge of the bed, planting my feet on the floor.

It gives the glass three more quick pecks.

My body shivers from the cold as I cautiously approach the window, keeping a watchful eye on the creature. "Tell me," I ask, my voice guarded. "Tell me ... tell me what you have seen."

The bird, intrigued, releases a clacking from its beak.

"I am certain you have witnessed what happens within these walls."

The hinges of the door squeal open behind me.

Startled, I swiftly turn around, and the bird reacts with shrill screeches and caws. The chambermaid bursts into the room, startling the creature and causing it to fly away.

I scan the green satin dress with crème lace on the neckline in her hands. *It is gorgeous.* The lush material draws my attention, distracting me from my tumultuous thoughts.

Quickly setting it on the bed, she rushes back to the hall and totes two large buckets of steaming water into the washroom.

I approach the dress, admiring the rich color and regal puffed sleeves.

The sound of the tub being filled resonates from the other room, capturing my attention. I hear the chambermaid's hand splashing in the water, and knowing it is my cue to make my way to her, I reluctantly leave the dress behind.

She waits with a rag in her hand, ready to scrub.

I approach her, and after she lifts my nightgown over my head, she helps me into the tub and immediately begins rubbing my back with suds.

As I hunch over, allowing her to bathe me, I cannot help but feel an odd sensation of déjà vu. Everything about the scene is identical to yesterday. Only, this time, there is no fight. I quietly go through the motions.

After she finishes, I rise from the tub, and she uses a towel to dry me. She then leads me to the bedroom.

I comply and step into my undergarments, allowing her to layer the hoop skirt around me. As she laces up my corset, my ribs, already accustomed, feel less tender. I barely flinch. She places the dress over my head and, securing the buttons, pushes me toward the vanity.

I sit down, facing the window.

As I stare into the glass, thinking of the raven, she pins up my curls, crafting a beautiful updo and securing satin ribbon bows. She swivels my body toward the mirror while applying the finishing touches of rouge on my cheeks.

I glance at my reflection.

She lowers herself to the floor to fasten the buckles of my shoes.

While she tugs on my feet, my attention remains fixed on my reflection. There's a certain allure to my appearance today, surpassing that of the previous day. A radiant glow emanates from my skin, giving me a more youthful aura, and the faint creases at the edges of my eyes are diminished. The chambermaid stands to place a last pin in my curls.

Is this what others mean when they say marriage changes you? I lightly touch my skin.

She finishes and slowly steps away. I grin. "Perfect," I say. Suddenly, I notice the quietness of the room. It is odd. I had been so consumed in my thoughts that, until just now, I had not noticed her silence.

It is quite refreshing to have a moment of solitude where I can engage in my internal dialogue without the distraction of another.

The chambermaid glances at me in the mirror. I make eye contact with her and smile. "I look perfect."

Fourteen

Fresh Start

As we approach the dining room, a peculiar sensation washes over me. It is a mixture of anxiety and confusion.

My dream last night seems to smear into the encounter with Hugh's family, blurring all the facts. Everything in my bones feels disconnected.

The closer I come to seeing them all again, the more my steps refuse to cooperate.

All I can think about is ingesting the ash of God knows what or whom and their heckling laughter. Last night, they were ready to dispose of me. The same people who were supposed to be my new family wanted me dead; they did not care about me. They have no morals and a complete disregard for my life—or any life, for that matter.

As we approach the opulent dining room doors, I am brought back to the moment Hugh and I took our first steps together as man and wife. Indeed, things weren't perfect, but what is? At least I felt optimism for what lay ahead—a feeling that, once gone, can never be regained.

The innocence that once thrived is now lost forever.

The closer I get to our reunion, the more my confidence wanes, and my palms sweat. Reality sets in. I am about to enter a room filled with individuals whom I do not trust and who, at the drop of a hat, will leave me for dead. *Deep breaths, remember what Clinton said ... yes, remember that kind man's words.*

My thoughts engage in an internal argument. *But how can you trust him? He was planning to kill you. He was no better than them. If it weren't for my intuition, I would be dead.*

The sounds of muffled chatter and cutlery scraping against porcelain pull me from my thoughts.

As the chambermaid opens the door, the smell of baked bread and roasted meat wafts into the hall.

I shield my eyes from the sunlight pouring through the large windows, making the room warm and bright. Suddenly, I hear a chair dragging against the floor and heavy footsteps rushing toward me. I lower my hand and see Hugh's smiling face quickly approaching.

The closer he gets, the more his smile grows. "There she is! My lovely bride has arrived!" His cheery tone resonates throughout the room.

I look him in the eye and force a grin. "There is my husband," I say, matching his energy.

He lunges forward and, with a laugh, grips my arm. "Is she not the most stunning bride you have ever seen?" he says, spinning me around; his excitement grows. "I daresay she is even more beautiful than yesterday!"

I eye the room.

All the wedding decor is gone. Clinton was right; it is like the prior evening never happened. The flower arrangements are bright and cheery, in royal tones, matching the color palette of my dress for the day.

Everyone pauses their meals to look at me; all are dressed in vibrant jewel tones.

"Daughter!" Adeline says, springing to her feet. Her grin stretches from ear to ear. "Yes, she is even more breathtaking than when I last saw her."

As I glance toward her, the others nod in agreement.

"Come sit, dear … I want my newest and favorite daughter to sit beside me for breakfast."

She quickly pats the empty seat next to her at the end of the table. Ettie and Hattie hide their sneers.

I glance at Hugh, and noticing him nod, I make my way toward the designated chair. He places his hand on my back, gently guiding me to walk faster.

Everyone puts down their golden utensils and smiles to greet me as I pass by.

I find myself avoiding eye contact with them, speculating about why they are being so kind.

Hugh races in front of me and pulls out my chair. "There you are, my bride," he says. I nervously glance at him before quickly taking my seat. His eyes lock on mine, giving me a smoldering look. Then, taking my palm in his, he lightly kisses the backside of my hand and motions to the enormous spread on the table. "*Chérie*, I hope this feast is to your liking."

The table is covered with a stunning golden tablecloth, and it is beautifully decorated with baskets and platters filled with a variety of bread, meats, cheeses, and fruits, artfully arranged to look like birds.

I glance at the section of plums and grapes; its design reminds me of the raven I saw in the window.

Hugh pulls out his chair and sits at the opposite end of the table. The rest of the group is seated in the same spots assigned during dinner the previous night. Their eyes are focused on me, eagerly waiting for my words.

I smile and release a light chuckle, playfully commenting, "It seems Hugh is quite the romantic, don't you think?"

They look at one another and break out with laughter.

I scan each of their faces and, noticing one missing, shift my attention to the empty seat next to Ettie.

Although there is a place set for Clinton, he is gone.

Ettie notices my look of concern, and her laughter fades. She averts her eyes to the table.

I analyze her face; her eyes appear swollen. My heart sinks in my chest; something is wrong.

Hattie turns toward her husband. Then, with a grin, she nudges his shoulder. "Lucius, why don't you do precious little things like that for me?"

He shrugs. "I suppose when one is married for some time, things can get a bit dull."

"Well, maybe if you tried a little harder." She sighs, rolling her eyes.

He glares at her. They exchange passive smiles with each other, and then they quietly start bickering.

I shift my attention back to the empty seat. Adeline notices where I am looking; she slowly leans in my direction. "Is something the matter, dear?"

I wince, nervously glancing toward her.

"Tell me, what has your attention?"

I clear my throat and smile. "I must confess, I did not sleep well last night. I believe I was too thrilled about the wedding and all the new things accompanying it."

"Oh?" she replies, studying my expression.

I straighten my posture.

She lifts her eyebrow and smirks. "I presume that can happen to a newlywed woman," she says.

I take a moment to gather my thoughts, then reply, "Yes, I suppose you are right."

Hugh looks at me across the table and grins.

I notice Ettie from my peripheral vision; she is still staring at the table in the same spot. I turn my gaze to her, and my smile fades.

Adeline leans closer and whispers, "You need not worry about that girl. Ettie will soon remarry so she won't be lonely for long." She stops, takes a bite of food, and loudly chews.

I cringe, confused. *How can she mention such matters when her husband was sitting beside her just yesterday, and there was no discussion about his absence?*

"There is no need for concern," Adeline affirms, continuing to eat. "Although she may appear melancholy now, I reassured her that women get married and remarry every day, and she should not waste time dwelling on what was, as change is quite normal. As women, we must adapt. It is simply the way of the world."

The sound of her fork scraping against her plate grates at my nerves. Trying to keep my composure, I dig my fingers into the seat and steal a glance at Ettie.

"We already have a suitor arranged for her to wed. They will be married by the end of the week." As Adeline leans closer to me, I can see her excitement growing.

Startled by her words, I turn to look at her. "Married?" I ask under my breath.

Her smile fades. "Don't be foolish, child." She angrily chews a bite of food. "Do you think she shall live like a spinster forever?"

The sound of her tense tone sends me into a panic. "No … um, no, of course not," I stutter, attempting to defuse the situation. Quickly gathering my thoughts, I look back to the empty seat and ask, "But what happened to—"

Mid-sentence, she abruptly stops me by kicking my leg under the table. I flinch, covering my pain. "When struck with adversity, child, it is important not to dwell. The best course of action is to keep moving forward." As she tips her nose to the air, she speaks louder. "And that is that!"

Hugh narrows his eyes, sensing a quarrel. "I cannot help but wonder … What topic has captivated the attention of my two favorite ladies?"

Adeline ignores the question.

"It seems filled to the brim with passion, and I must have a part of it!" Hugh exclaims.

Hattie and Lucious stop bickering as he slams his fist against the table.

Noticing all eyes on us, I gingerly place my napkin on my lap and coyly smile. "Oh, it is just hen chatter," I say. "That is all."

He chuckles. "If that's all there is to it, I won't be able to contribute, I'm afraid."

I anxiously look at my plate.

"What do you say, Lucius?"

Lucius laughs. "Indeed, I agree with you. If that's all it is, that leaves you with little to contribute."

I glance up and look at Hugh, relieved it is all put behind us. Light from the window softly brushes against his cheek as he turns to nod in agreement with Lucius.

My eyes widen as I notice a slightly ridged patch of skin. Even though nothing is making sense, it is the exact spot where he was wounded the night before. I squint to get a better look.

He catches sight of my attention and swiftly angles his cheek away from the light, attempting to conceal it from view.

As I watch him return to eating, I envision the gash that was on his face the night before. I do not doubt the exact placement, but what is odd is that it appears to be much more healed than I expected. Regardless, it is all the confirmation I need. Whether healed or not, now I know that within this horrific narrative lies a glimmer of truth.

Although it appears Clinton is no longer with us, I know in my heart that the events from last night occurred; Hugh's wound is all I need to prove it.

I pick up my fork and grab a piece of melon from the tray. Hugh watches me set it on my plate and glances at his mother. She grimaces, reaching with her fork for the tray of cold cuts. "No need to be shy, dear. You are part of the family now. Now go on, get a heap of the meat while it's still fresh," she says, picking up a slab and hovering it over my dish.

I watch the dark meat fall on my plate; it lands, touching my fruit.

Based on the coloring, it appears to have come from the same animal as the roast from last night.

I am not used to eating something so hardy at this hour of the morning; the sight of its marbled edges makes my stomach queasy.

The table falls quiet; everyone's attention is on me.

I glance up at their smiling faces. Obliging by curling the ends of my lips into a grin, I cut a piece from the meat and put it into my mouth. I look at them and, chewing, murmur, "Mmm."

Eagerly, they snatch for more food, filling their plates.

Sounds of sniffling infiltrate the chaos.

As I continue to chew, I find the texture of the meat much more arduous than I had remembered. Taking my time with my first bite, I look toward the sniffling.

Ettie slowly begins slicing her piece, and as she does, a solitary tear escapes her eye, landing on the porcelain.

"Is everything all right?" I ask my voice barely a whisper. Realizing I am not loud enough to be heard, I clear my throat to prepare to ask again.

Adeline intercepts my concern. "Every now and then, she feels sorry for the animals that must be slaughtered for our enjoyment."

"But she seemed in such high spirits at dinner yesterday," I say.

"Yes, like most ailments, it waxes and wanes," she replies.

I watch Ettie take her first bite; her body tenses as she starts to chew.

Adeline looks at her, and with a mouthful, she awkwardly grins. "The things we must do for beauty," she says, shoving another bite into her mouth.

I slowly cut the meat on my plate; something is trapped between my molars.

Everyone else is chatting among themselves.

I turn away from the table and use my fingers to extract the culprit lodged in my teeth—a coarse, curly black hair.

The texture is identical to Clinton's.

I jump, startled by a hand touching my back, and swiftly flick the strand away to the floor.

"We have finished eating, my love," Hugh says.

I slowly turn back around. My mind is racing, and I am unsure of what to think. *How did the hair get into my food, and what does it mean?*

People have already pushed their chairs away from the table and are now standing.

"Oh, dear." I awkwardly glance at him and chuckle. "It seems like time has slipped away from me."

"Would you like to finish?" he asks.

As he gestures toward my plate, a wave of dizziness overtakes me, causing me to sway. "No, that is quite all right. I'm trying to pace my appetite, for if I were to consume even a morsel more, my corset would surely burst at the seams."

He smiles. "Very well, then. Shall we?"

I look at his extended arm. Lightly grabbing it, he helps me to my feet. "Where are we off to now?" I ask.

"It's a surprise," he says.

Fifteen

The Drawing Room

As we walk toward the doorway, an array of noises cuts through the air.

The sounds of stacking plates, scraping forks, and swinging doors capture my focus. Glancing over my shoulder, I discover a crowd of servants infiltrating the room.

Hugh keeps dragging me along as I catch quick glimpses of them rushing around with trays, clearing the feast. The initial group fills their trays with dishes and promptly goes to the kitchen. Shortly after, a fresh wave of people arrives, repeating the same process. Once they finish, a final group of waitstaff, primarily women, swiftly enters the room. They carry large polishing rags to gather the cutlery, skillfully amassing piles of gold before returning to the kitchen. Their movements resemble those of a well-oiled machine.

As we are about to exit, I see something peculiar. A single maid lingers behind the others. Not only is she much younger, but her out-of-synch behavior also suggests inexperience.

Noticing her patting the table, trying to find the remaining cutlery, the sight of her petite stature and mousy brown hair pulled back into her bonnet stirs something inside me. "Fran," I loudly gasp.

Hearing my call, she pivots to face me. Her hips make a loud thud as they hit the table's edge.

I chuckle under my breath. "Some things never change. She is still the same clumsy girl."

She slowly lifts her eyes, giving me a better view of her features.

Her face is different; it no longer resembles the bright, lively girl I had grown to know—the friend who felt like a sister to me.

Once filled with youth and beauty, her face is now mangled, and her skin looks worn. Each wrinkle looks manufactured, not earned by age; it is like the Devil has sucked the life from her.

I scan the brutal extent of her injuries. "Dear God," I whisper, horrified by the sight. "What they have done to you?"

The bruising on her jaw has worsened since the last time I saw her.

The closer I look, the deeper my heart sinks in my chest.

Small sutures connect her upper and lower lips. Tightly laced together, her plump lips' flesh sticks through the taught threads.

As my guilt overwhelms me, I shift my attention to her eyes, and the sight of her eyelids sends panic through me.

Their skin is charred and fused.

I stare at the branded cross etched into each mound of flesh, unable to form coherent words. "What—what—what," I stammer, my voice trembling.

Her injuries bear a striking resemblance to the man who visited me the night before.

Hugh pulls on my arm. "Come on, dear."

My legs are frozen beneath me.

He turns, noticing my panic. "What on earth could have caused you to be in such a state of distress?"

I lift my shaking hand to point at Fran.

He looks at my finger and laughs. "Yes, I see … the staff are doing their job; it looks much tidier."

Fran does not move, staring in my direction.

Does he not see what I see?

Hugh yanks my arm, ready to exit.

I dig my heels into the floorboards, grunting as I adamantly refuse to budge. "But … Fran…

she—she's—" I stammer while frantically pointing toward the room behind me. "Don't you see?!"

He looks in the direction I am motioning, his face turning a shade of angry red. "What has gotten into you?!" he asks. "Why are you so fixated on your chambermaid? It's quite peculiar." He releases my arm and motions to the room. "Genevieve, has it reached such depths that you envision her?"

I turn to look and am confused by what I see.

The table is cleared, and everything is spotless. All that is left are the floral arrangements.

A young maid adjusts the flowers at the center of the table. Despite sharing Fran's petite and well-built physique, there is no sign of any disfigured resemblance between the two. I retract my hand as I analyze the freckles on her cheeks and light blond hair.

Inadvertently, she looks in our direction and, noticing our stare, averts her eyes to the floor.

Hugh glares at her, and she dashes back to the kitchen. He turns to me, his expression furious. "I permitted you to bring your maid to this estate, and this is how you show your gratitude?"

The spit projecting from his words nearly hits my eye, and I wince.

He sarcastically chuckles. "You know, Genevieve, you are a McKinley now, which means you need to act as such rather than make a spectacle out of us in front of the help."

I look past his shoulder at the empty hall; we are alone. "I … I'm…"

"Quite frankly, I blame myself for this mistake. There was a moment of weakness for me. I should never have brought that trash with us." Letting out a huff, he runs his fingers through his hair. "I will not tolerate such inappropriate behavior from my wife."

Despite being aware of the need to make amends, I struggle to articulate my thoughts. "She was, um … well, she…" My eyes dart around the room, taking in every corner before settling on the banquet table. She was standing right there; I can still feel her eyes on me. "I swear…" I blurt out.

"You swear? You swear what?" he asks.

My heart pounds in my chest, and I struggle to catch my breath.

Agitated, Hugh paces up and down the corridor, gesturing wildly with his hands. "There is no Fran. There is no one there!" He points to the room.

I recoil.

"If I have been deceived into marrying a deranged bride ... I will rectify the situation promptly. Just as quickly as I took ownership of you, I can end our arrangement." I wince, picturing the disappointment on my parents' faces if I am returned.

Hugh grabs my shoulders, pulling me closer to his body. "Let that sink into your thick little skull," he remarks.

His words flood panic through my veins, and the pressure of his hands on my bones sends shockwaves of pain through me. Trembling, I try to muster my words. "I swear she was—"

Hugh stops me. He spins me around and looks me dead in the eyes. "You swear she was what, Genevieve?!" he asks, slowly tightening his grip. "Huh?"

I look to the floor to avoid eye contact; I do not want to stir any more anger.

He releases his grip and shrugs, not getting a rise out of me. "Perhaps you are simply unwell and need a good ... long…rest."

What does that mean? The uncertainty of his intentions, whether it is just a nap or something more sinister, frightens me. I would not find it alarming if he had not uttered it in that tone and if I had not seen what I did the prior night. "What was that you said?" I ask.

He turns his back in silence.

I timidly talk faster. "No, really … I promise, there's no need for that. I assure you, I am perfectly fine. Please, trust me. And regarding Fran and my impetuous behavior toward the servants, I will not say another word."

Hugh turns to look at me. "You swear on your life?" he asks; his anger slowly subsides.

I nod. "Yes … yes, of course," I reply, much calmer than before.

His expression remains cold as he glances at me up and down. "Very well, then." He straightens his posture and clears his throat. "If you insist."

As his words end, a heavy silence fills the air, leaving me holding my breath in anticipation of his next action.

He extends his arm, and I nervously glance toward it. "Let us go to the drawing room," he says.

"Of course," I smile, delicately touching his hand. "Please, lead the way."

He shakes his shoulders and puffs out his chest. It is as if a switch flips inside him, making him a gentleman. Turning, he walks, and I breathe a sigh of relief as I follow.

"Did you notice our matching attire?" he asks. He pauses, waiting for a response.

I look at his green coat and cape, flapping from side to side as he walks. They perfectly match my dress.

"Well?" he asks.

"It is thoughtfully done," I say.

"Indeed." He glances down at his chest, then at my bodice. "That was precisely what I had planned."

I anxiously watch the passing walls from the edge of my vision.

The artwork progressively becomes darker with every step, displaying scenes of violence and warfare. I cannot help fixating on the brutality of the images, filled with gore.

"You know, it has become quite fashionable among the upper class," he says, his excitement growing. "Matrimonial couples wearing matching dress is said to be the latest trend in showing their commitment to one another. It's a beautiful way to express our love outwardly."

My attention focuses on one painting. It is of Hugh, in his younger days, slaying a bear. "You don't say?" I ask.

It is disconcerting how the image conveys his thirst for blood.

"Yes, it is all the rage," he says with a gritty laugh. "So, my darling, we are truly at the forefront of fashion."

I gulp, turning my head; the section of the hallway we are approaching is all too familiar. It has been permanently etched into my mind from the night before.

My body tenses as Hugh slows down. He releases my hand and, with a grin, glances toward me.

Catching his stare and unable to remember where the conversation left off, I apprehensively smile back. "That is just lovely. It is brilliant of you to think of these things."

He turns toward the doorway and sighs. "Here we are."

I notice him fishing for something in his pocket and anxiously chuckle. "This entrance looks so familiar," I say, pretending not to recall.

"I would be astonished if you did not find it familiar." He grins, pulling a key from his jacket. He holds it in the air, observing it.

I look at the design; each beveled edge reflects light particles as he turns it from side to side.

"It is the very room we had our cocktail hour in last night." He says.

The last time I saw that key, Clinton had just locked the door and put it in his pocket.

Hugh inserts the key into the lock and turns it to the right.

I flinch at the sound of it unlatching.

"Shall we go inside?" he asks. With a smirk, he slowly removes the key. Placing it back in his pocket, he opens the door.

I stare at the darkness inside.

"After you, my lady," he says.

Sixteen

Surprises

I see his motioning hand and having no choice but to step into the abyss.

As he closes the door behind us, the hinges loudly creak.

I scan my surroundings from left to right. *Why is it so dark? Where are the lights? Why are the curtains drawn? Where is Hugh?* Countless questions race through my mind; keeping track of my thoughts is impossible.

Hugh waits in the pitch-black near the entrance, not saying a word.

The silence is so profound that you could hear a pin drop. It gives me an unsettling feeling in my gut.

Suddenly, the stillness is shattered by a squeal from a floorboard.

As I turn to look, my mind spirals out of control. *What if he intends to do what he failed to do last night? Is it possible that my fate could resemble that of Clinton? What if he plans to trap me or, even worse, kill me? Could there be someone else in this room?*

Each morbid thought is more intrusive than the last. I think about the depiction of him hunting the bear, imagining him lurking in the darkness, preying on my every move. I envision the whites of his eyes glowing in the dark as he fixates on me with a killer's intent.

A soft chuckle echoes, reverberating off the walls, seeming to come from every direction.

I turn in circles as I chase every lead, scanning from left to right, feeling completely disoriented.

Suddenly, the curtains are yanked apart, causing the brass rings to scrape against the golden rods and flooding the room with sunlight through the windows. I stumble, catching myself on a piece of furniture. My legs give way, and a surge of dizziness overwhelms me, causing me to crumple onto the settee and bury my head in its soft cushions.

Laughter fills the room, and I timidly lift my head to look.

Hugh jumps at me and shouts at the top of his lungs, "Surprise!"

I clutch my heart, sliding down to a seated position on the floor.

Four more sets of curtains are instantly thrown open, and Adeline, Hattie, Ettie, and Lucius emerge from behind them. I press my back against the couch, my gaze fixed on the wall as the room spins around me.

As I listen to my heavy breaths, I try to compose myself, but my heart refuses to slow its beats.

Adeline races across the room. "I warned you this was a terrible idea," she says.

Hugh flinches as she whacks his arm. "Mother, please calm yourself," he says, gesturing toward me. "Just look at her; it's obvious that she enjoys it."

I stare back at him from the floor.

Hattie and Ettie cackle, watching the series of events.

"You have knocked the wind out of her with your childish behavior," Adeline says.

Hugh rolls his eyes as Lucius approaches. "Come on, brother." He glances at me. "You must be honest with yourself. She does not appear enthused by your charade."

I look at everyone's faces; they watch me like I am a startled animal. "What ... what is happening?" I ask. "Why are we here?"

They all look at one another.

"Help the girl up," Adeline says. Then, a wave of disgust crosses her lips, and she sneers. "It is improper to leave her on the floor like that."

Hugh reluctantly offers his arm. I accept his assistance and stand to my feet, brushing the wrinkles from my dress.

Ettie and Hattie sneak up behind me. Giggling, they tap my shoulder.

I quickly spin around, my attention darting as I scan the room. It appears very different from the last time I saw it. All the furniture has been removed from the walls and returned to its original position. The sarcophagus and table on which it rested have also been removed from the room, leaving no trace of the events from the previous night. The mere thought of the mummy makes me shudder, especially when I reflect on my narrow escape.

Hugh laughs at my confusion. "How do you like your birthday surprise?"

I look at him. "My birthday?"

"Yes, a little bird told me you just turned seventeen."

The lie sounds like a nail trolling against a chalkboard. "Oh, my birthday ... Yes... I nearly forgot," I say, nervously shifting my weight.

Their eyes are filled with judgment as they all stare at me.

"So, what is the surprise?" I ask.

With a smirk, Hugh watches as the door swings open.

The house staff rushes toward us, carrying golden trays of champagne glasses. I glance at the small dish with a golden spoon beside each brimming flute.

"Shall we start with some drinks?" Hugh says.

The group shrugs as the servants approach.

"It cannot hurt," Adeline says.

My eyes quickly dart toward them. "May I have the privilege of choosing first? Considering it is my birthday celebration."

They look at one another.

"Oh, why not?" Hugh says. "What could be the harm in that?" He snaps his fingers and gestures in my direction.

The staff quickly responds and instantly rushes toward me. As they approach, I swiftly analyze the liquid's surface.

Clinton's words play through my mind. *You must look at how the top fizzles. If it simmers, you are a winner; if it boils, you must recoil.*

"I choose...." Knowing I must act fast, I see and point toward one with little to no bubbles. "That one."

The man carrying the tray I select remains by my side.

"All right, it's my turn next, and then we will proceed in the order of age of the McKinley bloodline," Hugh declares, confidently making his selection. "Lucius, you will go last."

I watch as Adeline cautiously makes her pick.

The butler approaches with the clay container as the others claim their drinks. Moving from person to person, they each sprinkle a spoonful of ash into their effervescent liquid and stir it. Then, they turn their focus toward me.

Sensing the pressure, I look at the small canister waiting on the tray.

On the side of the container, a striking eye is intricately carved and decorated with bold liner, resembling the eyes engraved on the sarcophagus—a thin eyebrow over the top and two lines near the bottom duct. One line forms a curled tail that extends toward the left. The other one is oriented vertically and moves directly downward.

Fixating on the gleam of sunlight mirroring off the painted iris, I remove the lid from the small container and take the spoon into my hand. As I lift it from the tray, I am startled by my skewed reflection in the golden utensil. The others appear closer than I had realized, watching me.

Their chatter falls silent.

I clench my jaw, shifting the spoon slightly to examine each of their faces. *Like a pack of wolves, they are watching my every move.* A knot forms in my stomach, and with a gulp, I glance back at the tray.

Their whispers resume, quietly hissing among themselves as I slowly submerge my spoon into the ash.

The servant holding the tray lowers it closer so I can better see.

Hesitant to retrieve a scoop, I procrastinate by swirling my spoon in the chalky substance. As I sift through the soot, my utensil unexpectedly encounters a hard object.

Finding it strange, I skillfully bring it to the surface. Looking over the container, a wave of horror washes over me; it is a human tooth.

Startled, I fumble, almost dropping the spoon, and the molar slips away, disappearing into the depths of the decorative canister.

Adeline grows impatient. "What is taking so long?" she groans.

My heart races as I glance at the effervescence of the champagne. A simmering fizzle graces the surface, and I begin second-guessing my selection.

Holding my breath, I plop a teaspoon of ash into the glass and, stirring the contents, watch it partially dissolve.

Adeline leans closer to Hugh. "If you ask me, for someone seventeen, she is quite outspoken and seems to lack a youth's impressionability."

Her whisper cuts through the silence and puts prickles on my skin. Her questioning my age is more unsettling than discovering a human tooth.

Unable to contain herself, she whispers louder to Hugh. "Are you certain that she is what she says she is?"

He chuckles. "Mother, stop it; she will hear you." A sneer escapes her lips as he leans closer and lowers his voice. "Anyway ... who would lower themselves to lie about something so trivial?"

I wince, pick up the glass, and spin around to face them. "My apologies for the delay; I wanted to ensure I got the most excellent scoop," I say. Straightening my posture, I glance at Adeline and smirk. Her demeanor shifts. "This is supposed to be my birthday celebration. Is it not?" I ask, directing my question toward her.

"Of course," she says, with a forced smile, her jaw clenched. "Carry on, my dearest new daughter."

Hattie and Ettie snicker.

As Hugh lifts his glass, the staff exits with the empty trays.

"Let us raise a glass to Genevieve on her seventeenth birthday," he says, looking toward me. A grimace crosses his lips. "May it be filled with youthful memories and radiant skin, and we pray to God ... for her to be free of any unfortunate accidents."

Everyone joins him in laughter.

I glance over at them. Then I direct my attention to Hugh and smile. "To seventeen," I say.

They give me a puzzled glare as if questioning why I am speaking.

"I have one more point to mention," I say deliberately, making eye contact with each person.

They glance at one another, wondering what it could be.

"From this moment forward, may no one ever attempt to poison my drink again." I chuckle.

Hattie and Ettie halt their snickers, their mouths agape as the room falls dead quiet.

I grin, listening to the silence. Something about their lack of speech fills me with power.

Taking a deep inhale, I lift my glass higher. "Well, if no one else has anything more to contribute…" With a shrug, I say, "Cheers!"

They continue to stare, even more dumbfounded than before.

I slowly raise my champagne toward my lips. The closer it gets, the more stomach acid travels up my throat. Holding my breath, I tighten my grip around the stem of the glass and tip it to drink. The liquid drips down my chin as I drink the slurry in a single gulp.

Hugh breaks the silence. "You heard her," he says, lifting his glass. "Cheers!"

They all look at me and scan one another before cautiously drinking their elixirs.

I placed my empty glass on the table next to me. Hugh, Hattie, Ettie, and Adeline follow suit.

As Lucius takes his last sip, an odd expression consumes his face. His eyes bulge, and his pupils expand into white. He stumbles, missing the end table; his glass tumbles from his hand and shatters on the floor.

Hattie rushes toward him, grabs his arm, and nervously giggles. "Is everything all right, dear?"

She tries to maintain her composure while looking him dead in the eye. His eyes slowly roll to look at her. Then, as if possessed, they veer off in various directions.

She waves her hand in front of his face to get his attention. "You look a bit under the weather. Are you unwell?" she asks.

He staggers, catching himself on the couch. Regaining his balance, he wipes the sweat from his forehead. "Never … never felt better," he slurs.

As he continues to babble, the skin on his face breaks out into a rash, forming small hives, and his lips and eyes swell shut.

She stares at him in horror.

"Such a shame. Right when I was getting so accustomed to him," Hugh says, stepping closer.

Too weak to stand, Lucius's legs collapse beneath him. Frantically, he paws at the couch; his ballooning hands cannot stop his fall.

Hugh cocks his head, watching his body slide to the floor. "Yes, it is such a pity … I found him to be most pleasant at times."

Adeline steps beside her son to get a better view and chimes in. "He added an element we haven't had before."

"No, no, no, no, no." Hattie throws herself to the floor. "This is not happening."

Lucius coughs, gasping for air.

Hattie cradles his head, and his eyes bulge. Her panic makes it impossible for her to catch her breath. "It was not supposed to be my turn," she wails, tears streaming down her cheeks. "Why is this happening to me? Why?"

Twitches originate in his limbs, accompanied by a surge of convulsions emanating from his chest. She cradles her husband's head tighter. "He's all right … he's going to be all right," she mutters. With a grunt, she tries to sit him up.

I watch in horror as his convulsions worsen. As his tongue swells, he grabs for his throat; patches of his skin turn black and blue.

Ettie fights back her snicker.

Hattie winces, releasing her grip from his head.

His body makes a heavy thud as it hits the floor. I look at the pool of red building around his head; it is clear the fall has cracked his skull.

Hattie glares at me, anger flooding her eyes. "This is all your fault!" she screams, pointing at me.

"Me?" I ask, confused; I take a step back.

She springs to her feet. "It was Hugh's turn, not mine. You were supposed to be the one who died!"

I glance at the others.

Avoiding eye contact, they look away.

"We drew straws!" she says, rushing toward Hugh. "The person who drew the shortest straw lost, and that was you. You drew the shortest stick. Those were the rules!"

He shrugs. "Sometimes, unforeseen circumstances arise, and rules change."

Lucius hacks, and blood spills from his lungs.

Ettie observes with a sense of amusement. "What comes around goes around," she says.

Hattie points to her. "Did you influence her to do this?"

Ettie bursts into laughter, exclaiming, "That is absurd! Are you aware of how ridiculous you sound?"

Blood trickles from Lucius's nose.

I watch him trying to roll over and point at him. "He—he—he," I stammer.

Adeline looks where I am motioning; she is overwhelmed by disgust. "For God's sake, can someone just put him out of his misery? He's flailing about like a floundering fish."

Everyone stops their bickering.

"Do I have to do everything around here?" Hugh asks.

Lucius, desperately holding on, flinches as Hugh approaches him with heavy steps. He wiggles his body, trying to turn, but his hands slip on the blood.

With a grunt, Hugh lifts his foot and gives his head a weighty stomp. Lucius's skull collapses beneath his foot. "There," he says. "That is that."

I cringe, looking away.

Hugh turns to face his siblings. "Now, where were we?"

Hattie rolls her eyes and stamps her feet. "This isn't fair!" She screams.

Adeline sees the conflict escalating and makes her way toward them to intervene. She joins in, and their voices grow louder.

As their quarrel fills my ears, I turn my gaze away, only to find my eyes landing on Lucius's lifeless body. Although the gruesomeness is much worse than I had expected, it has an element of intrigue. The way the crushed bones puncture the flesh is truly extraordinary. Staring at it from afar, I imagine broken paintbrushes skewering canvas soaked in vibrant ruby hues. Nothing about it looks natural.

Hattie screams at Hugh, demanding he listen. In the background, each of their voices fills with more enthusiasm.

I find something alluring about the display and, filled with curiosity, take a step closer. Lucius looks so peaceful lying in his morbid state, contradicting the suffering he endured. It is hard to fathom that the grotesque creature before me was once handsome. If someone saw him in his current dismantled state, they would never know; they would presume him average at best.

With increasing intensity, Hattie and Ettie direct their anger toward each other. "How does it feel now? Huh?" Ettie asks, grabbing her hair. "You were so quick to get rid of my husband. Now look at you," she says.

With a grunt, Hattie paws at her shoulders, trying to free herself from her grasp. "You deceptive witch! We all know you cheated every time we had to choose sticks!"

"Girls!" Adeline squeals from a distance.

"If you recall, my husband made a valuable contribution to this family," Ettie says with disdain. "He's the sole reason we still maintain a decent appearance."

Engaged in a fierce catfight, they shove and grab each other, eventually falling to the ground and yanking at each other's hair.

Hattie grunts as she struggles to get back on her feet.

"Were it not for him," Ettie screams, shoving her back onto the floor, "you would have already taken on the appearance of the decrepit hag you are."

Hattie seizes her neck. "Well … my husband was just as valuable as yours. He was the only reason we received our supply through the harbor!" she shouts as the two persist in pummeling and scratching each other.

"Dear God, you must do something, Hugh; I fear they will kill each other!" Adeline wails, shaking Hugh's shoulders, trying to make him listen.

Happy that it is not him, he raises his hand, declining to budge, and shrugs. "Good," he says. "Since they are identical, we only need one."

"What an insufferable thing to say." Adeline fetches a handkerchief from her cleavage and huffs into it. "This could be your last moment with both of your sisters."

Ettie screams louder, grasping for Hattie's neck. "Everyone knows that harbor is as loose as a hedge creeper. It is the worst in all of Europe. You married him for vanity, not his cleverness; he was nothing more than a challenge. That man was as astute as a wet rag."

Gasping for air, Hattie's eyes bulge as she stammers, "You—you—"

Ettie digs her thumbs into her jugular and squeezes harder. "Admit it! You married a dud."

As they roll, they tighten their grips around the other's neck, squeezing with all their might.

Hugh is entertained as he watches them attempt to strangle each other.

Adeline races toward them, frantically waving her hands. "Stop it, children! You must stop this nonsense this instant!"

Each keeping one hand on another's neck, they swat at her to get away. She shrieks and flails her arms faster, trying to break them up. "It's time to put our differences aside and get along!"

I tune out the noise and stare at the grisly scene; their screams become muted beneath my thoughts.

The gruesome display holds my undivided attention. Before that moment, I had never witnessed a recently deceased body, nor had I encountered any form of a dead human being aside from my encounter with the mummified one. Apart from the fact that they are both dead, there is little similarity between them.

As I analyze the scene, the complete stillness of each lifeless limb continues to haunt my mind. Each brushstroke of deep crimson decorates the floor, resembling a meticulously painted masterpiece; the vividness is captivating. "It ... it's beautiful," I murmur under my breath.

Flowing from the skull, the ichor travels toward my feet. I lock my eyes on the injury and slowly approach, feeling the bottom of my dress pick up weight with each step. Glancing down, I see the eyelet lace soaking up the blood. I stop and stand over Lucius, looking at the mess.

Tiny air bubbles push through the fractured bone fragments. As they reach the surface, they pop like little balloons.

The imagery provokes something inside me. A giggle stems from my gut, quickly escalating into full-blown hysterical laughter.

Again, more bubbles escape to the surface and pop.

Unable to control myself, I laugh louder, snorting through my nose with every guffaw. Short of breath, my ribs ache.

Hattie and Ettie abruptly pause, their hands gripping each other's necks, before simultaneously turning to face me and bursting into laughter.

I clutch my ribs, trying to get ahold of myself, but nothing works. No matter what I do, I cannot seem to cease my cackling. It spills out of me with even more abundance than before.

Hugh stares at me for a moment, then bursts into laughter at the sight of my dress, drenched in blood.

As Adeline joins in, the two girls release their grip on each other and continue to laugh, rolling on the floor and wildly kicking their feet.

Their laughter echoes loudly from behind me, shattering my concentration. It resembles the high-pitched yelps of a pack of wild hyenas.

Ettie and Hattie clutch their stomachs as they try to catch their breaths. "Dear God, sister, how did we end up in this state, behaving like wild creatures?" Ettie says, casting a sidelong glance at Hattie.

Hattie snickers, thinking of their brawl. "Indeed, sister." She glances toward Ettie and sighs. "It is all so vexing, is it not?"

Ettie giggles, taking hold of her hand. "What a foolish argument. It was quite silly, don't you think?"

They burst into laughter again.

Hattie grins. "What is done cannot be undone. Let us never fight about such trivial matters again."

"Sisters?" they say, finishing their question simultaneously. Their eyes grow wide. "Jinx!" They sit up in unison.

Adeline adoringly watches as they wiggle their fingers together.

"Sisters for life. The best things happen twice," they cheer.

As they finish their handshake, Adeline lowers herself to the floor. "Let's hope the disagreement is now behind us," she says.

Standing quietly, I observe the scene when I suddenly feel someone grab my shoulder. I gasp and spin around. The sight of Hugh's proximity startles me.

He extends his arm and says, "Shall we … wife?"

I gaze at his wide smile, stretching from ear to ear. Then, taking his hand, I allow him to assist me out of the horrifying scene. Taking a moment to gather my thoughts, I glance downward, only to discover my dress has painted the floor, leaving a bloody crimson trail in my wake. A mix of dread and curiosity compels me to follow the gruesome path with my eyes, leading me back to the lifeless body of Lucius.

Hugh, seeing my preoccupation, clears his throat, wanting my attention. I lift my skirt to prevent creating a further mess and briefly look toward him; he appears anxious as he silently stares at me.

My attention shifts back to the corpse. Hugh pulls on my arm and chuckles. "Don't worry, my dear. The poison had already paralyzed him well before the smashing, so it was truly the best outcome for him," he reassures me. "Consider it as an act of charity."

My eyes remain locked on the blood and bone. The longer I stare, the more entranced I become.

"Trust me, he would have endured much greater suffering if we had waited for the poison to fully take effect. It was the humane thing to do."

As his words go in one ear and out the other, I notice him watching me while tapping the leg of his trousers. The eager expression on his face tells me he is waiting for me to speak. I break my silence and motion to the body. "It's quite exquisite," I say, tilting my head to admire it from a different angle.

He cocks his head to see from my perspective.

"The way the hues decorate the floor so effortlessly ... I've seen nothing like it. It is rather intoxicating," I say.

His smile is filled with intrigue as he adjusts his posture and stares at me. Feeling his stare, I turn toward him. He reaches for my face and grips my cheeks between his hands, looking deep into my eyes. My lips pucker together under the pressure as I gaze at him helplessly.

A twisted smirk appears on his lips. "Genevieve, you might be the most attractive woman I have ever seen."

His words are enchanting. I close my eyes and take a deep breath, holding onto his every syllable. He abruptly releases my face, and I look to see where he has gone.

Stepping aside, he dips a single finger into the blood, then slowly moves toward me. "Are you aware that fresh blood is believed to possess medicinal properties?"

His voice has a hypnotic effect on my ears.

"It is said that when you consume it, you are infused with the person's soul, enhancing your vitality.... Human blood is believed to restore youth and heal all ailments—even those you never knew existed."

I observe him whisking his tainted finger across his lips. Something about the action excites me; it is invigorating.

Then, leaning close beside me, he gently whispers in my ear, "Kiss me." His voice lingers as he moves in for a kiss.

The sensation of his lips on mine sends an electrifying spark from head to toe as he pulls me near, and we share a passionate kiss. As he releases me, I open my eyes and glimpse his devilish smile.

My pulse quickens at the sight of crimson stains around his mouth. I feel free like my soul has left and entered another world. It is a sensation I have never felt before.

He stares at me, licking the residue from his lips. I have never witnessed such a sparkle in his eyes; they glisten like those of a predator, fixated on me like prey as if he wants to devour me whole.

As the flavor of iron enters my tastebuds, everything in my core tells me I should be terrified, but my infatuation overrides all my common sense. There's a unique connection between us, a deep closeness that is difficult to put into words. Laced with euphoria, its potency is dangerous.

His mother and sisters sniff the air like wild dogs, and the overwhelming scent of ichor makes drool collect at the creases of their lips. It shifts something deep within them; their faces narrow, and their pupils dilate and darken, morphing into tones of black.

We continue to gaze into one another's eyes.

The light hitting their bodies casts a shadow onto the wall near us, emphasizing their approaching steps. Their elongated forms resemble slithering creatures, and their shadows' jarring movements appear almost possessed. Unable to hide my surprise, my eyes widen.

Instantly, the disturbing sound of gnashing teeth and ravenous eating surround me.

I try to glance around Hugh to see the cause, but he grabs my shoulders and pulls me closer, blocking the view. The unsettling din of slurping tongues, feasting on the bloody corpse, fills the room.

Seventeen

One of us

A s he embraces me with more force, the sound of their animalistic growls escalates.

Pressing his hand against my head, Hugh whispers, "Do not turn around."

I wiggle slightly, but his grip on me feels lethal as if one wrong move will end me.

"Trust me, you'll soon realize it is for the best," he says, taking hold of my hand. I follow him, carefully staying close behind as we approach the exit.

There is an inconsistency in the air—a deviating instability.

The commotion triggers a sickness in my gut and an ache in my bones; I feel it is a warning. Deep down, a nagging feeling tells me that even though it seems impossible, something is even more horribly wrong.

Hugh stiffens his posture.

Creaks and squeaks emanate from the floorboards behind me, followed by the unsettling noise of clicking tongues—suctioning against the roofs of their mouths, producing an ominous intonation. It is predatorial, like a flock of ravens preparing to swoop, informing the others of a meal.

Hugh places his hand on my back and pushes me to move faster.

As I quicken my pace, a loud thud echoes throughout the room. Startled, I turn around to look, little realizing that what was waiting for me would be even more horrifying than my worst nightmares.

Ettie and Hattie crawl through the gore, hovering over the body; blood trickles down their chins, dripping to refill the pool on the floor. Their gowns are drenched in a deep shade of red.

Ettie snarls. The socket cord of Lucius's eyeball dangles from her lips. Then, with the ferocity of a wild dog, she shakes her head, flinging the body part into the air and opening her mouth to prepare to catch it. Blood splatters her face as it descends.

Her jaw opening seems unnatural, with a looseness that resembles that of a marionette. She coils her tongue around the optic and pulls it into her mouth. Being careful not to squish it, she grips it between her teeth and opens and closes her lips, pretending it is blinking while releasing an unhinged cackle.

Based on their horrific appearance, it is clear that the sounds I had heard earlier resulted from unspeakable acts.

Hattie smiles at her sister, thick chunks of gore wedged between her incisors.

Ettie chews the firm texture and, swallowing, smiles.

With a snarl, their attention shifts to Adeline.

As she arches her spine, she pushes her face deeper into the body cavity—her back heaves with every bite, reminiscent of a lion feasting on an antelope. The sound of breaking cartilage and bone torments my ears.

Ettie and Hattie creep closer toward their mother. It is like pure evil has gutted their souls from their bodies. There is nothing remotely human about them; they are monsters.

Adeline tears off a mouthful of flesh, savoring the taste as she chews. As she swallows, she turns, and her tongue extends, slithering out of her mouth.

Drawing a long breath, I muster the courage to meet her gaze. Once familiar and, at times, reassuring, her eyes have now transformed into something I can barely recognize. They are now two large, ebony pupils that seem to swallow up all the light in the room, leaving only a cold emptiness in their wake.

I cannot help but feel like I am staring into the soulless portals of hell itself. There is no emotion or recognition in those coal-black orbs, making her feel like a stranger to me. I search for any hint of familiarity, but there is none. The alien-like gaze of her eyes fills me with terror as I find myself trapped in a sea of confusion and despair. She clicks her teeth, and the corners of her mouth twitch into a grin.

Although fear fills every ounce of my being, there is something so fascinating about her actions that I cannot peel my eyes away.

The sisters cock their heads toward the ceiling and fervently sniff the air. Catching my scent, they sneer as they turn and look at me.

Their animalistic nature induces a panic in me, as I can tell they are imagining stripping my flesh from the bone and devouring me whole.

They lick their lips and curl their legs into a crouching position to lunge.

I gasp, my body tensing as their smiles twist into the grins of impish tricksters.

Hugh wrenches my arm, causing me to stumble as he drags me through the doorway and into the corridor.

The door slams shut, and the hall fills with muffled, predatory growls behind it.

I spin around, clutching my chest, and rest my back against the wall. "Wha-what…" I stammer, my fear causing my words to scramble.

"That is what happens when they do not get their daily regimen," he says with a grimace. He reaches into his pockets and pulls out the skeleton key.

I glance at his hand; it is trembling.

He swiftly sticks the key into the lock and twists it. "You should give yourself a pat on the back," he mutters.

The latch clicks.

The sound startles me, and I nearly leap from my skin. I quickly straighten my posture, my mind racing, unsure of what to think about the horrific things I just witnessed. The uncertainty of the situation is overwhelming, causing me to tremble and sweat.

He shoves the key back into his pocket.

Panic floods my body, and I dart my attention to the door. The creature's gruesome appearances consume my mind. Although dressed identically to his sisters and mother, I cannot fathom them being one and the same. "Why did you lock them inside?" I ask, rushing toward the door. "You can't leave them in there with those…"

He clutches his fingers to stabilize his shaking hands.

I point toward the door. "Those things!"

Without looking up or saying a word, he pats his pocket to ensure the key is secure.

I turn around, breathing heavily. I watch him straighten the lapel of his jacket; his lack of trepidation is alarming.

Their howls become snarls on the other side of the door, each more voracious than the last.

"The answer to your question is quite simple," he says. Continuing calmly, he explains, "I locked the door not out of concern for their safety but for the well-being of the staff."

My eyes widen as I hear nails clawing at the door. He fights his snicker. "Quite frankly, we simply can't afford to *lose* any help in this place, and I am all out of energy and patience to find more. The process is excruciatingly dull, and grooming them to our liking is quite tedious, to say the least."

I flinch. "Lose?" I ask.

As he turns away from me, he paces, and I find myself anxiously listening to each of his footsteps.

"Yes, that is right, my lovely wife." Taking a moment of pause, he shrugs and, with a smirk, glances in my direction. "There appears to be a lot we do not know and much we need to learn about this type of remedy."

Although I hear his words, my mind is scattered; I cannot seem to control my train of thought. "'Remedy?'" I ask.

He waves his hand and continues to explain, "Yes, remedy … it involves using medication made from various forms of human flesh. It is known to cure nearly every type of ailment."

Suddenly, it is as if all the puzzle pieces have finally clicked into place as the memory of a term used the night before floods back to me. "Mummia," I utter.

He glances at me, shocked by my knowledge, and anxiously chuckles. "You continue to surprise me."

As he studies my face, I stare into his contemplating eyes. His smirk makes my heart patter.

"Yes, what you saw is quite reminiscent of the usage of Mummia. Both are ingested and have similar rejuvenating properties, but when the source is the newly deceased, it seems to elicit a bit more ferocity," he says, shrugging. "As far as I can tell, Mummia does not appear to have those concerns. Well, at least none that we observed. It is a pity that obtaining mummies has become so difficult, which is why the reveal on our wedding night brought such excitement. The entire upper class apparently knows the secret to preserving one's vitality. Now, you must pay a queen's ransom to get one, and the few mummies remaining obviously have defects. But on a positive note, we are quite handsome indeed. It is both a blessing and a curse."

The sensation of being released from his smoldering look sends shock waves through my body, and, woozy, I brace myself against the wall.

Taking a step, he resumes his pace. "So far, we have learned that after the first drop ingested of the freshly dead, if any dose is missed, it provokes an uncontrollable frenzy inside us … nearly, do I dare say…pushing us to the edge of madness."

I observe a noticeable change in his demeanor. The more he thinks about everything that has gone awry, the more his resentment toward the topic builds. His face turns red; he shakes his head and points at the door. "Just as you witnessed in there, it transforms one into a ravenous state!"

I slowly step back away from him to create space between us. I shift my attention toward the door.

He throws his hands in the air in frustration. "There appear to be only two ways to counteract the symptoms: ingesting a large dosage of desiccated mummy or a small serving of a fresh kill."

Each of his words sends a wave of horror through me at both their intent with me and what I may become.

With a defeated sigh, he rests a hand on his forehead. "There appears to be no cure—only ways to tide over the beast that looms inside us."

Dear God. As I lift my finger to the dried blood on my lips, my finger trembles. *What have I done? Is that what I will become? Is that who I have become?*

Silence plagues the hall.

He despondently looks at the wall. "Our bodies have become unable to function without it. Utterly dependent."

The image of the feral look in his sister's eyes floods my mind. *Is that what I am destined to be? Is that what I am to become?*

As I turn to Hugh, hoping to interrupt my train of thought, I see him wallowing in self-pity, and rage takes hold of me. "You … you!" Pointing toward him, I stumble over my words.

He turns away from me, avoiding eye contact. "Oh, do not act like one kiss is the reason for your demise," he says, his eyes fixed down the hallway. He appears to be planning his escape.

As I listen to him, I grit my teeth. The combination of his sarcasm and evasion sends fire through my veins.

"Were you not surprised by your appearance in the mirror this morning?"

His question strikes a nerve. *Was he spying on me? How else could he possibly know my reaction?*

I cringe at the thought of him peeping into my quarters. As my anger turns into paranoia, I replay my moment in front of the mirror, recalling the sensation of touching my soft, youthful skin while admiring my reflection.

He chuckles, amused by my silence.

"You are thinking about it, aren't you? How on earth did I look so much younger today?" he asks, amused.

I wince. Pushing through my flustered state, I can barely assemble a sentence, "It is impossible.... I ... uh... uh... But I did not take a single sip of my champagne yesterday."

"Clearly!" he sarcastically exclaims. Then, with a cynical laugh, he turns toward me. "You wouldn't be standing before me if you had."

As he looks me up and down, our eyes meet. "So, it is true ... you tried to kill me!"

Rolling his eyes, he says, "Yes, it is true." Tempering his rage, he continues. "Your accusations were correct." He shrugs. "Since it is no longer a secret that you were supposed to be dead by now, we should all feel relieved."

I watch his every move, more disgusted than before.

"I do not know about you, but personally, I feel like an enormous weight has been lifted from my shoulders."

"If not for you, I would not have been subjected to this mess. I would still be living a normal life," I say. "But now, I'm left to live like an animal! I do not feel a single grain of weight lifted off my chest! You … you have subjected me to whatever this hellish curse is!"

He smirks and, with a playful turn, says, "Oh, on the contrary."

I stand there watching him in disbelief.

"If I'm not mistaken," he says, suppressing a snicker, "you seemed to thoroughly enjoy your dinner last night."

Growing more frustrated, I stomp my foot and grumble, "How is that relevant to my concern? Just get on with it!"

He responds with a grin. "That meal, my dear, was made possible by the man who married us," he says.

Instantly, my mind is flooded with my dream from the night before. *In your stomach, I sit.* The man's words repeat in my mind, and a feeling of dread washes over me as I contemplate the grim possibilities. "What … what… is the significance of that?" I ask. My question is filled with apprehension, uncertain whether I want to hear the answer.

"Why else would a 'blessed roast' quip make sense?" He bursts into laughter, utterly enjoying his own wit. "It should have been more obvious than you are making it seem."

My gut churns, and I turn away as stomach acid fills my throat.

"Well, regardless of your sense of humor, you now know that I was not the cause of your fate. I did not force you to eat. You made your own choice when you ingested the food before you."

The revelation causes me to retch uncontrollably.

Hugh rushes toward me. "What a peculiar reaction," he remarks, stroking my back. "I expected that having that knowledge would make you feel much better."

As I focus on a single board, my sickness subsides. "'Better?!' Did you honestly believe that knowing I consumed the flesh of another would bring me solace?"

"Yes, because now you know your husband is not to blame if you experience strange cravings," he replies.

It astonishes me how he fails to grasp the subject that concerns me. Making matters worse, he abruptly leaves, his footsteps growing faint as he walks toward the exit, behaving as if all has been resolved, and I am satisfied with his answer.

"Wait, where are you going?" I ask, confounded. "I believe we are still discussing matters."

Hugh stops in his tracks and fixes his eyes on me. "Oh, is that so? Well, I am certain our conversation saw its end," he says, and playfully, spinning around, he continues to walk while calling out. "Besides, I have other pressing matters that demand my attention."

I quickly chase after him, shouting, "But … but…I have more questions!"

He halts, and his posture stiffens. I narrowly avoid a collision with him. "What else is there to know?"

I huff for breath. "Did I … I mean, did we…I must know, did we consume Clinton for breakfast? Was he the source of the meat?" I ask, my anxiety accelerating the pace of my words.

Hugh winces.

"Hugh, please answer me," I say, desperate for a response. "Was he the meat at breakfast?"

"Why do you care about him?" he asks defensively.

As I watch his reaction, I attempt to conceal my concern and assume an indifferent demeanor. "I do not care about him," I reply.

As his right eyebrow lifts, a slight smile tugs at the corner of his lip.

"I … I am just filled with an insatiable curiosity. Can you share the details of his death?" I anxiously glance past his shoulder down the hall. "It is all so exciting."

He slowly turns to face me.

"Was he murdered? Gruesomely disemboweled?"

His facial muscles stiffen; he can tell care hides beneath my words, and his manner falls cold. "If you must know, he was nowhere to be found this morning when we went to fetch him for breakfast."

I want to smile with relief but refrain.

He clenches his jaw. "Nothing was left of him except for the key and a note found on the drawing room table."

"Do you have any idea where he might have gone?" I ask. As I wait for a response, my fingers tighten around the fabric of my skirt.

His attention becomes fixed on something behind me, leading me to turn around and discover only the closed drawing room door.

"Bloody hell, how would I know?!" he angrily spouts.

"You surely must have some idea," I reply.

"The letter was vague." Each response that escapes his bloodstained lips reveals his mounting agitation. "It just mentioned something about having to get away … the rest was gibberish. His handwriting was very ill indeed. Only two things are certain: both he and the mummy are gone."

An icy chill frosts my skin.

"It is obvious to me," he says, "that he must have taken the mummy … You know, they are quite valuable and hard to come by."

I nervously glance from left to right. "The mummy has disappeared?"

He clenches his fists, and his face turns red. "Yes!" he says, sweltering in his rage. "Were my words not articulated well enough for your daft ears, woman?" I cower in fear as he screams and throws up his hands, huffing and puffing, about to explode. "Perhaps I shall enunciate more. The mummy is gone! Vanished! Just like Clinton … into thin air."

I reflect on my morning in the drawing room. Indeed, I had noticed the casket and mummy were missing, but rather than questioning their whereabouts, I believed the reason to be different. I assumed that the part of the story where the creature came to life was simply a terrifying figment of my imagination, a nightmare born out of sheer exhaustion. It seemed so unrealistic.

Then, as if he has read my mind, Hugh chimes in. "To be honest, at first, I was infuriated by all the money wasted on purchasing the thing and having it stolen. But then, I had the strangest dream where it came to life … and I could feel its icy breath on my neck as it tried tearing me apart!"

I cringe. Having the same recollection means none of it was a dream—all my flashbacks of the creature from the prior night are real. *It was real*… I gulp, trying to clear my head.

Hugh's emotionally charged shouting appears manic as he projects spit with every word. "So, I say, good riddance!"

He finishes his rant and walks away. With each heavy pace, he exudes a sense of pride, asserting his control.

His steps pull me from my thoughts. "Where are you going?" I ask. Glancing up, I see he is already halfway down the hall.

Without stopping, he lifts his hands above his head and loudly claps. "She is ready to be changed for dinner," he shouts, picking up his pace.

His tone tells me that his words are not directed at me; it is clear he is summoning my chambermaid.

As he exits from view, I clutch my dress tighter and stay put to wait for her retrieval.

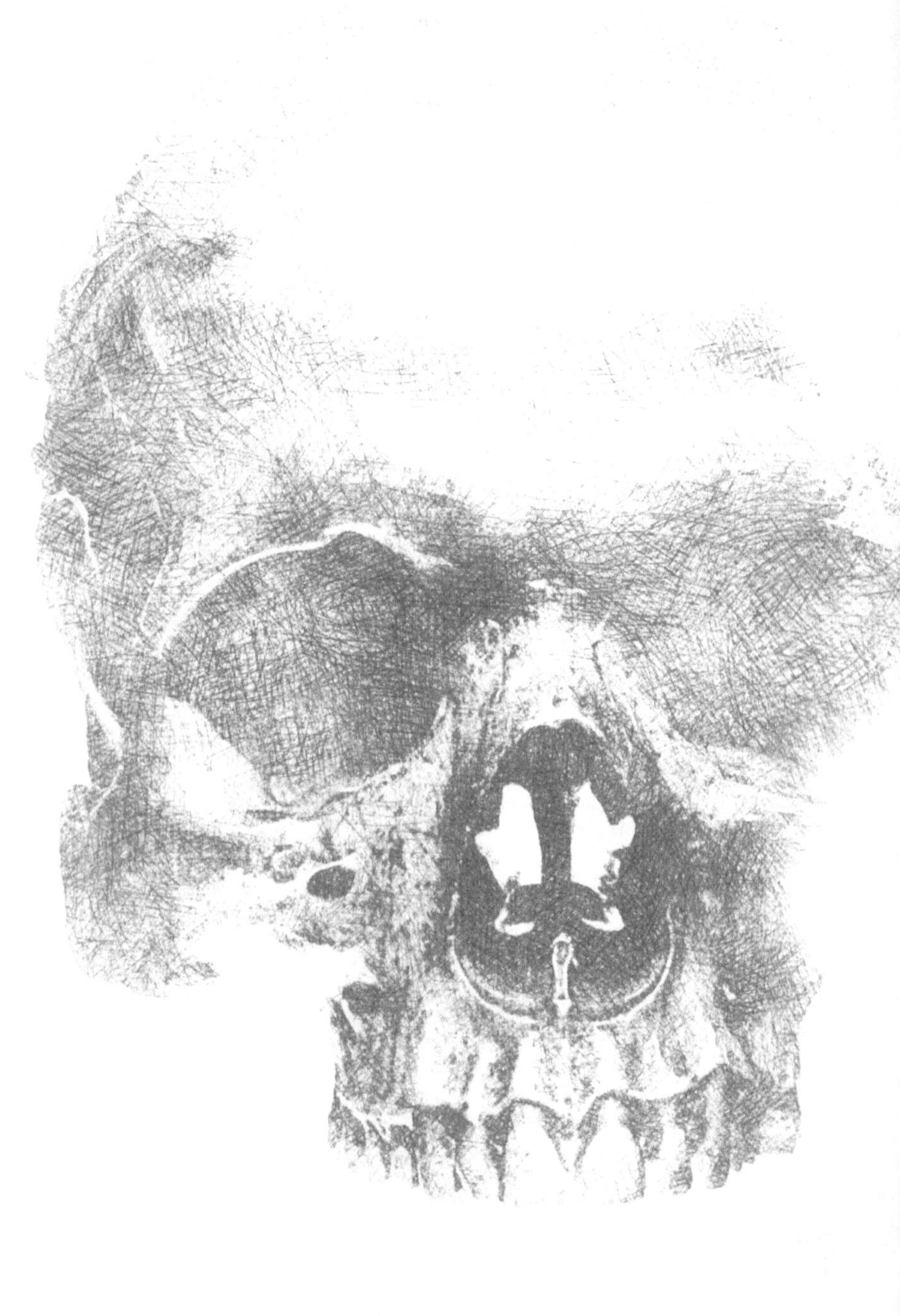

Eighteen

Who is There?

As my arms ache from the weight of my soaked underskirt, I restlessly scan my surroundings to pass the time.

The hallway appears less ominous as the natural light softly illuminates the space. The battle shields, adorned with intricate designs, and the diverse array of war memorabilia, including suits of armor, weapons, and miscellaneous historical artifacts, create a captivating and rich milieu.

My eyes land on a painting of a knight wearing a bronze-and-golden suit of armor. To the right of it, there is a portrait. The painting is colored in brown-and-autumn tones, giving it a somber appearance. In the center of the scene is a man dressed in battle attire, mounted on a magnificent stallion, his shield slipping from his grip. He appears to struggle to maintain control

of the horse with one hand as his body partially slumps off the charcoal steed.

I squint and move closer to better see the
dark burgundies splattering the family crest
on his chest. It appears he has been wounded
during the fight. Finding the depiction dis-
tasteful, I quickly shift my gaze to the next one.

Instead of improving, the image is more
gruesome than the last. Portrayed in the
scene is another war, wherein a man lies
helpless on the battlefield, begging for his life
as his adversary, with a sword in hand, stands
poised to inflict a fatal blow.

I take another step, and my eyes fixate
on the long row of portraits ahead, studying
every brushstroke.

While they also depict woeful themes,
they are much less graphic—most detail no-
blemen in mourning or expressions of grief
after the battle. Compared to their predeces-
sors, they are much more palatable. There
is something beautiful about seeing such
masculine figures show emotions other than
anger.

As I seek a momentary escape from their
sadness, my eyes land on the portrait just
ahead, triggering a flood of memories. I suddenly realize it is next to where I stood with
Clinton the previous night.

With a surge of sentiment, I step toward the artwork; I had not gotten a good look at it before.

As I continue to study the painting, I am struck by a sense of recognition that eluded me previously. The artist's portrayal of the man's dark olive-toned skin and the contour of his jawline evoke a strong resemblance to Clinton.

I lift my hand and trace his body, touching the canvas. "Clinton, it appears you were the smartest among us," I comment.

His tears shimmer in his fixed gaze, reflecting the light and producing a glossy sheen.

I move closer, stopping my finger at his shoulder. I stare deeply into his eyes. "You are the only one, it seems, who will ever break free of this madhouse."

With a sigh, I shift my attention to the sun's rays, peeking through the clouds in the sky, and notice something peculiar.

The subject's shoulders and chest emit an ethereal smoke that forms a noticeable human shape. Within the area of the head, distinct features emerge, including a mouth, lips, and ears. The way the apparition clings to the subject's body is captivating and makes it apparent that it does not want to leave.

With my fingertip, I delicately trace the ethereal image. "Fascinating," I remark. My digit crosses the painting's silver armor, creating a red smudge.

I pause and carefully examine my hand, feeling a rush of panic as I see a droplet of sweat on my fingertip. I am sure it is to blame. Looking back at the painting, I see the crimson spot has grown and is now effortlessly flowing across the canvas and dripping onto the floor.

Panic rushes through me as I realize what I have done. "Clumsy, girl." I gasp. Hiking my skirt, I hastily rub my toe against the floor. It only exacerbates the issue, causing the droplets to smear and spread.

With a frustrated grunt, I let go of my skirt, allowing it to fall. Then, hastily, I gather the edge of my sleeve in my hand and vigorously begin scrubbing the mess on the painting.

But the splotch only grows, contaminating the surrounding scenery with its crimson hue. With each additional swipe, it bleeds further, like an open wound oozing its iron-infused pigment over the surface.

My heart pounds in my head as I dread the possibility of being scorned for tarnishing the image, and I nervously rub faster. "Oh, Genevieve, what have you done? What have you done?"

Something rustles in the distance.

"What would they think if they saw you this way?" I ask, stiffening my posture. I talk faster, frantically scrubbing. "They would certainly view me as mad."

The hallway is filled with a sudden rush of cold air and murmuring voices. A swift prickle brushes my nape, sending a shiver down my spine. As I listen, I hear a mixture of dialects as the voices intertwine. Each utterance sounds closer than the last.

A creeping unease washes over me as I sense something watching me, their penetrating gaze scorching the back of my head. I try to remain calm and listen while taking slow, deep breaths.

Then, without warning, a piercing noise startles me from behind.

Realizing it is coming from the direction of Hugh's departure, I reluctantly glance over my shoulder, assuming it is him, but he is nowhere to be found.

The hall is empty.

The ambiance of the long hallway slowly shifts. It is much darker than before—too dark for the time of day.

But we just had breakfast. My thoughts run wild as I question the reasons for the sudden darkness.

Despite the passage of time since I arose, it has still not been long enough to make it nightfall.

I glance at the candelabras scattered between paintings. Their once shiny gold is now dull, accenting the worn look of the wicks' charcoal coatings. Someone or something has blown out all but one flame, leaving me with the most unnerving feeling.

I catch the blood-tainted portrait again from the corner of my eye. The neglected stain haunts me.

As I turn to resume scrubbing, a voice calls out, "Genevieve." It is immediately followed by movement at the end of the hall.

Fear grips me, and I stand frozen in place, listening to the unsettling scratching noises resonating from something scurrying from wall to wall in the darkness. With trepidation, I slowly turn toward the source while attempting to see through the murky surroundings.

"Who … who is there?" I ask. My trembling words are met with a deafening silence.

The longer I wait, the more unsure I am if I want a reply.

I freeze in place, my chest aching from my corset as I hold my breath. My attention is drawn to the subtle yet unmistakable sound traversing the hallway. Squinting in the dim light, my eyes finally come to rest on the farthest point of the corridor, where shadows seem to gather and whisper secrets.

An almost imperceptible patch of darkness stands out, its density noticeably greater than the surrounding shadows. I detect a subtle movement within the obscurity near the right wall.

A mischievous smirk plays on my lips. I stand tall, drawing in a deep breath before clearing my throat. "This isn't a game, Hugh," I call out while scanning for any sign of movement. "You can come out now."

My sly smile vanishes instantly as the murmurs disperse like tiny spiders skittering in every direction, leaving an unsettling energy in the air.

I take another step forward, my eyes straining to pierce through the dark. "Hugh?" I ask timidly, straining to see any movement ahead.

The air is sliced by a haunting shush reverberating off the walls as a spectral figure gradually takes shape. Its elongated limbs move in a ghostly dance as it scampers from one wall to the next, resembling a wisp of smoke.

I slide back silently, hoping to remain unseen, my eyes fixed on the ever-changing patterns of darkness.

My body trembles as I watch its spectral presence creep closer. I step back to further the distance between it and myself and gasp as the floor groans, fearing that it will draw attention to me.

My chest tightens while my eyes remain fixed on the hunched figure. I try to discern more details than just a silhouette, but I am unable. As it raises its head, it extends its elongated legs, dragging the rest of its body lethargically behind it as it steps into the center of the hallway.

Everything becomes quiet as the figure's upper body suddenly folds, collapsing further over his knees.

I cringe, observing the profile of its arched spine. The jagged ridge remains eerily motion-less.

"Hugh, if that's you, I no longer find this amusing. I am ready for his charade to end," I yell anxiously. I pick at the skin of my nails, my fear growing as I wait for a reply.

Suddenly, the figure's neck stretches until its head brushes against the ceiling, revealing its eyes glowing a vibrant yellow. Its strange movement gives it a ghoulish appearance as it advances toward me. At that moment, I realize that it is simply not possible for it to be a mere joke.

"It ... it is not him," I stammer, my eyes darting to the shadowy recesses of the hall, looking for an escape. "That is not Hugh."

I take a cautious step backward, the overwhelming urge to flee building inside me. Beads of sweat trickle down my forehead, a sign of my escalating fear.

As it inches closer, its neck undulates with a serpentine motion reminiscent of a slithering snake. Its head thrusts forward, and its frightening eyes lock onto mine with a piercing glare. "Genevieve..." it hisses the syllables rolling off its tongue.

I take another hurried step back, my breath catching in my throat. To calm myself, I steal a glance at the portrait hanging on the wall, hoping to find solace in the likeness of my friend Clinton.

The painting has been defaced with a gruesome overlay much worse than blood. Now visible are the intricate details of a woman, her face twisted in a tormented scream.

With disbelief, I scan her gory cheeks and prominent eyebrows, and in her terrified eyes, I glimpse my reflection as the entity creeps closer.

The creature points its gangly arm toward the portrait, and a twisted howl escapes its lips.

"You are the girl you see," it says, each word carrying the stench of rot.

I stare in shock at the thing before me and scream, "Lies!"

"Bound by desires, you will never leave. Trapped between these walls, ensnared by your misery. You will perish like the rest. Wait and see!" it screams.

The shrill tone ripples through the canvas, causing blood to drip from the painting onto the floor.

I monitor the creature from the corner of my eyesight. Its fingers wiggle, casting a sinister shadow over the portrait. Every movement mimics a puppeteer orchestrating a gruesome show, conducting the gore to spread and add more detail to the subject's face and bustline.

Horror engulfs me as I stare at the new revelation. "Dear God, it is me." I gasp.

As the pace of the macabre artistry increases, the intricate details continue to manifest, gradually assuming a more lifelike resemblance.

"Please ... please stop," I stammer. "Stop this instant." Frantically, I try to blur the strokes on the canvas, my breath catching in my throat as I attempt to erase them with my sleeve, but the faster I scrub, the more quickly fresh strokes appear, replacing the previous ones.

My mouth opens and releases a piercing scream.

The woman's mouth opens in perfect sync with mine, but instead of screaming, the canvas beneath her lips tears apart, unleashing a torrent of vivid crimson-red liquid.

The metallic taste of iron floods my senses, causing my stomach to twist with nausea. Desperately gasping for air, I wipe the fluid from my eyes and nervously use my hand to block the hemorrhage and erase the likeness. The torn edges of the canvas scrape my fingers as they slip through the gash and deep into her mouth.

With the strength of a vise, her lips close around my elbow, trapping me in her terrifying grip. I fight against her unyielding jaws, feeling myself being dragged closer. My shoulder aches as I fight to yank my hand away from her teeth.

Her nostrils flare as she inhales with determination, her lips pursed, and delicate wrinkles form on her cheeks.

As my body is pulled further into the void, I thrash my free hand above my head and jab its fingers into her eyes. Her face contorts in anger.

In a state of panic, I make another desperate attempt to remove the terrifying apparition using my sleeve, but the bloodstain on the painting continues to spread. As I scrub vigorously, the friction disrupts the image, revealing bits of the original portrait of the man underneath.

As I pull with all my might, her nostrils flare, and her cheeks puff out, and then, with a loud gasp, she finally relinquishes my arm.

A sinister laugh reverberates down the hallway, and I turn to look. The enigmatic figure slowly fades away and disappears into the darkness.

As I look back at the painting, there is no longer any trace of the woman, and in her place is a disturbing, swirling shadow that takes the shape of someone I know all too well.

"Phillip?" I whisper in a soft, trembling voice.

The mere thought of seeing him as an apparition makes me tremble uncontrollably. *What if he, too, is dead, and all that is left of him?*

Then, a moment of self-preservation consumes me, knowing I have barely escaped the same fate.

"This is all because of you!" My finger points accusingly at the painting, and I sneer in disbelief. "If only you were still here, you could have warned me ... You could have intervened!" Anger builds up as I lift my fist, preparing to swing.

A sudden, ominous hiss pierces the silence, coming from my right.

My muscles tighten, and my body becomes rigid, as if trapped in ice, hindering my movement.

"Genevieve," a voice calls.

A frigid gust of air caresses the side of my neck as my name is spoken. Startled, I inhale sharply and twist to look where the sound came from.

Only silence consumes the empty hallway.

My skin prickles with goosebumps as I force myself to look back at the portrait on the wall. I cannot help but stare at the void where I had imagined the image of my brother's twisted existence.

My heart quickens as whispers drift through the desolate hall. Soft, ominous clicks of a rattling doorknob reverberate, adding a chilling undertone through the vibrant tapestry of voices.

My eyes jump to the nearest door, and I notice its handle trembling. This sets off a series of reactions, prompting the others to join. One by one, each handle violently shakes. The rattling reverberates through the wood of each entry lining the corridor, resonating throughout the space.

Fleeting whispers drift and dance around me. I struggle to fill my anxious lungs with air as I desperately fumble through the suffocating darkness. I run my fingers along the walls until my eyes come to rest on the open drawing room door ahead of me.

As if on cue, the handles fall silent, creating a void that is instantly filled with a chorus of ethereal whispers that bring with them a forceful gust of wind that surges past me, pushing me closer.

With unwavering focus, I keep my eyes locked on the entrance, straining to catch any subtle movement from the gaping doorway.

The whispers abruptly stop, replaced by a bone-chilling, guttural growl emanating from the room itself.

The terrifying sound mirrors that of the mummy from my wedding night. My breath creates a delicate, frosted pattern in the cold air. *It can't be ... He said it was gone. He said it had been stolen.*

The creature's ponderous footsteps resonate from the room. With each step, a massive shadow emerges from the doorway, stretching into the hall, serving as a haunting reminder of the malevolence inside and the monster's effortless ability to rip a piece of flesh from Hugh's face.

My heart races as I desperately stare at the silhouette of the mummy creeping up the wall, along with the distinct outline of the crook in its hand. I visualize the curvature of the sharp edge against my neck. All it would take is one fell swoop to lop my head from my body.

Paralyzed by fear and a sense of powerlessness, I anxiously evaluate my choices for escape as the voice transforms into a whisper, breathing my name. "Genevieve…"

A powerful need to flee grips me, and knowing each direction faces its own peril, I choose to move forward and gather my skirt, preparing to run.

"Genevieve!"

The sound, much closer than before, stops me in my tracks.

"When I step outside, I will devour you whole; with each bite, I will savor the delight," it says.

I swiftly pivot away from the direction of the voice, and with a lunging step, I collide with something solid, sending me stumbling backward.

As I struggle to regain my balance, my gaze drops to the floor, where I notice the chambermaid's plain, distinct shoes and skirt. In a moment of panic, our eyes lock, and I meet her gaze. Her face is expressionless and cold.

"Thank goodness it's you," I exclaim, relief flooding me as I embrace her.

She does not budge.

"We must go this instant … that creature is going to destroy us," I plead, straining as I try to pull her along, but she remains motionless.

. "Why won't you heed my warning? Can't you see … it?"

Gasping for air, I stammer, "It is … right there in the doorway. You must see it!" I point toward the drawing room door. The chambermaid maintains an unwavering stare, her eyes focused beyond my shoulder, following the line of my outstretched arm.

I look at what has caught her interest, only to find the door closed. Sunlight streams through the windows, transforming the hallway, illuminating every corner, and dispelling lingering shadows.

"It appears that someone has closed it," I say. Feeling disoriented, I quickly glance at my dress to gather my thoughts, noticing that the ruffles remain drenched in a striking crimson hue.

The chambermaid seizes my arm.

My mind is a whirlwind of confusion, making it impossible to move from where I stand. Turning back, I steal a lingering glance at the door, and with each passing moment, my disbelief grows. "But it was open," I murmur, desperately trying to convince myself. "I promise you, I saw it with my own eyes."

The chambermaid's fingers tighten their grip as she exerts all her strength, forcefully trying to coax me into motion.

I inhale deeply and anchor my heels onto the floor. "It was right there ... I swear... the mummy was there," I explain. The scene is still vivid in my mind as I try to make sense of the situation.

She flexes her leg muscles and gives it another try, determination evident on her face.

As my feet refuse to heed my command to stop, I stumble forward, almost tripping, and glimpse the vexing portrait on the wall. "No," I gasp, my head shaking in disbelief.

The painting has been restored to its original state. I examine the heart-wrenching portrayal of a battle-scarred man lost in grief, his eyes fixed on the sky. Dark red streaks accent his eyes and ears, the consequence of his injuries. His frantic stance conveys the profound impact of his blindness, a result of the battle wounds he has sustained.

As I feel my sanity slipping away, I stare blankly at the canvas, my thoughts swirling like leaves in the wind.

The chambermaid ushers me to continue to walk.

I follow her in a catatonic state, catching my reflection in several mirrors tucked between the paintings as I pass by. Aside from the dried crimson stain on my lips, no blemish remains on my face. They appear much fuller than before; they are like the lips of a cherub.

The chambermaid looks at my disheveled appearance, grabbing a handful of my bloodstained skirt and lifting it from the floor. She urges me to move faster.

The sight of my reflection brings back the image of the creature's silhouette, making me question whether it is a trick of my mind or if the creature is present, as it appears in every reflection, just like me.

She pulls on my skirt, moving in front of me. "Maybe a little rest would do me good." I nervously chuckle. She hurries me along, and we pick up our pace.

Although this morning, it seemed convenient, now, I find her quietness unnerving. I would do anything for her to assure me everything will be okay.

With every breath, my lungs constrict, and the scent of iron beneath my nose makes me feel unwell. Lost in my thoughts, I lower my gaze to the floor, finding solace in the rhythm of counting my steps.

A whisper cuts through the air, trailing behind me, calling, "Genevieve…"

The gritty tone sends a shiver down my spine, and I catch myself turning my head.

Lurking behind me is the looming shadow of the man—the same one from my horrid nightmare: the clergyman.

Gasping, I desperately attempt to break free and flee, my feet nearly tangling.

He follows behind me, levitating off the floor. "In your stomach, I sit!" he says.

Focusing on the end of the hall, I pick up my pace. "Leave me alone!" I cry as his frigid breath tickles my neck. I wiggle my shoulders and break away, taking off in a sprint.

The chambermaid, still holding my dress, rushes after me, yanking on the material to slow me down.

Reaching the hallway's conclusion, I anxiously check behind me. The corridor, now empty, is filled only with the echo of his laughter.

With a heavy glare, the chambermaid readjusts her hold on my arm, and, walking ahead, she pulls me along.

We make our way to the staircase and ascend to the next floor without delay. Moving down the hallway, we promptly enter my room, and the chambermaid closes the door behind us.

The delightful fragrances of cedar and clean linens instantly put me at ease.

She quickly heads for the washroom, leaving me alone to savor the gentle crackling of the flames. The comforting warmth brushes against my cheek as I glance at the fireplace.

A heap of fresh wood burns inside.

I hear sloshing from the tub as I focus on the dancing orange blaze. "That was quick." I chuckle.

An ethereal voice slithers through the air, murmuring nondescript words as it passes. I run toward the bedroom door and fumble for the lock. The click of the latch causes the whispers to cease.

Taking a deep inhale, I hear the chambermaid splash her hand louder through the water, summoning me. Turning around, I lean my back against the wood. "You must calm yourself, or they will think you've gone mad," I say. I smile at the tranquility while reassuring myself. "You are safe. No one can hurt you here."

The glow from the fireplace creates a peaceful ambiance, allowing my mind to drift.

As I release my worries, my eyelids feel heavy, like a gentle weight is upon them. I focus on each inhale and exhale, sinking deeper into a meditative state.

Abruptly, the feeling of someone grabbing my arm sends a rush of adrenaline through me, robbing me of the tranquility I felt moments ago.

The chambermaid's grip on me tightens as she pulls me away from the door.

Annoyed, I follow her with a smirking expression. *One must always cleanse one's sins before sitting down to dinner.*

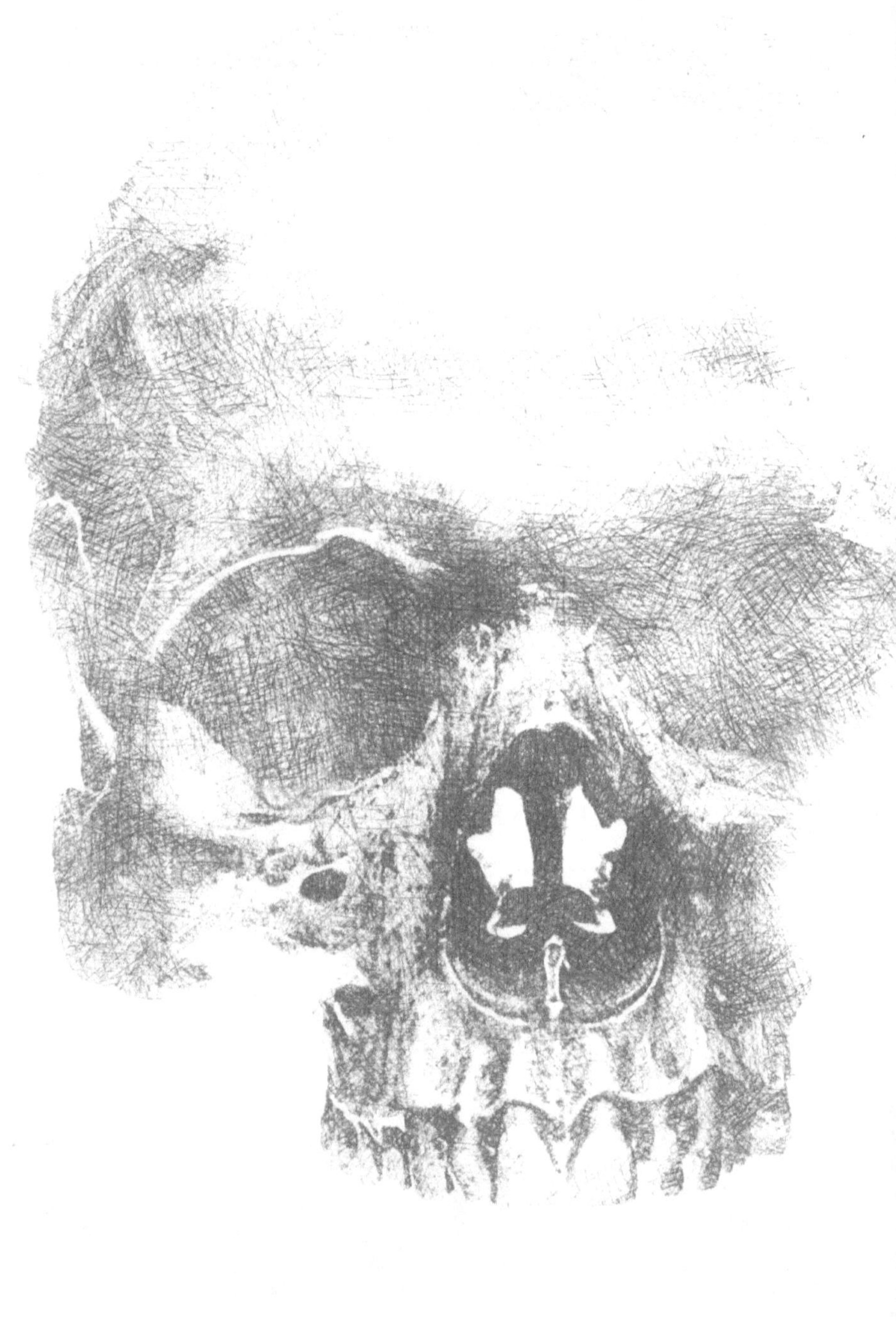

Nineteen

Where are you From?

As the sky turns dark and the stars twinkle, the dinner staff gather around the dining table, eagerly waiting to serve. However, there are two noticeable absences—Clinton and Lucious.

The silence at the table is palpable; I can feel the tension in the air.

A wave of servants rushes in carrying polished cutlery, breaking the quiet. The silverware clinks as they lay it next to the plates. Then, putting the finishing touches on the place settings, they make a mass exit for the kitchen.

Looking around the table, I notice how everyone's faces are pristine. It is hard to imagine that they were all drenched in blood the last time I saw them. Honestly, the contrast between their earlier and current appearance is astonishing.

Nonetheless, they seem not to care a bit; their behavior tells me they have done this before.

As they all sit patiently, waiting for the meal to begin, I struggle to keep from squirming as my stiff lace collar scratches against my skin. Though irritating, I choose to keep my annoyance at bay so as not to create a spectacle. I confidently meet each of their gazes and subtly nod to acknowledge their presence.

Besides the lilac choker around Ettie's neck and the sky-blue one around Hattie's, to set them apart, everyone is dressed in black.

Everything from the clothing to the decorations is somber in tone. Even the tablecloth has been chosen to match the theme. Despite the gloomy shade, the fabric is lavish and features a stunningly elaborate Gothic spiderweb design. The details of the web are mesmerizing. Each thread is meticulously woven together to create an elaborate work of art.

As I study the way the material covers the table beneath my plate, my eyes are drawn to the captivating sight of the floral arrangements before me. The large, decorative urns contain stunning bouquets of dark-maroon hollyhocks, their vibrant colors contrasting with the tangled vines cascading down the sides. Flawlessly dyed black ostrich feathers protrude from the dense greenery, stylishly draping over the prickly leaves.

I unconsciously fiddle with a nearby vine while stealing glances at Ettie and Hattie, attempting to divert my attention from the irritating collar.

The two girls sit facing each other, their arms crossed and their eyes locked in a fiery glare. Neither of them budges, determined to maintain their stubborn stance. The tension is so thick you could cut it with a knife.

The door of the kitchen swings open.

In unison, everyone turns to the men entering the dining room carrying additional chairs. They are closely followed by a line of waitstaff holding trays with extra place settings.

With the precision of a well-oiled machine, two extra staff members join in and move the girls' place settings over a few feet. Next, they lift the chairs with the sisters sitting on them and move them to create space next to their husbands' former seats.

The girls' eyes widen in surprise as they realize someone else may join them for dinner. The sudden revelation causes them to forget their disagreement briefly and wonder who their new companions might be.

Hugh clears his throat and, smirking, glances down the table at me. "I presume you are doing well, dear," he shouts, eyeing the bustline of my bodice.

The sound of his boisterous tone makes me skittishly jump as I make eye contact with him. "Yes, indeed … I am quite well, thank you."

Ettie and Hattie shift their attention toward me. "Of course, she is doing well," they say in unison and, cackling, look at one another. "Look at her; she is alive, isn't she?"

I tensely swallow, and the lace material scratches my neck.

Hattie watches me anxiously pull at it. "I wish that would finish the job by tightening its grip around your throat and robbing you of your breath. If it were not for you, Lucius would still be here," she says, disgusted.

I sink into my seat, shifting uncomfortably as I try to refrain from picking at the collar.

Ettie rolls her eyes. "I told you, Mother, that gown would have suited me far better than her." She huffs in irritation.

Hattie laughs at me. "It appears she is allergic to fashion…. Look at her neck."

I trace my skin around the collar, trying to relieve the rash. "It must be stress hives," I interject, feeling embarrassed. "I am ashamed to admit that it seems to be taking me a bit longer to adjust to my new surroundings than expected," I add. "I have not had them since I was a child." My voice trails off as my embarrassment lingers.

Hattie and Ettie look at each other and roll their eyes. "Disgusting," they say.

"That is enough, girls," Adeline says. As she glares at them, her black knitted veil partially drapes from her hair, covering a single eye.

"Look at the three of you bickering. I would think you were all blood siblings." Hugh laughs.

Ettie and Hattie's faces harden as they scowl back at him.

He clears his throat. "I suppose you all are wondering why there are two additional place settings at the table this evening."

Everyone glances at the chairs.

"Oh, dear God," Adeline says, stiffening her posture. "Please tell me this is not a memorial dinner. Usually, they do not occur for another week."

Hugh avoids her question. "Our guests of honor shall be here any moment."

"Memorial dinner?" I ask, confused.

"Brilliant question, Genevieve." He smiles, rising from his seat as the doors to the dining hall swing open. He turns around and adds, "We will need to come back to it later."

All eyes are drawn to the entrance as an elderly couple enters the room. They are dressed entirely in black, their attire devouring any trace of light that touches them. Their faces bear deep lines, and their exhausted, swollen eyes hint at days of relentless tears.

"There they are," Hugh says, rushing toward them.

They move slowly, with a palpable heaviness, as if the air around them is thicker than the rest of the room. The overwhelming sorrow emanating from them is impossible to ignore.

Hugh quickly turns around. "Let me introduce Blanche and Cyprian," he says, motioning to each of them. "These are the Burgesses … Lucius's lovely parents."

Adeline pushes herself back in her seat. "I knew it," she mutters. She quickly stands. Then, clasping her hands together as if praying, she looks at them with an air of sadness, "Please accept my condolences…."

I analyze their expressions as she speaks.

Retrieving a hanky from her bust, she gazes at the floor and sniffles. "Believe me … I never imagined our long-awaited meeting would occur under these dreadful circumstances. It makes me feel very ill indeed."

Blanche stands aloof, her eyes detached from the surroundings. Her hair, a shade of elegant gray, is styled in a towering updo, intricate in design and befitting of her graceful demeanor. The updo's grandeur is matched only by the width of her eyelet lace gown, an outfit that exudes sophistication and poise.

Cyprian appears equally joyless. His facial expressions are strained, and his body language suggests a profound melancholy. His outfit comprises a coat and knickers that are flawlessly crafted from the finest material, giving it a smooth and refined uniformity. The coat hugs his frame, accentuating his tall and slender physique and giving him a regal air that demands respect. His hair, which is as white as snow, is tied back meticulously with a black ribbon.

They both ignore her and simultaneously direct their attention toward Hugh.

"This is not the occasion to be smiling, boy," Blanche says.

Hugh attempts to regain his composure by glancing at the wall, his lips twitching.

Blanche tips her nose into the air to avoid eye contact with everyone in the room. "Adeline, did you neglect to teach him basic etiquette?" she says.

Offended, Adeline clears her throat, but Cyprian chimes in before she can speak. "That boy must wipe that smirk off his condescending face." He sneers.

Hugh glances at his mother.

"For God's sake, man, our son just died. Have you no decency?" Cyprian says. He observes the despondent expression on his wife's face and adds, "Give him the honor he deserves."

Adeline clenches her jaw and gives Hugh a subtle nod. He scrambles to speak. "Oh, yes, my apologies. We are so sorry for your loss," he says, trying to maintain a solemn demeanor; he extends his arm to assist them. "Please, would you be so gracious as to allow me to help you to your seats?"

Blanche glares at his arm in revulsion. "Do not touch me!" she shouts, batting his hand away. Her eyes bulge as she glances at the room's corners.

I follow her gaze, confused about what she is looking at.

She gasps, frantic for air, and grabs her chest. "Are you without a manservant?" she asks.

I can tell by Hugh's complexion that he is fighting back his anger. "Certainly not," he says. With a sudden clap of his hands, a staff member hurriedly enters through the kitchen door. Hugh snaps for him to hurry. "He will guide you to your designated seats."

Refraining from looking at them, the staff hurries to assist.

Hugh glares at the couple's back, his nostrils flaring with irritation as he restrains a sarcastic sneer.

The closer they get, the more noticeable the wrinkles on their faces. Even though they have a child near the age of Adelines, they do not mirror her youthful facade. Conflicted, I glance at Adeline's appearance for reference and then return to Blanche. *They should be around the same age. Should they not? Why does Blanche appear drastically more decrepit?* I cannot help but wonder if perhaps she is much older than I know.

Hattie's angst grows as they draw closer, her attention fixated on the space in front of her.

Blanche intentionally selects the seat adjacent to Hattie. As the servant pulls out the chair, its legs screech loudly, causing her to wince. She carefully settles into the seat, her back straight and her shoulders squared.

Hattie fights her annoyance as the woman sits down beside her.

Blanche discreetly steals a glance at her from the corner of her eye. "Pray tell, my dear, what seems to be the matter? You do not appear to be too upset," she comments, placing her napkin on her lap. She slowly turns her head and looks Hattie up and down. Hattie flinches. "I daresay you appear remarkably composed despite the circumstances."

Hattie speaks, searching for her words. "Well, I—"

Blanche swings a handkerchief in front of her face, cueing her to silence. "Following the death of my first husband, I could not appear in public for weeks." She dramatically sighs and blows her nose.

The familiarity of her movements and inflection strikes a nerve, reminding me of my mother. Oddly, I feel sympathy for Hattie.

Blanche lowers the square silk fabric from her face and flicks it once more. "Then, after my second—"

"I am afraid there are no tears left in my ducts," Hattie interjects, abruptly cutting her off in the middle of her sentence. She cannot stand to hear another comparison from the woman.

Blanche stares at her skeptically. "How fascinating, child," she says, uninterested; her expression falls cold. "Go on. Do tell us more. Your words have left us curious and eager to hear more about the challenging experiences you have encountered following the death of our son."

Hattie glances at her mother, looking for guidance on how to respond.

Adeline stands, coming to her rescue. "Let me explain," she says, her voice resonating.

Blanche glares at her and slams her fist against the table. "Hush, woman. Know your place!" she shouts. Adeline releases a deep exhale and calmly takes her seat before returning her attention to Hattie. "I believe I directed the question to your daughter," Blanche replies. "So, why don't we allow her to speak?"

Her husband nods in agreement.

Hattie's face turns flush as her words fall from her lips. "What I meant by my words is that I have spent the entire day in tears."

"And that would cause a dry spell, would it?" Blanche asks, uninterested in her response. A tense silence hangs in the air.

Blanche edges her chair closer to the table, and the sound of the wooden legs screeching against the floor makes everyone cringe.

"Mm-hmm," Hattie says through gritted teeth. "Yes, dear Mother-in-law, my melancholy has transformed my tear ducts into a parched desert."

"I see," she replies.

Thinking the confrontation is over, Hattie slowly lifts her head.

Blanche stares her directly in the eyes. "Well … then…dear," she says, enunciating every word. She pauses and, glancing at Adeline, smirks. "Since it is apparent that the woman over there—the one whom you call

Mother," she says, her voice dripping with disdain, "has failed to educate you on the proper way to deal with the death of a husband, I suppose I will take it upon myself to enlighten you."

With every word, Adeline's cheeks redden.

"When someone has died, especially a husband, the mourning period does not just occur at the hour of death. Nor can it be only a single day. The loss should bring on weeping and sadness that lasts for many weeks at the least." Blanche clears her throat, emphasizing each word as she sits taller in her chair. "That is the social etiquette of how one should behave when it comes to matters of death." As she finishes, she glances around the table.

All but Hugh look at their plate, avoiding confrontation.

As I digest the words of Blanche's forced opinion, I notice Hugh quietly moving toward the room's entrance. He appears to be waiting for something.

While I am focused on him, Blanche sees my distraction as a chance to interject. "And dear," she asks, "if you don't mind me asking, who might you be?"

Dread fills my chest as she speaks to me. "Endmill. I am from Endmill, London," I say.

"Oh, I see … But I am asking your name, dear, and I highly doubt it is Endmill."

"Yes, of course," I say with a slight nod. "My apologies for the confusion. My name is Genevieve."

"I presume you are betrothed to Hugh?" The look on her face appears snobbish.

"Yes, that is correct," I say, extending my hand toward her. "As you can see, we are newly wed."

She stares at the sparkle from the large, oblong diamond adorning my ring finger.

Hugh's lips curl into a grin as he listens to the conversation.

Blanche scans me from head to toe, silently judging my appearance. "I am surprised such a pretty thing can come from the countryside. Endmill is quite far into the country, is it not?"

"It is scenic," I say, placing my hands on my lap and coiling my fingers into fists underneath the table.

"So, I imagine these accommodations seem quite luxurious compared to the humble cottage you came from … Your mother must have thought she struck gold to secure such a pairing."

"I am uncertain I would go as far as voicing such opinions," I say, forcing a smile and maintaining my composure. "Often, things that come in the most beautifully wrapped packages conceal the darkest secrets."

I see her eyes widen with shock, and I cannot help but chuckle at her reaction. "Oh goodness, I hope you don't think I'm referring to this family's character," I say. "It's merely a witty remark I came across in a book once."

She slowly pans the table.

"Indeed, some may find this manor large, but I consider it comparable to the dwelling where I was raised. Both have walls and a fireplace. Wouldn't you say that is enough to make it a home?"

Blanche directs her attention to Adeline. "Do tell me, how did you find that girl?"

Hugh smirks at his mother. Adeline grins. "She came highly recommended by others." Keeping Blanche's attention, she leans forward. "Your youngest…"

"Yes, our beloved darling, Clarise."

"How is she?" Adeline asks.

"Very well," she replies. Her eyes uncomfortably dart around the room.

Adeline's smile expands. "That is wonderful to hear."

"Yes, it is," Blanche says proudly. "She is arranged to marry a respectable young man from the Endellion family. His name is Eamon. Eamon Endellion."

Everyone around the table glances at one another, fighting back their snickers.

"That name sounds so majestic!" Adeline exclaims. "It is absolutely splendid."

Miffed by their lack of respect, Blanche tilts her nose. "I presume you're familiar with the Endellion family."

"I cannot say that I am," Adeline replies.

Blanche continues, "The Endellion family manufactures all the best gowns. I can only assume that includes the ones you wear as well. They are highly regarded in the textile industry."

Adeline covers her mouth with her napkin and turns away to compose herself.

"I must tell you how thrilled I am that she has found a good match," Hugh says.

After taking a moment to compose herself, Adeline turns back around. "Yes, I couldn't agree more." She shifts her attention to her son. "I know how desperately you wanted Hugh to take a liking to her, so I am pleased to hear that she has attained a perfect pairing and can now happily thrive without him."

I cannot help but smirk at her sarcastic reply.

Blanche is struggling to find the right words to divert the conversation. Her gaze shifts toward the two vacant chairs across the table and the unoccupied seat beside her husband. "Will there be more joining us?" she inquires.

I glance at the empty chair Doc occupied during our first meal together. Then it dawned on me: I had not laid eyes on him since he retired early on the evening of my wedding day. Perhaps he had other obligations to fulfill or simply wanted to give my spouse and me some much-needed alone time. It is difficult to say for sure.

As I ponder the situation, I realize this is the modus operandi people follow in this household—they appear and disappear, sometimes without warning or explanation. They are characters in a story, fading in and out of the narrative.

I frequently contemplate whether I am merely an observer in the story of my life, authored by someone unknown, forced to watch the plot unfold with no ability to shape or control the outcome.

"Is one seat perhaps for your husband? Will he finally join us?" Blanche asks, and, waiting for a response, she leans forward. "You know, I've never met the fellow."

Adeline straightens her posture in response to the presumptuous remarks and sneers. "It is audacious of you to ask such questions to your hostess," she says. "Quite inappropriate indeed."

Her defensiveness amuses Blanche. Adeline's anger simmers as she listens to the woman snicker. Determined not to let her opponent gain the upper hand, she takes a moment to compose herself. Then, with a coy smile, she speaks, her voice soft and measured. "There will only be two," she says.

Blanche furrows her brow as she scrutinizes Adeline's collected demeanor.

Adeline catches her gaze. "Theodosia is to sit in the empty seat between your Cyprian and Hugh, not my husband."

Ettie and Hattie look at one another; hearing their sister's name makes their jaws drop in shock.

"Honestly," Adeline says through clenched teeth, "the chances of you meeting my husband are highly unlikely. He has not been himself for quite some time now. Ever since his health issues, he has lost interest in spending time with us. It's like he's become a mere shadow of his former self."

A pang of guilt washes over Blanche for her earlier remarks. "Please accept my sincere apologies for the inquiry. I was not privy to that information."

Hugh clenches his fists as he listens, eagerly awaiting the argument to end.

Adeline glances at him before redirecting her attention to Blanche across the table. "Why would you be? Privy ... that is?" she asks, her words trailing into silence. "Especially now ... Given the circumstances, we will probably never cross paths again," she concludes, her tone heavy with finality.

Still consumed by the news of their sister's impending arrival, my eyes remain fixated on the empty chairs. "Theodosia ... is coming?" I inquire, instantly thinking of my brother.

Happy to have a change of conversation, Hugh eagerly chimes in. "Indeed!" he shouts from across the room.

The girls gasp and look at him. "Are you certain?" they ask.

Hugh smiles. "Yes, sisters, I am quite certain. She wrote to me this morning, and I could tell by her letter that she was rather excited to visit. She should be here any moment, and in fact, I am honestly surprised she hasn't—"

As if choreographed, the door opens, and a sudden stillness blankets the room.

Twenty

Deceased

Ettie and Hattie turn their heads in unison toward the sound. "Theo?" they whisper.

The noise ceases from the slow squeak of the hinges as the door comes to a halt.

The girls stare through the open entrance at the shadows in the hallway, their faces pale. "Is that you?" they ask, trembling.

Slowly, an older couple emerges into the room, closing the door behind them. With his broad shoulders and confident demeanor, the man exudes authority, while the petite and graceful woman effortlessly moves beside him, radiating elegance. Although they are also dressed in black, they seem very different from the Burgesses. Their demeanors are much more modest and grounded.

With a burst of enthusiasm, Hugh throws his hands up and exclaims, "Looks like our other guests have arrived!"

"Thank God." Ettie and Hattie glance at one another, clutching their chests and chuckling.

I analyze the man's wild, curling gray hair. Each strand coils and twists in a unique pattern that adds to his overall chaotic yet intriguing look.

As he moves in their direction, the sisters glance to the floor.

"Allow me to introduce Colin's parents," Hugh says, instantly covering his mouth as he notices their perplexed expressions. "Oops! Oh, dear, please forgive me. I meant to say Clinton's parents." He chuckles. Then he gestures toward them and continues, "This lovely chap is Digory." He points to the woman. "And that's Huldah."

Why are they here? I thought this was only for those who have lost a son. Hugh said he had disappeared; there was never any mention of death. Their presence makes me question Hugh's account of the narrative regarding Clinton's disappearance.

I cringe, barely able to look at them. Their likeness to the only man in this estate who exhibited kindness toward me is uncanny. Overwhelmed with a mix of guilt and confusion, all my fluttering emotions cast an illness upon me.

Trying to find answers, I analyze Hugh's behavior, and his apparent lack of remorse makes my mind spiral. *What if he lied to me? What if his story had a more sinister truth than he let on?* Working to reign in my thoughts, I take a deep breath.

Adeline slowly stands. The sound of her clearing her throat to speak catches my attention. I turn to her, hoping she will bring clarity to my muddle.

She lowers her head and offers condolences before resuming her seat. "I am deeply saddened that you have been invited here under such dreadful circumstances," she says.

Blanche looks at her husband, confused.

What does that even mean? As I try to dissect her words, I shift my attention to Clinton's parents.

Huldah's graying, long, dark hair is pulled back into a slicked bun. While her dress is not fashionable, its unique empire-cut waistline and floor-length full skirt set it apart from the conventional style of a corset and wide hoop.

I gaze at the translucent black veil covering her face. Beneath it, her eyes are a delicate shade of pink, and her eyelids are swollen.

Feeling lost, I look to Digory, seeking solace in his familiar presence.

He is dressed in a black jacket, coordinating trousers, and a slightly contrasting shirt underneath. The lack of frills adds to his air of simplicity. His complexion and features closely resemble Clinton's. Dark circles are beneath his eyes. It's clear that something has been troubling him, leading to sleepless nights.

"Allow me." Hugh nods as he extends his arm. "I will show you to your seats."

Huldah looks at his hand and accepts his offer with gratitude. "Thank you," she mumbles, her gaze fixed on the floor. "That is very kind of you."

He glances at Blanche before responding. "Certainly. It is my pleasure to assist you in times like these."

Blanche sneers at him and rolls her eyes.

He contains his smile as he gestures to the table. "This way, please," he says.

Ettie beckons for her mother-in-law to sit beside her. "Come, Mother Huldah, sit by me," she says.

As she extends her hand, one of the male servants immediately springs into action. He rushes toward the designated seat across the table from her and swiftly pulls out the chair.

Huldah avoids eye contact, keeping her eyes forward while quietly taking her seat. Digory sits beside her, and Ettie's hand, still suspended in the air, drops with embarrassment.

Blanche and Cyprian cringe at the sound of his chair scooting against the floor. Then, they look at one another in confusion. Blanche shifts her gaze toward Huldah. "Are they here for our poor Lucius?" she asks, directing her question to Hugh.

The staff quickly fetches Hugh's chair from the table. Everyone shifts their attention toward him, watching him slowly take his seat. "I am afraid not," he says.

Blanche grabs hold of Cyprian's knee and squeezes it.

Hugh looks at her intently before continuing, "Regrettably, you both have experienced a tragic loss—the loss of a son."

"They, too, have lost their boy?" Blanche gasps.

A tear escapes Huldah's eye, and Digory leans closer to console her. "Yes, I am afraid so," he responds.

Blanche gestures toward Ettie and asks, "Was your son married to that girl over there?"

Ettie uncomfortably looks away.

"Indeed," Digory replies. "They were married for some time."

Blanche leans closer, her curiosity piqued. "May I ask, for how long?"

Adeline expresses her annoyance by rolling her eyes. "What is the importance of such insignificant details?"

"It was soon to be the fifth anniversary of their wedding day," Digory answers.

"It was over a year for my poor Lucius." Blanche sneers, her disdain clear in her tone. She looks skeptically at Ettie and then at Hattie. "Hmm … how strange."

Not wanting to be left out of the conversation, Cyprian joins in, briefly glancing at the two girls. "It is strange indeed," he says.

"Yes, it is, husband," Blanche replies, taking a moment to ponder.

Ettie and Hattie exchange uncertain glances, avoiding her gaze and unsure how to respond.

Blanche stares at their profiles; her eyes fixated on their strikingly similar features. She ponders aloud, "How is it possible that their faces mirror each other, and their husbands' life trajectories align so perfectly … even though these two boys had never crossed paths until their wedding days?"

As Hugh listens to the accusation, he leans forward in his seat, weighing every word.

I carefully observe his unshaken reaction and flushed cheeks, and an unmistakable feeling washes over me. *He lied. Clinton is dead.*

"Now that you mention it ... the circumstance is peculiar," Cyprian says.

"I cannot help but find it suspicious," Blanche says, her gaze lingering on Hattie.

Adeline turns to Hugh, hoping he will step in.

In a fit of rage, he pounds the table with his fists. He declares, "If you've come to my house to disrespect my family and insinuate things that only serve to tarnish the honorable reputation of the McKinley name, then I will politely request our staff to escort you to the door."

A hush falls over the room, intensifying the already palatable tension.

"Oh ... oh, dear," Blanche stammers, attempting to rectify the situation. "There seems to have been a misunderstanding regarding what I was trying to say."

"Your offensive notion, madam, is unmistakable. It is clear to everyone present in this room what you are suggesting. The assertion you have made is absurd. It is unfathomable to suggest that any member of this family could be involved in any wrongdoing. Your words not only cause offense but also profoundly disrespect our family name and expose a troubling flaw in your character."

Blanche's eyes widen.

Hugh's face turns bright red as he continues. "Only a heartless monster would allow their son to marry into such a family if someone held such strong negative feelings toward them."

She stammers, trying to speak.

"I am not finished," he says.

She looks embarrassed and flustered as she glances down at the table.

"If someone is so negligent about the well-being of their own family, it would naturally be assumed that they made the arrangement solely for personal gain, whether for status or financial reasons."

Blanche looks up at him, narrowing her eyes. "Allow me to clarify," she says, her voice slow and deliberate, each word carefully enunciated. "My thoughts are not influenced by emotion. They are the result of reflection, not malice." However, the slight furrow in her brow suggests she is not entirely convinced.

Hugh's unyielding gaze intensifies, causing the tension of their argument to permeate the room. He narrows his lids, matching hers, and revels in the silence.

I believed our relationship was improving, but as I look at my husband, the thought of another betrayal weighs heavily on my shoulders. *Is there not a single ounce of honesty to be found?*

My ears ring and my chest feels as though it is compressed by a cart of bricks.

Abruptly, there is a loud thud at the door.

I brace myself against my chair. *Oh, God, who may it be now?* I ask myself.

Everyone turns at once to look in my direction, directing their gazes past me to the door.

A feeling of relief floods me as I hear the hurried footsteps and clanging metal coming from the kitchen entry. The sounds grow louder as the staff hurriedly enters the room and gathers around the table.

Each server holds a golden dish. The metal is draped with black lace, matching the tablecloth's ornate cobweb design. On top are shiny gold domed lids covering the first course of the evening. Eager to serve, the attendants each stop beside a guest, waiting for their cue.

Hugh slowly rises to his feet to address the table. He directs his attention to Blanche, who stares in awe at her reflection in the polished lid. "Let us hope everything is now behind us, and we can enjoy our meal," he says.

Blanche's eyes reluctantly leave the glimmering object, and she sits up attentively in her chair. "Certainly. There are no adversaries here," she says, nudging her husband beneath the table. "Don't you agree, Cyprian?"

He winces as he clutches his throbbing knee. "Indeed, my love," he says, smiling at Hugh. "We are all family, united in grief."

Ettie and Hattie glance at their mother in amusement.

With smirks exchanged, Hugh clasps his hands and says, "That is wonderful to hear." His smile slowly dissipates as he takes a deep breath and prepares to speak.

Anticipation fills the room as everyone leans forward, awaiting his words.

"I would like to express my heartfelt condolences for the tragic loss of our two beloved individuals, Lucius and Clinton. As our saddened eyes fill with tears, we hope this meal can help us heal our broken hearts. At the McKinley Estate, we believe that dining is not just about satisfying our hunger but also about creating a memorable experience that will uplift our minds and bodies," Hugh says, pausing.

Huldah and Blanche glance at one another; they share a moment of sentiment.

Hugh's excitement rises as he speaks. He lifts his hands and says, "You may have noticed that our procedures differ slightly from most households. We prefer to take a unique approach to our meals. Unlike the standard dining protocol, we do not display the entire feast at once, providing our guests with the element of surprise with each course served."

The staff grips the lids, preparing to remove them.

"We aim to create a surprising element that will take your dining experience to the next level," Hugh says, gesturing toward the servers standing next to each seat. He nearly hits Cyprian in the face with his expressive limbs.

Blanche flinches as her husband dramatically ducks. She leans in and whispers under her breath, "Behave."

Hugh points to the table and clarifies, "As we embrace a new era of service, we have implemented a practice of serving dishes one by one, beginning with the first course at the start of your meal."

Hattie glances at Ettie and rolls her eyes. He glares at them, and they quietly chatter.

"Each dish is crafted with a unique combination of flavors and textures, creating a masterpiece for your taste buds," Hugh exclaims.

I watch Ettie. Her bored expression shows that she has been subjected to this sales pitch one too many times. As she mouths each of his words like a ventriloquist, she catches my stare and snickers.

"Surprise is crucial for a successful dining experience," he says. "A well-crafted presentation creates anticipation, heightens the senses, and makes each dish unforgettable." He takes a momentary pause and smirks at his sisters.

Uncertain if it is time, the servers look to each other for a cue.

Hugh hears them beginning to lift the lids and frantically waves his hands. "And it's not just about the food! That would be a bore!"

As the waitpersons carefully balance their trays, they glimpse Hugh's bulging eyes and stop. A sense of unease washes over them as they realize it is not yet time.

"Our approach allows ample time to enjoy each other's company, engage in meaningful conversations, and savor every moment of your dining experience." He shifts his gaze toward everyone at the table and then lifts his hands. "Therefore, if you're searching for a dining experience that is more than just a meal, we invite you to join us at the McKinley Estate."

Hugh stands in silence for a moment, his sudden pause in speech perplexing everyone around the table. To break the tension, I start a slow applause, and the rest of the table soon joins in.

As expected, Hugh bends at the waist, acknowledging our ovation. Adeline stands, continuing to clap as she glances at me. "Well said, son," she says, taking her seat. "Now, let's eat."

He exhales and says, "Yes, let us eat." The staff looks at each other to time their delivery, and Hugh sits slowly. He glances toward Digory and puts his hand on his shoulder, giving it a gentle pat. Startled, Digory winces, glancing at him from the corner of his eye.

"You know," Hugh says, "Clinton enlightened us about the psychology behind the art of serving food." He purses his lips, reflecting on the memory, and a smile forms on his face. "I must commend you. You raised an exceptional man. He was, without a doubt, one of the finest brothers-in-law I've ever had the pleasure of knowing."

Sadness swelters in Digory's eyes. He swallows hard and proudly looks at Hugh as he tries to hide his emotions. "Thank you," he says. "He was a good boy."

As I observe their interaction, I get lost in my thoughts until the sound of metal clanking snaps me back to attention.

"Exactly on cue," Hugh says, laughing. He points toward the staff members, motioning for them to lower their trays. "It is my pleasure to introduce our starter for this evening."

In a stunning, wavelike formation, they synchronously lift the lids, each person standing tall with their backs straight and heads held high. They hold the domes behind their backs and lean forward with utmost care, unveiling a breathtaking spectacle of vibrant shades of green. The layers of lettuce seem to have a life of their own as their glistening surfaces dance in the light, creating a mesmerizing sight.

"This evening, we shall begin our meal with something fresh to cleanse our palates," Hugh says. "It is composed of a well-thought-out formation of digestive leaves."

The staff leans forward, setting the perfectly constructed dishes before the guests. Each plate is accompanied by a small golden sauce boat. A collective gasp of admiration fills the air as the staff simultaneously lifts them and drizzles a delicate vinaigrette over the leaves.

The color instantly pulls my attention, and looking at the droplets falling from the spout, I am reminded of the ichor flooding from Lucius's skull. It is the same shade of burgundy.

With perfect timing, the staff gracefully raises their golden boats in the air. Swiftly flicking their wrists, they halt the pouring motion. Hugh gleams with excitement. "I call it greens with a splash of flavor," he says, excitement spewing from his lips.

As the staff exits with their trays back to the kitchen, I stare at my plate, fixating on the rich dressing draping the forest-hued vegetables. A low gurgle emanates from the depths of my stomach. It is not a normal noise but a curious blend of hunger and unease. I cannot shake off the nagging feeling that something, or someone, might have been blended into the suspicious concoction to add flavorful zest. The thought sends a shudder down my spine and a clammy sensation over my skin.

Hugh reaches for his fork, his eyes darting around the table, filled with anticipation. The corners of his mouth curl into a wide smile as he looks at each person seated beside him. "Enjoy!" he exclaims, clapping his hands and filling the air with excitement.

The group fixates on him. Their eyes brighten as they reach for their forks in unison. A sense of eagerness infuses the air as each member prepares to indulge in their meal. They stare at him as he stabs a forkful of lettuce and raises his fork to his mouth. He chuckles. "Don't be shy, my friends. I promise it will not bite you," he says.

Noticing no one moving, he wiggles the fork's prongs toward his lips, making muffled barking sounds that echo around the room. He pretends the fork is a restless terrier, eager to be set free, and he cannot help but grin at his playful imagination.

Everyone laughs and, glancing back to their plates, slowly spears the greens and places them into their mouths.

I listen to their crunching bites as I stare at my untouched dish. The way they devour the food is unnerving. The more they eat, the less they seem to chew. It is as if they are inhaling the food.

Blanche gnaws and smiles at the same time. With her mouth full, she says, "Excellent."

The sound of her enjoyment makes me second-guess my worry. With a deep breath, I carefully impale a section of lettuce that is noticeably less drenched in dressing than the rest.

Hugh grins to acknowledge Blanche's presence, and his attention lands on me. "Is something wrong, my dear?" he asks.

I nervously lift my hand toward my lips. "Not at all," I say, peeking up at him. We make eye contact. He sets his utensil aside and leans back in his chair, momentarily pausing his meal. Crossing his arms, he shows he is waiting for me to speak.

Thinking quickly, I spin my fork, analyzing the leafy greens.

I glance up from dissecting the consistency of the dressing and shrug. "I suppose … I'm simply appreciating the artistry of it all," I re-mark.

"Ah." He snickers. "I see." Then, sitting up, he grabs his fork. "Very well, then. As you were."

My hand trembles as I squeamishly place the lettuce onto my tongue.

Satisfied with my response, he returns to eating.

As I continue chewing and focus on him, my eyes slowly widen. Despite my initial wish to dislike it, I am delighted by the taste. There is nothing ghastly about it. In truth, the flavors possess a mesmerizing and nearly addictive quality. Even before my first bite is swallowed, I scoop up the next.

Blanche ravenously finishes her mouthful of food. "What is in this dressing?" she asks. "It is divine! I must have the recipe!" Her demand-ing tone carries a sense of urgency.

Adeline snickers and, noticing Hugh's glare, purses her lips to fight it.

I quickly swallow my bite and direct my at-tention toward him, curious how he will answer.

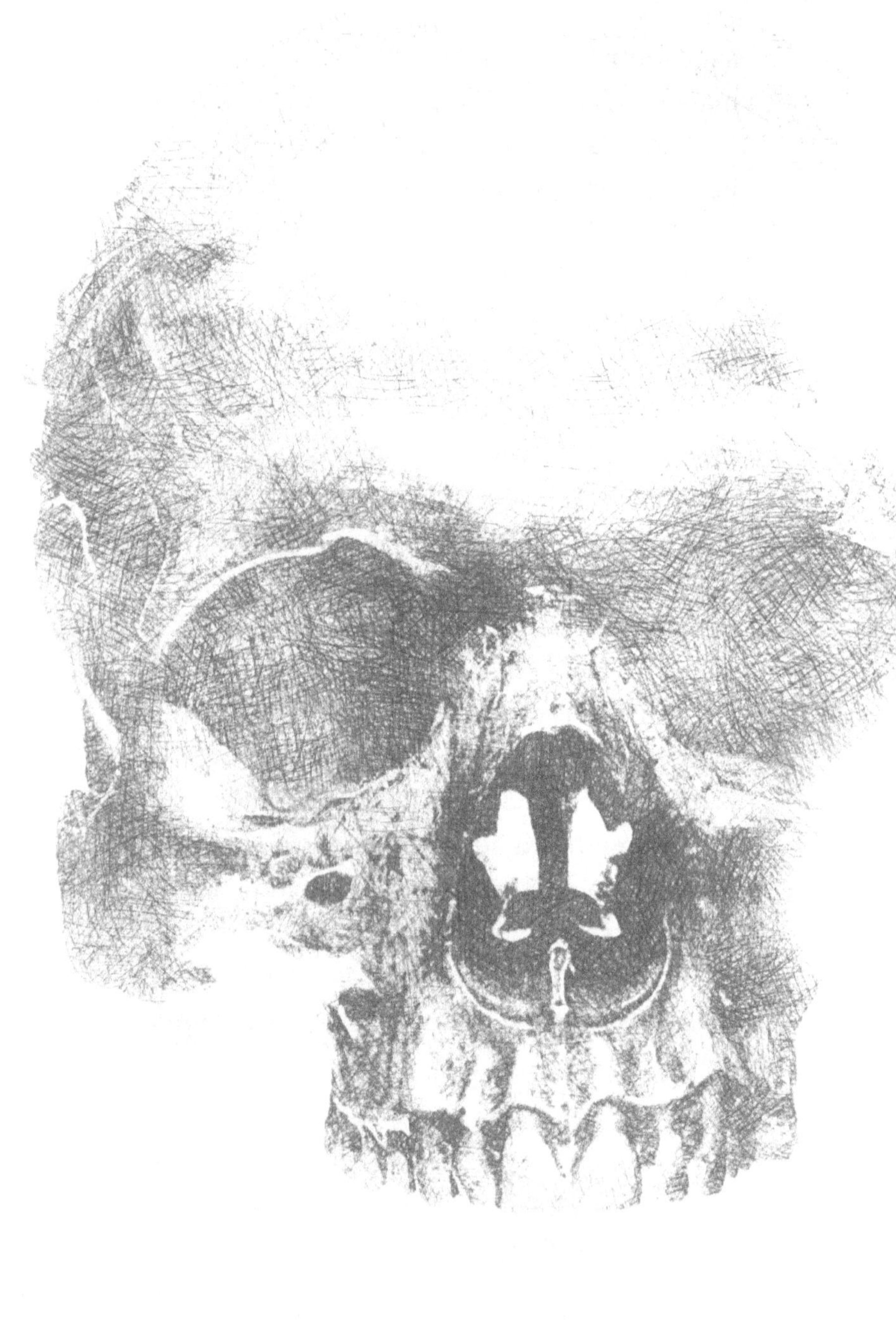

Twenty-One

Familia Secrets

As Hugh finishes his plate, he cannot help but notice Blanche's mouth, vigorously chewing, and the stubborn pieces of lettuce wedged between her teeth. Unable to look away from the tackiness of it all, he says, "I am afraid I cannot share the recipe. It is a secret passed down in my family for generations."

She notices a hint of superiority in his tone, and her mouth gapes open in offense. Interrupting him with a loud huff, she exclaims, "Are we not practically family?" Her voice grows louder with each word. "Even though we are not related by blood, we are connected through marriage," she says. "I would think that should be enough."

Hugh takes a moment to collect his thoughts. "I suppose you are right that there was one point in our lives when one could have made that argument," he says, his lips twitching as he listens.

Her eyes narrow, and she raises an eyebrow, unclear about what he is trying to say.

Everyone halts their side conversations, sets down their forks, and directs their attention to the end of the table.

Hugh clears his throat. "But I am afraid that would have only applied to your deceased son during his marriage to my sister," he says, sitting up in his seat and shrugging. "It was he who was connected to our family lineage, not you."

Her expression sours.

He continues to provoke her. "So, you see … you are not entitled to these family privileges you speak of."

Blanche's face is filled with frustration as she fumes, her expressions contorting and her eyebrows furrowing. But just as she readies to speak, the kitchen door swings open. A group of house staff emerges from the kitchen, all dressed in black and white. They approach the table, each picking up a plate and utensils from the first course and carrying them away.

Following their departure, the air fills with heavy, thudding footsteps. I turn to look and catch sight of more servers swiftly approaching from behind. As they come closer, I observe the trays they hold and hear the liquid sloshing beneath the domed lids that conceal the second course.

Hugh stands up and announces, "The next course has arrived!"

Blanche turns to gawp, and her attention becomes glued to the golden salvers carried by the staff. Immediately, her irritation is replaced with enthusiasm.

Hugh brings his hands together in a slow clap, capturing the attention of everyone in the room. With a gentle smile, he clears his throat and proclaims, "Ladies and gentlemen, I am delighted to present to you the second course of the evening—a sumptuous soup simmered for the better part of a day with only the freshest ingredients."

The dining room is alive with the bustling movement of waitstaff taking their assigned positions beside their designated chairs.

As Hugh waits for the chaos to subside, he turns toward Blanche and leans in. "This was one of your son's favorite dishes," he says.

As she stares at her reflection in the server's tray beside her, a look of ecstasy fills her eyes. "Yes, yes," she stammers, and, becoming impatient, she talks faster. "I am certain that when we are allowed to try it, it shall be our favorite as well." Unlike Digory's response, there is not a single drop of grief in her voice when her son is mentioned.

As Hugh studies her, he sneers. "We will get to that. You must be patient."

Then, with the table prepared, he lifts his hands. The servers remove the lids from their trays, and steam wafts into the air.

"We call this luck stew," Hugh says with a wide grin. "It is made by using the seasoned marrow of bones to prepare the broth. The warm collagen helps improve skin elasticity and restore its barrier." As he finishes his introduction, the servers place the bowls on the table, one in front of each guest. "Please enjoy," he says before taking his seat. "Its flavor is best before it cools."

As the servers quickly make their way back to the kitchen, their attention is drawn to the unappealing brown substance in the bowls.

"Very posh, indeed," Blanche says, her eyes widening in awe.

Ettie and Hattie pick up their spoons and ladle up a small helping. Then, they hold their utensils in the air, allowing the broth to cool.

I look at Diggory and Huldah, noticing them both gazing intently at their reflections in their soup. Huldah lets out a stifled sniffle, desperately trying to hold back her tears.

Hugh observes her reaction. "What is the matter? If you dislike the portion given to you, I can arrange for the staff to bring out another," he says.

"Thank you for the kind hospitality, but that will not be necessary. I have just suddenly been consumed by a bout of melancholy," she explains, wiping a tear from her cheek. "It is quite peculiar, really. The steam seems to have unexpectedly stirred up a whirlwind of emotions within me."

Digory gently touches her back, offering comfort, as Hugh continues speaking. "I assure you, I wish I could bring Clinton back. Truly. He was a great asset to this family." He rises from his chair and moves closer, kneeling beside her.

Her sniffling grows louder. "I am just missing my boy, that is all."

"His knowledge was truly ahead of his time," Hugh says.

Blanche and her husband noisily slurp their soup while locking eyes.

The cacophony of tiny slurps emanating from each person's lips becomes louder and more unbearable by the second. My stomach churns as I try to concentrate on my bowl, hoping to quell the nausea that threatens to consume me.

Suddenly, a small ripple in the atmosphere catches my attention. Starting from the center of the room, it quickly spreads to the outer edges, affecting everything in its path like a wave in the ocean.

Adeline gasps, staring at the movement forming in her bowl, and braces herself against her chair.

I glance toward her. "What is happening?" I whisper.

"Do you think I would be acting like a fool if I knew?" she hisses. "For all I know, it could be the revelation."

The floor trembles, prompting Hattie and Ettie to drop their spoons into their bowls

The vibrations worsen as a thunderous bang resonates through the dining room door. All eyes turn toward the entrance as Hugh stands up and playfully shouts. "Who is it?"

A disturbing silence takes over. The air is heavy with anticipation, as if everyone feels something significant is about to occur.

And then, slowly but surely, the quiet is broken by soft murmurs that spread throughout the room. Like a windstorm, they grow in intensity with each passing moment. The whispers seem to come from every direction, making it impossible to pinpoint their source while creating an atmosphere of mystery that lingers in the air.

Hugh adjusts his coat and steps closer to the entrance. "I demand to know who it is!" he shouts.

A low, unnerving roar stems from the hallway; its volume slightly dampened as it seeps beneath the door.

Hugh's commanding presence diminishes as he anxiously inquires, "I apologize, but I cannot hear you," he murmurs. "May I kindly ask you to reveal your name once more?"

Adeline bursting at the seams to interject, waves her napkin into the air. "Be a man and get over there!" she shouts.

The doorknob turns slowly, revealing its intricate design that sparkles under the chandelier's light.

Digory grabs Huldah by the arm and pulls her close. "Come here, my darling," he whispers, his voice trembling with uncertainty. His eyes dart back and forth to scan their surroundings, searching for a threat. "I have a terrible feeling about this," he says.

Huldah feels the tension in his body, and she knows in her gut that whatever is coming is not good. Clinging to him, she removes her veil as she whispers. "I as well."

The haunting murmurs come to an abrupt halt as the door slowly opens, its hinges emitting a long, drawn-out creak.

Hugh squints, straining his eyes to pierce through the hallway's inky blackness. His heart races as he glimpses a shadowy silhouette. He dashes back to the table and positions himself to better view the mysterious stranger lurking beyond the door from a safe distance. His gaze is fixed, and his body tense as he readies himself for whatever might come next.

The entire table gasps, catching sight of the intruder's large silhouette.

Adeline tightens her grip around the sides of her chair. "P-perhaps it is Doc?" she stammers.

"The stature does have a familiarity to it," Hattie nervously utters.

Ettie's breath catches in her throat as she gulps. Turning to her brother, she agrees and says, "Yes, I believe they are right. It must be him."

I stare at the murky form, trying to comprehend the situation. While the others seem confident about the visitor's identity, I am not. The only point of agreement is that its looming size suggests it is most likely male. The intruder's breathing is shallow and raspy, and the lack of movement feels dangerous. Its unsettling nature reminds me of the figure that tormented me in the hallway and my subsequent nightmare.

Hugh's eyes widen as he watches the door. "Do not be ridiculous!" he barks. "You know he was slain for the meal."

I gulp, feeling sick to my stomach. The thought of meeting him at our wedding dinner plays in my mind.

Ettie and Hattie look at their mother in a panic.

With a shrug, Hugh chuckles. "You were there, so tell me—how it can be him?"

Blanche frantically scans the table, her face paling. "What ... what did he just say?" she stammers.

As Adeline watches the chaos unfold, she leans on the table with her head in her hands, unable to believe what she has heard. "Dear Lord, silence my son's tongue," she murmurs.

I glance in panic at Hugh. The shadow figure is still looming in the hall.

"Did ... did he say that someone was slain for our meal?" Blanche asks, hastily pushing her chair away from the table. Just as she is about to leave, the kitchen door swings open.

The servers hurriedly enter, their heavy footsteps filling the room like a herd of stampeding elephants.

Suddenly, the clanking of porcelain and clanging silverware startles Blanche, causing her to pause and slowly sit back down; she watches as they deftly gather up the soup bowls, carefully placing them on the tray.

The group glides in a well-choreographed dance, each person moving purposefully while avoiding collisions. I focus on the sound of their footsteps and the rustling of cloth as they wipe the table clean. Then, I watch the liquid from my bowl slosh over the porcelain rim and onto their tray as they walk away.

Adeline lifts her head from her hands and, though wanting to scream, lets out an anxious chuckle. "Do not worry, dear Blanche. There is no reason to be concerned. It is simply the latest phrase the royals are using. When he says 'slain,' he does not mean it literally. Rather, it is a term used to describe someone extremely exhausted and needing to sleep. In Doc's case, he was too slain for dinner."

I glance toward the entrance.

Blanche releases a heavy sigh and manically chuckles. "Oh!" she says. "That makes perfect sense, does it not, Cyprian?"

He flinches as she grips his knee. "I knew there was no need for alarm," he says, reassuring her.

Ettie shifts her gaze back to the hallway and narrows her eyes. "It ... it... it..." she screams, standing to her feet. She stammers, lifts her finger, and points at the hallway.

Adeline rolls her eyes. "What is it, girl? Spit it out!" She hisses and, glaring at her daughter, enunciates, "You must speak clearly."

The figure takes a broken step toward the dining room. As it stumbles closer and collapses against the door frame, the light reveals its unmistakable masculinity.

Ettie's fingers tremble, and her body shudders as she cries out, "It's Clinton!"

My disbelief turns to horror as I glance toward the man. From a distance, I can see that dried blood has matted his wild black curls. His undone shirt is stained burgundy-red.

In a panic, Hugh scrambles backward, desperately trying to create distance. "Dear God!" he shouts.

"What have they done to you?" I whisper under my breath.

Huldah screams, frantically grabbing her husband and motioning to Clinton. "Digory, help him! You … you must do something! I beg of you!"

Digory scrambles to his feet and, steadying himself, holds the back of his chair. Still uncertain if it is Clinton, he analyzes the boy, trying to identify any familiar feature through the grim exterior.

Desperate for help, Clinton pushes himself through the doorway and into the light, reveal-

ing clumps of gory matter on his face. Dismantled and mangled pieces of flesh hang partially off the bone. Mounds of scabbing wounds
cover lacerations on his skin; his entire body is
severely battered and bruised.

With a horrified gasp, Digory suddenly rec-
ognizes him. "I … I cannot believe it. My boy!"

With a wailing howl, Clinton's knees buckle
beneath him, and his upper body takes the
brunt of the impact as he hits the floor. Clutching his ribs in agony, he struggles to rise to his
feet, but his legs betray him, causing him to
collapse onto the ground. His eyes roll back into
his head.

As I gaze at him, I recoil, transfixed on his
bloodshot irises; I cannot look away.

The bones of his breast bulge with each
of his breaths. His arms coil toward his chest,
trying to stop the torturous hyperventilation. He
froths at the mouth like a wild animal while his
entire body convulses with seizures.

Huldah, overwhelmed by grief, grabs her
chair and screams in despair. "My poor son!"
she cries. "Don't just stand there, Digory; he will
die!"

With a gulp, Digory stares at the barely
recognizable body before him. The horrific sight
is enough to make him shudder and squirm.
Trying to calm himself, he takes a deep breath

and says, "Do not worry, son. Everything will be just fine."

Clinton's body stiffens, and his muscles spasm uncontrollably. He arches his back, and his head jerks backward as if subjected to an electric surge. His eyes bulge, and pupils expand while his mouth gapes open, choking and gasping for air. The color of his irises takes on a yellowish hue, intensifying his disturbing appearance as a low growl emanates from his throat. It's as if a malevolent demon is trapped within his lungs, hungry for a soul to eat.

Digory nervously approaches with cautious steps. He extends his hand and, getting closer, slows his pace, not wanting to stress him further. "That is right—just breathe. I am coming to help you, and we will get this whole matter sorted out," he says, monitoring his every movement, sweat pooling on his forehead.

As Clinton swallows, he experiences a strange sensation in his throat—a solid lump stuck in his upper esophagus. With another gulp, the lump shifts down, obstructing his airway. The delicate, fleshy layer of his throat stretches, gradually thinning as something beneath presses against it, seeking an escape. Then, suddenly, the culprit reveals itself as the form of a massive beetle takes shape, accompanied by a piercing hiss.

I slowly stand to get a better view. It is both strange and unsettling.

Despite Clinton's efforts to clear his throat, the insect lodges firmly. His pupils return to his irises. There is a frantic look in his eye as he coughs and sputters.

Hugh takes another step back while Hattie and Ettie nervously stand up from their chairs.

Noticing the family's oddly skittish behavior, I look to my left and see Adeline is gone and hear the kitchen door close behind me—*bloody hell*. I think to myself. I glance at Blanche and Cyprian, gripped by terror; they are frozen to their seats with no clue of their surroundings.

Fraught with desperation, Clinton climbs to his hands and knees, his grip tight on his throat as he frantically tries to clear his airway. The harder he digs his fingertips into his trachea, the more his eyes water, and his face turns red. With each struggle to breathe, the lodged invader grows larger.

Digory stares in horror.

"Hurry, Digory!" Huldah exclaims. "You must make haste!"

Wincing, he clears the sweat from his eyes. "Clinton. I am here to help," Digory says. Abruptly, stopping in his tracks, he stares at his son.

Hugh nervously glances toward his sisters, who are leaving through the kitchen door.

Never having seen something frighten him quite like this, I follow his gaze and realize we are the only two family members left in the dining room.

Clinton takes a deep breath and releases a final huff of air before collapsing onto the ground. His chest rises and falls with great effort before ceasing altogether, leaving a profound stillness in its wake.

The sound of Digory's shouting and Huldah's sobs draw my attention to his limbs; they appear lifeless and limp.

As Digory rushes toward the body, Hugh sprints toward the kitchen door. Confused about where he is going, I spin around and run after him.

Suddenly, I hear a hideous growl behind me emanating from Clinton's chest. It reminds me of the dreadful noise that had come from the girls when feasting on Lucius's corpse. I run faster.

As I push my hand against the kitchen door, about to open it, I steal one final glance over my shoulder and see Clinton latching onto his father.

His eyes expand, and his pupils turn deep black, violating the corners of his irises. A glimmer of yellow tinges his stare, and his mouth hinges open.

Digory's gaze is fixed on his lips, slightly askew and revealing his jagged teeth. The gumline underneath does not match his son's complexion, creating an unsettling detachment, as if another entity resides within his fleshy shell.

Struggling to speak, Digory's eyes widen in horror as the enormous beetle wriggles out of Clinton's throat and onto his tongue, emitting a chilling hiss.

With an unrelenting grip on his head, Clinton pulls Digory closer to his gaping mouth. He lets out a piercing scream and kicks his legs in a desperate attempt to break free, but within seconds ... his body goes limp and screams cease.

"Digory?" Huldah cries, rushing toward them while pulling the cross pendant from her neck. "He ... he... he's biting him! Someone do something!" she sobs. "He's eating him alive!"

Blanche and Cyprian stand up in a panic from the table. They glance at the exit on the other side of the bloody massacre and then look toward the kitchen door.

My heart races as they stare in my direction.

Clinton slowly rises to his feet. I rush to the kitchen entrance and flee inside. As I turn to shut the door, I hear a loud slam coming from the dining room, accompanied by frantic scurrying.

Panicked, I fumble to find the lock in the dimly lit space, my fingers shaking as I finally grab and twist it.

Huldah lets out a bloodcurdling scream. Horrified, I press my ear to the door, desperate to listen.

The air is saturated with the unsettling sounds of an animal feasting on flesh and crunching bones.

The cries grow louder, now blending with hurried footsteps approaching.

Pushing myself away from the entrance, my eyes remain fixed on the door as the knob frantically spins.

"Help! Help!" Blanche sobs.

I step back while watching the door rattle with each frenzied knock until my back hits the butcher's block. I grab hold of the wood, trying to stabilize myself.

"Let us in!" she shrieks as she pounds harder. "That creature consumed Digory, and now it's devouring Huldah!"

Petrified, I watch the metal knob spin from left to right. "I—I can't," I stammer.

Cyprian kicks the door. "Open the door! It's trying to kill us!" he screeches.

Then, abruptly, they fall silent.

I hold my breath, listening, as their breathing shallows and shrieks transform into whimpers.

Then, a demonic roar echoes, turning into a menacing growl. The low guttural sound rumbles the pots and pans hanging from the kitchen wall.

In a frenzy, Blanche turns the knob faster and cries, "Please, Genevieve, if this is over what I said earlier ... I want to assure you that there was no ill intention behind my words!"

The sound of fear in her voice causes my eyes to pool with water. Wanting to be anywhere else but here, I scan the room to escape the relentless pleas. "I'm ... sorry," I say under my breath. "I can't."

Her pleading turns to rage as she pounds and kicks on the door. "You think you are above this? Just wait. Your fate will not differ from Lucius's! But unlike him, you will rot in hell!"

I grip the wooden block tighter and clench my jaw. The tears waiting to escape my ducts sting my eyes, and I quietly sniffle. I jump at the sound of Cyprian's scream as his body hits the wall and then is dragged across the floor.

"Oh, no, please don't! No!" Blanche cries, her words thick with anguish.

Her begging consumes me with guilt. To block the noise, I cover my ears and hum a tune I remember my mother singing to me from childhood.

The door trembles violently with each of her battering hits.

The horrifying snarls draw nearer.

"Cyprian ... What did you do to my husband?" she asks her back against the door and her words ridden with hysteria.

I stop humming as I hear a low gurgling sound resonating from Clinton's throat, almost like a demented cat's purr.

"Answer me!" she shouts.

I slow my breathing and keep my eyes on the shadows projecting from beneath the door.

I cautiously take a small step forward, fighting my racing heart.

"Please," she sobs. "My daughter will have no family left."

As I listen to her cries, I kneel and peek through the keyhole, glimpsing Clinton as he slowly approaches the woman.

Aside from a layer of fresh blood staining his clothing, all his wounds appear to have vanished, and his skin is no longer dangling from the bone. All that is left is a tiny gash on his head.

The man standing before me is a stark contrast to his earlier appearance. As I gaze at him, I cannot help but notice that this is the Clinton I know so well. His presence brings me a sense of comfort, and I reach for the doorknob, feeling reassured by his familiarity.

His eyes dart toward the keyhole as if he senses my movements, and his lips curl into a smile.

As I feel the cool metal of the handle against my fingertips, I reach for the lock.

But just as I do, someone grabs my wrist from the darkness. In a panic, I tear my eyes away from him and focus on my wrist, where I spot the weathered hand of a woman. A warm sensation radiates across my cheek, catching flickers of light from the edge of my eye; I turn around.

The chambermaid grips the slender candle in her fist. Each bobble of the delicate light dances across the contours of her face, casting shadows and highlighting her tired and worn-out countenance.

Looking at her, I cannot help but see the dark circles that have formed beneath her eyes. Just as I am about to speak, her hand covers my mouth, silencing me. I can feel the tension in her body as she looks around as if expecting someone to jump out at us from the shadows.

She slowly withdraws her hand and places a finger on her lips, whispering, "You must not let it hear you." Her voice is so faint that I am unsure if I even heard it; my heart pounding loudly is my only response.

She leans forward, tightening her grip. "Come, miss, we must go," she murmurs, louder this time.

I stare at her, my mouth agape and eyes wide open in shock. "You … you can speak?" I stammer in disbelief. A mixture of excitement and fear runs through me as I await her response, hoping I am not just imagining things.

Without saying another word, she gently tugs my arm, guiding me to stand.

My legs tremble beneath me as I rise to my feet. Blanche's bloodcurdling screams fill my ears, compelling me to take one final last glance at the door before giving into the force of the chambermaid's pull, knowing I have no other option but to follow.

I trail closely behind her as she guides me through the obscurity, and the unbearable wails grow louder behind us. I wince, imagining it being me, and pick up my stride.

With a sudden halt, the chambermaid stops at the end of a wall brimming with pans. The flame from her candle flickers as she raises it to the wallpaper adorned with clusters of sunflowers. She scans the intricate design with focused determination, her eyes searching for something amid the vibrant scenery.

I anxiously shift my attention to the dining room door upon hearing snapping bones. Thinking of their agony sends a shudder through my body.

Becoming impatient, I glance toward what the chambermaid is doing. The flickers of light reflect off something golden.

I approach her as she reaches for a small knob hidden in the center of a flower arrangement.

My eyes widen in surprise at the sight. The barely visible door blends seamlessly into the wall, almost like it does not exist. The sight catches me off-guard as I wonder where else hidden entrances may lie.

She turns the handle, opens the door, and gestures for me to crawl into the dark space.

A monstrous howl comes from the dining room, accompanied by a fierce clawing at its doorway.

I drop to my hands and knees, hurrying to get inside as the scratches intensify. The chambermaid follows me and swiftly shuts the door behind us.

I come to an abrupt halt, my chest heaving as I gasp for air. The darkness envelops me, and as I peer into the abyss, my eyes strain as they adjust to the lack of light.

As I rise to my feet, I quickly realize that this is no ordinary pathway. Deep below the estate, the cavernous portal connects to a sprawling network of winding routes that stretch in every direction. The walls appear naturally formed in stone, with stalactites jutting from the ceiling, casting strange and distorted shadows on the ground. The air is thick and musty, smelling of earth, with a dampness that clings to my skin and makes my hair unruly. There are no other sounds besides the soft patter of our footsteps and the distant drip of water echoing off the walls.

I stop, feeling apprehensive about what lies ahead. Just as I am lost in my thoughts, a forceful tap on my shoulder jolts me out of my daze. "Go!" the chambermaid says, shoving me forward. Her voice sends an icy chill through my body; I walk faster.

She races in front of me and guides us to a dead end, giving the wall a heave. It folds under the force, opening at the hinges.

I follow her into another dimly lit corridor. A chilling realization dawns on me as she shuts the passage door behind us. *Nothing is as it seems.*

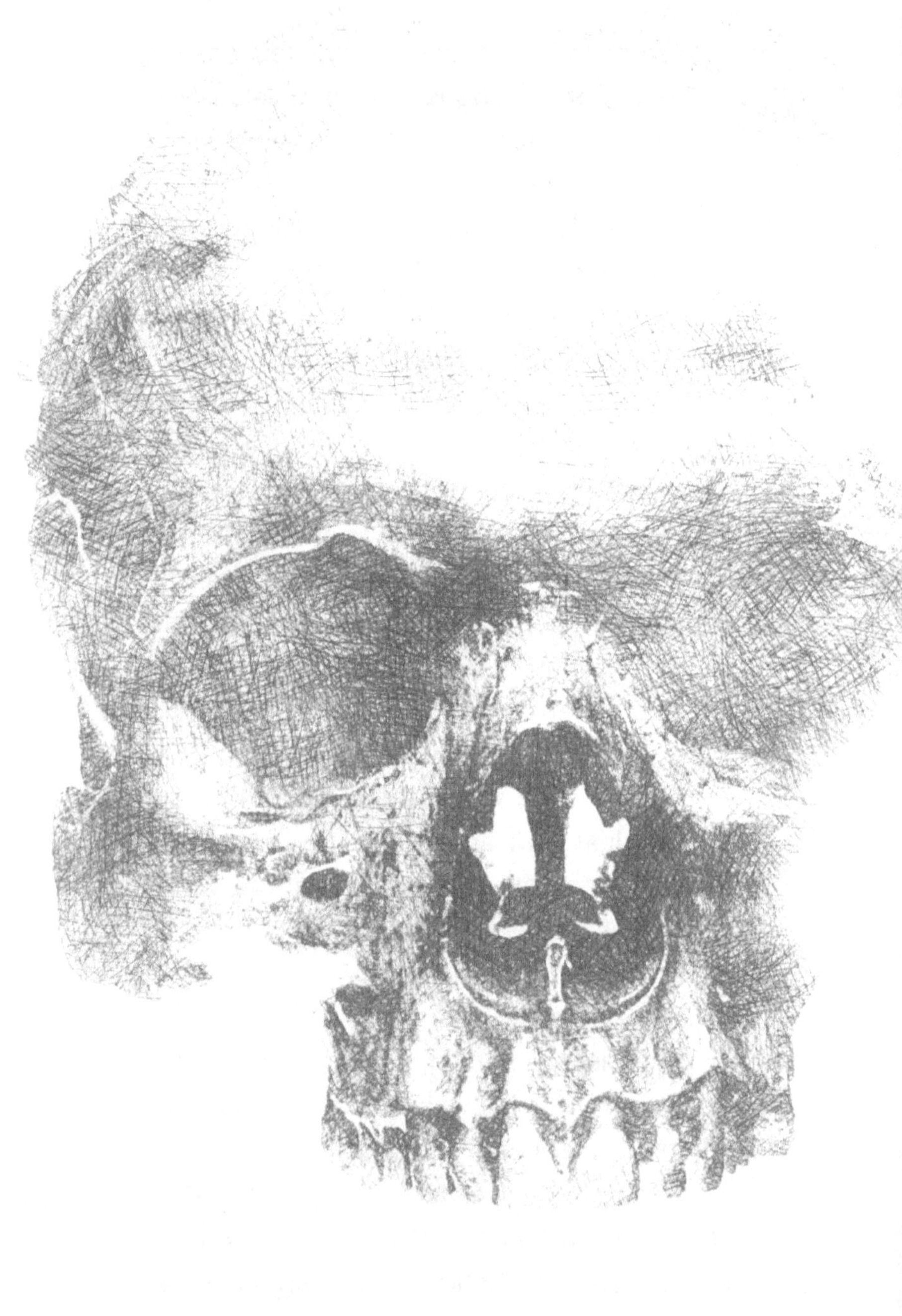

Twenty-Two

Lurking Shadows

With each passing moment, the gloomy corridor makes me more uneasy, and anticipation of the unknown causes my pulse to race. I nervously scan every nook and cranny, worried someone may lurk around the corners.

The chambermaid is at my side, her hand resting lightly on my arm as she guides me. We arrive at an iron spiral staircase with an open doorway at the top, exuding a soft glow. I carefully ascend the steps and am relieved to see that we have finally escaped the bowels of the estate and arrived at the home's familiar walls. I peer down the long, candlelit hall, searching for the outline of my bedroom door among the paintings.

My heart quickens at the sight of its wooden frame standing out against the subdued hues of the walls and canvases. I feel the chambermaid tugging harder on my arm, urging me to keep moving. Determined not to trip, I keep my gaze fixed on the floor, taking small, measured steps.

The soft moonlight filtering through the frosted windows casts a warm glow on the hallway, and a sense of comfort washes over me.

I quicken my pace, eager to reach the haven of my room. The chambermaid matches my stride, a slight smile playing at the corners of her lips.

Everything seems eerily docile compared to my experience in the dining hall. I find the lack of threat disconcerting because, in this house, I have found that it generally proceeds something to fear. I take a deep breath as we stop before the door and remain silent, praying we are safe from creeping dangers.

The chambermaid releases my arm and brings the flame closer to the keyhole, illuminating its metal facing and casting a warm glow on her face.

Her eyes remain fixed on it as she reaches into her apron pocket.

The hall's draftiness houses a slight breeze that makes the flame dance. As I watch the flicker, I realize that I didn't remember her locking the door earlier.

As the chambermaid's hand continues rummaging, I hear a footstep and catch sight of a dark figure lingering in the exact location of the entity I encountered earlier.

What is taking her so long?

With a gulp, I nervously fix my gaze on the chambermaid's hand, silently willing her to hurry. She appears to have no reaction to the noise. Her face clenches as she pushes her fingers deeper into the corner of the seams, searching for the key. Although her calm demeanor brings me some relief, it does not prevent my fear from fueling my paranoia.

I hear another footstep, but this time, amid the thumping sound, I catch a voice saying, "Genevieve."

As I stand there, my heart racing with a potent blend of fear and apprehension, I coil my fingers into tight fists, trying to steady my nerves. Swiftly, I turn my head, glancing at the shadowy figure lying in wait. The dim lighting makes it hard to see the face, but I can make out the subtle outline of its looming body.

Gradually, as my eyes adapt to the obscurity, the figure's male attributes are revealed—broad shoulders, tall frame, and muscular build.

The silhouette remains still, seamlessly merging with the shadows. Then, it sways ever so slightly, revealing more detail. *It is him! It is Phillip!* My hand instinctively covers my mouth to remain silent while I try to comprehend what I see.

He slowly directs his gaze toward me, tilting his head as if assessing me. His eyes meet mine, and for a moment, time seems to stand still.

A surge of emotions boils within me, ready to explode. I struggle to find the right words to convey my overwhelming anger and confusion. "What ... what sort of madness have you subjected me to? Is this some kind of twisted punishment? A cruel retaliation for a grudge from our youth, perhaps? Mother and father always favored you. They made it no secret that you were preferred, so why would you hate me so to subject me to this torment?"

There is no reply.

The silence is overwhelming, creating an unsettling atmosphere as if something ominous is about to occur. Abruptly, his head snaps to one side, and his eyes fixate on something behind me.

The longer I stare at his unnerving gaze, the more my stomach churns. I fear knowing what has caught his attention beyond my shoulder.

I stand frozen in place as the quiet is broken by a series of whispers. The voices, each coming from different directions, hiss and murmur in my ears, making me feel like a coven of witches encircles me. My heart races as a cold sweat breaks out on my skin, causing the bodice of my dress to cling to my body.

I close my eyes, hoping to shut out the frightening antagonists, but it does not help; the voices grow louder, their words indiscernible but their intent unmistakable.

I sense a suffocating presence behind me as if the darkness itself is infused with evil. A low gurgling sound emanates from it, resembling the saliva-filled groan from Clinton's throat.

It sends a wave of terror through me, but despite my fear, it also oddly provokes an air of curiosity. Taking a deep breath, I begin to turn around to look, but when I hear faint clinking noises from the bedroom door, I stop myself, and my attention darts to the chambermaid.

She finishes unlocking the bedroom door and glances over at me. The moment our eyes lock, a look of terror fills her stare as a door down the hall slams shut, causing me to jump and her too hastily open the entrance to my room and dart inside.

My heart races as I nervously scan my surroundings and find that the shadowy figure has vanished, and the unsettling whispers have ceased.

The chambermaid waves at me, gesturing to follow.

As I approach her, I am drawn to a sudden movement on my left. I quickly scan the disturbance from the corner of my vision.

My eyes shift to the portraits; beside them, peering through the pitch-black is a pair of yellow eyes and a set of sharp, glistening teeth. The corners of its lips slowly curl into a smile.

I rush into the room, my heart pounding. As soon as I am inside, the chambermaid shuts the door.

With a sense of urgency, she deftly slides the bolt into place, checking twice to ensure it is securely locked.

I am captivated by the ethereal beauty of the moonlight as it streams through the window. My eyes then drift toward the fireplace, which has not been tended to. It is strange—one would expect a fire to burn in the hearth, especially on a chilly evening like this. *Could it be that she was not expecting me to return from the meal?*

As she turns around, her eyes scan the room and land on the flameless firewood. She contemplates their charred remains for a moment. Then, cupping her hand around the candle wick to ensure the flame stays lit, she rushes over to ignite it.

She halts before the golden fireplace screen, carefully placing the candle between the logs and skillfully setting them ablaze.

As the fire comes back to life, the dancing flames highlight the intricate golden floral design cutouts, producing a mesmerizing play of light and shadow on the walls. I am captivated by its beauty; it brings me a sense of tranquility. The way the flecks warm my skin makes me temporarily forget my troubles.

With a tight grip on the candle, the chambermaid turns around and glances in my direction. Relieved to find me preoccupied, she hurriedly makes her way to the washroom, purposefully avoiding eye contact.

The sound of her footsteps jolts me from my contemplation, and I gasp as I am brought back to the severity of the situation.

She picks up her pace. I turn my head, following her movement. "Where are you going?" I ask, my voice tinged with confusion and concern.

She continues walking forward, ignoring me.

I look at where she is heading. The sight of the washroom prompts a sense of urgency to rise within me. I shake my head in disbelief. "Now is not the time to draw a bath. We must sit down and discuss everything that has happened," I firmly insist.

Her footsteps quicken with determination.

"I said stop!" I shout.

She hesitates at the entrance to the washroom doorway and takes a moment to pause. Skittish, her eyes dart the surroundings.

I anxiously clear my throat to gain her focus. "I have so many unanswered questions," I say while staring at her back, hoping she will turn around. "I implore you to speak to me."

She stands silent, her eyes focused on a distant point.

My emotions abruptly explode. "I command you to turn around this instant!" I shout. Each word sends speckles of spit flying.

She coils her fingers, digging her nails into her palms.

My body heaves, struggling to catch my breath. I cannot help but notice the tenseness in her body—her posture is abnormally rigid. Abruptly, she spins toward me, lowering her gaze to hide her inner turmoil.

There is something off about her. Her eyes have no shine; the reflection of the world around her has disappeared from her irises.

A subtle movement arises from her Adam's apple.

I shift my attention to the bottom of her frilled bonnet, watching for her lips to move. "You may speak," I say softly.

She glances up at me. As our eyes meet, I notice her pupils constricting in fear. I reach out my hand, offering comfort and reassurance. "There is no need to worry," I whisper, trying to calm her nerves.

Despite my attempts to engage her, she remains silent. The soft glow of the orange fire casts a warm reflection on her weathered skin.

Wanting to appear less threatening, I adjust my posture to mirror hers. "You know, I have already heard you speak in the kitchen, so I know you can," I say, attempting to keep my voice steady as I lean in closer.

She clenches her jaw.

"It can be our little secret, just between you and me," I whisper.

She continues to be uncooperative.

Desperation overwhelms me, and I sprint toward her, my pounding heart reverberating in my ears. With each step, my corseted lungs struggle to keep up with the frantic pace, and, coming to a stop in front of her, I gasp for air. "Please," I say, my voice quivering with emotion as I plead, "say something ... anything. I beg you to speak."

Her lips form a tight, concentrated pout that crinkles toward her nose.

My entire body freezes as I observe a subtle movement in her jaw. It appears as if she is chewing.

As she exerts herself, her nostrils flare, and her cheeks become more pronounced.

"That's it..." I say, encouraging her; I hear an agonized moan come from the back of her throat. My eyes widen, staring at her wiggling lips. "That's it ... now all you must do is open your mouth," I say, demonstrating. "Like this. It would be best if you parted your lips to articulate."

A loud wail emerges from her, causing her pupils to dilate.

"It shouldn't be this difficult," I say, reaching for her face. I grab hold of the skin around her mouth. "Let me show you."

She cringes in pain as I pull at her flesh. The soft skin of her lips is fused together.

"I know for certain I heard you talk earlier," I grunt, pulling harder.

She struggles to free herself.

I slap away her hands. "Stop it this instant! You must hold still!"

Muffled cries emanate from her throat and the color flushes from her face. Her eyes shimmer with tears as she struggles harder and swings the candle toward my face.

The scorching heat from the flames licking at my cheek ignites a rage I have never felt before. It is like a switch has flipped, unleashing a side of myself that I did not know existed. "You could have burned me!" I scream.

A look of panic infiltrates her pupils.

I question her with a narrow, fierce glare. "Are you trying to disfigure me?"

My sneer catches her off-guard, and she recoils.

I latch onto her wrists and tighten my grip. "What is wrong with you?!" I ask. With clenched teeth, I strained to drag her toward the fireplace, grunting with each heave.

Her muffled pleas grow louder as we draw nearer to the flames. She kicks her legs, trying to stop my pull.

Feeling her body tremble under my fingers, I yank harder. "Rest assured, I will free those lips if it is the last thing I do!" I say.

Her gaze darts across the room in a panic.

My eyes fixate on her mouth as I usher her toward the blazing fire. I bring her to a stop beside the hearth, then push down on her shoulders, prompting her to kneel. Her hands shake, and her breath quickens.

I wipe away the beads of sweat on my forehead from the exertion. "Now, all we need is something with a sharp point," I remark as I hurriedly approach the vanity. A smile forms on my face as I retrieve a carved-bone hair comb. "I believe this will suffice," I say.

The way light glints off the long teeth and inset jewels creates a sparkle that reflects on the wall.

She glances at the object; the sight of its piercing tips fills her with terror. Slowly, I move it from side to side in my hands. "Yes, you will do just fine," I say.

She claws at the ground, desperately trying to move her body backward to escape.

I swiftly turn toward her, meeting her gaze with a grin. Our eyes lock as I approach. "You will experience a newfound sense of freedom once I'm finished," I say with a sneer, raising the tool. I prepare to strike.

Hysterically, she scurries across the floor, trying to flee.

I lunge toward her and grab her bodice.

She swings the candle toward my face in defense.

"Stop that," I say, snatching it from her grip and pitching it into the flames. "I am trying to help you."

Her nostrils flare, and her pupils dilate further as I pin her to the floor with an irregular strength. The muscles in my arms quiver as I lift the jagged tool above my head, and clenching my jaw, I lodge the piercing tips between her lips. As I wiggle them through her fused skin, I slowly pry, ripping the flesh apart.

Agonizing screams stem from her chest, getting louder with each lengthening tear of the incision. Blood oozes from the tissue, falling into her mouth and dripping down her chin.

I clench the comb tightly between my fingers, sawing with more force, digging its teeth deep to ensure I separate the flesh to the corners of her mouth. Once satisfied with my work, I release my grip. The bloody surgical implement tumbles from my hand to the floor.

Her lips open with a gasp, and she immediately sits up. "You … you…" she says, trembling in pain.

I spring to my feet and motion for her to stop. "Do not say another word," I say, racing into the washroom.

Grabbing a towel, I clean the blood from her face and apply pressure to the wound. I carefully lower the towel from her lips as the ichor clots, creating scabs around the torn flesh.

She glares at me, her eyes filled with a mixture of fear and shock, as her distraught tears stream down her cheeks.

"Now, you must calm down and tell me everything you know," I say.

She nods, taking a deep breath.

Twenty-Three

A Nice Bath

Giving her a moment to compose herself, I listen to the sound of the snapping flames.

She takes a deep breath while climbing to her hands and knees and proposes, "Shall we continue our discussion while you enjoy a relaxing bath?" Rising to her feet, she continues, "It is crucial for a young woman to prioritize cleanliness and self-care."

I am surprised by her resolve.

"If we must," I reply. Staying near the fireplace, I watch her slowly move toward the washroom entrance.

Her feet barely lift from the polished wood floor, creating a shuffling sound as she travels across the room. The cadence of her steps strikes me as different from what I had previously observed. An unsettling determination to her movements leaves me with a sense of unease.

The flames leap and swirl behind me, radiating warmth over my body.

As her footsteps resonate into the washroom, the soft echo of buckets of water pouring into the tub fills the air. Gentle sloshing reverberates from the copper basin, creating a calming ambiance. She carefully prepares the towels and suds, ensuring everything is perfect before calling, "Miss, it is ready."

I fixate on the darkness beyond the ajar washroom door. "Coming," I reply. I gaze toward the fireplace, searching for any glimmer of hope that the candle might have endured the blaze.

Scanning the hearth, I am drawn to a clump of melted wax on a log's surface. Its molten form slowly drips and merges with the charred remnants below.

With her impatience mounting, the chambermaid forcefully splashes her hands through the water, scattering droplets across the marble floor.

The sound of splattering liquid catches my attention, and I quickly turn to look in its direction. I languidly approach her while reaching behind my back to unfasten the bodice of my dress. Seeing my approach, she rushes to assist me.

As she unbuttons and unlaces the back of my gown, I cannot ignore the stiffness of her fingers. Her touch feels rougher than usual. I am uncertain whether it is because of the wound on her face, but regardless of the reason, there is something about her behavior that makes me uneasy. I instinctually cover myself as my dress falls to the floor, and, noticing her reaching for my undergarment, lift my hands.

She pulls the material over my head and, kneeling, removes my shoes. "Let's tidy you up," she murmurs.

I nervously chuckle and glance at the tub, then tentatively walk toward the water. As I stand shivering from the cold, I feel the moist steam on my skin. The smell of soap is a refreshing change from the gore.

She grabs my arm to help me step inside. The moment the heat touches my nakedness, the sudden shift in temperature sends a sharp, prickling sensation surging through my limbs. I wince and straighten my legs, my focus fixed on the overwhelming discomfort in my feet; it is as if they are engulfed in flames.

The chambermaid pushes on my shoulders. "It is simply your body adjusting. There is no need for alarm," she says.

Her relentless pressure causes my knees to give way, and I grit my teeth as the scalding water erupts into the air. I shut my eyes tightly to shield them from the searing heat.

She retrieves a golden cup from a marble shelf near the tub and, filling it to the brim, pours the soapy water on the nape of my neck. The scorching temperature makes me cringe.

As it trickles down my spine, I glimpse her disfigurement. I quickly avert my gaze to escape the discomfort of the view. "Now," I say through clenched teeth, "I believe it is your turn to uphold your end of the bargain."

The cup slips from her hand, splashing into the water.

I hug my knees tightly to my chest.

She nervously chuckles. "Yes," she says, clearing her throat. "I suppose that is true. So, miss, tell me … What would you like to know?"

My mind races with questions. Suddenly, unable to contain my curiosity, I blurt out, "Why are you not allowed to speak?"

"The master of the house values his privacy greatly. He is concerned that granting too much freedom to someone risks them revealing family secrets, like a squealing piglet," she says, fishing the cup from beneath the bubbles.

"Hugh implemented this rule?" I ask.

With a bewildered expression, she pauses, empties the cup, and returns it to the shelf. "Who?" she asks, grabbing a small washcloth.

As her hands scrub my skin gently, I cannot help but feel frustrated by her lack of cooperation. "My husband," I remark with a trace of irritation.

She anxiously scrubs faster. "Oh ... yes." She chuckles. "Of course."

The rag's pressure abrades my skin. I frantically swat behind my back. "Ouch! You are hurting me!"

She hesitates. "Sorry, miss ... I didn't mean to cause any harm. I will try to be more careful. I was referring to Mr. McKinley, the housemaster." Silence engulfs the room as she resumes her scrubbing.

My knuckles tighten, turning white as I grip the tub's sides. My voice trembles as I hesitantly ask, "Hasn't he passed?"

"He is very much alive, miss."

I suddenly jolt upright as a vivid memory floods back to me. My eyes widen, and I sit taller, the water rippling around me. "But I saw him. There is no doubt the life had been sucked from his skin," I utter, my mind drifting back to the unsettling encounter on my first day at the estate.

She dips the soft rag into the water, watching it absorb the liquid. With a furrowed brow, she murmurs, "That was not him."

Taken aback, my eyes widen in surprise. "Excuse me?"

She carefully wrings out the rag and then looks at me to emphasize her words. "I said that was not him, miss," she repeats, her voice unwavering.

My breath catches in my throat as I gulp in disbelief. "Then who was it?" I ask, my voice barely rising above a whisper.

The world around me is enveloped in a profound silence, broken only by the slightest sound of rippling water.

My eyes dart nervously as my mind races. With a sudden surge of energy, I plunge my fists into the soapy water, shattering the eerie quiet. "Who was resting in his bed chamber if not him?"

Without uttering a word, she quickens her pace and continues to bathe me. Droplets of water trickle down my back, glistening in the fraction of light entering the doorway. As they land back in the water, each tiny drip creates a mesmerizing ripple, sending concentric circles dancing across the surface.

I am captivated by the gentle rain-like sounds reverberating through the marble surroundings. They weave an eerie symphony that fills the room, leaving a trail of goosebumps in their wake.

Whispers instantly fill the corners of the space. I anxiously hold my breath and fight the temptation to look, determined to ignore them as I persist in my search for clarity. "Well?" I ask, eager for a response. "I'm waiting!"

The murmurs persist, growing louder, making it impossible to ignore until the warm water cascading over my hair, accompanied by the soothing sensation of the chambermaid's fingers massaging my scalp, overwhelms my senses and quiets my mind. As the air fills with her rhythmic breaths, I close my eyes.

Little by little, her fingers tighten around the strands. "You are a murderer," she utters.

I gasp, and my eyes spring wide open.

Her fingers grip more intentionally, gathering fistfuls of hair.

Suddenly, she yanks me backward, causing my body to flail as panic consumes me.

I scream at the top of my lungs as her hands latch onto me like a shark's jaws, dragging its prey to the bottom of the ocean. My head submerges into the water; the soapy liquid infiltrates my mouth and lungs. A sharp sting penetrates my eyes as I peer through the murky abyss.

Shrouded in darkness, a figure looms over the tub, watching me with its piercing yellow glowing eyes. I quickly realize that my tormentor is the same monstrous creature that had been following me in the hallway. I gasp in fear; the sensation of water rushing into my throat escalates my terror. As my breath is stolen away, the mere thought of drowning floods me with adrenaline.

Closing my eyes, I try with all my might to escape while flailing my arms and legs with a burst of survival instinct.

Just as everything is about to go dark around me, I hear a sound.

"Genevieve," a voice calls; something about it has an uncanny familiarity to my own.

"Genevieve," it repeats.

My lids fly open to find the spectral figure has disappeared. Clutching the sides of the tub, I frantically pull myself up from the water, struggling to catch my breath as I cough violently, expelling liquid from my lungs. My eyes bulge as my attention darts around the washroom.

Both the chambermaid and the malevolent entity are nowhere to be found. Only the muffled crackling noises from the fireplace and whispering hisses remain.

My gaze lands on the washroom door, and a shiver rolls down my spine. I don't recall it being closed.

Listening closely, I try to decipher the surrounding voices, searching for the chambermaid's familiar tone amid the chaos. As I hear what I assume to be her heavy footsteps getting closer, I release a slow exhale of relief.

"I have finished my bath," I call out, my fingers tightening on the tub's edge. I twist to face the entrance.

The echoing footsteps gradually come to a halt just beyond the closed door. I anxiously glance down, straining to discern the shadowy outline of feet through the gap.

"Chambermaid, is that you?" I ask, my voice tinged with nervousness.

The room is filled with inaudible murmurs seeping in from the other side. "Murderer," they repeat before vanishing into nothingness.

"If it is you, give a single knock," I say.

While my eyes remain locked on the gap beneath the door, I am consumed by a haunting presence in the atmosphere. An unsettling feeling churns my gut as the scent of death permeates the air around me.

I watch in silence as the silhouette of the feet, bathed in the warm glow of the flickering fire, casts an unmoving shadow.

My voice fills the room as I speak faster. "And if it is not, knock twice," I say, warily examining the door. My teeth chatter as I slowly rise from the bath's warmth. "Chambermaid, is that you?" I ask, stepping out of the tub.

Without breaking my gaze, I feel for the silk robe hanging from the wall. I gently remove the garment from the hook and slip it on.

As I stand waiting for a response, I hear movement, intensifying my fear of what awaits me on the other side.

I wrap my arms around my chest, creating a protective barrier. Then, after a moment of careful consideration, I take a step.

In the faint light, I squint and see the outline of shoes peeping from under the door's gap, immediately identifying them as the chambermaid's. A wave of relief floods me, causing a wry smile to play on my lips. "I want to assure you, I never intended to upset you," I call out, attempting to mend the situation.

The feet remain still.

As I cautiously approach the door, a trail of water glistens behind me. Each drop echoes in the quiet room as it drips from my legs to the floor. Nervously reaching for the handle, I am startled by a tiny shock that shoots through my fingers.

I quickly retract my hand, and the sudden sound of two heavy knocks reverberates through the door. I am frozen in place, my mind recalling the question I asked just moments earlier, and a sinking feeling settles in my stomach.

The feet shift their stance, altering the shadow with the change in position.

My breathing shallows, and my heart pounds in my chest. "Who—who is there?" I stammer.

The movement abruptly stops, and then the feet pivot with deliberate slowness, retreating as if called elsewhere.

I strain to hear the fading footsteps while cautiously reaching for the doorknob as they grow more distant. The touch of the cold metal causes my hand to tremble. In a desperate attempt to silence the rattling door handle, I clutch my wrist to steady the shaking and guardedly crack open the door.

The fire is inviting, and sensing no immediate danger, I open the door further. I cautiously step into the room, calling out, "Hello?"

My eyes sweep the space, stopping at the warm glow emanating from the hearth.

However, rather than finding comfort, my eyes are met with a horrifying sight: a pair of lifeless legs sticking out from behind the armchair placed beside it.

I move closer, scanning it for any identifiable quality. Suddenly, my eyes fall upon something I desperately want to unsee—the weathered face of the chambermaid.

Her bonnet is pulled over her eyes like a mask. Beneath the ruffles, deep gashes disfigure the flesh at the corners of her lips.

I find it impossible to tear my gaze away as I stare in disbelief at her mouth. Apart from the torn corners, the rest appears entirely normal. The center where her lips meet remains unharmed; there is no sign of prior fusion.

As the color drains from my face, curiosity overwhelms me, compelling me to take yet another step forward.

The sound of the crackling embers grows louder.

I hesitantly extend the toe of my bare foot, gently nudging the top of her bonnet further back onto her forehead, uncovering her eyes. As they are unveiled, I gasp and stumble backward, my gaze fixed on a giant beetle emerging from her eye socket.

Suddenly, her body starts emitting a series of hissing sounds. I quickly take another step back, but my feet get tangled up, causing me to lose my balance and fall to the ground.

Beetles crawl out of her eye sockets, their tiny legs skittering across her face as they emerge from every orifice and open wound. Gathering momentum, they propel themselves from her body and onto the floor.

I recoil in horror while frantically scrambling on the floor to escape. I kick my legs as the insects scamper toward my feet. "Get back!" I scream, grimacing while crushing them beneath my shoeless feet. "Get away from me!"

And then, as fast as it began, the beetles depart, rushing back toward the fireplace.

Puzzled by their unexpected change in behavior, I rise to my hands and knees to observe as they crawl over the chambermaid, past the bloody hair comb, and into the fire. Little popping sounds permeate the room as their insides expand and hard shells burst.

As I draw closer, my thoughts swirl with concerns for the maid's dreadful condition. Her morbid appearance triggers vivid recollections of our past exchange, compelling me to shift my attention to her.

She lies there, completely limp, showing no sign of movement. With genuine sympathy, I inquire, "What has happened, my poor friend?"

Fleeting murmurs tangle with the snapping sounds emanating from the fireplace.

I lean in closer, fixing my gaze on her, then the comb. "I assure you, I had nothing to do with your demise. My intention was solely to offer assistance," I say.

Seeing the small fillets of flesh attached to the comb's prongs makes my stomach churn and sends a wave of nausea up my throat. As I fight to restrain my tears, I glimpse her chest slowly rising in my peripheral vision.

I gasp in shock, my head snapping toward her. As I observe the gentle rise and fall of her ribcage, I slide closer. "Can you hear me? Are you conscious?" I whisper. Then, gently resting my head near her heart, I strain to hear any sign of life.

The irregular heartbeat is scarcely audible but there. Each thump is accompanied by a shallow, uneven breath emanating from her nose.

With my ear on her chest, I continue to listen, my gaze fixed on her disfigured face. As I focus on the subtle movement of her nostrils, I cannot help but notice her one good eye staring back at me. Her once-vibrant and colorful pupil has transformed, dilating into a deep, impenetrable black.

The longer I fixate on her, the more a nearly invisible twitch materializes at the corner of her upper lip, almost as if it is struggling to remain hidden.

Her throat releases a quick, strained wheeze. "Murderer," she says. The stillness of her lips resembles the controlled speech of a ventriloquist operating a dummy.

I fix my gaze on her wandering eye, my disbelief at the accusation evident in my expression. "I did no such thing!" I shout. "I did nothing more than help you speak."

Her expression twists in pain and anger. "You … did this…to me." She forces out the words.

I push myself away while grabbing the bodice of her dress. "You listen to me, servant!" I assert, tightening my grip. "You are a liar! I am not a murderer!" I sneer, pulling her closer.

Her head hangs heavy, her eye rolling back in its socket, leaving only a bloodstained white.

I frantically pat her head, trying to get her attention. "Do you hear me?"

A sudden creak from the floorboard causes me to twist my body toward the door. I unintentionally release my grip on her, resulting in a forceful impact of her head against the marble fireplace, producing a sharp crack.

Other than shadows, no one is there.

My chest constricts with an overwhelming anxiousness. I raise my palm and, shutting my eyes, rest it over my heart. "Thud…… thud…… thud," I whisper, synchronizing with the rhythm. As I monitor the rapid beats, I let out a deep exhale to calm myself.

I fix my gaze on the chambermaid, taking in every detail with a fresh mindset.

Decomposition has turned her skin a shade of grayish blue.

I reach out and grasp her hand. "No one can know. This must remain our little secret," I whisper, and in a cathartic state, I retrieve the skeleton key from her pocket. Rising to my feet, I pull back the fireplace screen and roll the corpse into the flames.

The fire singes her flesh, forming bubbles beneath her skin.

With every layer that is peeled away, a putrid smell fills the air, and her organs slowly disintegrate into a vile, liquefied sludge. I grab the fire poker and forcefully push more of her remains into the blaze, stoking the heat.

"Yes … yes… it will be our little secret," I utter.

The flames roar, sending plumes of black smoke up the chimney.

Once I have double-checked that the door is locked by turning the key and giving it a slight push, I make my way to my bed. I take a moment to plump the pillows, pull back the covers, and lay down, feeling a comforting sense of security, knowing that everything is prepared for a peaceful night's sleep.

Twenty-Four

Innocent

T he rising sun casts a warm glow through the window as a persistent crow squawks and pecks at the pane, rousing me from my slumber.

I snatch the pillow from the bed and wrap it around my face, covering my ears. "Why are you tormenting me?" I grunt. I want to scream.

Its caws only get louder.

The burden of the night's occurrences appears to be taking its toll on me. I am overcome with exhaustion. With great effort, I push myself upright and survey the room, letting the pillow slip from my hands. Every muscle and joint in my body aches.

Not ceasing, the crow's squawks persist, inundating the room.

As I turn to give it a look of annoyance, I glimpse the fireplace.

What is left of the chambermaid's remains are coiled in a ball, lying on top of the wood in a fetal position. Not all has been turned to ash. Apart from a hand that appears to have escaped the flames, a portion of her skeleton remains.

The way her hand covers her face, one would think she had been trying to protect herself from the flames.

I gaze at the fiery red embers casting a warm glow around her. "So, it wasn't a figment of my imagination," I murmur, inching toward the edge of the bed. I plant my feet firmly on the floor. "At least I can take comfort in knowing I am not going mad."

A shrill scream pierces the air outside the window, causing a chilling sensation to run through my body.

I turn around and lock eyes with the imposing bird, its small, glossy black orbs staring back at me. Their piercing glare seems to penetrate my very being.

I narrow my gaze, swiftly rising to my feet, but before I can take a step, the sound of heeled footsteps reverberates through the hallway. My heart races as I remain frozen in place.

The melodic timbre of Ettie's voice fills the air, resonating through the hallway as she warmly greets Hattie. "Good morning, dearest sister." The familial affection appears authentic, but I would beg to differ after the things I have observed.

Hattie steps into the hallway and shuts her bedroom door. "The sun is shining, and the sky looks so blue," she muses, her gaze fixed upon the large windows, captivated by the picturesque scene outside. "It is a beautiful day, don't you think, sister?"

As their voices gradually fade, I hurriedly approach the window, urgently gesturing for silence. "Now is not the time. They will hear you!" I exclaim.

With a distinctive caw, the majestic bird spreads its wings and gracefully soars into the boundless sky.

I inhale sharply and pivot toward the fireplace.

I am taken aback as I glimpse my reflection in the vanity mirror. The familiar creases have reappeared at the corners of my eyes, and the youthful tautness of my skin seems to have dissipated. It is worse than it was before.

"What happened to you?" I gasp as I touch the lax skin and pull it up to smooth out the deep crease. Yet, the moment I let go, I am overcome with horror as gravity takes hold.

The jarring noise of a door slamming shut in the hallway reverberates, sending shockwaves through the surroundings. Adeline's commanding voice immediately follows. "I was told Genevieve's chambermaid was missing from the lineup this morning."

A surge of panic floods through me.

Adeline pauses outside my door and continues, "Ensure the girl is awake and ready for breakfast."

"No, no, no … What will they say when they see the dreadful condition of my maid?" I mutter as I nervously wait for the door to open, exposing the dark reason for her absence.

Unexpectedly, Adeline leaves. The clicking of her heeled footsteps disappears as she moves down the hallway and heads toward the stairs. I breathe out a heavy sigh, grateful for my escape from trouble.

However, my moment of relief is short-lived, abruptly interrupted by an annoying rattle emanating from the doorknob.

I stand in front of the mirror, my reflection staring back at me as I hold my breath, hoping no one will hear me inside. Suddenly, I am startled by three loud knocks. Someone is trying to enter.

In a panic, I shout, "You must wait! I am not decent!"

The knocking persists, growing more aggressive with each strike.

Desperately seeking a solution, my gaze falls on the fireplace. I squint as I analyze the hand that escaped the searing heat, resting just a hair's breadth away from the flames. Despite being partially covered in charred flesh, it remains the sole remnant of the body that has not been completely incinerated.

Tilting my head, I assess the meat on the bone—scents of cooking flesh and toasted iron waft in the air. My stomach growls with hunger.

"All I need is a tiny nibble," I utter, my heart racing as I hear the knocks. With each thud, I gather more courage and take a step closer.

The aggressive nature of the battering makes it hard to concentrate.

I wince, bringing my attention back to the hand. "Just a moment!" I shout. Then, taking a deep inhale, I sniff the air. The closer I get, the more intense the aroma becomes; my pupils dilate as I salivate over the meal.

With my eyes bulging, a fierce growl escapes from my lungs, and I uncontrollably lunge forward. Coming to a crouch on the floor, I seize the hand, and ripping it from the bone, I lift it to my lips; my jaw muscles relax, allowing for a larger opening reminiscent of an anaconda. Without a second thought, I shove the entire appendage into my mouth and swallow it whole. As it travels further down my throat,

I cock my head toward the ceiling, heaving to make room and provide it with the momentum it needs for its journey to my stomach.

A soft knock sounds at the door.

I glance at the mirror and observe my youthful features gradually reappearing. Then, with a swipe of my tongue, I clear away the charred remnants from my lips.

The longer I gaze at my reflection, the more I discern a feral quality in my appearance. The elongated lines of my face and the predatory glint in my eye send a surge of adrenaline through my body.

With a self-assured smirk, I turn toward the door, prepared to face whatever lies on the other side.

Twenty-Five

Pick a Straw

The breakfast scene radiates with a captivating beauty. The sun's golden illumination adds an angelic touch to the blooming bouquets of vibrant flowers and tall vases filled with lush greenery, creating a delightful contrast to the muted tones of the previous evening.

The vivid display masks the lingering remnants of the prior night's unsettling dinner.

As I make myself comfortable in my seat across from Hugh, I cannot help but marvel at the lavish spread that lies before us.

A captivating assortment of perfectly ripened fruits, including plump strawberries and sliced melon, complements the savory tray of prosciutto, salami, and roast beef. The aroma of freshly baked bread and pastries wafts through the air, adding to the sensory delight. All is elegantly presented on a vibrant lime-green tablecloth, creating a stunning tableau.

Everyone gazes at the display, avoiding eye contact. They sit in silence, their expressions reflecting deep contemplation.

I stare at the serving of meats; it is much more dwindled than I had remembered.

Hugh clears his throat with a sly smirk directed at me, his eyes twinkling mischievously. "We are thrilled to see you have made it to yet another delightful meal," he says, his voice tinged with cordiality as he unfolds his napkin and places it on his lap.

Listening, I slowly remove my napkin from the table.

Ettie and Hattie glance at each other; their eyes narrow, and their mouths down-turned. They are back to wearing their signatory colors.

I observe their peculiar behaviors with keen interest, carefully analyzing the subtle changes in their expressions as they interact. Their hesitant smiles and guarded glances reveal more than their words ever could. "Yes, I daresay I am quite lucky," I remark, my voice portraying a mix of resignation and defiance. "Following your abandonment last night, I was uncertain of what would become of me."

Their eyes shift in my direction, and a look of displeasure creeps onto their faces.

I quickly continue, "Fortunately for me, the other four guests were dreadful at running." I laugh.

Adeline shoots me a scathing look from the corner of her eye and mutters, "Praise God." Her voice is dripping with sarcasm.

The young women gaze at each other with expressions of pure hate.

I shift my attention toward the vacant seats beside the girls. "I'm surprised to see that Clinton isn't here with us. Is he not joining us on this lovely morning?" I inquire.

Ettie widens her eyes in shock as she turns to look at me, her complexion growing paler as the color drains from her face.

"As one might imagine … he is still feeling a bit unwell," Hugh says.

I cannot help but notice his self-satisfied expression as he answers my question.

"And what about the doctor?" I ask, casually reaching for a piece of fruit and placing it on my plate. "Will he be joining us?"

Hugh's hand, embellished with a gold ring, reaches out for the delicately arranged platter of meats. Without hesitation, he confidently interjects, "No … unfortunately, he will not. Like Clinton, he, too, is suffering with a dreadful plague of exhaustion."

I take a moment to collect my thoughts, carefully choosing my words. "Has he been unwell for some time?" I ask, feigning concern. "I noticed his absence at dinner."

Hugh aggressively stabs a piece of meat with his fork, then moves it onto his plate while pretending not to notice me.

As tension fills the room, Hattie shifts uneasily in her seat, her eyes darting back and forth as she tries to focus on the conversation. A furrow forms on her brow. Her growing sense of unease seems to weigh heavily on her mind.

I narrow my eyes and stare at Hugh, urging him to respond. "I apologize. Could you please repeat that?" I ask. A small chuckle escapes me as I add, "I did not quite catch your reply."

His eyes delve into mine with a look of obvious disapproval, leaving no doubt that he is unamused.

I look at Hattie, observing her lips pursed tightly together, a telltale sign of an impending emotional outburst. She reaches her breaking point and blurts, "We devoured him!" She gasps and quickly covers her mouth in shock over her imprudence as her words linger in the air.

In an instant, all eyes shift toward her.

Adeline releases a dramatic sigh, her voice filled with exasperation as she says, "Please, Hattie ... try to control yourself."

Hattie's eyes dart around the table until they meet mine. Her widened gaze exposes her embarrassment as she diverts her gaze to the table and mumbles, "Well, it is true … he was yesterday's dinner."

Ettie scoots down in her chair and surreptitiously kicks her sister under the table. Hattie lets out a surprised and painful "Ow!" she screams. Then, quickly regaining her composure, she reaches for a golden-brown pastry.

Ettie's eyes light up with mischief as she scans the display for the ripest, juiciest berries. She carefully selects each one, inspecting its color and plumpness before placing it on her plate. A smirk of satisfaction crosses her lips.

Adeline rolls her eyes at her daughter's exchange. "I suppose the secret is no longer a secret," she remarks. I shift my attention toward her. Seamlessly, she snatches the butter and applies it to her toast, showing no reaction, as if discussing this topic is normal. "It is no secret that we delight in eating the flesh of the living."

"I have noticed," I say.

She glances toward me, her eyes meeting mine, and then leans in to whisper, "I cannot help but notice the incredible youth and tranquility that graces your face this morning."

I nervously giggle while gently brushing my fingertips against my cheek, secretly appreciating the suppleness of my skin. "Oh, is that so? I had not noticed," I mutter as I avert my eyes, unable to meet anyone's gaze at the table.

Ettie pauses amid her bite and looks closer at my face, squinting as she carefully surveys me. "I must agree with Mother. You appear quite refreshed," she notes, a faint grin gracing her lips.

Hugh joins the conversation teasingly. "Could it be that she indulged in a late-night snack?" he asks, his eyes twinkling with amusement. "Adeline informed us that her chambermaid failed to appear for the morning lineup."

Ettie and Hattie snicker.

I try to hide my mounting irritation as I attempt to divert the conversation. "Did you have trouble sleeping last night?"

The two girls become silent. Hattie's expression quickly shifts to a look of confusion. She asks, "Pardon me?"

Ettie's posture stiffens, and she puts on a forced smile as she asks. "Why are you interested in such a matter?" Turning toward me, her curls bouncing near her cheeks, she tries to feign composure, but her eyes betray her, exposing her anxiety.

Hattie adjusts her demeanor to match that of her sister, and then, with a deliberate pause, she looks directly at me. "I must say, I had a rather satisfactory sleep. Thank you. Why do you ask?"

"Oh, there is no particular reason," I say with a shrug.

The two girls move in sync, leaning closer with eager anticipation, wholly engrossed in every word I speak.

"It is just," I continue, "as I look at you, I cannot help but notice that your complexion seems less vibrant than I remember."

Once full of life and energy, their faces turn pale with mortification.

Turning my gaze toward them, my eyes exude concern and empathy. "I am deeply concerned about your well-being given the tragic circumstances. I know you have both been through a lot of grief as of late, and as your new sister, I genuinely want to offer my support in any way I can. I'm here for you if you need someone to talk to or just a shoulder to cry on."

They simmer in frustration as they listen.

"The last thing I want is for this dreadful ordeal to age you," I say.

Ettie grabs her spoon from the table, her fingers tightening around it. "Sister," she says, her voice filled with dismay, "I distinctly recall you assuring me this morning that I did not look a day over fifteen." Her furrowed brow reflects her concern as she scrutinizes her reflection in the small gilded mirror.

"I ... I ... firmly stand by my assertion," Hattie stammers. "It is true. You look very young indeed! Pay no attention to her pointless rambling."

Ettie anxiously prods at the delicate skin beneath her eye. "Then what is this?" she asks, her gaze fixed on a tiny crease.

"Are you referring to your eye?" Hattie asks.

"No, you ninny!" Ettie exclaims. "Look ... look…can you not see it? It is a clear sign of old age!"

Disbelief washes over Hattie as she listens to her sister's accusations. In response, she tightly grips the table's edge, her knuckles turning white from the force while she grits her teeth in irritation. "There is nothing there! You are imagining things!" she exclaims. Then, turning her piercing gaze toward me, she venomously spits, "This is what she wants! She desires to create a conflict between us. She is trying to create a detergent!"

Ettie's face flushes red as she let out a boisterous laugh. "I believe you misspoke. It is divergent, not detergent! Do you know how dull you sound right now? Sometimes, you can be quite embarrassing, and I often wonder how we could have been birthed from the same sac."

A soft chuckle escapes my lips, as neither has gotten it right.

Hattie points at me with daggers in her eyes. "Look at the grin on her face!" she says. "Dressed in the brightest reds, she looks like the Devil himself. One might suspect they have formed a sinister alliance and are plotting our demise!"

I focus on the delicate ruffled sleeves of my dress, the fabric feeling smooth beneath my fingertips. As I contemplate their accusations, a daring thought crosses my mind. *If they call me the Devil, then the Devil is what they shall receive. I embrace the role if it means securing my survival.* A mischievous glint flashes in my eye as I toy with the thought.

Hugh interrupts just as Ettie opens her mouth to speak. "That is enough of that. We must get back to the topic of the chambermaid," he says.

His tone hits me like a fighter's blow, causing me to shrink back. I feel like a small, helpless child bracing myself for an impending whipping.

"I am confident that I know what happened, and fortunately for you, I will overlook it this time due to your inexperience in such matters. But ... be warned. I will not show the same compassion if it happens again. It is of the utmost importance that the staff be treated with respect and safeguarded from any harm. Having a constant fear of being the next victim not only creates a negative work atmosphere, but it is also morally unjust to exploit those of lower social status."

I raise my chin to meet his gaze.

He explains, "When we consume others, their souls reside within our bodies, influencing our thoughts and actions."

While I listen attentively, my curiosity piques, and memories of the terrifying entities I have witnessed wandering the dim corridors flood my mind. "My apologies. I did not know," I say.

"I am honestly surprised," Adeline says. I glance at her, curious about what she means. A sly and knowing expression appears on her face. "What I mean is, you have surpassed expectations and persevered for so long. One would assume you know it all."

Hugh furrows his brow.

"Yes … I daresay… I am certain she is part cockroach with her resiliency," Ettie says, bursting into laughter as she looks toward Hattie, who joins in with a loud, high-pitched squeal.

Having had enough, Hugh rises to his feet. His commanding presence fills the space as he raises his hands to end the conversation.

"Silence!" he shouts. Adeline, Ettie, and Hattie flinch as his booming voice echoes. "We must put an end to this immediately," he says. "There are more significant matters to discuss."

All eyes turn toward him.

"What is wrong?" Ettie gasps, her voice trembling. I look at her widening pupils; there is terror in her eyes.

"Yes, brother, what is it?" Hattie asks.

Stricken with despair, Hugh leans forward and places his hands on the table. With a firm stance, he clears his throat and points to the table. "Has it not occurred to you that our meat portion is shrinking?"

Adeline looks at the tray. "I assumed it was just a lighter spread because of our dwindling numbers," she says.

"No, Mother, it is not!" he screams.

Adeline's breath catches sharply in her throat, and her heart races as she grips her chest, feeling unsteady in her seat.

In an emotional rage, Hugh kicks the table. "All that is left is swine and sheep!"

"Where did all the meat from last night's meal go? There should be some left ... We did not even get to the main course," Adeline stammers, struggling to comprehend the situation.

Hugh paces back and forth. "Spoiled!" he shouts, angrily throwing his hands into the air. "All of it ended up spoiled!"

Adeline's lips part as she exhales a soft "No." The word barely escapes her mouth. Her eyes flit anxiously around the table, searching for an answer that eludes her.

"Last night was a catastrophe," Hugh says, his frustration evident in his tense body and clenched fists. "The kitchen and dining room were left in complete chaos as everyone fled for their lives, including the staff. Nothing was properly stored in the icebox, resulting in blood and body parts strewn about, leaving them to spoil. The stench this morning was horrendous. And the mess—nothing short of a disaster." He pauses, gesturing with his hands. "It was truly indescribable."

Ettie and Hattie slump forward, their foreheads resting on the table, conveying their obvious disappointment.

Their dramatic movements make Hugh anxious, prompting him to pick up his pace. "Of course, they cleaned everything up nicely this morning, but that did not compensate for what was lost. What are we supposed to do? Besides having animals to eat, we have nothing left." Continuing, his face loses color as he states, "And we all know the consequences of not eating the proper meat."

I nervously pop a piece of melon into my mouth as I listen.

Hattie's face lights up as a sudden idea strikes her. "What if we sought more husbands?" she suggests, glancing at Hugh, looking for approval.

"She … she can get one too!" Pointing at me as she adds, "It would help our odds!"

Startled by the statement, I involuntarily let out a loud cough and quickly reach for my glass of water to clear my throat.

Instead of responding to her comment, Hugh calms his irritation before turning to Adeline. "Did you drop her on her head at birth?" he asks.

She pays no attention to the question and carries on with her meal.

He sarcastically laughs and redirects his attention to Hattie, asking, "How can she can remarry if she is already married to me, you dimwit? We have already announced our betrothal, alerting everyone." As Hattie opens her mouth to speak, he lifts his hand to silence her. "I'm not finished."

She clenches her jaw.

"How do you propose we explain that?" he says. As she begins to reply, he talks louder. "Or the brilliant notion of you remarrying so close to the deaths of your husbands, not to mention the disappearance of both sets of parents, which will eventually get out to the public. It adds an incomprehensible level of idiocy to your plan."

Hattie's lips tighten as she struggles to find words, and then she slides down in her seat, defeated.

"Just as I expected," Hugh says with a crazed laugh, his eyes darting around the table. "There is not a soul in front of me who will enter a marriage anytime soon."

Ettie tightly grips the armrests of her chair, trying to process the shocking revelation. "But … what about the supply?" she stammers, her voice trembling with concern.

"I suppose we will have to get creative." Hugh shrugs.

The unsettling idea of the creatures we will become without human flesh lingers in my mind. I ponder how much time each person at the table has left.

Adeline's fork slips from her hand, creating a loud noise as it collides with the corner of her plate. "The staff? What about them?" she asks, her words faltering as she struggles to express herself. "There are plenty of them to go around."

Hugh shakes his head. "No, we cannot afford to lose another. After last night, many have fled, and I'm sure more will leave after they discover how Genevieve indulged herself."

The mere sound of my name makes my heart race. I quickly interject, "I thought they could not speak."

Ettie rolls her eyes in response. "They obviously talk," she remarks sarcastically. "Why would you even consider such a ridiculous idea? Are you out of your mind?"

The feeling of a tiny bead of sweat descending from my hairline, tracing a path down to my cheek, captures the moment's intensity. "But … Hugh said—"

She speaks over me, interjecting. "They are forbidden from engaging in any conversation, whether with us or each other. The notion that they are incapable is completely absurd."

"It is indeed true that they have the ability. I have heard their whispers from the servants' quarters through the walls." Hattie chuckles.

Looking at Hugh in confusion, I hear Adeline's chair screeching against the floor. She shifts in her seat, stiffening her back, her eyes focused and serious. "Hugh is right. We cannot afford to draw any attention to ourselves," she says. "If anyone has any beneficial ideas, now is the time to share them."

Amid the tense silence, I hear murmuring voices from the kitchen. Closing my eyes, I try to make out what they are saying. Finally, I capture a single word. "Straws?" I ask.

Hattie looks at me, bewildered. "Straws?"

Adeline turns her gaze toward me and nods with approval. Turning to face the others, she rests her hands on her lap. "She is right; we could draw straws."

The atmosphere is dominated by fear.

Terror is evident in Ettie and Hattie's expressions.

"What do you mean by drawing straws?"

Adeline ignores my questions. "Thank God someone in this family has some common sense," she says, and, with a grin, she sets her napkin on the table. Grabbing a grape from the fruit display, she pops it into her mouth and chews. "It is settled. We will draw straws, and the one with the shortest will be the first to go."

The initial gasps give way to a cacophony of whispers.

"It will be our sacrifice for one another," she says with a resigned shrug, her eyes reflecting the gravity of the situation. "What other choice do we have? I blame our entire predicament on those mummies the doctor acquired for us to consume in the name of youth. Now, just look at us; we are dependent. Though I would not change my appearance, there is a price to pay to maintain our youthful beauty. It is both a blessing and a curse. You have seen the revolting creatures we become. All I know is that we must act swiftly and precisely, or else we will have sealed our fate."

As he settles into his seat, Hugh slides his chair back from the table, his gaze lingers on the meat tray. "I suppose that if we are conservative with our portions, it will provide us with the time we need for any scandals to blow over."

"Are you implying that the solution to our problem requires us killing one another? What is the point of that if we are all dead?" Ettie inquires, her expression filled with concern.

Hattie's eyes bulge in disbelief, almost popping from their sockets. "Is that truly your plan?" she asks, bewildered.

"Well, not all of us will perish," Hugh says as he looks at the fruit basket with a contemplative expression, then shrugs.

I fix my gaze on the flower arrangement, feeling a surge of emotions as the weight of the situation sinks in. My mind races as I try to make sense of everything. *"Not all of us will perish?" What does that even mean? Three, four, perhaps one survivor? Knowing this lot, the outcome seems grim indeed.*

Adeline's smile falters as she anxiously scans the others, stating, "I agree with Hugh. We must creatively navigate these difficult times until all is forgotten about our tragedies not to arouse suspicion. I am certain it won't take long."

As her words linger in everyone's minds, the room fills with a heavy silence. Everyone stares at different points on the table, their faces reflecting deep introspection. It is as if they are all lost in a maze of thought, wholly absorbed by their inner worlds and their own best interests.

Hugh breaks the tense silence with his low and steady voice. "So, it is settled. We will draw straws to keep it fair," he murmurs, his eyes searching mine.

As our gazes meet, I cannot help but gulp.

Twenty-Six

Run

The dining room is filled with the haunting resonance of Hugh's words, creating a tangible tension that mirrors the compression of air in a sealed tomb. An eerie stillness weighs heavily upon the eating place, intensifying even the slightest sound to a piercing clarity.

Each person remains absorbed in their thoughts, their eyes fixed on their plates as they struggle to come to terms with the unsettling truth.

As the morning light filters through the windows, casting a gentle glow over the breakfast table, one by one, they reluctantly return to their meals. The weight of the new reality is evident in the furrowed brows and contemplative silence that envelops us.

The gentle clinking of utensils against plates creates a soft reverberation, yet everyone is reluctant to disturb the peaceful atmosphere further with any form of debate or discussion. I am struck by the absence of opposing viewpoints or a sense of urgency. It is perplexing to witness how they readily appear willing to sacrifice one of their own.

Hugh exudes a disturbing calm as he surveys the dwindling selection of meats, grinning while choosing another slice.

As I watch him, I cut the melon on my plate into perfectly sized bites, hoping to distract myself from the overwhelming feeling of unease at the table.

Ettie tears a small piece from her pastry, lifts it to her tongue, and lets it dissolve without chewing.

While the gravity of the situation weighs heavily on me, I cannot let go of another revelation: Ettie's unsettling clarification: the staff can speak.

The eerie image of the chambermaid's disfigured lips flashes through my mind, sowing seeds of doubt about the reality of what I witnessed.

As the buttery flake melts on Ettie's tongue, I struggle to gather my thoughts. I fix a piercing gaze on the girls, questioning whether they are toying with me or if the statement holds validity.

Hattie, deeply absorbed in her contemplation, mirrors Ettie's every move with a sense of profound focus. As she plucks a tiny bite from her croissant, her mind seems consumed by a whirlwind of thoughts. With great care, she lifts the morsel to her tongue, savoring the fleeting taste as the flavors engulf her tastebuds.

Observing their interactions, my thoughts continue to be drawn back to the topic of the staff, and I find myself compulsively dishing up more food.

The sisters are seated across from each other at the table, their eyes never meeting, yet their movements are in perfect sync. When they both reach for their napkins, it's as if they are attuned to each other's slightest gestures, seamlessly timed.

I find myself brooding over how Hugh casually brushed aside the topic. It seemed deliberate as if he intentionally avoided addressing the issue clearly and concisely. While there may be more important things going on, I can't ignore my concern about how his lack of opinion influenced my actions.

Adeline's eyes flick anxiously between her plate and the meat tray. A burst of air fills her cheeks, and she releases an exasperated exhale. Her complexion pales as she sets her fork on the table. "It seems that my appetite has disappeared," she says.

Hugh blots his lips with his napkin. "I suppose such topics can be unsettling to the stomach," he remarks.

In an effort to regain my mental composure, I find solace in eating the fruit from my plate, using it as a distraction while admiring the stunning bouquet on the table.

Hugh places his napkin on the table and then turns his gaze toward me, a sly smirk forming on his lips. "Some of us remain completely unfazed," he remarks.

I chew rapidly, entirely unaware of my surroundings—Adeline winces at the sound of my teeth grinding. Ettie and Hattie turn toward me, their eyes widening with disgust.

As I savor the succulent sweetness of another bite of melon, Hugh's smirk gradually transforms into a wide grin.

I delicately tap the tines of my fork against my plate, searching for another delectable piece of fruit to savor. The sharp, rhythmic clinking resonates through the room, creating a sense of anticipation as I stab for the perfect bite.

He cringes. "It appears that Genevieve has finished," he remarks.

As the fork hovers just inches from my mouth, his deep voice interrupts my thoughts, pulling me back to the present moment. I sense the heaviness of everyone's gaze upon me. "I guess I am," I mumble as I nervously glance at the empty plate before me. Carefully, I set the fork down, filled with embarrassment.

"Capital!" Hugh exclaims, and clasping his hands together, he smiles. "All right,… Shall we adjourn to the drawing room?"

As a slight nod is exchanged, each person slowly pushes their chair back and rises from the table, indicating their compliance.

I come to a brief halt, carefully studying their movements and facial expressions, absorbing every detail.

Their eyes radiate doubt as they scrutinize each other's faces, searching for any sign of deception. With cautious precision, I rise from my seat, keenly aware of the stifling tension in the room. Their narrowed gazes expose their systematic approaches as they painstakingly devise their survival plan.

As Hugh approaches the exit, the gentle light from the hallway highlights the exquisite details of the green baroque pattern adorning his well-tailored jacket. With a flick of his wrist, he extends his hand to adjust the sleeve, ensuring that every subtle curve, seam, and detail aligns perfectly. I narrow my eyes, discerning the fabric he holds between his fingers. It did not strike me until now that, for the first time during my stay at the estate, our clothing does not complement each other.

He stands with a proud and imposing posture. "Let's get this over with," he says with a contemptuous sneer.

Ettie and Hattie exchange a nervous glance, swallowing hard as they gaze toward the door.

As Hugh steps into the hall, they rush to follow him. Adeline trails along with excitement.

At that moment, I stand completely still, my muscles tense with the effort of resisting any movement. I watch in silence as the crowd departs, the clicking of their footsteps imprinting themselves on my consciousness like the ticks of a doomsday clock.

As the women move, the opulent fabric of their gowns gracefully sways, creating a mesmerizing spectacle. It is akin to observing an elegant dance, with each ruffle flowing like a beautiful and poetic expression. Each of their stunning ensembles exudes an air of significance, perhaps symbolizing the conclusion of an era.

It may be the last statement they make in this world.

In the dimly lit hallway, Hugh raises his hand and snaps his fingers sharply. The sound echoes off the walls, commanding the attention of everyone around him, signaling for them to pick up their pace.

As their footsteps gradually disappear, I allow myself a moment of quiet reflection. I close my eyes with a deep breath and let the tranquility envelop me. "If only I could seek solace in my thoughts for the rest of my days. It would bring such simplicity to everything," I whisper.

An unexpected creak of the kitchen door, followed by footsteps, interrupts the serenity. I wince while stubbornly keeping my eyes fixed straight ahead, determined to savor the moment of peace. However, my ears detect a nuanced change in the waitstaff's presence that piques my curiosity.

The once-familiar sounds of clinking trays have been replaced with slow, raspy breaths, and the usual purposeful pace of footsteps has transformed into slow and dragging ones.

I take a step back away from the table. "My apologies," I murmur light-heartedly. "I can hear your approach. Allow me to make way for you to continue your duties."

The footsteps abruptly cease, casting an eerie stillness over the room.

I pause, straining to catch even the faintest sound. "Hello?" I call out, the word hanging in the air, filled with an uneasy anticipation for a reply.

The unsettling sound of gravelly breaths intensifies, filling the room and sending an icy chill down my spine.

My heart pounds.

"Genevieve," a voice says.

The barely discernible whisper slices through the harsh exhalations. I swiftly turn around, clutching my chest as I take a sharp intake of breath.

"Genevieve," it says much louder than before. The deep, booming tone reverberates through the room, causing the porcelain dishes on the table to rattle.

"I'm not afraid of you," I declare, bracing myself with feet firmly planted on the floor, ready to confront whatever may come my way.

The room is suddenly enveloped in a subtle glow, casting shadows beside me that dance and sway in the stillness.

A dark mist forms at the edge of my sight, gradually transforming into the distinct form of a tall, slender man, the details of his figure becoming clearer with each passing moment.

As I stare in silence, the air is heavy with a sense of foreboding, then a tentative wave of relief washes over me. *The silhouette is so familiar. Could it be?* I grit my teeth as I call out to the figure. "Phillip? Is that you? You know I ... I will emerge victorious from this ordeal. You will bear witness to it, brother. Our destinies shall not be intertwined, nor will our outcomes be the same. I will make sure of it!"

The face, still cloaked in shadows, features drawn-in cheeks and lips that curve into a gentle smile. Its presence brings with it melodic whispers emanating from every crevice and corner.

The eerie chorus inundates my ears, creating an unsettling pressure on my eardrums. I strain to focus and see the man's glowing eyes through the darkness. The moment I see their yellow color and peculiar shape, fear rushes over me as I realize I am wrong about the intruder's identity.

"Dear God ... you're not my brother." I stammer.

A sinister shift in energy fills the room, adding demonic laughter among the whispers. The figure edges a step forward while shaking its head in emphatically no.

I tightly coil my fingers into my palms, trying to suppress the tremors coursing through me. "If not him, then I must know who you are!" I say, my voice quivering with a blend of worry and determination.

At that exact moment, the multitude of voices stops, and the entity disappears.

Though the figure is no longer visible, its energy remains, enveloping everything in a thick cloud of gloom that shakes my resolve.

Panicked, my eyes dart toward the exit, preparing to take immediate flight. Just then, the sound of movement emanates from the kitchen door.

I nearly leaped from my skin as the waitstaff burst into the room, each carrying a gleaming golden tray high above their heads. The space was filled with the sound of their hurried footsteps as they scurried around, clearing the dishes. I stood stock-still amid their chaos, observing their every move.

The kitchen door flies open again, causing me to look, dreading that it could mean the return of the horrifying creature. I nervously scan the area, hoping that my fears are unfounded. To my relief, I discover it is merely a servant carrying a stack of table linens. My eyes stay there momentarily, captivated before the clattering silverware and clinking plates pull me back.

Suddenly, I hear Hugh's booming voice from the hallway. "Genevieve!" he calls.

I cringe. With my heart racing, I glance at the exit that leads to the corridor. "Coming!" I reply.

I gather my skirt and sprint from the room. The exquisite paintings on the walls blur, turning to mere smudges as I swiftly pass by. I quicken my pace, the sound of Hugh's heavy footfalls ahead guiding me through the darkness.

As I stride down the long corridor, the sight of the inviting open door of the drawing room beckons, encouraging me to hasten my steps.

Upon entering, I take a moment to steady my breath. With a loud slam, the door closes behind me, the sound bouncing off the walls of the cavernous room, escalating my anxiety.

A female servant with a stoic expression and rigid stance stands beside the large wooden doorway. Out of nowhere, a sudden snap of fingers startles her, prompting her to spin around and lock it.

"I am pleased that you have finally decided to join us," Hugh remarks.

I scan the room, tracing his voice until I see him. He lounges comfortably on an elegant loveseat, savoring a glass of champagne and the gentle heat from the crackling fire. His fingers trace the condensation-covered patterns adorning the gold chalice clasped in his hand.

I am captivated by the elaborate group of cocktail stirring sticks protruding from the rim, their golden accents shimmering in the light.

"How did you arrive here so swiftly?" I ask.

His features twist into a perplexed expression as he asks, "Could you elaborate on what you mean?"

Ettie and Hattie are engaged in lively conversation by the expansive window, their voices creating an energetic buzz in the air.

I step forward, my eyes immediately drawn to Adeline, seated in an elegant armchair across the room near the grand piano. As I approach, her posture stiffens in response to my footsteps. She turns to acknowledge my presence, and I can sense the heightened anticipation of what I might say.

Nervously, I clear my throat before addressing Hugh. "You called my name in the hall just now," I say, taking a deep breath.

Hugh leisurely raises his glass to his lips, taking a small sip. "I assure you, I have been sitting in this seat the entire time. I came straight here from the dining room and have not moved since," he asserts.

His condescending smile grabs my attention while the sound of the sisters whispering permeates the air, growing louder. It ignites a sense of discomfiture, as I cannot shake the feeling that they are discussing me.

"The others can vouch for my exact whereabouts," he says, raising his drink and swirling the liquid inside, creating a symphony of clinking sticks against the sides of his chalice.

Sensing the start of a disagreement draws the girls' attention. They turn simultaneously to observe, eagerly awaiting my reply.

I fidget nervously, shifting my weight from one foot to the other. "That is quite all right; confirmation is unnecessary," I say softly, avoiding eye contact as I glance down at the floor. I clench my jaw, the memory of the dining room flashing through my mind. "Perhaps it would be best to redirect our attention toward a more agreeable topic," I say, hoping to steer the conversation away from the uncomfortable subject.

Hugh smirks, a glint of anticipation in his eyes as he shifts forward in his seat. With a sense of satisfaction, he leisurely savors the last remnants of his drink, relishing each sip before placing his empty cup on the marble-top table.

His movements twist my intestines in knots.

With an air of mischief, he snatches the stirring sticks from his chalice and taps them against the side, filling the room with tink … tink…tink before returning them.

The women eagerly gravitate toward him, akin to a herd of cattle homing in on the sound of a feeding bell. They settle onto the chairs and sofas arranged in a graceful crescent around the hearth.

Hugh pats the cushion beside him and says, "Genevieve, please join me so I can explain the protocol for what is about to occur."

Seeing no other choice, I reluctantly approach him and take a seat.

His eyes sparkle with eagerness as he lifts the chalice toward my face. "Contained within this vessel lies the destiny of us all," he proclaims. He theatrically gestures toward the identically carved stirring sticks, each adorned with a tiny touch of color at its tip.

"To ensure fairness, a staff member has coated all but one stick in pristine white, while the exception glistens with a vibrant red," he explains. "Interestingly, the color matches perfectly with the shade of your elegant dress, Genevieve."

Ettie and Hattie bite their lips and clench their fists to keep themselves from bursting into laughter.

With unwavering composure, I ignore them, my eyes darting back and forth between the sticks and the shade of my dress.

Ettie lets out a hopeful giggle and exclaims, leaning closer to Hattie. "This could be a favorable sign for us, sister," she says. "I believe she shall be the first to go."

Hugh's intense gaze silences the room as he directs his attention toward me and explains, "As you might expect—the person who draws the stick with the red tip shall be the unfortunate soul whom we shall eat."

My gaze fixates on the cup that holds my fate. "I understand," I mumble.

His face lights up as he exclaims, "Excellent! Moments like these reaffirm my decision not to marry a woman with a small brain."

Hattie parts her lips to speak, but before she can utter a word, Hugh continues, "In the past, when selecting which spouse would go next, we used sticks of different lengths. Considering that our fates are at stake, I thought it wise to come up with a more reliable process. Therefore, I devised a foolproof method using painted tips instead. This was particularly inspired after *Hattie ... and... Ettie* passionately expressed their opinions following the last round of selections."

"Yes, brilliantly thought out, son," Adeline chimes in, stroking his ego with compliments. "I suspect there shall be no more quarrels."

Ettie and Hattie huff in annoyance and exaggeratedly roll their eyes.

Hugh's gaze shifts toward the group as he lifts the cup above his head and gently shakes it, softly rattling and mixing the metal sticks inside. "So, who would like to go first?"

"Why don't we begin with the oldest and then move on to the youngest?" Adeline suggests.

"Does anyone have any objections to the proposed idea?" Hugh scans the room, eyeing each person's reaction for signs of opposition.

All eyes turn in my direction, filled with anticipation, as they wait for me to break the silence.

I nervously avert my gaze, my mind racing about revealing my true age. The thought of being at a disadvantage compared to the twins in the upcoming drawing of straws weighs heavily on my mind. Even though it could help my odds, the risk of disclosing this information now feels daunting, as I fear being labeled a liar and triggering an automatic extermination. It is a delicate situation, and I must carefully strategize my next move.

The snapping flames highlight the room's silence.

"It is settled," Hugh announces as he extends the cup toward Adeline. "We'll begin with

Mother and then go down the line. Everyone, close your eyes as you draw a stick. When you pick one, shield it with your hand. This way, we can all reveal our results at once."

Adeline's gaze is captivated by the shimmering golden rim.

After confirming that everyone understands, Hugh smiles. "Excellent," he says. "You can draw yours now, Mother."

She takes a deep breath and closes her eyes. As she reaches out, her fingers brush against the cold metal tops until she finds one. With a delicate touch, she plucks it from its place and swiftly covers it in her fist, her heart racing with anticipation.

Without hesitation, Hugh mimics her, doing the same, and with his pick tucked away in his fist, he extends the cup toward the girls.

Ettie and Hattie exchange glances, their eyes locking for a moment before simultaneously closing them. With anticipation, they reach for the cup, their fingers brushing against the smooth surface as they each select a stick. As they withdraw their hands, a subtle smirk forms on their lips, and they cup their hands around the sticks, eagerly awaiting what fate has in store for them.

Hugh turns his gaze toward me. "I suppose, since only one stick remains, you don't have a choice. There's no need to close your eyes, my dearest," he says, extending the cup toward me with a glint in his eye.

My focus turns to the last remaining stick. "I suppose you are right." I nervously gulp, attempting to calm my angst by focusing on the snapping sounds from the flames.

As I carefully lift the stick from its place, Hugh commands, "All right, everyone, show your hand."

The room brims with gasps of mixed emotions.

My hand trembles as I fix my gaze upon the sharp ivory-colored point of the stirrer resting in my palm. I am overcome with disbelief as I reflect on my triumph over the odds. I close my lids, savoring the moment.

Hugh's voice, barely above a whisper, reaches my ear. "It seems we have both dodged peril, my dear."

I glance toward the white-tipped stick in his hand, my lips curling into a tentative smirk. "What are the odds?" I sigh.

He turns his attention from me to the others, his eyes scanning each face before he asks, "Out of all of you, who chose the stick of death?"

Ettie and Hattie, their faces beaming with relief, wrap their arms around each other, grateful to have escaped a carnivorous fate. As they hold each other tightly, they suddenly turn to face him. In perfect unison, they declare, "Not I."

I turn my attention to Adeline.

She sits in stunned silence, her eyes locked on the end of her stick. As a soft sniffle escapes her, her pupils dilate, and her complexion turns ashen.

With a chuckle, Hugh turns to his mother and remarks, "Ah, Mother, it seems you are the one who does not quite fit in. Everyone else is so cheerful, but I'm afraid you ... well, you are filled with gloom, and I am certain I know the reason."

Worriedly, she blurts out, "There must be a mistake." She desperately searches for her words while vigorously shaking her head. "As the matriarch of this household, I ... I demand a retrial."

Ettie and Hattie hold each other tightly as they look at their mother.

Hugh rises from his seat and utters, "I am afraid that would not be fair, Mother." He carefully places his stick back in the chalice and then extends it toward me with solemnity.

I quickly toss mine into the cup, hoping never to see it again.

Hugh strolls over to his sisters. "Rules are rules," he says, directing his attention toward them. "Wouldn't you agree, ladies?"

With apprehension, they slowly reach for the chalice, their hands trembling. Both take a deep breath while sensing the weight of their sticks, leaving their hands and tapping the bottom of the cup.

Hugh strides toward Adeline, his presence commanding as he stands in front of her. Tears well up in her eyes, blurring her vision as she frantically glances downward as if searching for something on the floor.

Hugh leers as he grips the thick stem of the cup. Slowly lowering himself, he squats and delicately lifts her chin, peering into her eyes. "Do you have any last words, Adeline?" he inquires.

Hyperventilating, she mumbles under her breath.

He chuckles, getting a thrill out of her struggle. "You must speak up if you expect us to hear you," he says. Glancing toward his sisters, he chuckles again.

Adeline's pupils dilate as they share delusional glances, reflecting a crazed expression. Then, in a single frenzied motion, she thrusts her hand forward, plunging her stirring stick deep into his jugular and giving it a twist for good luck.

His widening eyes reflect sheer panic as he struggles to draw breath, frantically clutching at his throat as blood pulsates from his torn artery. The chalice slips from his grasp, causing stirring sticks to scatter and clatter across the floor.

Ettie and Hattie grip the armrests, their bodies pushed against the soft cushions of their seats as they attempt to comprehend what is happening before them.

Hugh's body slumps to the ground.

Adeline smirks as she slowly crawls toward him, leaning close to his ear. "You should think twice before treating your mother that way," she whispers. "Ungrateful boy." Her words seethe with resentment.

Stunned, I reach for the chalice, rolling toward my feet, fetch the sticks and put them back inside. Returning to my seat, I fixate on the final stirring stick lodged into his neck. I analyze its position. She struck her blow with the precision of an assassin, perfectly hitting his artery. His eyes bulge as he lies on the ground, bleeding profusely and nearing death.

With a grunt, Adeline pulls the stick from his neck, raises it to her lips, and licks it clean. Ichor paints her teeth as she smiles. "Till death do us part," she murmurs, motioning for me to bring the chalice closer.

I extend my hand, and she tosses it inside. Her last words replay in my mind as I return the cup to my side.

Ettie and Hattie's expressions are of fear and panic, as though an uncontrollable surge of emotions overwhelms them. I am taken aback by the intensity of their reaction to Hugh's murder.

As Hattie weeps, looking at the lifeless body, she turns to Ettie and cries, "Father ... is he dead?"

"Yes, sister, he is dead," Ettie replies.

"Father?" I murmur under my breath, feeling confused.

Hattie lets out a high-pitched wail, causing Ettie's body to tense up as she feels the impact of the scream. In a surge of anger, she turns sharply toward Adeline and confronts her. "Mother, how could you?!"

Adeline's eyes blaze with intensity as she glares at them. "What other choice did I have? You saw the look in his eyes. He was going to kill me!"

A growing unease consumes me as I observe the life draining from the man's eyes and his blood staining the floor. The words of the chambermaid reverberate in my mind: *If that man is not Hugh ... then... there is far more to her words than she revealed.*

A chill runs down my spine. The sorrowful wails of the girl, crying out "Father, father," evoke a feeling that what I once believed was fading from existence.

Catatonic and unable to move, I sit collapsed in my seat, silently observing the spectacle of grief unfolding before me. Amid the somber atmosphere, I should feel shaken over the death of my husband or filled with rage at the news of my fictitious matrimony.

Instead, my mind remains apathetic about the situation, racing with only one troubling question: *If this is Mr. McKinley, then whose lifeless form lies in Mr. McKinley's bed?*

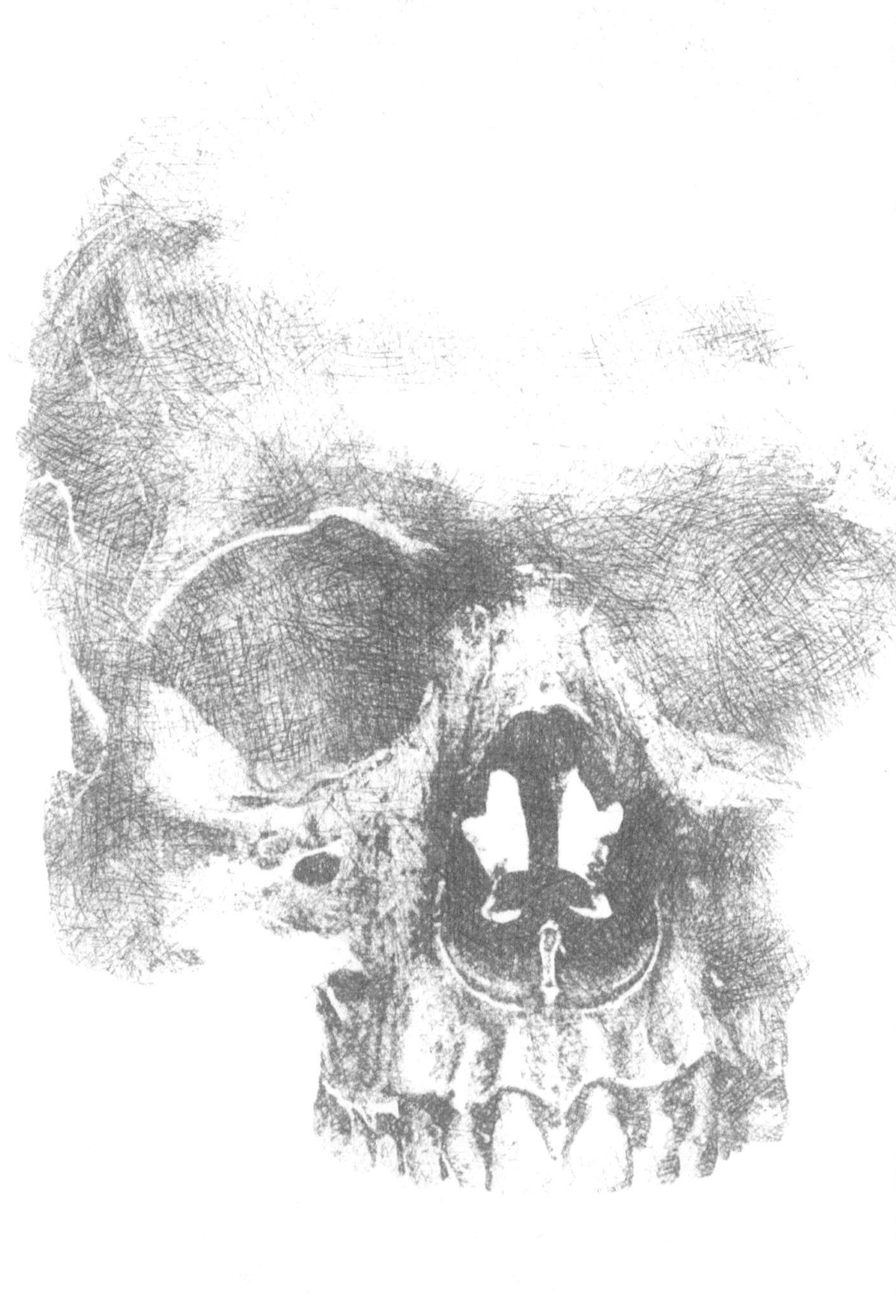

Twenty-Seven

Soft Whispers

Adeline's eyes glisten with a wash of budding tears as she takes one last lingering look into Hugh's lifeless eyes. Her once-sorrowful expression transforms into an unyielding mask of detachment and resolve. "I suppose we shall leave him for the staff," she declares, punctuating her words with a brisk snap of her fingers.

The servant standing by the door rushes to her. Adeline stands motionless, her eyes fixed on the floor.

"Kindly take him to the kitchen. The kitchen staff will provide the necessary assistance to care for him. They will know what to do," Adeline instructs.

The servant's eyes remain lowered as she nods in agreement, demonstrating her obedience.

Adeline's lip curls into a sneer as she lifts Hugh's hand and calmly releases it, watching it descend limply to the floor. "You may want to enlist some extra help … he will prove quite the weight to handle."

With a last nod, the maid hurriedly approaches the door. She swiftly unlocks it and exits without looking back.

I fix my gaze on the lifeless figure, taken aback by Adeline's lack of empathy.

Ettie wipes the tears from her cheeks, her voice quivering with emotion. "Mother, you cannot expect us to indulge in his remains," she says, glancing at her sister for reassurance.

Hattie gulps, her eyes wincing shut as her body shudders. "Ettie is right. You cannot, Mother. It would not be right," she adds.

Adeline listens to them pensively, her hand brushing phantom dust from her flowing skirt as she slowly rises. "What's done is done," she replies callously, her voice tinged with finality.

Gazing at her with wide eyes, their mouths agape, soft whimpers escaping their lips.

Adeline gestures for silence, raising her index finger. Then, surveying the room, she ensures everyone is paying attention. "Are you proposing that we waste this opportunity and allow ourselves to age prematurely? Let us not forget that he wholeheartedly endorsed this idea—with much enthusiasm, I might add—when he was upright and in an agreeable state."

Ettie and Hattie sniffle, exchanging glances before standing up from the couch. I rise from my seat, emulating their actions as I try to mask any hint of apprehension. Nervously, I interject, "Your mother is right. He was in complete agreement with the plan. If it weren't for him, the obligation would have fallen upon one of us. I genuinely question whether he would have extended the same level of consideration if our positions were reversed."

Ettie raises her nose haughtily while Hattie pointedly averts her gaze, feigning ignorance.

Adeline abruptly turns in my direction, a sly look on her face. "Listen to Genevieve, girls," she says. "She speaks the truth ... You could learn a lot from her."

They look at each other, exchanging smug smiles before responding in unison, "Yes, Mother."

Adeline gracefully pivots and makes her way toward the door with urgency. "I will see you all at dinner," she declares. Then, pausing under the doorframe, she looks back at us and firmly instructs, "Ensure that you are punctual!"

"Yes, Mother," Ettie and Hattie reluctantly respond.

Expressing my understanding and willingness to comply, I nod in agreement while softly saying, "Of course."

Adeline purposefully ignores their gazes and locks eyes with me, flashing a mischievous grin before turning and vanishing from sight.

They exchange disgusted looks before making their way toward the door.

Ettie shoves Hattie, determined to get through first. "You're blocking my path," she declares, and they find themselves stuck while attempting to squeeze through simultaneously with their hoop skirts.

"I think someone might have overeaten at breakfast," Hattie grumbles and shoves her back.

"Do not touch me!" Ettie's voice resonates with fury as she forcefully pushes back, causing herself to lose her balance. With a grunt, she tumbles into the hallway, her breath escaping in sporadic gasps.

"Oh, dear," Hattie chuckles as she lifts her skirt and steps over her. "You mustn't be so clumsy, sister," she says, tilting her nose upward as she heads down the corridor.

Ettie scowls and hastily picks herself up from the ground. "It was your fault!" she shouts and then angrily chases after her.

I pause for a moment and close my lids as the sounds of their bickering gradually recede.

Once again, I am alone. "Thank God," I whisper, soaking in the blissful solitude.

A chuckle breaks the silence.

I slowly open my eyes, trying to adjust to the scant light filtering between the curtains. As my vision becomes clearer, a sense of unease creeps over me. "Who is it? Who is there?" I call out, my voice unsteady with fear and frustration.

I scan the room, my heart pounding, searching every inch for any sign of an intruder trying to ruin my happiness.

There is no one in sight. I am alone.

I freeze in surprise as a sudden fit of laughter fills the room. The sound rumbles against the walls, creating an unnerving resonance. I reluctantly turn to follow the noise, and my eyes are led to the corpse sprawled on the floor.

Just the sight of it, motionless, surrounded by blood, and with its eyes wide open, is enough to make anyone feel unsettled.

I tremble as I take a tentative step closer, feeling the weight of his gaze upon me. "You lied to me," I mutter, the words heavy with contempt. "You lured me here with the false promise that I would be the mistress of this grand estate once you departed from this world." The bitterness of the betrayal ignites a fierce heat within me. "Now that you are gone, what do I find? Nothing. Adeline is the one who inherits it all, not me. Because, of all things, you were already her husband. I was deceived into believing in our marriage, only to discover that it was all a ploy for you and the despicable residents of this estate to consume my flesh to sustain your own. You have left me and abandoned me in this hellish place, trapped in your cruel and twisted drama."

My thoughts quickly flip from disdain to torment. I frantically scan the room, my eyes darting from corner to corner, searching for any sign of escape from this nightmarish existence. As I speak, my words pour out in a desperate rush. "I cannot go home; it would be a disgrace. If it were discovered that I married a man with an imaginary identity, my chances of ever finding happiness in another betrothal would cease to exist. I would be ruined…. My family name would be tarnished, and we would be the laughingstock of London."

The mocking laughter gradually subsides, replaced by hushed whispers of conversation.

I pivot to look back at Hugh and clench my fists. "Honestly, my death would have been more desirable than this life you left me with." Spitting with rage, my words hiss through my teeth. "The idea of eating flesh until my last days brings me little pleasure."

His fingers convulse, gradually contorting and curling inwards.

As I stare blankly into the distance, the thought of my life mirroring that of the creatures around me makes me wince. I continue talking faster. "In your absence, the depth of my misery surpasses any suffering I experienced in your company."

His hand clenches, pressing harder into the cushions of his palms.

I close my eyes and am enveloped by the cacophony of voices swirling the space, their intensity building like an approaching storm.

"Genevieve." Hugh's voice reverberates through the room, causing goosebumps to flood my skin. I stand frozen, focusing on the wall as if permanently rooted to the spot. "Behind you." He says.

The sound of his call strikes my eardrums like a knight's sword. "It is not possible," I murmur. "You cannot be here. I watched her steal the very essence from your eyes, leaving nothing but a lifeless shell."

His voice undergoes a dramatic transformation that is haunting and guttural.

I spin around to face him.

He is no longer sprawled on the floor; he has shifted his position, sitting up with his back firmly against the chair, his eyes fixed on me.

I gasp, unable to look away as I fixate on the deep puncture wound in his neck. My throat tightens as anxiety takes hold, and in that instant, the mummers fade into complete silence.

A subtle, almost imperceptible movement tugs at the corners of his lips, coaxing them into a grin. With a trembling sensation coursing through my body, I lean forward, carefully scanning him for any hint of breath. "Are you still in there?" I inquire with hope and apprehension.

His chin mechanically tilts upward, resembling the orchestrated movement of a marionette.

"May I ask you something?" As I nervously ask my question, I notice his head subtly nodding in response. I struggle to maintain a steady voice as I continue. "Why did you choose me? Was I simply an easy target? Or is it implying something about my weight?" With a hint of anxiety, I chuckle while pinching my waist. "I have never considered myself plump, but it makes sense that if you're putting in the effort, you would want to get the most out of it."

His lips slowly part, unveiling a trace of sentimentality. "Phillip…" he mutters.

The barely audible words pierce through me, stirring a profound emotional ache. Taken aback, my eyes widen in shock. "My ... brother? ... You must be mistaken. He would never do such a thing."

As he exerts energy to speak, the tear in his neck shifts, causing a surge of blood to spurt from his wound. "It was a ... trade," he mutters, his voice struggling to escape his lips.

"Trade?"

Struggling to maintain consciousness, he presses his hands against the floor and forces himself to straighten up, his chest heaving desperately to take in the air. "He traded your life ... to ensure his immortality."

My breath catches in my chest as my mind swirls from the horrible accusation to thoughts of my brother's well-being. *It cannot be. He would never do such a thing, but could madness lead him to such an act? Is he still clinging to life? Is he still among the living? Is he here in this God-forsaken place?* As I struggle to process the possibilities, the air is imbued with a heavy silence.

Hugh's head hangs with exhaustion, succumbing to the invisible pull of eternal sleep.

I throw myself onto the floor, my hands trembling with desperation as I crawl toward him, every movement a struggle for answers. I grab his jacket in both hands, my voice cracking as I shake him and scream, "Where is he?!"

His mouth tightens, his head slowly tilts to one side, and his eyes close gently.

Desperately, I shake him again and ask, "Where is Phillip? You must tell me!"

The sound of footsteps resounds through the hall.

I freeze, listening for their approach. I hear a faint jingle from Hugh's pocket as I release my grip. Curious, I reach inside, and my fingers close around a cold metal key. I carefully remove it and tuck it between my breasts. I turn toward the door, the key's significance weighing heavily on my mind.

Swiftly and purposefully, the maid enters the room, followed by two male servers she fetched from the kitchen.

The sight of her familiar face triggers my nerves. "Hello," I say, quickly rising to my feet. I move out of the way so they can take the body.

They look straight past me, reach down, and lift him from the floor. His lifeless limbs dangle, swaying with every step as they carry him out the door.

I make my way back to the fireplace, taking a seat in the very chair from which I had witnessed the horrific murder. I can't help but stare at the floor, now coated in a thick pool of blood, a chilling reminder of the family's bloodthirsty tendencies.

The gentle warmth of the flames dances across my body, creating a comforting sensation. Simultaneously, I notice the sudden increase in the temperature of the metal tucked in my cleavage, and I fumble as I retrieve it.

As I hold the skeleton key to the light, I ponder its intricate design and question,

What secrets do you hold?

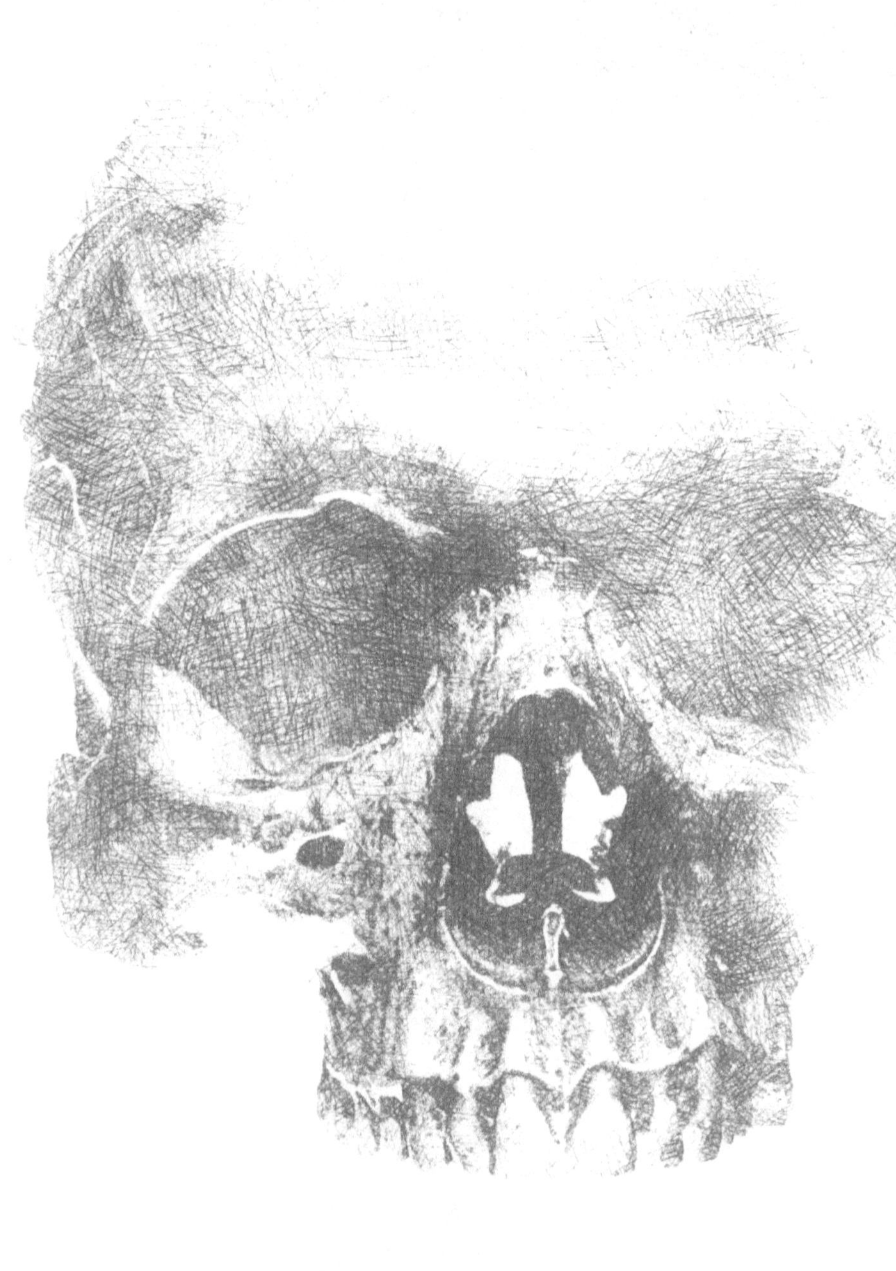

Twenty-Eight

Mummified Lies

As I examine the key's intricate baroque pattern, a sense of familiarity stirs me as if tugging at a long-forgotten memory. Intrigued, I lean in closer, studying the elaborate details, hoping to unravel the mystery of what it may be.

I sink deeper into the plush seat, feeling it yield to my weight and embrace me with its soft down filling as I tighten my grip on the key.

In that instant, it is as if a veil of forgetfulness is lifted as a flood of memories from my first evening at the once-enchanting McKinley Estate come rushing back to me, triggering epiphany after epiphany.

Everything about Hugh's erratic behavior suddenly makes sense. He was merely pretending all along, solely driven by his insatiable craving for his upcoming meal.

I was sure that Hugh kept the key to Mr. McKinley's room on him out of a sense of duty to his beloved father. However, upon my recent discovery of his character, I am certain there is a darker reason behind his actions. A sinister secret that he is desperate to conceal.

The uncontrollable urge to laugh grips me. "Foolish girl," I murmur. "You have been influenced by far too many romantic tales. It wasn't lust or love that engrossed him, nor was the weight of disappointing his father the reason for his hurried marriage. It was solely his turn to find the next participant for the family's sacrificial rotation that compelled him to act with such urgency."

As I rise from my seat, my eyes are drawn to the closed curtain. Through the break in its fabric, I steal a glimpse of the world outside the window.

The once-vibrant blue sky is now shrouded in dense, billowing clouds, casting a melancholy shade of gray over the world below. There is a majestic black bird, its wings outstretched, soaring gracefully through the boundless sky, heading toward the far-off horizon. As it passes, its haunting cry is softened by the barrier of the windowpane.

Lost in thought, I yearn for freedom as I gaze at the world beyond. In this fleeting moment, I long to soar like a bird. With a wry smile, I encourage it. "Set your spirit free and take flight. Soar high into the endless sky. It is the courageous souls who endure and thrive. Only the brave of heart survive," I murmur, a trace of admiration in my voice.

Without its distraction, I realize that precious seconds are slipping away; I wrap my fingers tightly around the key. A sudden surge of urgency courses through my veins, propelling me toward the door with unrelenting determination. With each step, my heart beats a thunderous rhythm, echoing my mounting excitement. Every passing moment carries the weight of anticipation as I eagerly contemplate the mysteries that await beyond the threshold.

The moment I enter the dimly lit hall, the floorboards groan under the pressure of my steps. I take a right turn, the clicking of my heels echoing through the corridor.

Despite lacking a clear direction, I am propelled forward by an unspoken intuition originating deep within my core. I press on, the arches of my feet throbbing with a dull, persistent ache, each step a reminder of the distance traveled. The seemingly endless landscape unfolds in a repetitive pattern, each turn revealing a scene indistinguishable from the last.

Surrounded by a serene stillness, I take a moment to close my eyes and tune in to the symphony of my thoughts. Amid the tranquil silence, I discern faint whispering voices calling me. Their echoes weave a tapestry of sound that leads me toward my journey's end.

"Right foot, left foot," they jeer, conducting my steps.

As I meticulously adhere to every directive, I head deeper into the unknown, driven by an unyielding curiosity. I am consumed by the question of who or what the enigmatic force leading me along this path is. It is a thought that permeates every fiber of my being, leaving me with an insatiable desire to unravel the mystery.

Abruptly, all falls silent, instantly snapping me from the hyper-focused state.

Tremors quiver through my body as I stand frozen, trying to anchor myself with controlled breaths. I close my eyes, seeking refuge from the crushing weight of reality that engulfs me, allowing the gravity of the situation to seep into my consciousness.

Amid the charged atmosphere, a solitary voice surges forth with overwhelming intensity, commanding attention with its profound force. "Left foot!" The voice shouts.

I lean forward to take a deep, calming breath and feel the sensation of someone's gaze fixed upon me. I slowly muster the bravery to crack open one lid.

Through the tiny slit, I see the figure of a man in the distance, his presence casting a foreboding shadow against the backdrop. With each authoritative "Left!" that leaves his lips, His torso undulates with a serpentine fluidity. The amber glow emanating from his eyes pierces into the depths of my soul, triggering an overwhelming sense of terror within me.

I clench my eyelids shut, afraid to look while remaining acutely attuned to every subtle sound that signals his presence.

Pressing forward with each unsteady step, I mindlessly heed his call, venturing through the dimly lit and narrow passage. The acrid odor of mildew assaults my nostrils, filling the surrounding air. Every breath brings a sharp cough as thick layers of dust settle in my lungs, leaving me gasping for air.

As the man's silhouette disappears, his voice shatters into a chaotic symphony of overlapping tones and pitches emanating from different directions, colliding in a disorienting cacophony. It is as though a multitude of voices are intertwining and scattering, creating a sense of urgency, like a swarm of beetles fleeing from a ravenous predator.

I stand still, taking a moment to clear my mind.

The air grows heavy with the putrid stench of decay. Reluctantly, I turn my attention to the source, and there it is—the looming, all-too-familiar door, its presence casting a foreboding shadow that seems to engulf everything around it.

I recoil, shifting my weight backward and clutching my chest. I feel the key in my hand—a stark reminder of what I came to accomplish.

I nervously glance at the portraits hanging on the walls as I stand in the dimly lit corridor. Each subject has an eerie mask created by the delicate tendrils of cobwebs casting their shadows. In the dimness, the portraits take on an unsettling, lifelike appearance. The haunting expressions on their faces are brought into sharp relief by the mysterious glow, and their gazes shift uncomfortably, appearing to track my every movement.

A sense of disbelief washes over me as my gaze falls on the image I once thought bore a striking resemblance to Hugh. It now seems like a cruel joke, and I cannot help but feel irritation at my naivety.

I swiftly move toward the door, inserting the key into the lock and turning it while monitoring the painting's mocking expression.

The unsettling click reverberates through the hall as the latch disengages with a distinct sound of metal against metal. It elicits a twisted pleasure in the subject, instigating its lips to curl into a devilish smile.

With anticipation building inside me, I carefully extend my hand toward the gleaming knob, letting my fingers curl around its icy, polished surface. I cautiously give it a twist.

With slow anticipation, I nudge the door ajar, only to be greeted by a stench even more overpowering than I remember. The disgusting odor engulfs my senses, causing a searing sensation in my throat and a sharp sting in my lungs. I gasp for air, my chest burning as I struggle for breath.

With all my might, I strain against the weight of the heavy door, my determination fueling an extra surge of adrenaline. The door slowly groans open, and I guardedly peer from the threshold into the darkness.

There is a profound silence in the room.

Out of nowhere, a piercing sound behind me causes me to nearly leap from my skin as angst courses through my veins.

"Genevieve," a high-pitched voice screeches.

I spin my gaze toward the source, my heart pounding in anticipation. The air suddenly turns chilly, causing goosebumps on my skin and every hair to stand on end. The slender, towering figure slides out of the portrait, gliding gracefully until it comes to a halt at the far end of the hallway.

I am paralyzed with fear, unable to move as I stare into the void at the silhouette with piercing yellow eyes. "You," I murmur, my heartbeat rattling in my chest. "It … it is you."

Its body contorts, and its eyes squint, creating space for a sardonic smile to emerge.

I pivot and charge into the chamber, the door slamming shut behind me with a mighty thud. I stand motionless, taking in the ominous symphony of ricochets that fill the room. A prolific, raspy, guttural laugh joins in, adding to the mayhem encircling me.

Then, as suddenly as it began, the room falls silent, as if the lightless void has swallowed the very sound.

Gasping for air, I hear only one thing—the thump, thump of my terrified heart. I close my eyes, feeling a drop of sweat trickle from my hairline down my cheek.

A rhythmic click-clack of heeled footsteps joins in from the hall, resonating like a syncopated musical beat against the wooden planks with perfect precision.

My gaze remains fixed on the abyss as I absorb every sound.

Searching for stability, I press my palms against the sturdy, weathered wood, feeling its rough texture beneath my fingertips. My eyes widen in desperation as I struggle to identify the approaching presence.

A torch in the hall casts a beam of light, creating a wavering shadow beneath the door, giving a glimpse of the figure lurking on the other side.

Suddenly, the air is filled with an eerie clatter of metal scraping against metal.

Unease twists my stomach as I quickly glance at the rusty lock. A sudden moment of realization strikes me with the force of lightning: the key to my freedom is no longer in my hands.

"No, no, no," I cry. Gripping the doorknob, I jostle it, frantic for it to open.

The delicate rustle of the sheets drawn taut against the bed produces a soft wisp.

I abruptly halt, gaze darting from the obstinate door to the bed.

The cotton friction intensifies, growing in abundance, accompanied by the haunting squeak of wood.

An overwhelming sense of panic washes over me, causing sweat to collect in the creases of my palms, making my fingers slippery. I pound on the exit, consumed by desperation. "I demand that you open this door! You must let me out of here!"

With each forceful blow, the door trembles, loosening the lock's hold on the key. As it comes free, the distinct clinking of it hitting the floor rings through the air.

I kneel, drawn by the sound. My heart pounds against my chest as I peer beneath the door, the moment's urgency making my breath come in uneven, shallow bursts.

The surface of the key reflects speckles of light, creating an enchanting allure.

Furrowing my brow in concentration, I slide my hand through the narrow opening, wiggling my fingers toward the prize.

I strain, stretching as far as I can, pushing my fingertips until they are merely the breadth of a thumb away from the object. "I am certain it is only a bit further."

While I attempt to grasp it, the splintered edge of a floorboard tears into my hand, eliciting a sudden, intense pain and peeling away the delicate top layer of skin.

As I feel the cool touch of the key against my fingertips, I press down on it and slowly drag it toward me. Scraping sounds resonate in the air as it glides across the floor.

A heavy silence ushers in a haunting, raspy moan from the darkest depths of the room. As the sound permeates the space, the rustle of covers suddenly ceases, leaving behind an unsettling stillness.

I pause, slowly shifting my gaze toward the bed. In the dimness, the outlines of the furniture blur into the shadows. The tension is palpable as I strain to listen, acutely aware of the surrounding hostility.

The stillness of the night envelopes everything, casting a profound silence that pervades every inch of the surroundings. I cannot hear a single rustle or whisper, as if the world is momentarily holding its breath. Knowing I must make a choice and understand the key's vital role in my escape, I refocus on retrieving it and pray that the room's occupant will hold off on their arrival until I finish.

As I apply increasing pressure with the tips of my fingers on the icy metal, a sharp, electric jolt of unbearable pain shoots up my arm. With a sudden surge of panic, I attempt to pull back my hand but encounter an unexpected resistance. I come to an abrupt halt, pressing my cheek against the floor, frantically trying to discern the source of the obstruction.

The soft glow from a nearby torch illuminates the fabric of a woman's dress.

My gaze nervously shifts from the delicate, ruffled lilac hem of the woman's skirt to the piercing, unbearable sensation of pain coursing through me.

The force of her sharp heel's point has embedded itself into the skin on the top of my hand, tearing through my flesh.

A rush of adrenaline surges through my body. I scream, glancing back at the color of her skirt. "Ettie?" I scream. "What are you doing? You … you are hurting me!"

Her joyous laughter slowly transforms into a loud and witch-like cackle as she exerts pressure with more of her body weight.

I wince as I try to pull my hand from her grip, feeling the skin tear further, revealing muscle. I wail for her to stop as I helplessly watch in horror as her skirt lifts slightly higher from her ankles. A bone-chilling sound escapes her lips as she grunts and presses her lilac buckled heel down harder.

I struggle to catch my breath, choking on my saliva. My skin turns red as the pressure crushes my bones, sending excruciating shockwaves through my entire being. "Stop it!" I scream, my voice strained with pain.

She hums a cheerful tune while keeping her foot firmly in place. "With each playful step, I listen to her weep, waiting for her to succumb to her pain so I can feast," she sings. With a labored heave, she shifts her weight and then squeals. "It is solely your flesh that can satisfy me. You have outstayed your welcome. Now, return the key. Your fate is determined, with no means to flee!"

"It does not have to be this way," I plead. My voice quivers as tears cascade down my cheeks, begging her to cease.

All at once, a deep and unsettling moan escapes her lips, filling the air with a disturbing sound. It is chased by a piercing howl as she releases her hemline from her grasp, and it falls to her shoes.

Crimson droplets trickle from above, trailing down her dress, leaving a dark, glistening puddle on the floor.

The door obstructs my view, letting me see only to the level of her calves. The sight of blood dripping down the bottom of her gown makes my skin turn clammy. "I beg you to stop…" I cry, feeling her dead weight shift onto my hand.

I speak rapidly, my words tumbling out in a torrent. "If we join forces, we could establish a better existence in this estate. Just imagine if we create our own rules without answering to anyone. We would oversee this household without yielding to other's whims regarding whether we live or die."

As I battle the pain, my breath becomes rapid, and I fight to stay conscious, my thoughts drifting in and out like a passing dream.

Suddenly, she screeches, "Your flesh I will eat … blood and meat!" Her voice modulates through various octaves, producing an unsettling, inhuman sound.

The moment her words reach my ears, my eyes widen in terror. I instinctively reach for my elbow, desperately trying with all my might to free my arm. As I pull, my limp hand slips free from beneath her foot, and as it makes its way to me, the skeleton key catches on my sliding fingers. My adrenaline surges as I hear its metal scraping against the floor all the way to me.

When she realizes what has occurred, she lets out a guttural howl; her body presses against the door as she frantically twists the handle, desperate to gain entry. "Let me in!" she screams, with the voice of a demonic beast.

Writhing in pain, I hold my mangled appendage. Blood gushes from my wounds as I try to maintain my grip on the key. Finally, my grasp gives way, and it tumbles to the ground.

I quickly snatch it from the floor with my uninjured hand, clutching it tightly as its metallic edges press into my palm. With anxious precision, I conceal the prized object within the safety of my bosom.

She hollers, her voice echoing through the air and abruptly becoming a piercing shriek as she realizes I have escaped.

Breathless and in pain, I clutch my throbbing hand, my eyes locked on the door. As she forcefully rams into the wood, a bewildering symphony of taunting whispers engulfs the room, spiraling and weaving through the air, incessantly disrupting my focus.

"I will get in," she says menacingly, "and when I do, I will devour you!" Her tormented words reverberate through the air as she claws and pounds her fists on the entry with increasing intensity.

I peer into the darkness, and my eyes are immediately drawn to the billowing curtains across the room. Still uncertain of what may be in the room with me, I stay close to the ground, cautiously approaching the large windows while scanning for a secure hiding place to shield myself from all that may lurk.

As I inch closer to the opulent velvet drapes, the relentless pounding abruptly ceases, plunging the room into an eerie and unsettling silence. The unfamiliar surroundings induce a wave of unease within me, triggering a flurry of disturbing thoughts about what my future may hold.

Despite the overwhelming uncertainty, I gather every ounce of strength to push forward.

Ettie's bloodcurdling scream pierces the air, shattering my resolve. Different from before, it is laced with terror.

With mounting angst, I snatch the velvet tie from the curtain and hastily bind it around my broken hand. Despite the excruciating pain, I force myself to concentrate on the commotion in the hall, straining to hear any snippets of what is taking place.

Ettie's voice quivers as she pleads, her arms thrashing about, hitting the base of the door in a frantic attempt to escape. "Please, don't do this to me. Let me go," she begs.

A haunting hymn emerges, its ancient, unintelligible words accentuated by her desperate screams.

My heart pounds in my chest as I frantically propel myself backward, my feet scrambling against the floor until I hit the wall behind me. I reach for the curtains and curl the heavy fabric around my shoulders and back. Wrapped in the comforting embrace of velvet, I cannot help but tighten my grip as the air fills with the sound of bones cracking and bloodcurdling screams.

I pause and listen, straining my ears to distinguish any sound amid the lingering whispers, but there is silence in the hall, not even a whimper.

Suddenly, a low, gravelly moan sends a vibration through the floor.

I peer through the darkness, attempting to discern the culprit, and faintly make out a mysterious figure on the bed.

My lips quiver as I struggle to part them, finding it difficult to form coherent words. "Who ... who are you?" I stammer.

Amid the all-encompassing darkness, the surrounding sounds shift, merging into a single word: "Genevieve."

The voice's breath lingers, causing my pupils to dilate with nervous anticipation of the next word.

"Genevieve," it says again.

In a sudden rush of panic, I pivot, gripping the curtain in my fists, and wince as the twisting motion triggers a sharp, shooting pain in my right hand.

As the curtain is raised from the window, I am dumbfounded by what I see. Instead of being bathed in sunlight, the sky is adorned with a rich crimson horizon as the setting sun completes its descent. *How can that be? How can what I am sure was no more than an hour become an entire day?*

The voice grows increasingly aggressive, repeatedly calling out my name: "Genevieve … Genevieve…Genevieve…". " Each word is accompanied by the earsplitting screech of metal grinding against metal.

I whirl around in terror. With the room now bathed in the ominous red hue of the sunset, there is just enough illumination to see. My focus abruptly shifts to the empty bed. The covers have been peeled back, partially hanging off the end, with the wooden bed posts catching their fall.

I gaze upon the deep indentation left behind on the disheveled sheets, a testament to the mummified body that had rested there.

My eyes dart anxiously as each small sound fuels my paranoia. I step backward, colliding with the icy window; its frigid condensation sends a shiver down my spine, making me struggle to capture a deep breath.

Twenty-Nine

Deadly Eyes

The pungent smell of decay overwhelms my senses.

My eyes dart from side to side in the eerily quiet room until a skittering noise, as if something large is dragging itself across the floor, shatters the silence.

Terrified, I conceal myself in the musty folds of the curtain, listening but too afraid to look.

Each scampering sound is accompanied by the delicate pattern of tapping fingers, evoking the image of a giant spider scuttling across the wooden surface.

I gulp nervously, my throat tightening with anxiety as I avert my gaze, unwilling to confront the source.

Suddenly, all movement ceases.

I peek out from behind the fabric, believing the intruder has left. But as I do, paralysis overcomes me, and my eyes widen in terror.

A mummified figure, wrapped in aged linen, lies sprawled on the dusty floor at the center of the room. Its bony fingers are frozen in a haunting pose, clawing at the worn wooden planks beneath them.

As I gaze upon its sunken eyes and hollow cheeks, the whispering voices return louder than before. The ethereal sound of each chant causes a subtle tremor in its shoulders as if infusing life into its crumbling limbs.

Monitoring the movement, a growing feeling of dread takes hold. I shift my attention to the door, ready to sprint, and notice a large pool of liquid seeping from the hallway beneath the entrance. The crimson glow of the sunset casts a glossy sheen, intensifying the vivid cherry-red hue of the puddle and making it unmistakable that it is blood.

Unease washes over me, churning my stomach to the point of nausea as I attempt to make sense of the situation. I am sure that my injuries alone could not have produced such a mess. As I stare at the gruesome sight before me, questions about Ettie's fate creep into my mind, wondering if her slaughter created the horrific scene.

Seeking solace, I retreat further behind the heavy velvet, hoping to gather my thoughts, but to no avail. With a harsh snap, the mummy's shoulder blades curve inward, sloping toward one another, and its ribs expand as its chest fills with air.

The distressing sounds seize my attention, and I slowly look.

As the crimson glow reflects off the pool of blood, it casts a pinkish hue, highlighting the fragile texture of his skin.

I experience a wave of lightheadedness as fear floods through me. My face gives me away as my jaw falls open, leaving my mouth agape.

There is a sense of familiarity about him I had not noticed before—a haunting resemblance to someone I know.

A sense of disgust creeps over me, causing my face to squeeze in horror as I realize with dread who it might be.

"Phillip? Is that you?" I immediately recall Hugh's words about my brother's bargain for immortality.

His mouth stretches open with a grimace, revealing a menacing display of teeth and blackened gums. He extends his sinewy limbs and cracks his neck.

I press myself further against the window while scrutinizing the undeniable familiarity of his facial contour beneath the bandages.

I shift my position, and the gentle friction between my corset and the glass produces a piercing screech that immediately catches his attention. He stops, and I hold my breath, frozen in place. His blackened tongue press-es against the roof of his mouth as he listens intently.

I struggle to allow the word to cross my lips. "Brother?" I stammer, carefully watching his reactions.

Paralyzing fear washes over me as I wit-ness his chest rise and fall. With each exhale, the overpowering odor of decay lingers in the air, permeating the surroundings with its sickening presence.

I lock my gaze on his face, meticulously examining every detail, hoping to find some sign or confirmation to debunk my suspicion, but to no avail.

His desiccated skin twitches erratically, contorting his lips into a tormented grin. With a slow, deliberate movement, his shoulders rise, and he flexes his fingers one knuckle at a time.

Staring at the crevasses where his eyes should be, I clear my throat, trying to find my words. "Is this the life you traded me for, Phillip?"

I find myself deeply disturbed by his condition. Memories of our carefree childhood flood me as I watch the bandage fluttering over his nose with every breath.

Uncertain of his next move, I reach into the warmth of my bosom. My fingers tremble as they contact the key nestled against my skin. I find comfort in its presence, knowing it offers me a way to escape.

He remains entirely still, staring silently in my direction.

Looking at him, I feel a surge of compassion pulling at my soul, and my voice trembles with emotion. "Phillip … what have they done to you?" I find it challenging to grasp the changes in him and why he would have chosen such a horrific life.

His head tilts ever so slightly as he instinctively tracks the sound of my voice.

I clear my throat and speak louder. "How did we become so distant? What caused this poison to seep into our bond?"

His mouth twitches ever so slightly as if a shiver is coursing through his body. As his lips curl, a hint of his gumline emerges, revealing the intricate dance of his emotions playing out across every tiny muscle in his face.

Taking a tentative step forward, I extend my hand, my fingers trembling with fear and empathy. Tears gather at the corners of my eyes as I gaze at him, unable to fathom his state. "I should have seen the signs. I should have recognized my flesh and blood on the first day of my arrival."

He wets his parched lips with his tongue, and A hiss leaps from the back of his throat as he prepares to speak. "Phillip is no more," he growls.

The unfamiliar tone makes me nervously study his face for any sign of reassurance, my gaze resting on his trembling lips.

"I consumed his heart and devoured his soul," he continues. "Though his carcass lives for eternity, he no longer inhabits it." His decaying visage, devoid of emotion, exudes a tangible air of malice and betrayal.

I keep my eye on him while glancing at the door from the corner of my eye. With great effort to conceal my intent, I reach for the key in my blouse, careful not to draw any notice. But my cautious approach is not enough; the moment the metal grazes my fingertips, he looks at me, hearing the jostle of my ruffled lace undergarment.

Swiftly, I take out the key and hide it in my palm. He rears his head, and a wild, loud howl escapes his lips.

I clench my fists, causing a sharp jolt of pain to shoot through my arm, a grim reminder of my fractured bones. Fighting my agony, I hold on to the small metal liberator for dear life.

The bandages hanging over his nostrils retract as he sniffs the air for my scent. While remaining stagnant, his mouth twists further into a demented grin.

I pause, watching his unmoving body. He is awaiting my next move. I know he will snatch me into his grip if I charge forward. He stands directly in the middle of the room, blocking my path.

I take a shallow breath, feeling the need to buy some time to think. I carefully shift my weight and step back, wincing at the unexpected creak of a floorboard beneath my foot.

With a sudden, erratic jerk, his body convulses as he contorts grotesquely, his mouth gaping wide open. A primal, bone-chilling wail tears through the air, striking fear into anyone within earshot.

Then, with a fierce and frantic motion, he hurls himself forward, exuding a terrifying and intense energy.

His body collides with the ground, narrowly missing me, while the sound of his chattering teeth biting at my legs fills the air.

The windowsill's rough edge scrapes against my back as I leap backward, prompting me to turn and look. At that moment, I glimpse the sun as it completes its descent, enveloping the landscape in a magnificent golden glow. The reddish-orange sphere dips below the horizon, casting everything into shadows and making it increasingly difficult to see.

Frantically, I scurry along the wall, desperately searching for a way out.

He rushes, crawling close behind me, following the sound of my steps while sniffing the air. The metallic grommets scrape against the rod as he searches the curtain that holds my scent, and his chilling, animalistic snarls fill the room.

My breath quickens as I desperately try to escape.

I shift my gaze toward the door, noticing how the distance to it seems more daunting than it did just moments ago.

As I realize that reaching the door and unlocking it in time is impossible, I step back further into the embrace of the heavy velvet curtains. I fix my eyes on the tousled sheets of the bed, the fabric appearing like a relief map made up of hills and valleys.

His guttural roar gains intensity as he tracks even the slightest sounds.

As I watch his thrashing fists, my adrenaline surges, and I slowly take off my shoes, clenching them in my left hand. Realizing that the door is not a safe option, I am left with only one alternative. Holding my breath, I shift my weight onto my tiptoes and navigate toward the bed.

I slide swiftly underneath the sheets, hoping to find a sanctuary where the ominous figure cannot smell or see me. Beneath the blankets, the darkness envelops me, and my heart thuds loudly in my chest. I pull the covers over my head, creating a snug cocoon around myself as I listen, attempting to quiet my shaking breath.

The abrupt cessation of the curtains' movement frightens me, and I hold my breath, trying to still the trembling that has overtaken my body.

His deliberate, ponderous footsteps reverberate through the bedroom, each growing louder than the last, conjuring up whispers that relentlessly assail my ears.

My chest constricts as I shut my eyes, helplessly waiting for his rotting fingers to peel back the covers.

His heavy footsteps echo through the room, stopping beside the bed with a single resounding thud.

I slowly crack open my eyes and catch sight of his shadowy figure through the sheer veil of the sheets.

He shifts his weight, each movement causing the floorboards to groan beneath his feet. As he crawls onto the mattress, it yields beneath him.

Every muscle in my body tenses as the fabric beside me shifts, creating a noticeable indentation. I am frozen in place, my gaze fixated on the ceiling, determined not to move a muscle. The feeling of his motionless body sends a tremor down my spine, and the vile odor emanating from him quickens my heart with fear.

My jaw clenches as I strain to hear the laborious slowing of his breath, each wheeze fading into a raspy rhythm. I cannot help but notice the repeated pattern, and I gaze up at the ceiling, my view obstructed by the semi-translucent material veiling my face.

I lie perfectly still for the remaining hours of the night, afraid to move, keeping a vigilant watch over his movement as he lies beside me.

Morning comes, and the air is pierced by the caw of a raven outside while the sunlight slowly filters through the sheets.

Unable to ignore his presence, I gather every ounce of courage to move. I delicately pull back the covers from my face and look toward the window.

A large, sleek black bird perches on a sturdy tree branch just outside the window, its piercing gaze fixed intently on something within.

I stare into its beady eyes, and it suddenly flaps its wings to convey a message. Shifting my body to get a better look, I feel a gentle movement beside me on the mattress and the weight of something pressing against my side.

Panicked, I kick the sheets away from my body, the image of the decaying mummy's face still fresh in my mind.

With every gasping breath, I feel my body gravitate closer toward the indentation on the mattress. At that moment, I glimpse tangled chestnut strands of hair, and my eyes widen in recognition. I pause, staring in horror at the lifeless body beside me.

Clumps of gore smudge the corpse's mangled face, making the woman's features nearly unrecognizable.

With a nervous gulp, I fix my gaze on the delicate lilac-stained lace of her dress. "Ettie?" I whisper, my hand trembling as I reach out gently to feel for her breathing.

Her eyes are open, staring at the ceiling. Her torn skin resembles that of a victim of a crazed slasher.

I shift my weight, moving closer to observe her purpling skin and lips. "What monster did this to you?" I quake, analyzing the severe bruises on her neck and torn clothes.

A vibrant blue bow, contrasting with the delicate lace, subtly emerges from a tangled and messy clump of hair.

"Hattie?" I murmur, my heart pounding as I gaze into her clouded, milky pupils. Feeling dampness under my palm, my eyes shift to the heavy pool of blood soaking the mattress underneath her body.

I swiftly propel myself away, my mind racing with confusion. I lift my trembling hand to my mouth, desperately trying to stifle the scream that threatens to escape.

The bird's cries grow more insistent, filling the surroundings and heightening the tension in the room.

With my breath quickening, I can vividly imagine the mummy's gnashing teeth, eager to feast on my flesh. I pull my knees to my chest and nervously scan the room, not wanting to be next.

There is no danger to be found—no soul is in sight. There is only the gentle glow of the sun's rays casting warmth across the interior, creating an eerie contrast of light and dark.

The vast emptiness of space feels even more unnerving than if my brother's presence were here to fill the void. I tremble involuntarily, my senses reeling as I attempt to reorient my-self within the unfamiliar, disorienting place.

The symphony of birdcalls comes to an abrupt halt as I cast a wary glance toward the blood trickling from the bed.

A pool of red liquid has spread across the floor, originating from the hallway and seeping under the door. Besides the gore, the scene's lack of vibrancy suggests that the space has been undisturbed for quite some time.

I stare at the scene before me, remember-ing the chaos from the previous night. I cringe, attempting to replay the details in my head. As my mind becomes clouded with delusions, I glance down at my bloodstained garments, a chilling reminder of the evening, and cautiously inch toward the edge of the bed. I fix my gaze on the bedpost before me, afraid it might vanish if I look away. I take a deep inhale to calm myself.

The unpleasant odor seems to intensify with each breath. As the horrific stench enters my nostrils, I am once again reminded of the scent of death and decay, and I cover my mouth, trying to filter the stench as my feet touch the floor.

The foul smell is more intense than I remember. It smells fresh, reminiscent of the zing of a recently deceased giant rat rather than the mustiness of an ancient mummy.

Reluctantly rising to my feet, I wrinkle my nose and balance my weak knees against the bed's frame. I silently stand in place, surveying the room. Despite not seeing the desiccated corpse, I feel an unsettling sensation deep within me. The haunting image of his eyeless face pervades my mind, making me shudder.

The room is so quiet it is unnerving.

I crouch to the floor and peer under the bed, scanning the shadowy underbelly for infiltrators. The neglected wooden floor is adorned with dust balls and wispy cobwebs.

Staring at the emptiness, I turn back to glimpse the pool of ichor; it appears to have gotten thicker with time.

The screams that filled the room gave me all the answers I needed to identify the owner of the slaughter's remnants. Ettie's horrific cries will forever plague me. Just the mere thought of them causes a rush of adrenaline to flood my veins.

The act of pushing myself up to a standing position is met with a wave of pain coursing through my right hand. Still feeling disoriented, a shudder runs through me as I recall the excruciating agony and the sickening sound of my bones breaking the night before.

Wanting to flee the place and the smell of rot, I hasten toward the door. No matter how hard I try to fight it, the sight of the gore obsessively draws my attention, and the muscles of my face twinge with excitement.

There is beauty in the way it paints the floor.

I reach for the metal key nestled in the warmth of my bosom. As I take hold of it, I glide my fingers along the beautifully crafted iron surface. The intricate scrollwork captivates me, and I cannot help but feel building anticipation as I approach the exit.

However, I also imagine the possibility of the terrifying creature that killed Ettie waiting on the other side with blood dripping from its menacing jaws.

I shake my head, trying to clear the haunting image from my mind while acknowledging the weight of the impending challenge ahead. "Whatever misery awaits, I must stay strong," I reassure myself, sealing my resolve. My breaths hasten, mirroring the rapid pace of my pounding heart.

The temperature suddenly plummets, and an ominous sensation fills the air.

I clench my jaw to prevent my teeth from chattering and glare at the door with hatred. "They may try to undermine my resolve but can never take away my resilience. It is an intrinsic part of me, a source of strength that cannot be eliminated by anyone but myself," I whisper.

I stand tall and determined, holding the skeleton key as I carefully insert it into the lock. While turning it, I extend my hand toward the knob, paying close attention to the clicking sound as the catch relinquishes its grip on my freedom.

As I stand on the verge of crossing the threshold, I find a faint glimmer of solace in the belief that, despite enduring relentless torment from this family, there is a limit to how much worse my situation can become. With this fragile comfort, I draw a steadying breath, allowing the moment's weight to settle upon me.

Then, with grim resolve, I prepare to confront whatever awaits me beyond the door.

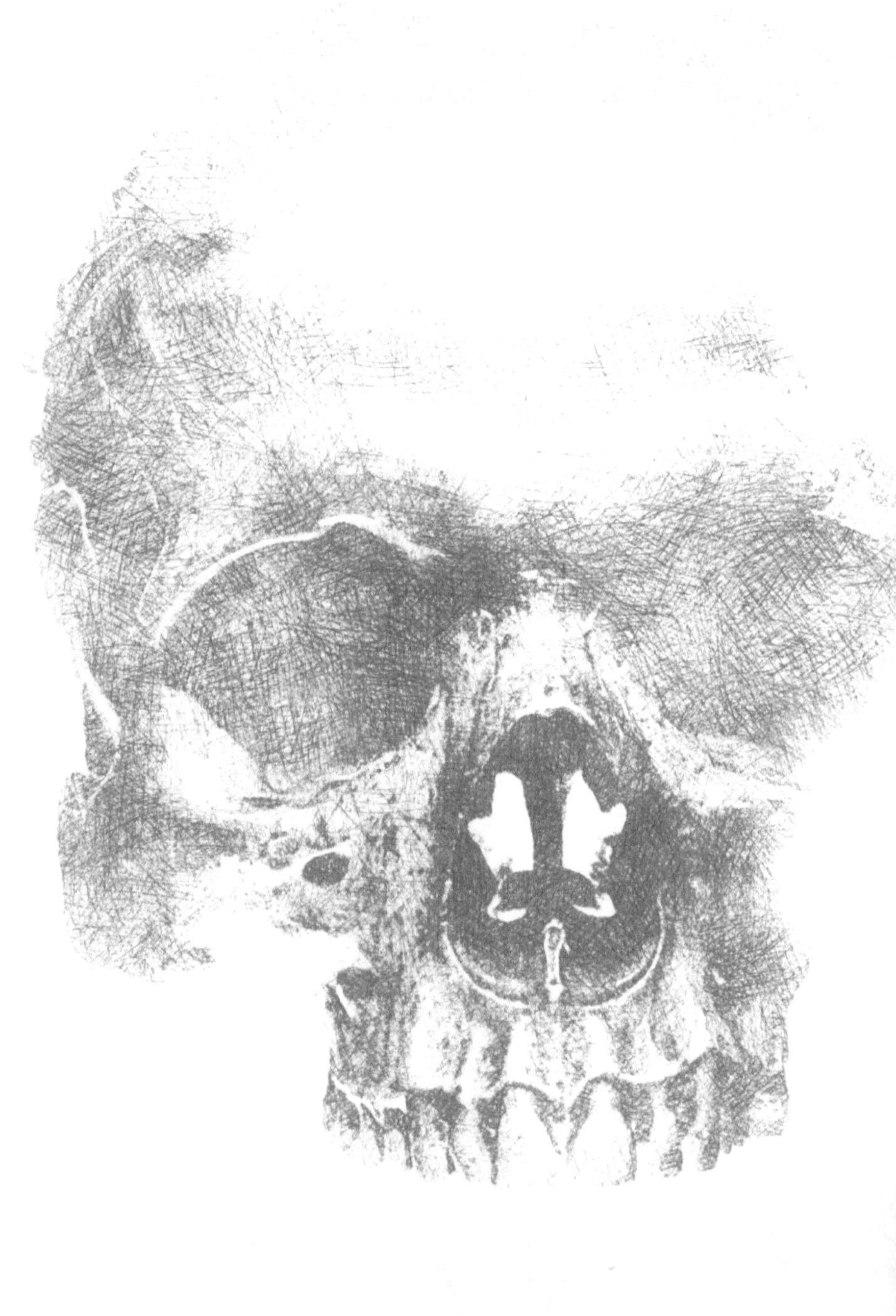

Thirty

Shattered Portraits

I tightly grip the door's cold metal handle, feeling its pitted texture against my palm. With a determined pull, I yank the door open, causing it to swing forcefully and crash into the wall.

The collision creates a jarring ring that batters my ears, further disorienting my mind. My lack of sleep and emergence from the poorly lit room makes my irises sensitive to the torchlight, and as I step through the door into the hall, I wince, covering my eyes.

Disregarding the state of my dress, I let it drag through the mess, leaving a trail of scarlet behind me.

As I look back through the entrance, a wave of whispers fills the room, each delicately calling out my name. "Genevieve."

In a frenzy, I grab the handle and slam the door shut, twisting the key to lock it with a comforting click. A heavy sigh escapes me as I exhale and slowly turn around. I press my back against the sizable door, seeking reassurance from its stability.

My eyes flit nervously around the corridor, meticulously scanning every nook and cranny for signs of peril. The portraits on the walls surrounding the room's entrance are saturated with deep, vibrant reds, which appear to have flowed from the paintings down the wall like streams of blood. The family crest, adorned with shields, is marred by a matching mix of splatters.

Despite the morbid nature of the scene, the rich red hues provide a stark and captivating contrast against the gold surfaces, creating a beautiful yet haunting display.

I move away from the comfort of the wood, the pool beneath my feet rippling as the thick liquid spreads with each step.

There are no corpses or body parts left behind, only puddles of gore, each telling a story of the struggle that has occurred. The gruesome surroundings compel me to hasten my steps.

As I observe the portraits from the corners of my eyes, their unsettling change halts me in my tracks.

Someone has added to the art, using blood as a medium, like finger paint, to etch a frown on every subject's face.

As I step closer, the exaggerated downturn of the lips catches my attention. The dried, hardened blood around the eyes creates a disturbing, shadowy look that brings to mind the empty voids of the mummy.

In the detailed portrayal of Mr. McKinley, he is dressed in a striking black outfit with a meticulously crafted formal coat adorned with a ridged, ruffled collar. His longer hair is slicked back, adding to his enigmatic presence. With one knee bent, his shined buckled shoe is perched on the stump of a tree; he exudes a sense of quiet power. A drawn sword rests in his hand, highlighting his readiness for battle.

The longer I stare at the painting, the more the hidden features of the subject become pronounced, almost as if they are calling out to me.

A taunting murmur emanates from the thick clusters of paint. I cringe, attempting to shield myself from the din, and as it intensifies in aggression, a surge of unease floods me. "Hateful man!" I shout, lunging toward the wall and wrenching the artwork from its nail. Gasping for breath, I hurl it to the ground, cringing at the jarring sound of the wooden frame splintering into countless pieces.

The fragments scatter across the floor. I scream, trying to catch my breath while glimpsing the jagged pieces of wood lying in the thick pool of blood near my feet. The candlelight reflecting off their crimson accents makes it easy to visualize them lodged into my flesh.

The suffocating surroundings overwhelm me, causing waves of agony to ripple through every fiber of my being. In a panic, I propel myself down the hallway, my frantic footsteps drowned out by the disquieting whispers that seem to emanate from the walls, casting doubt upon my tenuous grasp on reality.

"Genevieve, come this way ..." A chorus of voices echoes with every twist and turn, trying to sway my choices. "Turn right ... Turn left..." they cry. The haunting voices only compound my disorientation, each command adding to the confusion of the labyrinthine path.

I recoil in distress, my fingers reaching for my tangle of curls. With a pained expression, I attempt to control the chaos, my voice escalating into a plea for silence. "Hush! Silence!"

With each step I take, the sound of my heels clicking reverberates through the corridor. As I venture deeper into the hallway, the shadows grow thicker along the maze of walls, and my mind conjures illusions.

In the distance, a woman's ominous silhouette looms motionless. Her tall stature and billowing skirt create an aura of imposing mystery. Unsure if my eyes are playing tricks on me, I squint and concentrate, attempting to confirm the form's authenticity.

Her entire body stiffens as she assumes a rigid stance. With a cold and judgmental tone, she locks eyes with me and says, "Where have you been? You missed dinner." Her face twists into a scowl. "Mother is not pleased!"

I am nearly certain it is Ettie's voice, sending a shiver down my spine and making my eye nervously twitch.

But I must be sure.

As I move closer, my view becomes less hazy, and I recognize the delicate lavender adornments in her hair. A wave of unease washes over me, causing my stomach to drop and the pink to drain from my cheeks. "Ettie?" I ask.

With a callous tone, she responds, "Yes, dimwit. Who else would it be?"

I anxiously laugh.

She glances at my bandaged hand, then takes in my disheveled appearance. "What happened to you? Did you get into another scuffle with a maid?" She chuckles.

Consumed by paranoia, I find myself unable to tear my gaze away from the floor, my mind racing with fearful thoughts.

Her eyes narrow, watching me with a look of skepticism. "I advise that you quickly tidy yourself up before Mother catches you looking like that. If she suspects that you have murdered yet another member of the staff, her reaction will not be pleasant." She sneers, eyeing my blood-soaked dress. "She might even be angry enough to kill you."

My gaze shifts toward the trail of blood extending behind me. "It … it is not what you think… I…" I stammer.

Her perfectly arched brows shoot up in a dismissive expression. "Silence," she interjects, raising her hand. "Frankly, I couldn't care less, and I simply don't have the time to entertain your excuses," she declares.

She exudes a calculated and poised demeanor, her hand resting on the doorknob of the dining room door.

"Oh," I murmur.

She maintains a cunning smile, adding, "I must keep in Mother's good graces, so if you'll excuse me." With an air of smugness, she pushes open the door. "I would suggest you do the same."

As I stand there, the image of the blood in the hall creeps into my mind, and I tighten my jaw, unable to tear my eyes away from her. Her lavender dress sways with each stride, almost hypnotizing me as she glides through the entrance.

Abruptly, she stops and glances back at me with an expression of annoyance as the door slowly closes behind her, "Oh, and one more thing: if you come across Hattie, let her know I am still not speaking to her!"

Gravity seizes control and forcefully slams the heavy wooden door closed with a deep, resounding thud.

I stand frozen, my eyes locked on the dining room entrance, my ears alert to any sound behind me.

Nervously, I hurry toward the staircase; the memory of the woman's lavender-accented heel crushing my hand flashes vividly in my mind. *If it wasn't Ettie, then who?* The question gnaws at my thoughts as I rush up the steps, my heart pounding.

I dart past the large bay window and sprint up the remaining stairs to the hallway.

The air is filled with a cacophony of breathy chatter, creating a sense of unease that sweeps over me. I cannot resist shifting my gaze toward the portraits on the walls, their eyes tracking my every movement. I hasten my pace, trying to ignore the world around me as the sound of voices echoes louder in the corridor.

As I round the corner, the portraits of Ettie and Hattie enter my view. I come to an abrupt halt, a sense of unease creeping up my back as I scan the eerily realistic images.

In the paintings, they are shown from the waist up. Ettie is dressed in a white gown adorned with delicate lavender lace accents and ribbons, while Hattie wears a similar dress with charming sky-blue details. Both women are depicted holding parasols, shielding their fair, unblemished skin from the sun's rays. Their chestnut curls are meticulously styled.

I am captivated by the haunting beauty of each brushstroke and intricate detail in the portrait, but something feels amiss, prompting me to slow my approach.

Looking closer, I observe a thin film of blood coating Ettie's eyes. Her voice echoes in my mind, transporting me back to the encounter from last night. As I shift my gaze to her lips, a wave of panic washes over me.

Suddenly, fresh droplets of blood trickle from her gaze, glistening as the crimson hue flows down her cheeks and settles into the crevices of her lips, stretching her smile lines into a cynical frown.

I stand there, my breath caught in my throat. "No," I say. My eyes grow wide as I frantically turn toward my room.

A figure emerges from the end of the hallway, shrouded in darkness. "You have failed the test. You are next," it calls in a high, raspy tone.

Paralyzed with fear, I tremble while a multitude of whispered voices surround me, merging to create an eerie wail.

A sense of foreboding hangs in the air as the figure sways back and forth. It slowly extends its long, spindly fingers toward me, and its neck kinks to the side.

The temperature in the hallway plummets, flooding my skin with an icy chill and stinging my nostrils and lungs.

Abruptly, the mysterious figure defies the laws of gravity, slowly lifting from the ground. It looks down at me as it floats through the dimly lit hall, moving with a spectral grace.

I struggle to breathe, my chest tightening as I am lifted upward, pulled by an unseen force toward the ceiling. Fighting the act, my arms and legs thrash wildly. A sense of panic grips me as the voices grow louder, swirling around me like a cyclone.

My heart races as the shadow draws nearer, its nails dragging along the walls. Its chilling voice shrieks, "You are next!"

I desperately try to avert my gaze but cannot. Beads of sweat trickle down my forehead, and the veins in my neck pulsate, straining against my skin.

With deliberate slowness, the shadow raises its sinewy fingers and points toward my bedroom door. The voices, resonating in different dialects and tones, intensify, creating a mounting sense of foreboding.

As I slowly regain control over my mobility, I look toward the familiar sight of my bedroom. The previously bare space beside the door now features a beautifully framed portrait from the most special day of my life—my wedding day.

I am captured from the waist up, adorned in my wedding gown. The pristine white attire is accompanied by a delicate, sheer veil covering my deliberately scratched-out eyes. The unsettling alteration shatters any illusion of happiness from that day, emphasizing the truth of my nightmarish reality.

I stammer, looking at the bloody letters covering the canvas: *KILL.*

"K-kill..." I whisper, the word lodging uncomfortably in my throat.

The term is freshly written, and tiny droplets are still trailing from the block letters. As they settle at the corners of the wooden frame, they drip, pooling on the floor.

The voice shrieks, "In your stomach, I sit!"

With a sudden surge of adrenaline, every muscle in my body tenses as the invisible force releases its grip, causing me to plummet to the ground. Acting on instinct, I reach out with my hands to break the fall and instantly regret it as a sharp, unbearable pain surges through my arm.

Tears well in my eyes as I frantically crawl toward my room. "Please, leave me be," I beg, keeping my eyes low to avoid meeting the specter's gaze.

"You are next," it replies.

I try to block out the sound, my cries growing more intense as I ask, "Why are you tormenting me?"

The figure hovers above me, casting its shadow against my face, paralyzing me with fear.

"Leave me alone!" I cry out.

In response, a bloodcurdling scream pierces the air, and I shield my gaze as my wedding portrait flies off the wall, nearly hitting me as it crashes to the ground.

My eyes scan the floor, strewn with fractured wood, creating a treacherous minefield. The fear of a sharp edge grazing my skin lingers with every careful move I make.

Once clear of the debris, I tightly shut my eyes to gather my thoughts and calm my nerves. The unsettling voices slowly fade away. With caution, I open my eyes, and a wave of relief washes over me. The menacing shadow that was hovering above me has also disappeared.

I spot the ajar bedroom door and scramble to enter, my mind racing with questions and a creeping sense of unease.

Thirty-One

Ichor Smiles

The inviting crackle of the fireplace envelops the room as I step inside, wrapping me in its warmth. With a swift motion, I close the door behind me, the click of the latch providing comfort in the serene atmosphere.

I reach for the lock. The cool touch of the iron briefly steadies my trembling hands. Leaning against the door for a moment of quiet reflection, I place my hand on my chest, savoring the steady rhythm of my heartbeat—a tangible affirmation of the vitality within me.

The flames leap and sway, illuminating the surroundings with a mesmerizing spectacle of light and shadows. The enchanting display gradually intensifies, filling the space with a growing heat and making me sweat. It feels as though I have descended into the depths of hell, with the constant fear that the Devil himself will enter through the washroom door.

I take a deep breath to calm my nerves but quickly choke on the unmistakable smell of charred hair and burned flesh. I slowly shift my attention toward the fireplace.

At the edge of the flames, a skull rests, its scorched covering gone, allowing the fire to dance through its vacant eye sockets. The image of the chambermaid's hand jutting out from the logs remains vivid in my mind, and the memory of her desperate screams, pleading for someone to help her, pierces my thoughts.

Suddenly, a haunting memory resurfaces—one I had tried to bury deep within. It transports me back to a distressing moment from my childhood when I stumbled upon the remains of our cherished hunting dog amid the charred embers of our fireplace. The heart-wrenching discovery rattled me to the core.

When we were children, our mother gave us a lively, furry companion named Winston. She entrusted him to keep us company when we were without the presence of our care-givers. Our mother's disengagement during our formative years was intentional; she asserted it would contribute to developing us into re-spectable adults.

As time passed, the dog won the hearts of every member of the household. He was especially fond of me, and we formed a deep emotional connection.

Winston quickly became my most loyal companion and had a peculiar habit of refusing to sleep by any door but mine. He would emit a low growl whenever anyone, including Phillip, dared to approach. It was almost as if he possessed an uncanny ability to discern envy, making him particularly protective of his chosen spot.

I smirk, thinking of my brother's visible irritation as the dog consistently obeyed my commands, much to his chagrin.

I remember the event so clearly that it seemed to have happened only yesterday. Phillip, worn down by the dog's constant ill temper toward him, expressed his concerns to our mother about his misery. It was a bitterly cold winter day, and the wind howled, swirling small snow flurries through the trees.

To improve the situation, she suggested Phillip take my beloved Winston on a hunting expedition to search for pheasants. The idea of venturing into the wintry landscape and bonding with Winston while doing something they both enjoyed, seeking wildfowl, brought hope to the dreary situation.

Upon Phillip's return from their outing, I was overcome with despair when I discovered that poor Winston had not returned as well. It was as if he had been swallowed by the pristine white blanket of snow, vanishing into the vast and unforgiving landscape. My brother told me that his absence was attributed to his relentless pursuit of a large ebony-colored crow whose raucous caw had captivated his attention. According to him, the devilish creature had led him on a quest into the wintry unknown.

As the golden light of the setting sun poured through the front door, I refused to accept his absence and stood in the open entry, surrounded by a soft, knitted blanket. With each passing moment, I anxiously awaited Winston's return, knowing that if our roles were reversed, he would stand there for me just as I was for him.

Time passed slowly, and as evening fell, casting a somber hue over the estate, I wrapped the comforting woolen blanket tighter around my weary body, seeking respite from the day's exhaustion. Feeling hopeless, I found my way to the crackling fireplace in the drawing room. Its warm glow beckoned me to sit and contemplate.

Amid the dancing flames, a glint caught my eye, drawing my attention to an enigmatic piece of metal.

As I rubbed the sleep from my eyes, I leaned in closer, intent on unraveling the mystery of what it could be. I anxiously retrieved the fire poker and pulled the object from the flames. The surface was discolored and warped, making it difficult to recognize, but then, to my dismay, I caught sight of something I wished not to see - the word "Winston" engraved on its surface.

The revelation evoked a surge of emotions, making me feel sick to my stomach and causing my heart to sink into my chest. Memories of him flooded back as my body reacted with hyperventilation upon seeing further proof: the discolored buckle on his collar.

Following that day, everyone presumed he was forever lost in the snow. His name was never uttered again, and I discreetly retrieved his collar to conceal the secret.

I crafted a story in my mind, imagining that after wandering through the snow, he somehow found his way past us and sought warmth from the fire. However, in his haste, he accidentally got too close and tumbled inside with no one knowing.

In a remarkable epiphany, I realized that the chambermaid and Winston shared striking similarities, particularly in their quiet and unwavering loyalty. Our relationship resembled my bond with Winston; though brief, it held a rare and profound significance.

My mind briefly emerges from its reminiscence, and I am once again captivated by the fire. A soft sizzling echoes from the flames, entrancing me, sounding like a devil's whisper as if it is trying to speak through the fire.

Drifting in and out of the now and then, I sit in the middle of the floor, engulfed by the comfort of the memories as they seep from my bones and envelop me in a cocoon of nostalgia.

Suddenly, a sharp, piercing sound shakes the air around me, startling me and nearly making me jump out of my skin.

Through the burnt orange glimmer, haunting words emerge. "You devoured me."

I recoil, wrapping my arms around my knees. "I did nothing of the sort!" I sneer, fixing a fierce gaze on the hearth. My words roll from my tongue with a sharp edge.

The flames grow taller with fury. "You consumed my flesh!" The scream creates a heavy wave of smoke that floods the room.

Howling wind slices through the air, and I desperately shield my eyes.

With each hiss, a savory aroma fills the bed chamber, accompanied by the lively banter of voices emerging from every corner, overwhelming any remnants of stillness that may have sought refuge in the shadows.

I grit my teeth, my jaw tightening as I spit, "Watch your tongue." My voice cuts through the surrounding din. As my feet thrash about, I struggle to take a breath, the toxic fumes of soot filling my lungs.

The eerie voices chant in unison, "Kill, kill, kill." Their sinister tone casts a dark shadow over the fire.

I squeeze my eyes closed, struggling to form coherent words amid the mayhem. "No…" I say. It is the only word I manage to release through a series of violent coughs and labored breaths.

The fireplace emits another billowing surge of charcoal-filled air, covering the nearby space in a fine layer of soot.

As I roll over, I feel the heaviness of suffocation bearing down on my chest, making it difficult to breathe. With a wheezing gasp, I push my hands against the floor, clawing to escape, desperate for relief.

Amid my affliction, a faint echo of a dog's distant bark reaches my ears, triggering a cascade of swirling thoughts within my mind.

The sound intensifies, becoming deafening, and I fervently hope it ends. My fingers curl into tight fists, my nails cutting into my palms as I feel the fur of Winston's neck within my grip and his jugular collapsing beneath my fingertips.

The faint glimmer of hope emanating from the dog's heartfelt whines gradually transforms into increasingly urgent and piercing squeals of desperation as I squeeze with all my might.

Then, with a final crushing grip … there is silence.

An uncontrolled screeching wail erupts from my mouth, causing panic to course through my veins as I realize what I have done. Tears cascade down my cheeks, leaving streaks of charred mud in their wake.

I curl into a tight ball as a relentless hacking fit overwhelms me. Each cough robs me of precious breath, and my eyes bulge from their sockets, straining under the pressure. Desperate to escape the voices, I scream as best as I can. "Silence!"

The voices scatter, taking the smoke with them and creating an unsettling stillness.

My body lies amid the tranquility, trembling from the ordeal. I take a slow, deliberate inhalation and find relief in the ability to breathe freely again. I focus my attention on the only sound in the room—the gentle, rhythmic fire popping.

Shaken and disoriented, I hesitantly look around.

The remnants of the chambermaid are gone.

"Good … riddance," I stammer. "There's simply no need for you anymore."

Slowly, I regain my composure and rise to my feet. The weight of urgency is bearing on me as I focus on the washroom. "I must make haste … They are expecting me."

With determination, I push myself to take a step. An unsettling feeling of being watched grips me, causing me to steal a glance from the corner of my eye.

A majestic raven sits perched just outside the window, its sharp gaze following my every move.

"Oh, not now," I mutter. "I do not have time for you." Then, with a determined stride, I continue, shaking my head to dismiss the intrusion.

It hops closer on the branch, delicately tapping the glass with its feet.

I stop and reluctantly turn to confront it. "What is it? What do you want?" I ask.

Delicate whispers float through the air in response, weaving in and out of the crackling fire, creating a tingling sensation that sends goosebumps rippling down my limbs.

With a gentle fluttering of its wings, the bird taps again, this time with its beak.

A sense of unease takes hold of me, and I try to brush it off with a quip. "If you have nothing to say, I must be on my way."

Just as I turn around, a hideous groan reaches my ears. "Killer," it says.

Fueled by antagonism, I clench my fists, but as I notice the absence of pain in my right hand, I abruptly halt. Taken aback, I gaze at my wounds. The impromptu velvet brace has vanished, along with my torn flesh and broken bones.

Suddenly, a powerful gust of wind forces the window open, allowing a blast of icy air to fill the room. Amid the chill, the sleek black raven glides into the space, its dark feathers contrasting sharply against the light.

The fireplace pops and sputters as the wind stirs its ashes. Startled by the noise, I twist around, and my eyes meet the bird sitting on the mantel of the fireplace, its piercing gaze looking back at me.

I hurry toward the intruder, flailing my hands to shoo it away. "Shoo … shoo… back outside!" I shout. Across the room, I glimpse the vanity mirror.

The ebony bird lets out a raucous and piercing squawk, but the creature fades from my mind as I approach my reflection. Dark circles form a stark contrast around my tired eyes and mouth, mirroring the weariness I feel inside. I hesitate, my voice wavering as I reach up to touch my skin, feeling the desperation welling up inside me.

An overcast of darkness washes over the room.

I swallow nervously, knowing that consuming something would be the only way to dispel the unsettling attributes. "Yes, a good meal should vanish those pesky things," I mutter.

The creature tilts its head, and the clacking of its beak echoes in the air.

I turn to face the bird, forcing a smile to hide my inner turmoil. My eyes become wide with excitement. "Come here, my little songbird," I call as I anxiously wring my hands.

The bird repeatedly squawks, "Killer ... killer... killer." Its wings flap furiously as it adjusts its grip on the fireplace.

I cringe, wanting it to stop.

With each squawk, the bird's voice grows louder, filling the air with an unsettling sound.

As I rush forward, the bird lifts its wings and begins to flap them. Without hesitation, I reach out and seize its body. I quickly slide my hands up to its neck, my fingers closing in a firm grip.

The creature fights for its life, its cries growing fainter, silenced by my tightening grasp that squeezes the breath out of its tiny lungs. Its head falls to the side, and its body goes limp.

I stand holding the dead creature, its dull, unblinking eyes reflecting a ghostly sheen in the dim light. "Sweet dreams," I whisper.

Slowly, I crouch down, plucking the feathers from its body. As I do, my eyes widen with anticipation—a thin line of saliva forms at the corner of my lips.

Then, with a feral snarl, I feast on its warm flesh, savoring its taste while gnawing on its skin and bones. Shifting my eyes toward the window, I glimpse the vanity, and a chilling reflection stares back, revealing the person I have become.

My heart races in response to the sight of blood dripping from my lips to my chin. I avert my gaze, unable to bear the sight of the delicate bird's mutilated form in my grasp. "You … you are a monster," I whisper, the weight of the words causing me to wince. "You cannot hide from what you have become," I say. With my voice barely audible, I reluctantly turn to get a closer glimpse of my reflection.

With each hesitant step, I approach the mirror, my conflicting emotions churning inside me reflected on my skin. As I look deeply into my eyes, a haunting sadness lingers that refuses to dissipate, no matter how intently I stare.

I scrutinize the persistent dark circles and prominent veins around my gaze. "Damn it, Genevieve," I growl, pounding my fists against the vanity counter. "Human flesh ... human, not fowl. Only human meat is the cure for such things."

I fling the chair out of the way, then walk to the hearth and toss the bird inside. Then, rushing to close the window, I secure the latch and make my way to the washroom.

I reach for a soft washcloth from the shelf and clean the sticky crimson residue from my mouth; the metallic tang lingers on my tongue.

Suddenly, my senses heighten as a peculiar, almost otherworldly noise echoes in the enclosed space. The room is filled with a woman's laughter bouncing off the polished marble floor.

My muscles tighten as fear takes hold, causing the washcloth to slip from my trembling hand and land near my feet.

In a quivering voice, I muster the courage to whisper, "Who is there?"

Every giggle resonates off the walls within the unsettling stillness, taunting me, weaving an intricate tapestry of erratic sounds. The tone carries a hint of Hattie's voice, unsettling my mind and leaving me with a sickening feeling.

I pivot slowly, my heart pounding and my eyes flitting nervously about. The delicate floral print on the walls seems to mock my unease, each petal and vine a silent observer of my escalating anxiety.

Just the thought of Hattie sends a wave of anxiety crashing over me, bringing back memories that make my skin crawl.

My hands shake, and I grip the sides of my skirt to steady them. Summoning every ounce of courage, I clear my throat and shout, "I demand to know!"

The laughter abruptly disappears.

I pivot around in a sharp, disorienting circle, my mind filled with uncertainty. The dim light catches the forgotten washcloth on the floor as I narrowly avoid slipping on it.

I lean in, pressing my ear against the wall, my senses heightened as I strain to detect even the faintest sound. The world around me is unnervingly silent; not even a leaf's rustle or bird's chirping breaks the stillness. As the minutes tick by, the looming prospect of dinner hangs over me like an oppressive burden, intensifying my discomfort.

Grunting in frustration, I make my way out of the washroom. "I do not have time for this nonsense," I say, seeing the vanity mirror; I hurriedly approach it, eager to assess my appearance.

Getting closer, I glimpse the puffed stool lying on its side across the room; I sneer. "I have no time for you either…. I'm running late." My legs shake as I crouch down to better view myself in the mirror.

Although the bloody mess is gone, the dreadful dark circles and spider veins still linger.

Even with the other blemishes, my skin is oddly supple, illuminated by a gentle smile. "This is something we can work with."

I reach for the powder purposefully, carefully blending it into my skin to create a flawless canvas. Next, I apply rouge to my cheeks, adding a touch of warmth and radiance to my complexion.

Opening the vanity drawer, I search for hairpins and pin down my unruly locks. As I fasten the last strand in place, I declare, "There. That will do."

A sharp ache shoots through my legs as I rise to my feet. Glancing down, I notice I am still wearing the same outfit. I look toward the door, expecting someone to arrive with a fresh gown at any moment. But no one comes, and not having a wardrobe full of clothes at my fingertips only increases my impatience.

Suddenly, my eyes land on an ancient trunk at the foot of my bed. With a surge of urgency, I approach and eagerly open it to find out its contents.

A stack of exquisite dresses is neatly arranged inside, displaying a beautiful array of vibrant colors and intricate lace combinations. Each evokes a sense of joy with its delightful hues. As I gaze down, I am especially drawn to a beautiful jade-green satin gown. Its elegant draping captivates my attention.

"It seems you are the one."

With a grimace, I grapple with the task of removing my multiple layers of clothing alone. Despite the struggle, I remain determined, un-hooking the last button and allowing my stained red dress to descend to the floor.

Retrieving the fresh gown, I savor the sen-sation of the luxurious fabric as I slip it over my head and onto my skin, embracing the new-found comfort and cleanliness it brings. After securing the garment's last button, I gaze to-ward my feet. The hem, which is longer than what I am used to, gracefully sweeps the floor, skillfully hiding the slip stained with scarlet and mismatched shoes.

A smile creeps onto my face as I admire how seamlessly everything falls into place. I adjust the intricate lace overlay adorning my chest, lift my skirt to avoid potential tripping hazards, and hasten my steps toward the exit.

I warily push the door open and peek into the dimly lit hall. My gaze is drawn to a portrait hanging on the wall—a frozen moment from my wedding day. I cannot help but cringe at the sight of it, meticulously preserved in its pristine state, a stark contrast to the tumultuous emotions swirling inside me. The painting is impeccable. Even the frame exudes a lustrous sheen. Every trace of gore-laden defacement has vanished.

I feel a knot rise in my throat as I stand facing it.

A gentle draft meanders through the hallway, its faint whispers tickling my ears. As the frigid chill brushes against my skin, I quicken my steps and continue down the corridor, ready to join the family for dinner.

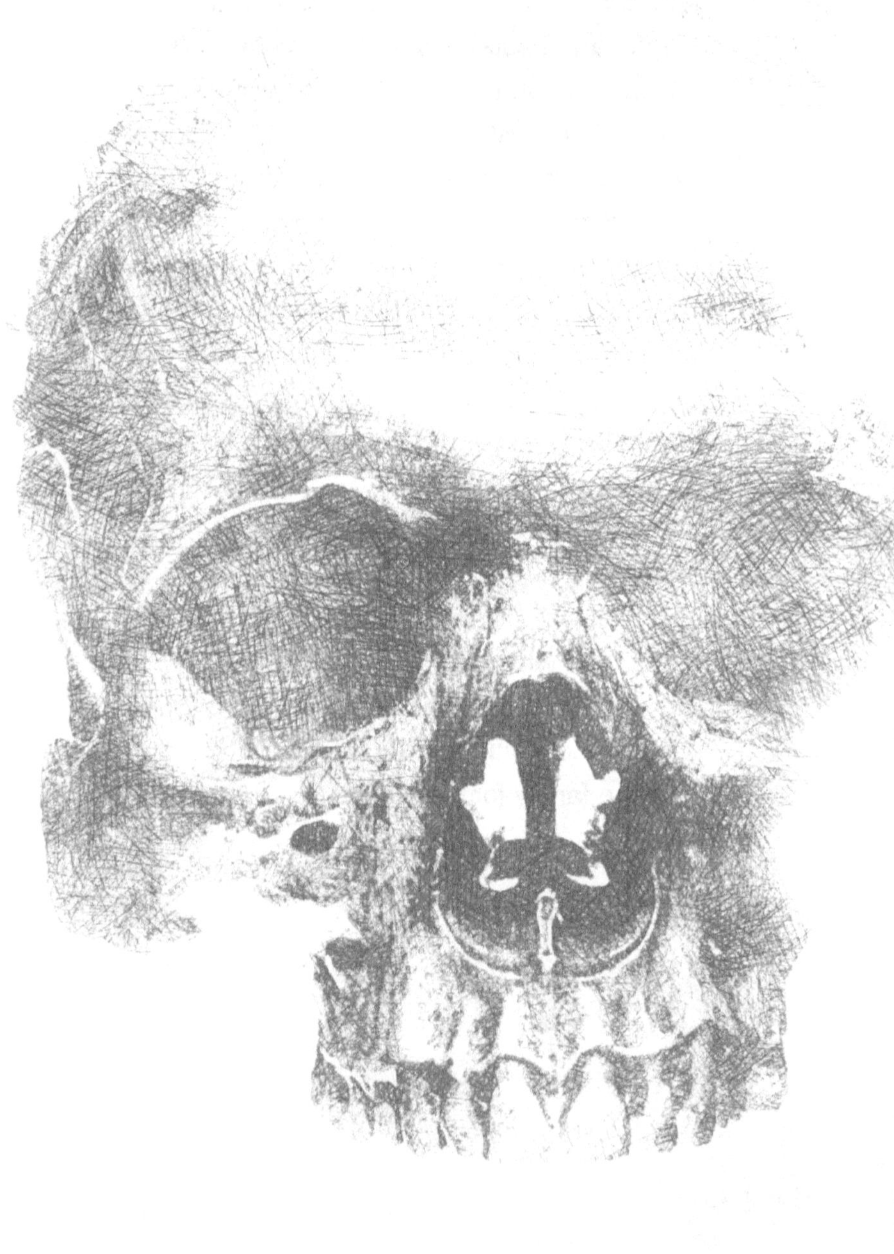

Thirty-Two

Dinner Plates

The unsettling feeling of being watched intensifies, urging me to quicken my pace. The click of each step resonates around me. I am consumed by the overwhelming desire to escape the suffocating grasp of paranoia as I tentatively approach the imposing entrance to the dining room.

I can hear Adeline's voice from inside, and I summon all the power in my muscles and the focus of my mind. The silverware makes clinking sounds, and the opulent hall is filled with animated chatter, creating a lively symphony in the air.

I muster all my strength, exerting force against the massive wooden door until it finally gives way, emitting a slow creak as it swings open. I cautiously step inside, bracing myself for the unknown.

The door slams shut behind me with a loud bang, followed by profound silence.

I find myself frozen in place, mesmerized by the exquisitely crafted banquet table that dominates the center of the room.

The jade-colored satin table runner is adorned with an array of brightly colored flower petals, adding a burst of vibrant hues. In the middle, a shimmering silver center-piece is crafted from an abundance of lush foliage and blossoms.

I steal a quick, nervous glance at the assorted colors filling the room and realize that my outfit unwittingly harmonizes with the dinner's color palette. It is as if the table runner has been fashioned from the same fabric as my gown.

Adeline's chair emits an ear-piercing screech as she quickly pushes herself away from the table. "I told you she would come down for dinner," she says.

Her high-pitched tone abruptly yanks me from my deep contemplation. As I turn my attention to her, I cannot help but notice something peculiar about her eyes. The pupils are strangely dilated, resembling bottomless craters. Her countenance brightens gradually, revealing a knowing smile. "I had a feeling you would join us," she says. "But did anyone believe me? No!"

With palpable excitement, she sneers and pats the table before turning to Ettie, seated across from her. "Didn't I tell you she would return?" she asks with conviction.

I am left in bewilderment as I gaze at her and slowly shift my attention to the meticulously arranged place settings.

The table has been arranged unconventionally, with only four place settings in our originally designated spots, resulting in an uneven distribution because half the group is missing. Each elegant stack of porcelain is topped with a vibrant fern, adding a natural and elegant touch.

Ettie's lips are tightly pressed together, her eyes shooting daggers, and her arms firmly crossed. "Yes, Mother, you did," she says.

I turn to look at her, perplexed by her hostile demeanor.

What could have happened?

Then, almost as if she has read my thoughts, she responds with a sneer. "Don't pretend that you are clueless," she says.

I attempt to respond, but my mind goes blank, making it difficult to articulate my thoughts.

Adeline pats the seat between them. "Come and sit, dear," she calls.

The sight of the familiar seat makes my mind race. I cannot help but imagine Hugh sitting at the opposite end, and I catch myself dwelling on the memories of everything that is no longer present.

Taking a moment to collect my thoughts, I am suddenly jolted by the sound of the door's deadbolt clicking into a locked position behind me. With trepidation, I move forward, my heart racing as I approach the table lit by flickering candlelight, casting eerie shadows that dance upon its surface.

Adeline settles into her seat, her gaze following my every movement.

As I approach my chair, every fiber of my being screams at me to escape. Despite my instincts, I find myself rooted in place, knowing no refuge exists.

Adeline snaps her fingers, creating a sharp staccato sound that fills the room. An ominous resonance of heavy footsteps emerging from the shadowy corner follows. A servant rushes toward me, pulling out my chair. I lower myself into its stiff embrace with apprehension and resignation.

"Well done. That's my girl," Adeline says in praise. Her eyes widen, raising her eyebrows.

I adjust my posture in the seat and avert my gaze toward the table to avoid making eye contact with her. "What is ... what is the occasion?" I stammer.

Adeline's hands clap loudly, drowning out my voice as she stares toward the kitchen door. In response to her signal, the air is suddenly filled with the roar of hurried footsteps approaching.

I leap from my seat, but before I can stand, a powerful grip wraps around my shoulders, forcefully pushing me back into my chair. My chest heaves with panic as I struggle to catch my breath. "What ... is the meaning of this?" I scream, fighting their restraining grip.

As the chaotic scene unfolds, Ettie cannot help but smirk. She retrieves her goblet of wine from the table, stroking its smooth surface with her fingertips. Leaning back and settling into her seat, she releases a contented sigh, savoring the moment.

Desperate, I look toward her, fervently hoping for her aid.

Adeline's pleasant expression quickly fades. "Restraints," she shouts, her face devoid of emotion.

Her authoritative hiss cuts through her clenched teeth, filling me with such fear that I am stupefied, unable to move. "Re-re-straints?" I stammer.

The room becomes silent as a staff member rushes over to me, skillfully threading a large leather belt beneath the chair and securing it around my upper thighs.

My arms flail as I scream, "Stop this at once!"

With malicious intent, they tighten the straps, disregarding my plea. Their stares hold no trace of remorse for their part in this while tears pour from my eyes, streaming down my cheeks like tiny rivers.

Ettie struggles to contain her amusement; a mischievous glint dances in her eye, and a smirk plays on her lips as she lifts her glass to take another sip. "How delightfully entertaining," she remarks. Finding it difficult to suppress her burgeoning chuckle, she talks faster. "The amusement alone has made this charade worthwhile."

With a harsh yank, the men secure the silver buckles. The restraints on my lower body are unyielding as I writhe to break free. "Release me! Now!" I shout.

As I swing my arms, they grab my wrists and press them down onto the arms of the chair.

Reinforcements pour in from the kitchen, bringing another set of restraints. They quickly secure them around my flailing limbs, lashing them to the wood.

Adeline, visibly frustrated, gestures toward her mouth as she struggles to express herself. "Do something ... I do not want to hear another word... Silence her at once!" she demands.

With my body rendered immobile, they fasten a tight restraint around my head, securing it in place. Then, without hesitation, they grab the napkin before me and stuff it into my mouth. I panic as the material lodges further in the back of my throat with each gasping breath. My face reddens as I choke.

"Just look at her," Ettie laughs, raising her glass to her lips to savor the last drop of her wine. "With that thing in her mouth, does she not bear a resemblance to a Christmas-suckling pig, Mother?"

"Enough!" Adeline's voice reverberates as she waves her hand, commanding them to stop. "The intent is to restrain her, not kill her!"

After loosening the leather straps, they pull the napkin forward, freeing my throat.

"Much better," Adeline says with a grin.

They slowly back away while maintaining a watchful eye on me.

Her smile vanishes, transforming into an angry scowl as she notices the individuals still lingering in the room. With an edge of irritation, she utters, "You are dismissed."

The staff exchanges nervous glances, then rushes toward the kitchen.

As their footsteps fade, a sense of dread washes over me, realizing I will now be alone with the worst of the lot. I contort my jaw, desperately trying to dislodge the cloth so I can scream, but not a sound escapes my lips. My efforts are futile.

"That will not work, little piggy," Ettie remarks. She reaches for the bottle of wine and helps herself to another pour.

I lock eyes with her and then turn my attention to Adeline, observing her every move. She stands silently, her gaze unwavering as she watches the staff depart through the kitchen.

As the last person leaves, the door swings shut with a loud slam.

The sensation of sweat trickling down my forehead makes me cringe. I inhale deeply through my nostrils, feeling the cool air fill my lungs as the bony ridge of my spine presses against the back of the chair. I yearn to create more distance, but the restraints won't allow it.

Adeline stares at me. Leaning in closer, focusing on me like a hawk, her lids narrow with great intensity. We lock gazes.

Then, suddenly, her eyes dramatically widen, making her pupils appear to swim in a vast sea of white.

"Theodosia, are you in there?" she asks.

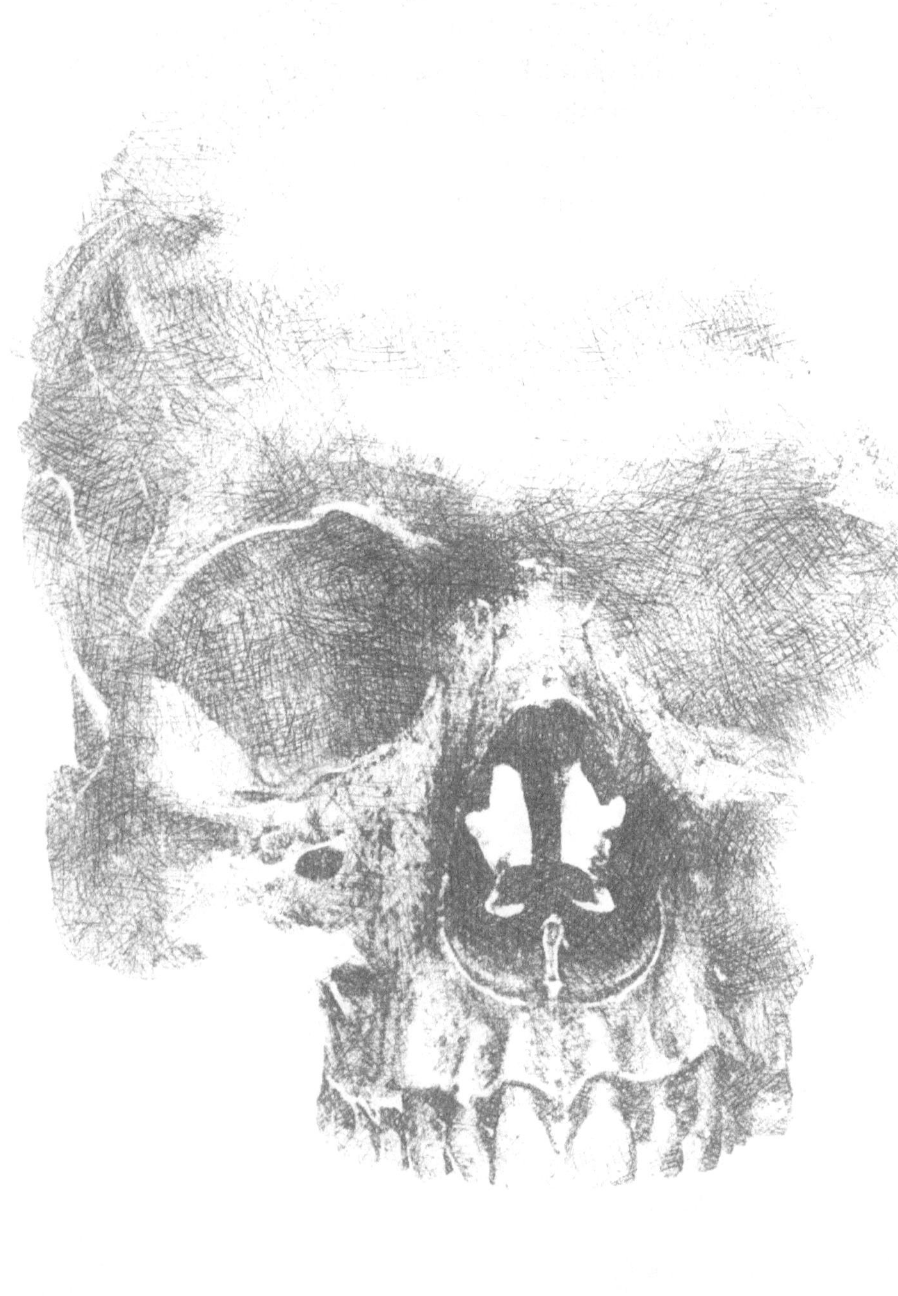

Thirty-Three

Blink Twice

Ettie's eyes fixate on me, her anticipation palpable as she waits for my reply.

In the dimly lit room, I nervously flick my gaze between the women's faces, searching for any sign of understanding. After what feels like an eternity, I turn my attention to Ettie, hoping to find a shred of compassion in her expression. Her once-pale cheeks now display a noticeable flush, a clear indication of the alcohol coursing through her veins.

Adeline clears her throat; her angst is palatable as her eyes widen further, anticipating my response. She grabs my hand, her grip firm and intentional. "Well?" she asks.

My eyes shift away from her face, and in that moment, a sudden and intense wave of panic washes over me, like a rush of icy water engulfing my entire body.

Ettie's piercing gaze follows my every move, her critical eye dissecting each action. "I do not believe your little experiment was successful," she proclaims, injecting tension into the room's already-charged atmosphere.

Adeline's eyes become daggers as she snarls, "But she is wearing her dress." Lunging forward, she grabs a fistful of my gown's fabric and, shooting a fierce glare toward Ettie, continues, "How could she have known which to choose if it wasn't her in the flesh?"

"I do not know, Mother. Perhaps her choice was sheer luck?" Ettie retorts with a hint of sarcasm.

Adeline clenches her jaw in frustration.

With a shrug of indifference, Ettie transitions the conversation to a more pressing matter. "I am famished. Can we proceed with dinner and discuss her later?" she says. "Once we finish eating, we can turn it into a game. Let us make her a post-meal hunt."

My eyes dart toward the exit, yearning to escape.

Adeline's delicate fingers tremble with desperation as she opens her hand, releasing the soft material of my dress from her fingertips. Her eyes, filled with anguish, remain fixed on the fluttering fabric as it descends to the floor.

Our gazes lock in a fleeting moment of connection. Adeline's breath catches in her throat, making it difficult to form words. "Theodosia?" she whispers. Her voice quivers with desperation as she clings to the fragile hope within her.

As I contemplate my answer, I feel the weight of Ettie's intense gaze on me. At that moment, her ominous suggestion of my demise comes rushing back, triggering a tightness that grips my chest, suffocating me with anxiety.

Adeline leans closer, her eyes filled with anticipation, waiting for my response.

Struggling against the restraints, I tilt my head back slightly, allowing me to raise my chin up and down in a subtle nod, showing, "Yes."

Adeline propels herself back, her eyes bulging in astonishment. "How glorious!" she exclaims, her hands lifting toward the sky as she looks up, immersing herself in the mural's beauty above. A deep, reverent sigh escapes her lips. "Thank you, thank you. I am eternally grateful to you for returning her to us!"

I feel a sense of unease as I find the task at hand to be deceptively simple.

Ettie places her empty glass on the table and chuckles. I slowly shift my attention toward her. Drawing closer, she gives me a once-over, noting every characteristic. "Mother, have you lost your mind?" she says. "That is surely an impostor."

I clench my hands into tight fists and pull at the restraints. They cut into my skin, eliciting a whimper.

Adeline glares at Ettie. "Hush now, jealous girl!" she says. Taking a brief pause, her demeanor becomes sterner. "I have made countless sacrifices for you and your sister, giving up everything so both of you can thrive. I have even gone as far as disregarding my flesh and blood for your benefit."

Ettie purses her lips, about to speak, but Adeline continues, not letting her get a word in edge-wise. "The decision to set aside my Theodosia was solely to ensure that your beauty would pave the way for your success in society," she utters.

"But…" Ettie tries to interject.

"I am not finished, girl!" Adeline hisses, cutting her off.

Ettie cowers in her seat.

Adeline's eyes bulge with fury as she points a finger at Ettie, her face flushing crimson. "I agreed to the sacrificial ritual with an understanding of the consequences and the promise of her return." Her lips curl into a sneer, her words dripping with venom as they escape through her clenched teeth. "Those were the explicit terms of the agreement. I will not entertain another word on this! As promised, she has made her return, and that is the end of it!" Her chest heaves with the weight of the effort she has just exerted, conveying both physical and emotional exhaustion.

Without a word in response, Ettie shifts her gaze toward the table, her expression unreadable.

The atmosphere shifts as a heavy, hushed silence descends upon the room.

Adeline's unexpected disclosure only adds to the weight of Hugh's last words regarding my brother, reverberating in my mind. Each syllable hangs in the air, sending a chill down my spine as I contemplate the lengths these individuals will go to for eternal youth. It is still difficult for me to grasp that, like them, Phillip was willing to make a horrifying sacrifice in pursuit of immortality.

Was he aware of this plan? Or is it possible that we are only pawns in a deadly scheme, manipulated with calculated precision by this family, or, God forbid, something darker? That he might have been deceived doesn't make it any easier to accept his betrayal, but it introduces a hint of grim satisfaction that the tables may have turned.

Adeline collects herself with a few deliberate breaths, then fixes her gaze upon me as she summons a brief, forced smile. "Let us bring this matter to a conclusive resolution," she states.

As I watch her, I cannot help but think of my brother, suffering and languishing in a hellish state for his foolish choices.

Pausing for emphasis, Adeline cups her hands around my restraints and clears her throat.

I wince, staring her dead in the eyes. My body is drenched in nervous sweat as I wonder what she will do next.

She steadies her movements and lowers her voice. "Theodosia … blink twice if you are truly present within." She falls silent, scooting closer to the edge of her seat, her eyes full of anticipation, eagerly awaiting my response.

Swiftly, I blink twice to signify my agreement, releasing a soft whimper as I wiggle my fingers to ease the discomfort caused by the tight leather restraints against my wrists.

"Ah, just as I suspected," Adeline declares, a mischievous glint in her eye. Ettie bites her tongue, suppressing the urge to speak.

Adeline enthusiastically claps her hands, capturing the staff's attention. Suddenly, the room is flooded with urgent footsteps streaming through the kitchen door. Adeline gestures toward me, saying, "She wants to speak! Someone, assist her!"

As the restraint around my skull loosens, I wince at the pulsating ache as circulation is restored to the back of my head. I resist the urge to choke as the napkin is removed from my mouth.

I see the radiant sun dip below the horizon from the corner of my eye. Its fading glow paints the room with deepening shadows, starkly contrasting the palpable sense of relief I feel inside.

Adeline and Ettie are hushed in tone and add to my growing unease.

My eyes dart frantically to the room's corners, my mind fraught with the fear of something lurking. The room's stillness amplifies the sound of my heart pounding, and every creak and whisper makes me startle as I strain to see through the darkness.

Ettie gestures toward me and says, "Mother, look at her. If she were Theodosia, she would not be so skittish." Her tone is sharp. "You know as well as I do that the girl terrified all of us. She displayed little empathy or remorse for even the most heinous acts." The haunting recollection makes her shudder. "Had it not been for her alarming demeanor and the fear she instilled in me, I would not have resorted to locking my door at night, a precaution I had never before deemed necessary."

I attempt to concentrate on her concerning words despite the sound of murmuring voices. As she rises to her feet, the piercing sound of her chair grating against the floor resonates in the room.

Adeline turns toward her, her lips twisted with irritation.

"You must listen to me, Mother ... I mean... Look at her! Her expression conveys intense discomfort as if she yearns to shed her skin and flee." She observes me, adding, "It is quite dreadful to watch."

Adeline delves into deep introspection as she shifts her gaze back toward me. Her thoughts weigh heavily on her as she processes Ettie's speculation.

Her look of uncertainty ignites panic within me.

Ettie's eyes twinkle with a glimmer of loathing. "Playing Devil's advocate, let's assume it is Theodosia. Knowing her tendencies, I see no benefit in adding her to our current predicament. In fact, it would be quite ill-advised indeed. Let us just get it over with and kill her," she says.

My heart races as I struggle to defend myself; I stammer in response, "Surely you ... you are not questioning my integrity." The tremble in my voice belies the emotions churning inside me.

Adeline turns her head slightly, fixing her eyes on me intensely, her eyebrows arching upward.

As my emotions surge, my speech quickens, the words flowing like a rushing river, barely taking shape before they pour out. "Mother, please tell me you recognize me. You mustn't listen to her."

Tears glisten as they form tiny pools in the corners of Adeline's eyes, mirroring the depth of her inner turmoil.

I lock eyes with her, desperately seeking a connection through my empathetic stare. Despite my attempt, she meets me with resistance, her gaze expressing only apprehension. Frustration washes over me as I glance toward the restraints, realizing my efforts may be in vain.

Her lips curve into a sly grin as she maintains a watching silence, scrutinizing me.

"How can it be that my own mother does not recognize me? Please look into my eyes. It is your dearest daughter, Theodosia. I have returned to you, drawn back to this place by an unyielding force that has brought us together once more."

"She is lying!" Ettie screams as she slams her fist against the table. The force sends ripples through the porcelain and silverware, the clatter emphasizing the frustration in her words.

Despite her continued tantrum, I cannot help but be distracted by the growing whispers emanating from the dimly lit corners of the room.

Filled with anger, Adeline glares at Ettie and, commandingly, shouts, "Hush!" Her voice catalyzes the whispering voices, instigating them as they swirl and dance more aggressively around me.

I steal a nervous glance at the door, my heart pounding with the desire to escape. I give a light tug, testing the strength of my restraints. They do not budge.

Adeline takes a deep, lengthy breath, feeling the weight of the moment pressing on her.

Darkness continues to sweep the corners, creeping closer to the center of the room.

As I refocus on Adeline, my anxiety restricts my breathing to quick, shallow breaths. The haunting whispers consume my mind as I struggle to stay composed. "How did you do it? How did you bring me back?" I ask.

She blinks multiple times as if trying to regain focus. "You are not cross with me for what

I did to you, are you?" she asks, searching my face for any sign of displeasure.

I nervously clear my throat before responding, "No, of course not, Mother. Not at all."

"Given the circumstances, you had no choice but to find solutions, as you were under an overwhelming amount of pressure," she says.

"What's done is done, and now I'm back, which is all that matters. I must say that I am quite fascinated to hear how you brought me back."

After a moment of silence, a mischievous grin spreads across her face. "Ah, yes, of course," she remarks. "It was quite simple, really," she says; a chilling calmness takes over her tone. "With Clinton's guidance, we preserved your body and stored it in the icebox."

Ettie's lip curls in disdain, her eyes narrowing at the sound of her husband's name. Her fingers wrap around the delicate stem of her empty wineglass as she leans forward, eagerly anticipating another pour of the luscious crimson.

"Your circumstance was unique, and your temporary sacrifice allowed your sisters to enhance their appearance and attract more desirable partners. Clinton told me that by following the correct protocol, we could not only bring you back, but you would return even better than before. He was right. Just look at you - not only are you present, but you have gained a physical appearance that far exceeds your original one. Each day, we would take small bits of your flesh, carefully choosing the specific body part required for the concoction we were preparing," she reminisces, reflecting on the process. For example, we used parts of your head to tackle issues related to the face and segments of your torso to handle matters concerning the body.

I acknowledge her with a nod, suppressing my disgust and sinking deeper into my chair.

Adeline continues, proud of her doings, and gains more animation in her words. "Every part of you, not consumed by your sisters, was used to make everyday items for potential hosts. It was hoped they would absorb your essence and entice you back to your new body. The cosmetics and fragrances were crafted using fat extracted from your cheeks. The bath soaps were made by combining herbs and lard from your gut. To aid absorption, I commanded the chambermaid to mix your rendered fat with the bathwater and softly scrub the host's skin, sometimes twice daily."

As I listen, my jaw clenches, and the heavy, putrid makeup feels even more oppressive on my skin.

"We spritzed every piece of fabric incorporated in the elaborate gowns such as the one you are wearing, with an enchanted potion made from you, ensuring that the mystical concoction permeated each fiber. It is as if the clothing captures your essence, preserving the individual within it," Adeline says.

"Was she … um, Genevieve… the target of your plan?" I say, struggling to conceal my growing disgust.

With a lighthearted laugh, she replies, "Oh, no, we experimented with several others before her. However, each time, it became clear that the process had some hitches to overcome."

"At what moment did you realize the endeavor was a success?" I nervously ask, picking at my nails.

"It became quite clear early on that her consistent ability to predict our every move, along with her clever remarks, showed your influence on her." She explains.

I wince as the whispering hisses sting my eardrums, growing louder.

"Then, after I killed your stepfather, the coldness of your reaction told me all I needed to know." She chuckles. "No one harbored a deeper resentment toward him than you, which is completely understandable. He consistently treated you with cruelty and malice simply for not being his natural-born child."

As the unsettling ambiance surrounds me, my attention is drawn to a faint stirring in the shadowy corners of the room. With every word Adeline utters, the shadows grow taller, creeping closer to the heart of the chamber as if they are eavesdropping.

She briefly gathers her thoughts and continues, "At that moment, I was ready to confirm your identity and have this talk, but Ettie and Hattie were adamant that we should subject you to one last test."

Ettie's knuckles turn a shade of white as she clenches the stem of her glass with growing intensity.

"Before Genevieve returned to her bedchamber, I directed the staff to place a trunk of your old dresses in her room. The timely demise of your chambermaid eliminated any chance of outside interference. When you arrived in your favorite gown, there was no question. It was quite the perfect test." Adeline smirks, thinking back on it all.

As I absorb the intricate details of the plan, vivid recollections of my time at the estate inundate my mind. "I see," I murmur. "What was the fate of those who failed in the experiment?" A shiver courses through me at the mere thought of what outcome might have befallen the others.

Ettie's laughter erupts in a tumultuous wave of cackles. "We devoured them." She snorts. She leans back in her seat, looking quite relaxed as she says, "Of course, the first step was to poison them."

Adeline leans in, her eyes gleaming with amusement. "Don't let her harsh account concern you," she says. "We were always kind." With a casual shrug, she adds, "I assume most barely felt a thing—just a minor poke."

As their eyes meet across the table, a shared, secret joke sets them off into fits of laughter.

The eerie chorus of whispers surges, intertwining with one another, permeating every inch of the surrounding space. I am entranced by their mysterious dialects and sinister laughter, unharmoniously blending to create a tumultuous melody.

Ettie ceases her crowing and dramatically frowns. "The only exception, Mother, was that unfortunate chambermaid Genevieve insisted on dragging along with her."

The mere thought of Fran makes me shudder as I desperately attempt to distance myself from any part I had in the horrific treatment she suffered upon coming to the estate.

"She arrived with her body as stiff as a board and stuck to the driver's seat," she explains. "In fact, she was frozen solid, like a pond in winter, making it nearly impossible to pry her free. And, dare I say, her flesh ... well... her flesh was frostbitten to the bone. Not a spot of pink or porcelain remained!" she exclaims excitedly. "Unlike the others, she was completely inedible. It's such a shame. What a waste."

The haunting image of Fran's disfigured face, which I had glimpsed in the dining room, plagues my thoughts. "Did she survive the ordeal?" I ask, hoping that I misinterpreted the seriousness of the situation. As I anxiously await the response, a knot twists in my stomach.

Adeline shakes her head with disappointment. "I am afraid not. It was truly a waste. We could have used the extra supply."

Consumed by a suffocating sense of guilt, I am unable to make eye contact with anyone. I struggle to control my tumultuous emotions, diverting my attention to the undulating shadows in the distant corner.

Ettie's stare lingers on me, and noticing my behavior, she edges nearer. "Is there something bothering you?" she inquires, her lips quivering in anticipation of my reply.

I wince and grip the armrests, trying to calm my nausea.

A soft, barely audible whisper weaves itself into the chorus of ethereal voices surrounding me. "Genevieve," it says.

There's a peculiar familiarity in the way my name is spoken, causing a prickling sensation to flood my skin.

With a mocking tone, Ettie asks, "Theodosia? Are you listening to me?!"

The corners of my mouth turn up into a smile. "Yes, of course. On the contrary … nothing is bothering me," I say, carefully choosing my words as I look at her. "I am simply envisioning her body frozen in a seated position. Without question, the driver must have been rather surprised to discover her icy state. It must have been quite a sight to see."

With a loud grunt, Ettie looks at the table and crosses her arms.

Adeline, her patience wearing thin, punctuates the air with a commanding clap—the signal for the commencement of the meal. "Now, let us eat!" she announces, her voice booming as she fervently motions for the servers to begin their duties.

The dining staff bursts into the room, moving swiftly and gracefully, each carrying a silver tray containing the first course of the evening high above their heads.

As hurried footsteps approach from behind me, I glance toward the empty place setting and ask, "Aren't we waiting for one more?"

With a worried expression, Ettie shifts her gaze toward the vacant seat. "Mother," she says, "do you think we should wait for Hattie?"

Adeline disregards her concerns, her voice firm. "That will not be necessary," she says. "You know how important punctuality is to me; if she is not here, it is her loss." She picks up her fork and gestures to the servants to clear the extra plates from the table.

The staff moves in unison as they lift the lids from their serving trays, revealing vibrant, fresh salad greens underneath. With fluid precision, they place a colorful dish in front of each of us, the crisp vegetables and tangy dressing enticing our senses.

Ettie observes as the server presents her meal, attempting to comprehend her mother's statement. She glares across the table and asks, "What do you mean it won't be necessary?"

Adeline repositions herself, adjusting her posture to better articulate her thoughts. "I am not sure, Ettie." She arranges her napkin on her lap. "What do you think I mean?"

"Where is she?" Ettie's eyes dart toward the empty chair as if she expects Hattie to materialize at any moment.

A disturbing laugh escapes Adeline as she stabs the lettuce on her plate. Her eyes fixate on the torn leaves, revealing a chilling indifference. "How should I know?" she says.

Caught up in the drama, I forget about my predicament and reach for my fork, only to be reminded of the resistance from the restraints pressing against my wrists. I wince, feeling a sharp jolt of pain.

Ettie's jaw clenches tightly, her teeth grinding together as she fights to hold back her emotions. "You monstrous bitch!" she says, her voice quivering. "I demand to know what you did to her?"

The waitstaff hurriedly leaves the room, exiting through the kitchen door.

Adeline chews her food slowly, her expression cold and calculating. With chilling composure, she utters, "Hold your tongue, girl. You are making a spectacle of yourself."

As they continue to argue, I notice another movement. This time, it is much closer than before.

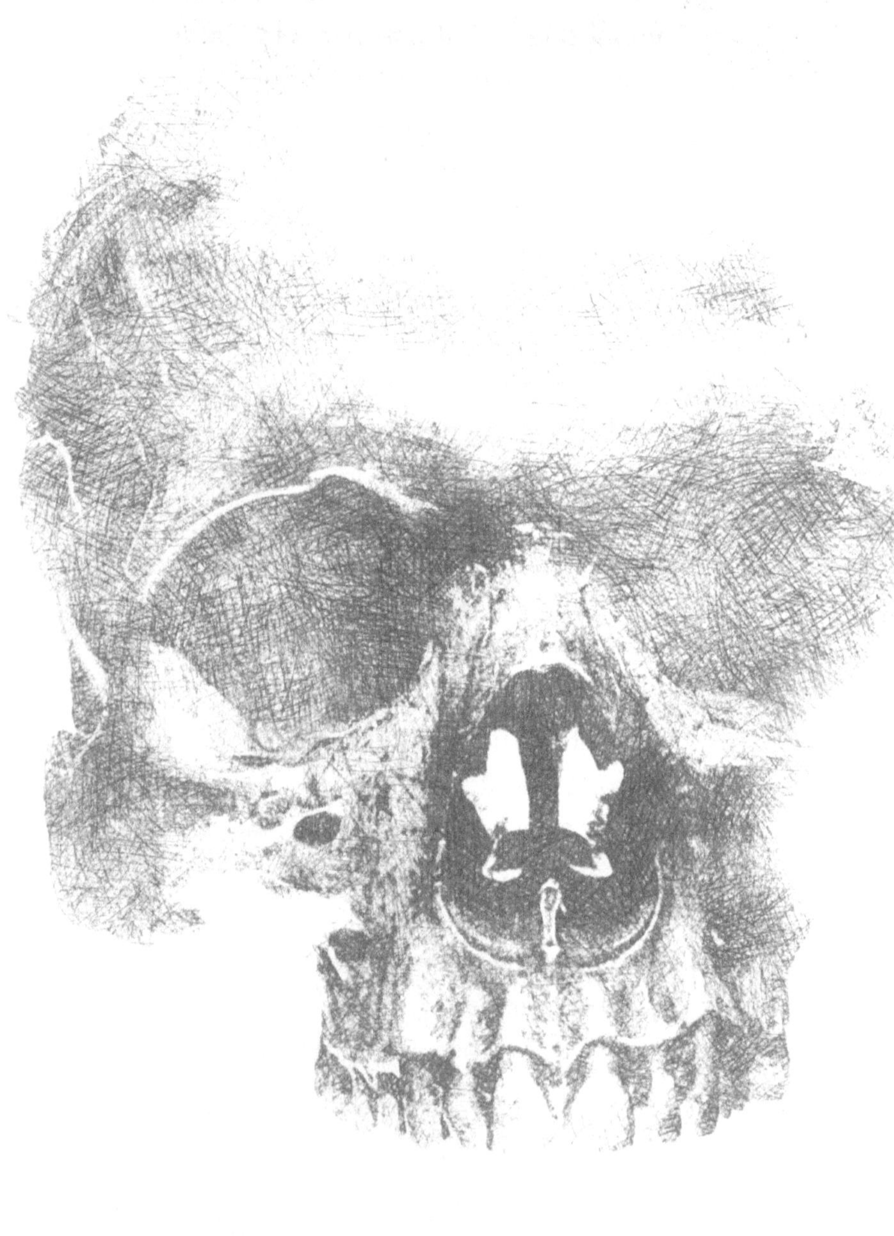

Thirty-Four

Do not Move

An icy chill infiltrates the air as I monitor the shadows from the corner of my nervously twitching eye.

"Now, eat your food," Adeline commands, her voice filled with impatience as her eyebrows furrow.

"You should know your sister's stubborn nature by now. It is best to let her be if she is staging another dinner boycott. Do not allow her spoiled behavior to damper your appetite."

Ettie's eyes narrow in fury as she observes her mother's lettuce-filled fork swinging back and forth, punctuating every word.

In an impulsive act, she pushes her salad plate from the table.

The delicate porcelain explodes into shards as it crashes onto the floor, filling the room with shattering glass.

Adeline's hand trembles as she slams her fork onto the table. "What is the meaning behind this spoiled behavior?" she asks, scowling, her voice seething with anger. "Remember your manners!"

Ettie, filled with hateful defiance, refuses to relent. Her voice carries the weight of accusation as she demands, "Mother, I know what you are capable of! I insist you tell me this minute: Did you kill her? Did you kill Hattie?"

In the perimeters darkness, a swift and subtle form slithers near the window, its curved silhouette barely discernible as it glides through the shadows.

As they bicker, I remain silent and motionless, studying the lithe figure's every action, my heart pounding in my chest with each passing moment.

"Are you aware of how absurd your accusations sound?!" Adeline says with offense. "Good God, child!" she exclaims. "What reason would I have to harm her?"

Ettie springs from the table, and her pupils widen. "She wouldn't be the first of us you killed." She sneers.

Adeline's fury explodes in response to her accusation. "You vile, ungrateful child!" she shrieks, her words leaving traces of spit in their wake.

The room grows colder, causing a light frost to blanket the flowers with a shimmering layer.

The elusive creature maintains its stealthy presence, fixating its unsettling gaze upon us. Its eyes emit an unearthly yellow glow that casts an eerie light amid the opaqueness. "Genevieve," it calls.

I dig my fingers into the smooth, varnished surface of the armrests. The way they clench at the wood only intensifies the uneasiness swirling in my gut. I remain silent and motionless, my eyes fixed on the threatening figure concealed by the shadows.

The women's conflict intensifies, and they close their eyes to the malevolent force at play, which, in comparison, makes their disagreement seem insignificant.

Finding that screaming no longer brings her satisfaction, Ettie sneers and, barring her teeth seizes a knife from the table and storms toward Adeline. The hem of her skirt trails behind her, collecting glimmering glass fragments along the way.

Adeline's voice reverberates through the room as she vehemently denies the accusation. Frantically scrambling to her feet, she uses her plate to shield herself. "Get back!" she shouts.

Ettie slows her approach, her nervous chuckle betraying her intent.

A gentle draft weaves beneath the crack of the hallway door, carrying muffled whispers and the pungent stench of decay.

With each languid step, the being emerges, inching toward the center of the room.

Restrained by leather and consumed by fear, I listen to their argument growing, knowing they remain oblivious to the frightening intruder lurking in the room.

Ettie's footsteps' aggressive pursuit grows louder as they round the table.

Adeline's eyes remain fixed on her daughter as she hurriedly grabs the half-empty wine bottle from the table and flings it across her path. "Stop this immediately! You are not in the right state of mind. You are intoxicated!" she exclaims.

The bottle explodes into countless fragments, releasing a torrent of vibrant red that cascades across the floor.

In a state of distress, Adeline screams, "You must stop this instant!"

Ettie's hand moves swiftly, the knife's edge glinting in the candlelight as she gets closer. "You are a murderer!" she snarls.

Adeline's flowing dress catches on the edge of a chair as she steps back, halting her graceful stride. As she struggles to untangle the fabric, her breathing quickens, and in a determined yet exasperated voice, she declares, "I am no such thing!"

Ettie's heart pounds as she sprints the last few steps toward her target. With a fierce determination, she raises the gleaming knife above her head. "This is for Hattie!" she screams.

Adeline tries to retreat, but her heel gets caught on the hem of her dress, causing her to lose balance and tumble to the ground. In her panic, she flails her hands to protect herself. "I command you not to do this! This is not how it is supposed to end! I am the matriarch of this household! It should be you in my stead!".

The chilling whispers dance through the air with the force of a raging wind, conjuring a swirling vortex in their wake.

Ettie looms over her, lifting the blade even higher as her mother cowers in fear. "The moment you took that first bite, a dark cloud descended upon us, suffocating us with a fate worse than death. Admit it, Mother, your thirst for youth has drug this family to hell."

"I beg to differ," Adeline replies, her tone laced with offense. Your father was the one who introduced Mummia to this place, not me.

"It's typical of you, Mother," she says bitterly, "to hold accountable someone who can't defend their name because … he's dead! Or have you conveniently forgotten that you killed him, just like my sister? Well, the moment has arrived for you to face the consequences. It's time for the reaper to claim what belongs to him—you."

With that, Ettie drives the blade deep into her mother with the force of two.

Adeline's screams of agony fill the air as the knife edge pierces her dress, slicing through the ivory boning of her corset as if it were butter. "You're … making… a grave mistake!" she cries out amid gasps for air.

As her terrified shrieks resound, the figure slinks back into the shadows, out of sight, while the chorus of hissing voices grows louder.

I close my eyes as my ears fill with the sound of the blade ripping through fabric, muscle, and bone over … and over… and over again.

Fear grips me as I helplessly await my turn, my heart pounding as if ready to explode. No matter how hard I try, I cannot capture a meaningful breath.

Ettie swings her weapon, the sound of metal slicing through the air as she unleashes her well-groomed anger. Then, as if a switch has been flipped, she stops, rises to her feet, and lets out an uncontrollable wail.

I slowly open my eyes, my gaze fixated in her direction.

She hovers over Adeline's body, every inch of her drenched in blood. A coat of crimson spray engulfs everything around her, spanning from the floor to the ceiling.

Utterly devoid of humanity, her pupils expand to the corners of her eyes, covered in an eerie glaze. Her eyes shift from the carnage to me with a fierce intensity, her focus unyielding, and she is sightless to everyone around her.

The elusive shadows multiply, slowly creeping closer to the edges of my vision, carrying the putrid stench of death.

Her words are heavy with accusation; Ettie murmurs, "This is your fault. You brought mayhem to this house." The knife shakes in her hand as she takes a deliberate step closer.

I cringe at the grating sound of glass crunching beneath her feet, each tiny shard adding to my uneasiness.

Whispering emanates from the creatures as they dart about within the shadowy landscape beyond the window's edge.

I nervously glance in their direction.

Ettie's voice breaks through the tension, demanding notice. "Look at me, Genevieve!" She points the glinting blade at me while slowly continuing her approach.

A low, guttural growl emerges from the foreboding chasm as I stare into the unsettling darkness.

My eyes widen as I strain to see beyond Ettie.

She stops abruptly as the sound of heavy footsteps approaches from behind. Her forehead glistens with sweat as fear takes hold.

Abruptly, a creature's commanding voice rings out above the rest. "You have consumed your fill, and now it's time for you to go. We are here to welcome you to your eternal hellish home. Forever hungry and in torment, you will join the others to atone for what you can never again possess ... sinew and bone."

Ettie's knuckles whiten as she tightens her grip around the knife's handle.

Hissing beetles echo from the dark recesses beneath the floorboards as they scurry, frantic to join in.

With a sudden, heart-pounding movement, she spins around, her breath catching in her throat as she is confronted by the creature's putrefied form and amber-glowing eyes. It continues approaching from its shadowy lair, its eyes gleaming with an unsettling intensity that mirrors a cobra ready to strike.

A piercing scream leaves her lungs. She staggers backward as the beetles hiss and skitter through the floor's cracks. They scurry up her feet, wriggling and squirming as they ascend her legs. "Get off me!" she screams, frantically slapping her skirt to rid herself of the hissing horde.

Her movement has the opposite effect of what she desires, drawing more insects to her. As their numbers grow, they swarm her, making quick work of tearing at her skin and devouring her flesh bite by bite.

She staggers back, swinging her knife. "Make it stop!" she screams.

The foreboding creature advances into the light of the fading candles, elongating its once-arched back before unleashing a bone-chilling, primal howl that echoes through the dining chamber.

Startled, Ettie's eyes widen as her leg catches on the corpse of her mother, and she trips, plummeting to the floor. "No!" she bawls, frantically kicking her feet; she propels herself backward, slipping and sliding on the blood-soaked floor. She gazes at the distorted visage and swallows hard. "It cannot be. You … you are not real," she stammers.

The creature's body is in clear view for the first time, revealing a female form.

The skin of her breasts hangs from her mummified chest. A large chunk missing from the bare stomach exposes fetid organs. Extensive decay consumes her limbs, and the fleshy parts of her face have been torn away, skewing her identity. The sight of her body reveals that she has been mercilessly harvested, chewed, and left half-eaten.

I remain still, my eyes widening as I observe her sharp and erratic movements.

"It wasn't me. It was her," Ettie cries, kicking more frantically to scoot away. She points to her mother's corpse. "She is the one responsible for your slaughter. That is who you want!"

The desecrated carcass hovers over her.

I gaze upon her eyelids, their delicate folds sewn shut. As I behold the sight, a wave of horror engulfs my thoughts.

The woman staggers forward, then stops and sniffs the air. The edges of her dissected lips twinge, forming a paralyzed smirk.

Ettie watches her while matching her stagnancy.

I shallow my every breath, my gaze fixed on the creature's unnerving stillness. Her body is perfectly motionless, creating an unsettling presence that resembles a horrifying statue preparing to come to life.

Ettie winces as the beetles scurry from all sides, searching for any opening to reach her tender insides. Tears spill from her eyes and trickle down her cheeks as she whispers, "Theodosia."

At the name's utterance, the ethereal voices stop.

Ettie places her hands against the floor behind her back, feeling the sharp glass fragments dig into her skin as her palms seek stability.

Theodosia lunges forward with a quick and exacting act, instinctively following the sound. The force of her body's impact embeds Ettie deeper into the shards of glass as a swarm of beetles engulfs her face. She gasps in horror as they crawl into her mouth and down her esophagus, leaving her choking and flailing her limbs for air. Her eyes bulge as she clutches her throat, struggling to take even the slightest breath, but to no avail.

After a moment or two, there was silence.

Theodosia slowly lifts herself from Ettie's sprawled body, gnarled fingers closing around her ankles as she drags her across the floor. With each forceful tug, the beetles release themselves from Ettie's flesh, uncovering a horrifying sight - her muscles stripped and her expression locked in fear.

As Theodosia nears Adeline, she pauses and grips her lifeless wrist before continuing, pulling a body with each hand. The air is heavy with the scent of iron as shards of bloodstained glass gather beneath their corpses, emitting a grating screech reminiscent of nails on a chalkboard as they are heaved toward the door.

Once more, a rustling in the shadows sends my mind spinning, imagining all the terrifying possibilities of what it could be.

To my horror, the mummy from my wedding night emerges, its body dissected and bandages trailing along the floor as it steps into the glow of the flickering candlelight. I hold my breath, hoping to avoid being noticed, while trembling in anticipation of its approach, fearing it will tear me apart bit by bit. However, it gives no indication of its malicious intentions. It simply turns away, disregarding my presence, as it follows Theodosia with a lumbering gait.

Just when I believe it is finished, the shadows spring back to life, seething with energy as if the depths of hell were about to pour into the room.

The air fills with a suffocating stench of decay as one corpse after another appears, their mummified and decaying forms creating a nightmarish procession. Though only some are familiar, all share one commonality aside from death, their state of incompleteness, indicating that they were once used as macabre ingredients in the McKinley family's meals.

They move with an unnerving slowness from every corner of the massive room, making their way toward the door. *Could this be nothing more than a figment of my imagination or a dreadful nightmare? Are they the ones who have been relentlessly tormenting me with their whispers, driving me to question my sanity?*

As Theodosia draws nearer to the dining room exit, it swings open ahead of her with a loud screech, allowing her to heave Ettie and Adeline's bodies into the hallway. The others follow closely behind.

Upon the last victim's departure, the weighty door slams shut. The resounding bang leaves me shaken, and I find myself staring blankly at the solid wood dining room exit.

From the kitchen, a single waitstaff member bursts into the room with an elegant golden tray cradling the second course. They glide to the table and remove the salad plate from in front of me, then carefully set a hot bowl of soup in its place, filling the air with a tantalizing aroma. In their wake, a servant with a dish towel over their arm swiftly follows, ready to address any spills or mishaps and ensure everything is in perfect order.

As they tend to me, a horde of employees assemble, carrying mops, rags, and buckets, determined to restore order. In what seems like a mere blink of an eye, they attend to the cleanup, meticulously returning the room to its original spotless condition before exiting back to the kitchen.

Wisps of steam slowly ascend from the simmering liquid, carrying the fragrance of herbs and spices. The warmth caresses my face, igniting a faint growl in my stomach, signaling its eagerness to partake.

Taking a brief pause to steady myself, I clear my throat and establish eye contact with the two remaining servants standing on either side of me. "I cannot eat if I am bound," I state firmly.

Their faces flush with embarrassment as they hurriedly remove the restraints from my wrists and lap and arrange them on the polished tray. They then make their way back to the kitchen with purpose; their footsteps joined by the gentle, rhythmic jingle of buckles. The distinct sound of the kitchen door closing signifies their departure.

Left in solitude, I am captivated by the faintest ripples on the broth's surface. As I swirl my spoon through the rich, aromatic liquid, my eyes are drawn to a subtle movement at the bottom of the bowl, and an unexpected sight greets me—a pair of human eyeballs emerge, revealing themselves.

Their buoyancy causes them to flip over as they bob, exposing their cloudy pupils and frostbitten whites. I gaze at them momentarily, feeling at ease in their familiar presence.

Then, leaning in closer, I gently scoop them up with my spoon and transfer them into my hand. "There you are," I say. With a tender touch, I gently kiss each one and bring them to my cheek as I whisper, "Oh, it's delightful to see you again, my dear friend! You won't believe the company I've been keeping. So much has happened since we last spoke, and I am bursting with excitement to share it all with you. Come now. " Carefully placing them in my mouth, I swallow them whole.

Then, leaning in closer, I gently scoop them up with my spoon and transfer them into my hand. With a tender touch, I gently kiss each one and whisper, "Oh, it's delightful to see you again, my dear friend! You won't believe the company I've been keeping. So much has happened since we last spoke, and I'm bursting with excitement to share it all with you. Come now, I won't let you out of my sight again." Grinning, I swallow them whole.

Afterword

'Mummia' - A Cannibalistic Movement of Europe

Have you ever wondered why there are substantially more sarcophagi than corpses on display in most exhibits showcasing ancient Egyptian culture? Many factors have impacted the preservation of ancient Egypt over the centuries. Sure, acquisitions of power and wars are partially to blame, but those broadly advertised culprits hide a much darker narrative—one rarely discussed. During the 12th through 18th centuries, Egyptian mummies were being unearthed and sold across Europe to be ground up and consumed for medicinal purposes or unwrapped as entertainment at parties and social gatherings.

You may ask yourself how ingesting embalmed flesh could be deemed the cure-all for a variety of medical ailments, including, but not limited to, upset stomach, headaches, healing wounds, scar fading, sicknesses, and hysteria. Unfortunately, a few errors were made over time, and words lost in translation sparked a craze that directly contributed to the plundering of artifacts, desecration of the dead, and subsequent reduction of mummies left in Egypt. Some have speculated that the number of mummies lost may range in the thousands.

The products resulting from this horrifying practice became so popular and in such high demand that the trade of mummia was banned in Egypt in the 16th century because of the decreasing availability of ancient corpses.

Abd' el-Latif al-Baghdadi (1162-1231), an Arab physician and philosopher, discussed 'mummy' derived from the Persian term for the mineral bitumen, which was found 'oozing' from the ground. Latif addressed the difference, claiming, 'The mummy found in the hollows of corpses in Egypt differs but immaterially from the nature of mineral mummy; and where any difficulty arises in procuring the latter, may be substituted in its stead.'

Later, Gerard of Cremona (1114-1187), an Italian translator, went on to define *mumiya*, the Arabic word, as 'the substance found in the land where bodies were buried with aloes by which the liquid of the dead, mixed with aloes, is transformed, and it is similar to marine pitch.'

Although both Gerard, Latif, and a few other philosophers, including the Arab physician Serapion the Younger, Simon Geneunsis, and popular author and teacher at Salerno medical school Matthaeus Platearius, noted the term's stressing point of bitumen being the particular 'sludgy black liquid,' residue found, something became lost in translation.

As time went on, the meaning of the term became distorted, and numerous translation errors compounded the confusion. European philosophers argued that mummia did not refer to the substance found in preserved corpses, the surrounding soil, or the preserving agent, but rather encompassed the entire ancient mummified body itself.

Giovanni da Vigo (1450-1525), an Italian surgeon, was one of many with the viewpoint. Vigo described mummia as: 'The flesh of a dead body which is embalmed, and it is hot and dry … it has virtue to heal over wounds and staunch blood.' Vigo's opinion quickly became the popular philosophy of the time.

Mummia, the substance derived from ground mummies, rapidly became one of the most in-demand items listed in medical catalogs. It received praise and was endorsed by many of the greats. Francis Bacon (1521-1626), a philosopher and pioneering scientist, declared, 'Mummy has great force in staunching of blood,' and Robert Boyle (1627-91), notoriously referred to as the 'father of modern chemistry,' made the bold claim that mummia was, 'one of the most useful medicines commended and given by our physicians for falls and bruises.'

The movement quickly caught with European royalty, including French king Francois I (1494-1547), who claimed, 'no accident if he had a little of that by him.'

According to Dolan's article, "The Gruesome History of Eating Corpses as Medicine," featured in the Smithsonian Magazine, "the 16th-century German-Swiss physician Paracelsus believed blood was good for drinking, and one of his followers even suggested taking blood from a living body. While that doesn't seem to have been common practice, the poor, who couldn't always afford the processed compounds sold in apothecaries, could gain the benefits of cannibal medicine by standing by at executions, paying a small fee for a cup of the still-warm blood of the condemned."

From there, not only did the consumption of ancient mummies become a fad, but wealthy households began collecting artifacts from ancient Egypt. Growing in popularity in the

19th century, the French abbot Father Géramb commented in 1833, 'It would hardly be respectable, on one's return from Egypt, to present oneself without a mummy in one hand and a crocodile in the other.'

This led to 'mummy unrolling,' or 'unwrapping,' occasions, an after-drink game in which the elite would literally unwrap the mummified corpse as the partygoers watched for entertainment. The Victorian practice of 'fun,' didn't just stay in England; Théophile Gautier, a French novelist and literary critic, recorded a detailed account of attending a 'mummy unwrapping,' in France in 1857. Gautier, bewildered by the state of the corpse, describes, 'Two white eyes with great black pupils shone with fictitious life between brown eyelids. They were enameled eyes, such as it was customary to insert in carefully prepared mummies. The clear, fixed glance, gazing out of the dead face, produced a terrifying effect; the body seemed to behold with disdainful surprise the living beings that moved around it.'

Besides the ancient, mummified corpses used for medical purposes, display, entertainment, and artifact collections, in the 16th and 17th centuries, ground mummies were used to create a distinct paint color known as 'Mummy Brown,' or 'Egyptian Brown,' or 'caput mortuum.' The 'rich brown pigment' would be created by mixing white pitch, Myrrh, and the ground corpses of ancient mummies.

With the growing demand for mummies and the dwindling supply, black market sellers turned to selling 'counterfeit mummia.' This fraudulent mixture was made by utilizing the corpses of recently deceased individuals, animals, and even prisoners, as well as stolen bodies from graves.

It has been noted that mummified corpses were used in creating the select brown paint color until 1893. Despite claims that only a small quantity of corpse material was used in the crafting of this unique hue, Roberson's of London, the renowned color manufacturer, continued to stock the pigment until it was finally removed in 1963.

Despite its waning popularity, the medical substance Mummia could still be found listed in the price catalog of Merck & Co, a prominent pharmaceutical company, until 1924.

The historical significance of medicinal cannibalism infiltrating various civilizations throughout history is profound. While it raised awareness about different cultures, it also destroyed aspects of their rich historical heritage.

Given the prevailing lack of awareness, I strongly believe it is crucial to shed light on the history of 'Mummia' and medical cannibalism. This dark movement was once accepted and integrated into European society, causing irreparable damage to the remnants of an ancient culture and often hindering the study of history.

References

Castleton, David. "Mummia - How Ground Egyptian Mummy Cured All Ailments & Painted Masterpieces." *David Castleton Blog - The Serpent's Pen*, 26 Sept. 2023, www.davidcastleton.net/mummia-ancient-egyptian-mummies-medicine-mummy-brown-paint/.

"Curiosities of Medical History: Ingesting 'Mummy Powder' for Health." *Medical News Today*, MediLexicon International, www.medicalnewstoday.com/articles/mumia-the-strange-history-of-human-remains-as-medicine#A-controversial-practice. Accessed June 2024.

Hinson, Ben. "Mummy Issues • V&A Blog." *V&A Blog*, 16 May 2023, www.vam.ac.uk/blog/museum life/mummyissues#:~:text=Due%20to%20demand%2C%20and%20the,corpses%2C%20often%0Othose%20of%20criminals.

Joy, Darrin. "Magic, Medicine and Eternal Love: Why Mummies Still Mesmerize." *News and Events*, 31 Aug. 2023, dornsife.usc.edu/news/stories/why-mummies-still-mesmerize/.

Magazine, Smithsonian. "The Gruesome History of Eating Corpses as Medicine." *Smithsonian.Com*, Smithsonian Institution, 6 May 2012, www.smithsonianmag.com/history/the-gruesome-history-of- eating-corpses-as-medicine-82360284/.

Brigitte, "Gitte," Tamar was born in a small rural Oregon town. From a young age, she was enthralled by scary tales featuring poetic tones and gravitated towards writing her own dark narratives. Upon graduating from Jesuit High School in Portland, she pursued her studies in Film, Television, and Media at Texas Christian University in Fort Worth, Texas.

However, her path took a different turn when she was crowned Miss Oregon USA in 2015. Following her Miss USA experience, she pursued further education and earned a business degree from Southern New Hampshire University, an MA in Law Studies from the University of Southern California, and graduate certificates in business law and entertainment law and industries.

As an author, she fearlessly delves into the gritty truths of modern society, unearthing the depths of peer pressure, addiction, homelessness, mental illness, childhood trauma, discrimination, loneliness, the allure of fame, and the horrors of abuse. She strongly believes in the importance of sharing narratives that don't sugarcoat the difficult topics society tends to shy away from and she does so in a brilliantly haunting fashion.

Aside from being an Amazon New Release Best Seller, her work has garnered recognition from Mystery Tribune, POPSUGAR, On-line Book Club, and Broadway World. She has also received the prestigious Mom's Choice Awards® Gold and many of her works have been awarded a five-star rating by Reader's Favorite.